THE SANATORIUM

THE SANATORIUM

SARAH PEARSE

WHEELER PUBLISHING
A part of Gale, a Cengage Company

Wheeler Publishing Large Print Hardcover.
The text of this Large Print edition is unabridged.
Other aspects of the book may vary from the original edition.
Set in 16 pt. Plantin.

LIBRARY OF CONGRESS CIP DATA ON FILE.
CATALOGUING IN PUBLICATION FOR THIS BOOK
IS AVAILABLE FROM THE LIBRARY OF CONGRESS.

ISBN 13: 978-1-4328-8869-5 (hardcover alk. paper)

Published in 2021 by arrangement with Viking, an imprint of Penguin Publishing Group, a division of Penguin Random House LLC.

Printed in Mexico
Print Number: 01   Print Year: 2021

For James, Rosie, and Molly,
It's a long way to the top
(if you wanna rock 'n' roll . . .)
— AC/DC

On nous apprend à vivre quand
la vie est passée.
They teach us to live when life has passed.

— MICHEL DE MONTAIGNE

I have loved constraints.
They give me comfort.

— JOSEPH DIRAND

PROLOGUE

January 2015
Discarded medical equipment litters the floor; surgical tools blistered with rust, broken bottles, jars, the scratched spine of an old invalid chair. A torn mattress sits slumped against the wall, bile-yellow stains pocking the surface.

Hand clamped tight around his briefcase, Daniel Lemaitre feels a sharp wave of revulsion: it's as if time has taken over the building's soul, left something rotten and diseased in its place.

He moves quickly down the corridor, footsteps echoing on the tiled floor.

Keep your eyes on the door. Don't look back.

But the decaying objects pull at his gaze, each one telling stories. It doesn't take much to imagine the people who'd stayed here, coughing up their lungs.

Sometimes he thinks he can even smell it, what this place used to be — the sharp, acrid scent of chemicals still lingering in the air from the old operating wards.

Daniel is halfway down the corridor when he stops.

A movement in the room opposite — a dark, distorted blur.

His stomach drops. Motionless, he stares, his gaze slowly picking over the shadowy contents of the room — a slew of papers scattered across the floor, the contorted tubes of a breathing apparatus, a broken bed frame, frayed restraints hanging loose.

He's silent, his skin prickling with tension, but nothing happens.

The building is quiet, still.

He exhales heavily, starts walking again.

Don't be stupid, he tells himself. *You're tired. Too many late nights, early mornings.*

Reaching the front door, he pulls it open. The wind howls angrily, jerking it back on its hinges. As he steps forward, he's blinded by an icy gust of snowflakes, but it's a relief to be outside.

The sanatorium unnerves him. Though he knows what it will become — has sketched every door, window, and light switch of the new hotel — at the moment, he can't help but react to its past, what it used to be.

The exterior isn't much better, he thinks, glancing up. The stark, rectangular structure is mottled with snow. It's decaying, neglected — the balconies and balustrades, the long veranda, crumbled and rotting. A few windows are still intact, but most are boarded up, ugly squares of chipboard scarring the façade like diseased, unseeing eyes.

Daniel thinks about the contrast with his own home in Vevey, overlooking the lake. The contemporary, blockish design is constructed mostly of glass to take in panoramic views of the water. It has a rooftop terrace, a small mooring.

He designed it all.

With the image comes Jo, his wife. She'll have just gotten back from work, her mind still churning over advertising budgets, briefs, already corralling the kids into doing their homework.

Daniel imagines her in the kitchen, preparing dinner, auburn hair falling across her face as she efficiently chops and slices. It'll be something easy — pasta, fish, stir-fry. Neither of them are good at the domestics.

The thought buoys him, but only momentarily. As he crosses the car park, Daniel feels the first flickers of trepidation about the drive home.

The sanatorium wasn't easy to get to in the best of weather, its position isolated, high among the mountains. This was a deliberate choice, engineered to keep the tuberculosis patients away from the smog of the towns and cities, and keep the rest of the population away from them.

But the remote location meant the road

11

leading to it was nightmarish, a series of hairpin bends cutting through a dense forest of firs. On the drive up this morning, the road itself was barely visible — snowflakes hurling themselves at the windscreen like icy, white darts, making it impossible to see more than a few yards ahead.

Daniel's nearly at the car when his foot catches on something, the tattered remains of a placard, half covered by snow. The letters are crude, daubed in red.

NON AUX TRAVAUX!! NO TO CONSTRUC-
TION!!

Anger spiking, Daniel tramples it underfoot. The protesters had been here last week. Over fifty of them, shouting abuse, waving their gaudy placards in his face. It had been filmed on mobile phones, shared on social media.

That was just one of the endless battles they'd had to fight to bring this project to fruition. People claimed they wanted progress, the tourist francs that followed, but when it came down to actually building they balked.

Daniel knew why. People don't like a winner.

It's what his father had said to him once and it was true. The locals had been proud at the start. They'd approved of his small successes — the shopping mall in Sion, the apartment block in Sierre overlooking the Rhône — but then he'd become *too much,* hadn't he? Too much of a success, a personality.

Daniel got the feeling that in their eyes he'd had his share of the pie, and was now being greedy by taking more. Only thirty-three, and his architectural practice was thriving — offices in Sion, Lausanne, Geneva. One planned for Zurich.

It was the same with Lucas, the property developer and one of his oldest friends. Midthirties, and he already owned three landmark hotels.

People resented them for their success.

And this project had been the nail in the coffin. They'd had it all: online trolls, e-mails, letters to the office. Planning objections.

They came for him first. Rumors began circulating on local blogs and social media that the business was struggling. Then they'd started on Lucas. Similar stories, stories he could easily dismiss, but one in particular stuck.

It bothered Daniel, more than he cared to admit.

Talk of bribes. Corruption.

Daniel had tried to speak to Lucas about it, but his friend had shut the conversation down. The thought nags at him, an itch, like so many things on this project, but he forces it away. He has to ignore it. Focus on the

13

result. This hotel will cement his reputation. Lucas's drive and his compulsion for detail have propelled Daniel to a spectacularly ambitious design, an end point he hadn't thought possible.

He reaches the car. The windscreen is thick with fresh snow; too much for the wipers. It will need scraping off.

But as he reaches into his pocket for his key, he notices something.

A bracelet, lying beside the front tire.

Daniel bends down, picks it up. It's thin, and made of copper. He twists it between his fingers, noticing a row of numbers engraved on the interior . . . a date?

He frowns. It has to belong to someone who'd been up there today, surely? Otherwise it would already be covered in snow.

But what were they doing so close to his car?

Images of the protesters flicker through his mind, their angry, jeering faces.

Could it be them?

Daniel makes himself take a long, deep breath, but as he pushes the bracelet into his pocket, he catches a glimpse of something: a movement behind the ridge of snow that's built up against the wall of the car park.

A hazy profile.

His heart races, his palms sweaty around his key fob. Pushing down hard on the fob to open the boot, he freezes as he looks up.

14

A figure, standing in front of him, positioned between him and his car.

Daniel stares, briefly paralyzed, his brain frantically trying to process what he's seeing — how could someone have moved so quickly toward him without him noticing?

The figure is dressed in black. Something is covering their face.

It resembles a gas mask; the same basic form, but it's missing the filter at the front. Instead, there's a thick rubber hose running from mouth to nose. A connector. The hose is black, ribbed; it quivers as the figure shifts from foot to foot.

The effect is horrifying. Monstrous. Something scraped from the darkest depths of the unconscious mind.

Think, he tells himself, *think.* His mind starts churning through possibilities, ways to make this something innocuous, benign. It's a prank, that's all: one of the protesters, trying to scare him.

Then the figure steps toward him. A precise, controlled movement.

All Daniel can see is the lurid, magnified close-up of the black rubber stretched across the face. The thick ribbed lines of the hose. Then he hears the breathing; a strange, wet sucking sound coming from the mask. Liquid exhalations.

His heart is pounding against his rib cage.

"What is this?" Daniel says, hearing the fear

in his voice. A tremble he tries to stamp out. "Who are you? What are you trying to do?" A drip slowly trickles down his face. Snow melting against the heat of his skin, or sweat? He can't tell.

Come on, he tells himself. *Get control of yourself.* It's some stupid prick, messing around.

Just walk past and get into your car.

It's then, from this angle, that he notices another car. A car that wasn't there when he arrived. A black pickup. A Nissan.

Come on, Daniel. Move.

But his body is frozen, refusing to obey. All he can do is listen to the strange breathing sound coming from the mask. It's louder now, faster, more labored.

A soft sucking noise and then a high-pitched whistle.

Over and over.

The figure lurches closer, with something in hand. A knife? Daniel can't make it out — the thick glove is concealing it.

Move, move.

He manages to propel himself forward, one step, then two, but fear makes his muscles seize. He stumbles in the snow, right foot sliding out from under him.

By the time he straightens it's too late: the gloved hand clamps over his mouth. Daniel can smell the stale mustiness of the glove but also the mask — the curious burnt-plasticky

16

odor of rubber, laced with something else.

Something familiar.

But before his brain can make the connection, something pierces his thigh. A single, sharp pain. His thoughts scatter; then his mind goes quiet.

A quiet that, within seconds, tips over into nothingness.

Press Release — Under Embargo until Midnight March 5, 2018

Le Sommet
Hauts de Plumachit
Crans-Montana 3963
Valais
Switzerland

5-STAR HOTEL SET TO OPEN IN THE SWISS RESORT OF CRANS-MONTANA

Located on a sunny mountain plateau above Crans-Montana, high in the Swiss Alps, Le Sommet is the brainchild of Swiss property developer Lucas Caron.

After eight years of extensive planning and construction, one of the town's oldest sanatoriums is set to reopen as a luxury hotel.

The main building was designed in the late nineteenth century by Caron's great-grandfather Pierre. It became renowned worldwide as a center for treating tuberculosis before the advent of antibiotics forced its diversification.

More recently, it gained international recognition for its innovative architecture, earning the elder Caron a posthumous Swiss Art Award in 1942. Combining clean lines with

18

large panoramic windows, flat roofs, and unadorned geometrical shapes, one judge described the building as "groundbreaking" — custom designed to fulfill its function as a hospital, while also creating a seamless transition between the interior and exterior landscapes.

Lucas Caron said: "It was time we breathed new life into this building. We were confident that with the right vision, we could create a sensitively restored hotel that would pay homage to its rich past."

Under the guidance of Swiss architectural firm Lemaitre SA, a team has been assembled to renovate the building and also add a state-of-the-art spa and event center.

Subtly refurbished, Le Sommet will make innovative use of natural, local materials such as wood, slate, and stone. The hotel's elegant, modern interiors will not only echo the powerful topography outside, but will draw on the building's past to create a new narrative.

Philippe Volkem, CEO of Valais Tourisme, said, "This will doubtless be the jewel in the crown of what is already one of the finest winter resorts in the world."

For press inquiries, please contact Leman PR, Lausanne.

For general inquiries / bookings, please visit www.lesommetcransmontana.ch.

1

January 2020
Day One
The funicular from the valley town of Sierre to Crans-Montana scores a near-perfect vertical line up the mountainside.

Slicing through snow-covered vineyards and the small towns of Venthone, Chermignon, Mollens, Randogne, and Bluche, the route, almost three miles long, takes passengers up the mountain in just twelve minutes.

In off-peak season, the funicular is usually half empty. Most people drive up the mountain or take the bus. But today, with the roads almost stationary thanks to heavy traffic, it's full.

Elin Warner stands on the left in the packed carriage, absorbing it all: the fat flakes of snow collecting on the windows, the slush-covered floor piled high with bags, the lanky teenagers shoving through the doors.

Her shoulders tense. She's forgotten how kids that age can be: selfish, unaware of anyone but themselves.

A sodden sleeve brushes her cheek. She smells damp, cigarettes, fried food, the musky-citrus tang of cheap aftershave. Then comes a throaty cough. Laughter.

A group of men are jostling through the doorway, talking loudly, bulging North Face sports bags on their backs. They are squeezing the family next to her farther into the carriage. Into her. An arm rubs hers, beer breath hot against her neck.

Panic pushes through her. Her heart is racing.

Will it ever stop?

It's been a year since the Hayler case and she's still thinking about it, dreaming about it. Waking up in the night, sheets damp with sweat, the dream vivid in her head: the hand around her throat, damp walls contracting, closing in on her.

Then salt water; frothing, sloshing over her mouth, her nose . . .

Control it, she tells herself, forcing herself to read the graffiti on the wall of the funicular.

Don't let it control you.

Her eyes dance over the scrawled letters weaving up the metal:

Michel 2010

BISOUS XXX

Ines & RIC 2016

22

Following the words up to the window, she startles. Her reflection . . . it pains her to look at it. She's thin. Too thin.

It's as if someone's hollowed her out, carved the very core of her away. Her cheekbones are knife sharp, her slanted blue-gray eyes wider, more pronounced. Even the choppy mess of pale blond hair, the blur of the scar on her upper lip, doesn't soften her appearance.

She's been training nonstop since her mother's death. Ten-K runs. Pilates. Weights. Cycling on the coast road between Torquay and Exeter in the blistering wind and rain.

It's too much, but she doesn't know how to stop, even if she should. It's all she's got; the only tactic to chase away what's inside her head.

Elin turns away. Sweat pricks the back of her neck. Looking at Will, she tries to concentrate on his face, the familiar shadow of stubble grazing his chin, the untamable dark blond tufts of his hair. "Will, I'm burning up."

His features contract. She can see the blueprint of future wrinkles in his anxious face; a starburst of lines around his eyes, light creases running across his forehead.

"You okay?"

Elin shakes her head, tears stinging her eyes. "I don't feel right."

Will lowers his voice. "About this, or . . ."

She knows what he's trying to say: *Isaac.* It's both; him, the panic, they're intertwined, connected.

"I don't know." Her throat feels tight. "I keep going over it, you know, the invitation, out of the blue. Maybe coming was the wrong decision. I should have thought about it more, or at least spoken to him properly before we let him book."

"It's not too late. We can always go back. Say I had problems with work." Smiling, Will nudges his glasses up his nose with his forefinger. "This might count as the shortest-ever holiday on record, but who cares."

Elin forces herself to return his smile, a quiet sting of devastation at the contrast between then and now. How easily he's accepted this: the new normal.

It's the opposite of when they'd first met. Back then, she was peaking; that's how she thinks of it now. At the pinnacle of her twentysomething life.

She'd just bought her first apartment near the beach, the top floor of an old Victorian villa. Bijou, but high ceilings, views of a tiny square of sea.

Work was going well — she'd been promoted to detective sergeant, landed a big case, an important one, her mother was responding well to the first round of chemo. She thought she was on top of her grief for Sam, dealing with it, but now . . .

Her life has contracted. Closed down to become something that would have been unrecognizable to her a few years ago.

The doors are closing now, thick glass panels sliding together.

With a jolt, the funicular lurches upward, away from the station, accelerating.

Elin closes her eyes, but that only makes it worse. Every sound, every judder, is magnified behind her eyelids.

She opens her eyes to see the landscape flashing by: blurry streaks of snow-covered vineyards, chalets, shops.

Her head swims. "I want to get out."

"What?" Will turns. He tries to mask it, but she can hear the frustration in his voice.

"I need to get out."

The funicular pulls into a tunnel. They plunge into darkness, and a woman whoops.

Elin breathes in, slowly, carefully, but she can feel it coming — that sense of impending doom. All at once, her blood feels sticky moving through her, yet also like it's rushing everywhere at once.

More breaths. Slower, as she'd taught herself. *In for four, hold, then out for seven.*

It's not enough. Her throat contracts. Her breath is coming shallow now, fast. Her lungs are fighting, desperately trying to drag in oxygen.

"Your inhaler," Will urges. "Where is it?"

Scrabbling in her pocket, she pulls it out,

pushes down: *good.* She presses again, feels the rush of gas hit the back of her throat, reach her windpipe.

Within minutes, her breathing regulates.

But when her head clears, they're there, in her mind's eye.

Her brothers. Isaac. Sam.

Images, on loop.

She sees soft child faces, cheeks smattered with freckles. The same wide-set blue eyes, but while Isaac's are cold, unnerving in their intensity, Sam's fizz with energy, a spark that draws people in.

Elin blinks, unable to stop herself thinking about the last time she saw those eyes — vacant, lifeless, that spark . . . snuffed out.

She turns to the window, but can't unsee the images from her past: Isaac, smiling at her; that familiar smirk. He holds up his hands, but the five splayed fingers are covered in blood.

Elin extends her hand, but she can't reach him. She never can.

2

The hotel minibus is waiting in the small car park at the top of the funicular. It's a sleek dark gray, the smoky tint of its windows smeared with snow.

Discreet silver lettering is etched on the bottom left of the door: le sommet. The letters are lowercase, understated, a fine, blocky font.

Elin allows herself to feel the first twinge of excitement. Up until this point, she's been carelessly dismissive of the hotel in conversations with friends:

Pretentious.

Style over substance.

In truth, she'd carefully peeled off Isaac's Post-it, taking pleasure in the pristine brochure beneath, running her fingers over the thick matte cardboard of the cover, savoring the novelty of each minimalist, photographed page.

She'd felt something strange, an unfamiliar mix of excitement and envy, a sense of having missed out on something indefinable, something she wasn't even aware that she wanted.

In contrast, Will had been openly effusive, raving about the architecture, the design. He'd scoured the pages, then gone straight online to read more.

Over lamb Madras that night, he'd quoted details at her about the interior design: *Influenced by Joseph Dirand . . . A new kind of minimalism, echoing the building's history . . . Creating a narrative.*

She's always been amazed by Will's capacity for absorbing this kind of intricate detail and fact. It makes her feel safe, somehow, secure that he has all the answers.

"Miss Warner? Mr. Riley?"

Elin turns. A tall, wiry man is striding toward them. He's wearing a gray fleece embossed with the same silver lettering.

Le Sommet.

"That's us." Will smiles. There's an awkward fumble as the man reaches for Elin's suitcase at the same time as Will, before Will extracts himself.

"Trip okay?" the driver asks. "Where have you come from?" Scooping up the cases, the man hoists them into the back of the minibus.

Elin looks to Will to fill the gaps. She finds small talk like this an effort.

"South Devon. Flight was on time . . . never

happens. I said to Elin that it's Swiss time-keeping keeping EasyJet on point." Will smiles — dark eyes rueful, eyebrows raised. "Shit, that sounded clichéd, right?"

The man laughs. This is Will's modus operandi with strangers — neutralize them with a mix of sheer enthusiasm and self-deprecation. People are invariably disarmed, then charmed. Will makes moments like this easy. But then, she thinks, hovering behind him, that's what first attracted her to him — it's his thing, isn't it?

Effortless.

To him, nothing's insurmountable. There's no bravado in it, it's just how his mind works — rapidly breaking an issue down into logical, manageable chunks. A list, some research, a phone call or two — answers found, problem solved. For her, even easy, everyday things became something to be agonized over until they swelled out of all proportion.

Take this trip: she'd stressed over the flight — the close proximity to other people at the airport and on the plane, the possible turbulence, delays.

Even the packing bothered her. It wasn't just the fact that she'd needed to buy new stuff, but the questions over *what* she should buy — what weather eventualities should be covered, the most suitable brands.

As a result, everything of hers is brand-new, and feels like it. Pushing her finger down her trousers, she tucks in the itchy label she meant to lop off at home.

Will had simply thrown things in his bag. It had taken less than fifteen minutes, but he still somehow manages to look the part: battered hiking boots, black Patagonia puffer jacket, North Face trousers just the right side of worn-in.

Somehow, though, their differences complement each other. Will accepts her and her foibles, and Elin is acutely aware that not everyone would. She's grateful.

With an expansive, easy gesture, the driver slides open the door. Elin clambers inside, casting a sidelong glance at the back.

One of the families from the funicular is already there: a pair of glossy-haired teenage girls, heads down, watching a tablet. The mother is holding a magazine. The father, thumb to screen, is scrolling through his phone.

Elin and Will settle into the middle two seats. "Better?" Will says softly.

She nods. It is: clean leather seats; no loud, abrupt voices. And best of all, a marked absence of damp bodies packed tight against hers.

The bus crawls forward. Turning right, it bumps over the uneven ground and out of the car park.

When they reach the end of the road, they come to a fork. The driver takes the right turn, windscreen wipers moving rapidly to dislodge the falling snow.

All's fine until they meet the first bend. With one quick movement, the bus swings around to face the opposite direction.

As the bus straightens with a jerk, Elin stiffens.

The road is no longer flanked with snow or trees, not even a strip of grassy verge. Instead, it's clinging to the very edge of the mountain, with only a thin metal barrier between her and the vertiginous drop to the valley floor below.

Beside her, she feels Will tense, knowing what he'll do next: he tries to cloak his unease with laughter, a low whistle between his teeth. "Bloody hell, wouldn't fancy my chances driving this at night."

The driver shakes his head. "No choice. It's the only way to get to the hotel." He glances at them in the rearview mirror. "It puts some people off from coming."

"Really?" Will puts a hand on her knee, presses too hard, and gives another forced laugh.

The driver nods. "There are forums about it online. Kids have put videos up on You-Tube, filmed themselves going around the bends, screaming. The camera angles make it look worse than it is. They stick their phone out of the window, point it over the edge, down the drop . . ." His words fall away as he

31

looks intently at the road ahead. "This is the worst part. Once we're through this . . ."

Looking up, Elin's stomach plummets. The road has narrowed further, barely wide enough to take the minibus. The tarmac is a murky white-gray, shiny with ice in places. She forces herself to look toward the ragged horizon of snowcapped peaks ahead.

It's over in a matter of minutes. As the road opens, Will's grip on her leg eases. Fiddling with his phone, he starts taking photographs through the window, forehead creased in concentration.

Elin smiles, touched by the care he's taking. He's been waiting for this moment — the views of the landscape, the first glimpse of the hotel. She knows these images will be toyed with on his laptop later. Critiqued. Tweaked some more. Shared with his arty friends.

"How long have you been working for the hotel?" Will says, turning back.

"Just over a year."

"You like it?"

The driver nods. "There's something about the building, the history, it gets inside your head."

"I looked it up online," Elin murmurs. "I couldn't believe how many patients actually —"

"I wouldn't think too much about that." The driver cuts her off. "Digging up the past,

32

especially with this place, you'll send yourself mad. If you go into the details about what went on . . ." He shrugs, trailing off.

Elin picks up her water bottle. His words echo in her mind: *It gets inside your head.*

It already has, she thinks, picturing the brochure, the photographs online.

Le Sommet.

They're only a few miles away.

3

Sliding her phone into her pocket, Adele Bourg pushes her vacuum cleaner through the door of room 301.

Not that it's actually called 301. Le Sommet is too . . . self-aware for that.

They'd rejected just about every Alpine cliché — the faux-fur chalet vibe, "traditional" menus — and that included getting rid of the mundanity of room numbers.

Instead, this room, like the others, is named after a peak in the mountain range opposite.

Bella Tolla.

Adele can see it now. Through the vast windows, its jagged summit punctures the sky. The sight burns. It was one of the last climbs she did before she became pregnant with Gabriel. August 2015.

She remembers it all: sun, a cloudless sky. Neon-framed sunglasses. The scrape of the harness against her thighs. The gray rock, cool beneath her fingers. Estelle's tanned legs high above her, contorted into an impossible

34

position.

Gabriel, her son, now age three, was born the following June, the result of a short-lived fling with Stephane, a fellow student and mountain lover, during a weekend in Chamonix. Everything stopped then — climbing, hiking, studying for her business degree, pissed-up nights with her friends.

Adele loves her son wholly, absolutely, but sometimes she struggles to remember who she was before. What her world was like before it had been deconstructed, reassembled into something else entirely.

Responsibilities. Worry. Collection letters stacking up on her desk. This job; the mundane rhythm of her days — changing sheets, wiping surfaces, the sucking up of other people's debris.

Adele swallows hard, bending down to plug the vacuum into the wall. Straightening, she looks around. *It won't take long,* she thinks, assessing the damage.

Adele likes this bit, the calculation of time and effort required. It's an art, the one part of the process that requires her to engage her brain.

Her eyes slide across the minimalist setup: the bed, the low-slung chairs, the abstract swirls that count as paintings on the left-hand wall, the cashmere throws in muted shades.

Not bad, she thinks.

These people were neat. Careful. The bed

is barely rumpled; the complex arrangement of throws arranged across the bottom still undisturbed.

The only visible mess is the half-empty cups on the bedside tables, a black jacket slung on the chair in the corner. She studies the woven badge on the upper arm. Moncler. Probably three thousand francs for that.

Adele always thought that kind of carelessness — flinging the jacket on the chair — only came with wealth. It was the same with the rooms. Most of the guests seemed oblivious to the intricacies and detail that elevated these rooms — the bespoke furniture, marble bathrooms, the tufted, hand-woven rugs.

She was always dealing with somebody's thoughtless filth — stained bedsheets, sticky food trodden into rugs. Adele pictures the slimy, wrinkled sack of the condom she'd fished out of the toilet last week.

The thought stings, like a graze. Adele pushes it away, plugs her headphones into her ears. She always listens to music when she works, fixes her tasks to the beat.

Her favorite playlist is old-school rock, heavy metal. Guns N' Roses, Slash, Metallica.

She's about to switch it on, then stops, noticing a change outside, a subtle darkening to the sky, the very particular leaden gray that precedes heavy snowfall — ominous in its uniformity. Snow is already falling relentlessly, drifts forming around the hotel signage, the cars parked out front.

Tiny darts of anxiety flicker in her chest. If the storm gets any worse, she might have problems getting home. Any other night, it wouldn't matter — her childcare was flexible, but today Gabriel leaves for his week with his father.

She needs to be back in time to say good-bye, a good-bye that always sticks in her throat as Stephane watches, face impassive, his hand already enclosing Gabriel's.

A dark, irrational fear engulfs her each and every time he leaves — that he might not come back, might not *want* to come back, that he might choose, after all, to live with Stephane.

Adele can see that fear now, reflected in the glass. Her dark hair is scraped back into a high ponytail, revealing a pinched face, her almond-shaped eyes narrowed with worry. She turns away quickly. Seeing yourself like that, shadowy, distorted, it's like looking into the darkest parts of your soul.

Glancing back at her phone, she's about to press play when, from the corner of her eye, she notices something on the balustrade.

A sliver of something shiny among the snow.

Adele pushes open the door, curious. Freezing air fills the room along with tiny flakes of windblown snow. Walking over to the balustrade, she picks it up.

A bracelet.

As she turns it between her fingers, she can see it's made of copper, similar to the ones people wear for arthritis. Tiny numbers loop the interior. An engraving.

It must be one of the guests', she decides. She'll put it on one of the bedside tables so they'll see it when they come in.

Adele goes back into the room, closing the door behind her. Putting the bracelet on the nearest table, she steals another glance at the heavy snowfall, the growing drifts circling the balcony.

If she's late, Stephane won't wait for her. All she'll find is a silent apartment and an emptiness that will consume her until Gabriel is home.

4

"Elin, are you going to come . . . ?" Will's last word is lost against the sound of the flag above, flapping in the gusting wind.

Thick flakes of snow plummet from the sky, settling on her face. Her stomach clenches. Despite Will's presence, and the hotel in front of her, she can't help but be struck by their isolation — the absolute remoteness of the location. The drive from town had taken more than an hour and a half. With each minute ticking by, the winding roads drawing them farther up the mountain, Elin couldn't shake her growing sense of unease.

The journey was protracted because of the snow, but she still can't escape the fact that they're a long way from civilization. Apart from the hotel, all she can see is a mass of trees, snow, the shadowy bulk of the mountains looming over them.

"Elin? Are you coming?" Will starts walking, bumping their cases across the snow toward the entrance of the hotel.

She nods, hand locked tight around the strap of her bag. Standing there in front of the hotel, she can feel the strangest thing — a disturbance in the air, a curious restlessness that has nothing to do with the falling snow.

Elin looks around. The driveway and the car park beyond are empty.

No one's there.

Everyone from the funicular has gone inside.

It's the building, she thinks, absorbing the vast white structure. The more she looks, the more she senses a tension.

An anomaly.

She hadn't noticed it in the brochure Isaac sent. But then, she thinks, those photos were taken from a distance, highlighting the scenic backdrop; the snow-covered peaks, the forest of white-frosted firs.

The images hadn't focused on the building itself, how savage it looks.

There's no doubting its past — what it used to be. There's something brutally clinical about the architecture, the air of the institution in the stark lines, the relentless rectangular planes and faces, the modernist flat roofs. Glass is everywhere, dizzying, whole walls of it, allowing you to see right in.

Yet, Elin thinks, stepping forward, something's at odds with that clinical feel, details not visible in the brochure — carved balustrades and balconies, the beautiful stretch of wooden veranda on the ground floor.

This is the anomaly, she thinks, the tension she's picked up on. This juxtaposition . . . it's chilling. Institution butting up against beauty.

Probably deliberate, she thinks, when they designed the building; the intricate decor an attempt to conceal the fact that this was not a place where someone came for fun.

This was a place where people struggled with illness, a place where people died.

It makes sense now, her brother celebrating his engagement here.

This place, like Isaac, is all about façades.

Covering up what really lies beneath.

5

"Shit," Adele mutters, wiggling her key in the lock. Why wouldn't it turn? It's always like this when she's in a hurry . . .

The door to the changing room swings open, a rush of cool air. Adele flinches, drops her keys.

"You okay?"

A flicker of relief. She knows that voice: Mat, a white-blond Swede, one of many foreign staff whom the hotel employs. He works behind the bar. Overconfident. Pale green eyes that first rake over you, then look right through you.

"Fine." She crouches, scoops up the key fob. "I'm in a rush, that's all. It's Gabriel's week with his dad. He takes him to his place tonight. I wanted to be back to say good-bye." Finally managing to open the locker, she pulls out her bag and coat.

"They've just announced the funicular's down." Mat jams his key into his locker. "Won't be running until morning."

Adele looks through the window. The storm is raging now, wind howling as it batters the side of the hotel.

"What about the buses?"

"Still running, but they'll be busy."

He's right. Biting down on her lip, Adele checks her watch.

She's meant to be in the valley in an hour. If she hurries, she might make it.

Adele says good-bye, and lets herself out the side door. She pauses, shivering, stunned by the force of the wind. It's strong, blowing icy pellets of snow into her face and eyes. Her cheeks are burning from the cold.

Pulling her scarf up around her nose, Adele walks out onto the small track leading to the front of the hotel.

With every step, her feet sink into the snow. It immediately starts seeping through the thin leather of her boots. *Idiot.* She should have worn her proper snow boots. Her feet will be soaked in minutes.

Carefully avoiding the bigger mounds of drifting snow, she keeps walking. A few feet on, she feels her phone vibrate in her pocket. She stops, pulls it out. It's a message from Stephane: *Leaving work now. See you soon.*

Work.

The word stirs up a familiar, bitter resentment. Adele hates herself for it.

She knows it's no good dwelling on what might have been — the climb up the career ladder, the accompanying salary, the travel, but she can't help it.

However she tries to position it in her mind, make justifications, it's blatantly clear that it's she who has made the sacrifices, not Stephane. He didn't have to give up his plans when Gabriel was born, his place at college. He graduated with top honors and got a job right away at a multinational in Vevey working in brand management. Stephane was highly rated, doing well. Earning even better.

His girlfriend works for the same company, pulling in an equally impressive salary, Adele can tell. Lise isn't flashy, but the subtly expensive grooming and innate confidence speak for themselves.

This, she can just about cope with — it's a petty, silly envy, nothing more, but it's the potential effect on Gabriel that bothers her. Adele knows it won't be long before Gabriel starts noticing the differences between his parents' jobs.

Part of her is scared that he'll look down on her — that he'll see her, and what she can give him, as inferior to what Stephane can provide.

Adele knows it's stupid to think ahead like this, because at the moment everything Gabriel loves has nothing to do with money: snuggles and books before bed. Hot chocolate with whipped cream. Joint play in the sandbox. Sledding.

She smiles to herself as she remembers the trip last week. Squeezed onto the sled together, the two of them had built up so much momentum that they'd careered out of control into the fence at the bottom of the hill. Gabriel ended up spread-eagled on top of her, laughing hysterically.

The memory instantly puts her anxieties into perspective. *Pull it together,* she tells herself, stepping sideways to avoid a fallen branch. *Stop thinking the worst.*

It's then that she feels something on her ankle, a pressure.

Has she caught it on something? Another branch?

Glancing down, she freezes. A gloved hand is around her ankle.

There's a sudden tug, jerking her backward.

Adele lands face-first in soft, powdery snow.

Tiny, icy particles fill her mouth and eyes.

6

The white pendants dangling from the ceiling remind Elin of a hangman's noose.

The wires are so long they traverse for several yards, cable hanging slack in the middle before descending farther on. The pendant itself is nothing more than a violent spasm of wire forming an intricate loop.

Undoubtedly hideously expensive, an artistic statement she doesn't "get," but however you see it, it's strange, Elin thinks, to have that in a hotel reception.

Something so sinister, in what's meant to be a welcoming space.

The rest of it isn't much better — leather chairs arranged around a narrow wooden table, a large slab of gray stone for the reception desk. Even the painting over the fireplace is bleak; swirls of gray and black paint angrily smeared across the canvas.

"What do you think?" Elin nudges Will. "An architect's dream?" She can already predict the words he'll quote later: *boundary pushing, soulful, immersive.*

Elin's absorbed these words by osmosis because to her they hold a kind of poetry. How Will talks about architecture, how he finds all that wonder in bricks and mortar, reveals so much about how he thinks and feels.

"Love it," he replies. "Buildings like this had a massive effect on twentieth-century architecture. Features people associate with modernism were used for the first time in sanatoriums." Will stops, taking in her expression. "You don't like it, do you?"

"I don't know. To me, it feels cold. Clinical. Such a big space, and there's hardly anything in here. A few chairs, tables."

"It's deliberate." Elin hears the slight tension in his words — he's frustrated that she doesn't get it right away. "The white walls, wood, the natural materials. It's a nod to the sanatorium's original design."

"So they want it to seem sterile?" It seems strange to her: that anyone would deliberately design something to be devoid of any warmth, comfort.

"It was a hygiene thing, but they also thought that whitewashing helped bring an 'inner cleanliness.' " He makes quote marks with his fingers. "Architects then were experimenting with using design to influence how people felt. A building like this was used as a medical instrument in itself, every detail

47

custom designed to help patients recover."

"What about all this glass? I'm not sure it would help me." Elin looks through the vast window at the snow being whipped into a fury, the drifts creeping past the frame. Hardly any barrier between her and the outside world. Despite the warmth coming from the fire, she shivers.

Will follows her gaze. "They thought natural light, the big views of the landscape, were healing."

"Maybe." As she looks past him, her eyes alight on a glass box hanging from the ceiling by a thin metal wire.

Walking over, she finds a small silver flask inside. A few words of text are written below, in both French and English.

CRACHOIR — SPITTOON. Commonly used by patients to reduce the spread of infection.

She beckons to Will. "You're telling me that's not weird? Hanging here, like some strange art installation."

"This whole place is an installation." Touching her arm, he softens his tone. "It's not that, is it? You're nervous, aren't you? About seeing him again."

Elin nods, leaning into him, breathing in the familiar, comforting smell of his aftershave — peppery basil and thyme, a slight

48

smokiness. "It's been nearly four years, Will. Things change, don't they? I've got no idea who he is, not anymore."

"I know." He holds her tight. "But don't overthink it. Put the past in the past. You coming here, it's a fresh start. Not just with Isaac, but with the Hayler case too. It's time to draw a line."

It's so easy for Will, Elin thinks. As an architect, every day is a blank page. He's always starting over, creating something new.

It was this quality that struck her the first time they met. How *fresh* he seemed. Unjaded. Elin wondered if she'd ever met anyone truly like that before — optimistic, excited by life. Excited by every little thing.

The day they'd met, she'd been running. She'd finished her shift, a shift she'd spent mainly at her desk churning through paperwork, and had decided to run the coast path, from her apartment in Torhun toward Brixham. An easy 10K there and back.

Stopping to stretch on the promenade above the beach, she'd spotted Will by the wall, smoke coiling around him, suspended in the salty still of the air.

He was barbecuing — fish, peppers, chicken that smelled like cumin and coriander.

Elin felt his eyes on her right away. A minute or so later, he called over, made a joke. Something clichéd. *Looks like I've got it easier than you.* She'd laughed, and they'd started talking.

She was attracted to him immediately. There was an unusual complexity about his appearance, something that had simultaneously intimidated and excited her.

Scruffy blond-brown hair, black Scandinavian-style glasses, a short-sleeved navy chevron shirt buttoned up to the neck. *Not her usual type.*

It made sense when he told her what he did — an architect. He told her details, eyes lighting up as he spoke — he was a design director, his special interests were mixed-use developments, waterfront regeneration.

He pointed out the new restaurant/housing complex along the seafront — a gleaming, grounded, white cruise liner of a building that she knew had been feted, won awards. He shared that he liked peanut butter and museums, surfing and Coke. What struck her was how easy it was. There was none of the usual awkwardness you got with strangers.

Elin knew it was because Will was completely at ease with himself. She didn't have to second-guess — he was an open book, and so she, in turn, opened up to him in a way she hadn't for a long time.

They exchanged numbers; he called her that night, then the next. No angst. No game playing. He asked her questions: demanding questions about policing, the politics of the force, her experiences.

Elin soon got the sense that he didn't see her the way she had always seen herself. The effect was almost dizzying; it made her want to live up to what he saw in her, or what he thought he saw.

With him, she did new things: galleries, museums, underground wine bars off the quayside in Exeter. They talked art, music, *ideas.* Bought coffee-table books and actually read them. Planned weekends away with minimal fuss.

None of which she was used to. Her life had, up until this point, been resolutely uncultured: Saturday nights watching TV, reading trashy magazines. Curries. The pub.

But she should have known it couldn't last, that the real Elin would come out eventually. The loner. The introvert. The one who found it easier to run than give her hand away.

It made her angry, in a way, how loosely she'd held it all, those few months where everything *worked.* If she'd known it was all so finely balanced, so close to crashing down, she'd have held it closer, tighter.

Within weeks, everything changed: it all came together, a perfect maelstrom. Her mother's treatment stopped working. She got a new boss, a challenging case.

Under pressure, she defaulted — closed up, refused to confide what she was feeling. Almost immediately she felt something shift in their relationship. Who she had become, it wasn't enough for him, didn't make sense.

The boundaries she'd put on the relationship, boundaries he'd seemed happy with at first — the fact that she needed her space, her independence, certain evenings where she simply just wanted to *be* — were no longer working.

Elin felt him subtly testing her, like a child probing a wobbly tooth — a work night out, a holiday with his friends. More nights staying over at his.

She sensed that if he couldn't get what he always had from her, then he wanted something else to put in its place — another part of her she hadn't offered up before. Commitment. Certainty.

Will wanted their lives to mix, merge, become enmeshed.

It came to a head six months ago. In their favorite Thai spot, he asked what she thought about moving out of their respective places, finding somewhere together.

We've been together over two years, Elin, it isn't unreasonable.

She put him off, gave excuses, but she knows his patience won't last forever. She has to make a decision. Time is running out.

"Els . . ."

She turns, sucks in her breath.

Isaac.

Isaac's here.

52

7

Adele scrabbles forward on her knees, fear surging through her.

The grip on her ankle slackens. She hears a grunt, frantic rustling — no words of apology, nothing to indicate that it was an accident.

Someone had been lurking in the darkness. Waiting to trip her up.

Questions crowd her head, but she pushes them aside. She has to get away. Escape.

Hauling herself forward, Adele pulls herself to her feet, starting to run. She doesn't dare turn back. Her eyes rake over the inky black of the landscape around her.

Think, Adele, think.

Going back to the hotel won't work. She'll have to dig out her pass when she gets to the door — it'll take too long. Her attacker will catch up.

The forest.

If she can get into the trees, the darkness of the tree canopy, then maybe she'll lose them.

Running as fast as she can up the small incline leading to the tree line, Adele hears footsteps behind her.

She might have the advantage here: she knows this path — she's walked here in the summer. The trail winds lazily up through the forest, over streams that gush down the hillside, bringing the glacier meltwater down the valley.

Several tracks lead off the main one. Mountain bike paths in the summer.

She'll divert, head onto one of them. Try to lose her attacker that way.

Adele runs up the path, adrenaline pumping, boots sloughing through the snow. Within minutes, her chest is heaving, her breathing fast, erratic, but she's losing them, she can tell. She can't hear them anymore.

Twenty yards on, she puts her plan into action. She darts left, tucks in behind a small cluster of firs, plunging into shadow. Sweat trickles down her back inside her coat. She hardly dares to breathe.

What if her attacker makes out her footprints in the snow? She might lead them directly to her. . . . She can only hope that the inconsistent snow cover, piled up in drifts around rocks and fallen branches, has acted as a foil.

Finally, she hears them go past, the soft, steady thuds of someone running, kicking up snow. She decides to double back on herself, and sprints across the path, diving onto the small track on the right. She glances behind her to try to see where her pursuer is, but her eyes just find more trees, snow. The forest is too dense.

Pushing aside branches with her arms, Adele moves slowly, carefully through the trees. She freezes. A sudden movement on the left. Her eyes flicker toward it.

Relief floods through her as a marmot springs out of a mound of snow. Twitching its fur, dislodging a few white flakes, it pauses, looking at her, then darts off between the trees.

Another movement. Another sound.

This time: a muffled cough.

Shit. They've found her.

Her mind races.

The hut . . . the one the hotel uses for storage. She's sure it's just below, parallel with this path. If she can make it a few yards farther, she could hide there. It might be locked, but there's a chance.

More sounds. Breathing.

Keep calm, she tells herself. *You're close now.*

Adele inches backward.

Silence.

She decides to make her move.

She walks slowly downhill, her eyes scouring the gaps between the trees for the hut, but there's nothing there. Only more forest.

55

More snow.

Adele curses softly under her breath. She's come too high, hasn't she? Too far up the first path. This is a different track entirely. . . .

Tears sting her eyes. It's the snow. That's why she's made the mistake. It's filled in all the usual landmarks; the familiar rocks, tree stumps, clearings. She'll have to go back onto the main path. Back the way she came.

Hearing the dull crack of a twig snapping, Adele whirls around.

A figure is standing in front of her. A faceless figure.

She blinks, the tears in her eyes making her vision go in and out of focus. *A dream,* she thinks, wiping her eyes. *Perhaps that's all this is.* Maybe she'd lain down on the bed in that last room, fallen asleep . . .

But when her sight clears, Adele realizes that this is no dream, no half-awake hallucination.

The reason the person is faceless is because he or she is wearing a mask.

From the side, it resembles a surgical mask; thin straps bisecting their cheek, pulled taut around the back of the head, but from the front, Adele realizes it's more than that. *A gas mask,* she thinks, with a cold feeling of dread, taking in the wide, ribbed tube extending from the mouth to the nose. A kind of peculiar gas mask . . .

56

It's huge, completely obscuring their face. She can't make out any distinguishing features.

The figure is stepping forward now, moving toward her. Adele feels her knees give way.

No more running. She can't run anymore.

8

Elin stiffens. *This is wrong,* she thinks. She shouldn't have agreed to come.

Isaac takes a step forward, hesitating, then finally pulls her toward him.

A shock wave moves through her. His hair is against her face, longer, dark curls nearly past his jaw. He smells different, too, tobacco, an unfamiliar soap.

Elin closes her eyes. Too late. Images rush in.

A glimmering, white-capped sea. Water, thick with seaweed, sloshing inside red buckets. Seagulls caterwauling.

Withdrawing, Isaac meets her gaze, a strange mixture of emotions in his eyes.

Love? Fear? It's impossible to tell. She can no longer read his face; time has blurred her sense of him. The idea stings — the only real family she's got left, and part of him is strange to her.

As he clears his throat, his fingers come up to his eyelid, scratching into the corner, near the tear duct. A familiar gesture: he's got eczema. Flare-ups throughout childhood. A variety of triggers: heat, synthetic clothing, stress.

"We saw people getting off the funicular. Laure was convinced you wouldn't have made this one, but I wanted to check."

"We ended up getting the earlier train." Elin forces the words out. She looks past him. "Where's Laure?"

"She had to go and see her boss about something for the party. She won't be long."

Isaac turns to Will. "Good to finally meet you, mate." He vigorously pumps Will's hand before leaning in — a half hug, which Isaac dominates, his left hand coming around to Will's back. Two, three hearty pats. A blokey gesture, but a power move all the same. The subtle movement into his body space, the taking of control.

Will's oblivious, his face open, smiling. "Good to meet you, too, and congrats. Big news . . ."

"I could say the same. You've done the impossible, haven't you?"

Will hesitates, uncertain. "What do you mean?"

"Elin." Isaac nods to her.

There's a pause. Will stiffens, doing the things he only does when he feels threatened — pulling back his shoulders to broaden his chest, jutting out his jaw.

Color rises in his cheeks. An unfamiliar color, because Will doesn't do embarrassed, but then Isaac's always been able to do this: wrong-foot people. Put them on edge.

"You've managed to pin my sister down." Isaac's laugh splinters the silence. "I thought it would never happen. Mind you, she always was a dark horse."

It's a clichéd joke, so they laugh, but Elin knows what he's doing. He's showing her that he still knows her, can read her. He's showing her who is in charge.

"I could say the same, couldn't I?" she retorts, but as soon as she says the words, she regrets it. Her response is delayed, louder, brittler, too obviously laced with something, and falls flat. She looks away, her neck burning.

Will changes the subject. "When did you arrive?"

"A few days ago. We were going to ski, but they closed the lifts." Isaac gestures at the swirling snow outside. "It's been like this since we got here."

Skiing. He's good, Elin remembers; a gap year in France before his post-grad, then holidays. He did it the hard way — worked, saved, worked again. Neither of them had it easy — no inheritance or parental fund to draw on.

He looks fit, she thinks, examining the lines of lean, sinewy muscle visible through his shirt. Strong. Like her, his face is thinner, more defined, new lines, but his blue eyes are unchanged; wide, guileless. Unreadable. Her school friends would say he hadn't changed. Still looks subtly stubbled, disheveled. Forever the indie boy drummer.

"When does everyone else arrive for the party?"

"A few days." Isaac shifts from foot to foot. "We thought it would be nice if you came out first. A pre-engagement party. Some family time."

He lightly touches her necklace. "Still wearing it?"

Flinching, Elin nods, instinctively enclosing the soft loop of silver in her hand, away from his touch.

"So what do you think of this place?" Isaac moves his hand away, gestures around him. "The hotel."

Elin stiffens. She knows this tone; he wants a reaction. The fact that it used to be a sanatorium, the studied minimalism . . . he wants her to find it uncomfortable.

"It's fantastic. Unique." Reaching up to push her hair away from her face, she realizes how short it is. A new thing, after her mother died.

"And Will? The architect's view?"

Will's back on familiar ground, using all the words she predicted and more — *crisp, well-executed, a perfect restraint.* While he's speaking, she watches Isaac.

Part of him hasn't changed, she thinks. His attention's already wandering, his gaze imperceptibly moving to her. A single, loaded glance. So much is going on in it: he's showing that he's bored by Will, that he knows she's aware of it, and even worse, that he knows Will hasn't clocked it. *He's on top.*

A few minutes later, Will turns. "Elin, I was asking Isaac about the proposal."

"Yes," she replies, "I —" But she doesn't get the chance to finish.

A voice: "Functional . . . that's how I'd describe it. A ring, in my ski boot."

Laure. There she is, behind Isaac. Smiling, slightly flushed. She loosely embraces Elin before stepping back, greeting Will.

She notices Will take her in; a microexpression of approval that he swiftly squashes. Elin feels a bolt of jealousy. She's seen recent photos of Laure, but they didn't do her justice: she has the type of face that only comes alive in person. Her features are bold, uncompromising; dark eyes, a perfectly straight fringe stopping just short of thick, well-contoured brows.

She's changed. There's a poise, a composure to her that she didn't have before. The Laure she remembers was more relaxed, her face artless, full of an easy openness. Now her features seem on a tighter leash.

She's wearing things Elin would never have

considered, she thinks, trying not to stare at the arty ensemble; high-waisted gray jeans, several tank tops, layered. A fine-knit lime-green cardigan is slung over the top. A scarf, also gray, is draped loosely around her neck. Silver bracelets loop her wrist.

"Sorry for the short notice." Laure shrugs. "It was all so last-minute."

An understatement. Elin had received the invitation only a month ago; a parcel, and inside, a neon Post-it stuck to the top of the simple, matte brochure:

Isaac Warner and Laure Strehl are engaged & having a party. Here . . . An arrow pointed to the brochure beneath. *You only need to pay for flights — Laure works in the hotel. Let me know. Isaac.*

The invite was unexpected. Since Isaac left for Switzerland over four years ago, contact had been sporadic at best. A few e-mails, a rare phone call. He'd told them bits and pieces — getting together with Laure, his lecturing job at the university in Lausanne, but that was it. Months could pass without them being in touch.

Even their mother's funeral hadn't drawn him back. Flimsy excuses: *Can't leave work. Emergency with a student.* The memory, sour, rough edged, makes her want to swallow hard; like a piece of gristly meat she can't get down.

63

Laure's watching her with a quizzical expression. "You don't look like" — she hesitates, rearranges her words — "I remember . . ." Again, she trails off.

"What?" Elin replies, voice brittle. "You remembered what?"

Laure smiles lazily. "Nothing. It's been ages, that's all."

Will gives her a sharp look. She knows why: she hadn't told him that she knew Laure. That they had history.

"We were wondering, do you want to have dinner together tonight?" Isaac says. "If you're tired, we can always take a rain check."

"No. We'd like that. What time?" She flushes, embarrassed by her eagerness.

"Sevenish?" He shrugs. "Before that, we'll give you the tour. I —"

He doesn't get to finish his sentence. There's a loud bang, the sound of glass shattering. A blast of cold air floods the room. The low hum of chatter stops.

Silence.

Elin turns, heart pounding. A side window is swinging wildly on its hinge. Shards of glass litter the floor along with a spreading pool of water, huge white lilies.

Even though she knows there's no threat — it's a window blown open, a vase knocked over — her pulse is still racing, adrenaline flooding her body. Elin feels her hands clench, fingernails digging into her palm.

64

A staff member appears, closes the window, moves people away from the debris. Elin unfurls her hands, looks down at them.

She can make out the imprint of nails on her palm.

Half-moons. Perfect crescents.

9

Outside, the storm is building. Snow is being whipped by the wind into a fury, sending it lashing against the glass. It doesn't distract Laure. She's slick, efficient, seamlessly moving them around the hotel. Restaurant to lounge, library to bar.

More glass. The same stark white walls, austere design.

"Last but not least." Laure leads them to the end of the corridor, pushes open a door. "The spa."

Inside, the reception space is vast, one wall clad in huge slabs of gray marble, veined with dark streaks. Another abstract installation hangs from the ceiling above the receptionist — a complex tangle of metal wires, studded with tiny lights.

Laure runs her finger over one of the walls. "The walls are all finished in Marmorino plaster. It's made of marble dust and lime putty. The effect, it's like suede. It's designed to catch the light, change as the day goes on.

It's similar to the effect they tried to achieve on the sanatorium walls — they were matte to reduce glare for the patients, but still light."

Despite the space, the high ceiling, it's unbearably warm, the air thick with the scent of mint and eucalyptus. Elin's eyes dart to one corner of the room. Another glass box is suspended from the ceiling. Inside, there's a helmet with a peaked brim made of what looks like brass. Walking over, she reads the text inside.

CLIAS HELMET. A fireman's helmet adapted to become a weight helmet. Used for strengthening neck muscles.

Isaac follows her gaze. "Part of 'the narrative.' " He makes quotation marks with his fingers. "All the communal spaces have them. Artifacts from the old sanatorium."

She nods, disconcerted.

Laure murmurs something to the woman at the desk, turns back. "Margot, our spa receptionist, will do a proper tour later, but I'll just show you the pool. The showpiece." Her voice is loud, patrician. As assistant hotel manager, she's clearly used to taking charge.

Elin imagines her with guests, staff. Answering questions. Issuing instructions. Watching her, she's seized by a sense of inadequacy: *Are we really the same age?* Laure seems older; a grown-up, a leader. But then, she thinks, maybe she always was.

She remembers the first time they met; eight-year-old Laure small and wiry, two thick plaits like ropes down her back. Laure instinctively knew her role in the world: commander, planner, the one to think up games, designate roles. *You're the mermaid. I'm the pirate.* Other kids would immediately acquiesce, desperate to be part of the game.

Elin knew why; Laure gave off a vibe she'd never mastered. *Not giving a shit.*

Laure was secure in who she was. There was something definite about her, a solidity anchoring her to the world that Elin envied. She was the opposite; she cared too much, fretted about every little thing: Was she too quiet? Too loud? Not enough?

Yet their differences never came between them. Their friendship was tight, fiercely protected by them both, by Elin especially, because Laure was her first proper friend. The first girl who got her, didn't try to change her, laugh at her for not being like them.

And look how you repaid her, a voice grinds out in her head. *She accepted you, befriended you, and look what you did.*

Laure opens a large door on the right. Following her inside, Elin blinks, blinded by the light flooding the space. Floor-to-ceiling glass wraps the pool on all sides, so the first thing

68

she sees isn't the water, but the swirling snow outside, the vast expanse of steely sky.

Just beyond the glass, she can make out a wooden terrace and several outdoor pools. The first, sitting just beyond the glass, is steaming, blurry coils snaking lazily into the air.

Will whistles between his teeth. "I wasn't expecting that."

"They extended at the end of the building to maximize this view." Laure's voice echoes out. "All this glass, it's deliberate. When the weather's good you've got a 360-degree view of the mountains, the natural light . . ."

"I was telling Elin about the focus on light in the original design." Will's still looking out. "They thought it helped recovery, didn't they?"

"Yes." Laure turns. "The standard of care for TB at the time was mainly environmental. Fresh air, sunlight. Ultraviolet rays were believed to be healing, so they sat patients out on the balconies and terraces, even through the winter, to take in the sun."

Elin is struggling to take it all in: Snow. The shimmering water.

It's dizzying. She still feels horribly exposed; that nothing separates them from the storm raging outside. She rubs at her temples and turns away from the glass, the swirling mass of snow.

"El? You okay?" Will says.

"Fine. Just a bit lightheaded."

"It's probably the altitude," Laure says. "We're high, for a hotel. More than seventy-two hundred feet."

"I don't think it's that," Isaac says slowly. "You used to be like this as a kid, if we went somewhere new, you felt uncomfortable."

"Isaac, stop." The words are sharper than she intended. "How is that relevant? I'm hardly a child anymore, am I?"

He holds up his hands, flattens his palms in surrender. "Chill, I was just . . ." He shakes his head.

Watching him, anger spikes in her chest. This brotherly concern, it's an act; she'd clocked the fleeting, superior smile.

As kids, he'd do this all the time: flip the conversation to expose her, lay her bare. She remembers telling her mother over dinner about a friend she'd made, Isaac immediately countering with something derogatory: *Isn't that the new girl? That weird one, who's always on her own?*

Will takes her hand, squeezes. "Shall we go?"

Grateful, Elin nods, looks to the pool itself. It's big for a hotel, floor and walls patterned with the same gray marble tiles. Tiny veins flicker up them like flames. Shimmering mirages of the snow-covered trees outside are reflected in the water.

A lone woman in a black swimsuit is doing

lengths, her muscular body illuminated in the spotlights beneath the water. Her limbs slice rhythmically through the water: an athlete's freestyle.

Isaac frowns. "Isn't that Cecile?"

Following his gaze, Laure stiffens.

"Cecile?" Elin echoes, intrigued.

"Cecile Caron. The hotel manager," Laure says. Her voice is tight. "She's the sister of the owner. She swims every day. She competed at a national level."

"She's good," Elin says, transfixed by the woman's easy prowess.

"Do you still like swimming?" Laure changes the subject.

Elin shakes her head, flushes, heat chasing up her back.

That familiar rush of feeling consumes her: embarrassment, fear, frustration.

As she turns away, it hits her: Isaac never told Laure how things changed after Sam died.

He hasn't told her any of it.

10

It's a relief to exit the pool area. Exhaling hard, Elin leans against the wall. Her breathing is heavy, labored.

What's wrong with her? This is meant to be a break, a chance to relax. It's the disadvantage of not working, her mind simultaneously overactive and underused.

But that's my choice, she thinks, her mind leaping to the e-mail she received from her detective chief inspector, Anna, a week ago.

Spoke to Jo. Need your decision at the end of the month xx

Two weeks. Two weeks to decide if she wants to end her leave, to go back.

Elin hasn't replied yet. Doesn't know what the answer is. She remembers the last time she spoke to Anna, the frustration and disappointment lacing her voice.

You're too good a detective to let this take over, Elin.

Detective.

Even the word is raw. It means too much. Not just hopes and dreams, but blood and sweat and slog — time in uniform, exams, interviews.

Now it's all in question.

Pushing the thought away, she follows Laure back down the corridor. Just ahead two men are deep in conversation.

Laure slows. Elin notices her exchange a glance with Isaac.

"Who's that?" she asks.

"One of the staff, with the hotel owner, Lucas Caron." Laure brushes a nonexistent hair away from her face. Her hand is shaking.

She's flustered. Why?

"Wasn't he meant to be away?" Isaac murmurs.

Laure nods. "With Cecile. They weren't due back until next week."

Will's still looking at one of the men, the blond with the beard. "So that's the man . . . Lucas Caron . . ."

His gaze lingers. Elin follows it, sees immediately what's caught his interest.

Lucas Caron is striking; very obviously someone powerful, important. *A boss.*

He's tall, athletic looking, but it isn't his stature that's giving off the power vibe; it's his wide-legged stance, the big expansive gestures. Only people with influence, money, possess that kind of inbuilt belief that they have the right to take up that much space.

His hiking boots, the casual, technical clothes — gray fleece, climbing trousers — only add to it, a calling card: *I'm important so I don't need to signal that I am.*

"You've heard of him?" Isaac replies.

Will nods. "There's chatter in the architecture world . . . the disruption in his style, approach." He hesitates. "If it's not too much trouble, it would be good to get an introduction at some point."

"I'm sure Laure can sort it, but I'd be careful." Isaac's tone is light. "He doesn't have much luck with architects."

"Isaac." Laure flashes him a warning look.

"Daniel Lemaitre?" Will says quickly.

Isaac raises an eyebrow. "You know about it?"

Will smiles. "Architecture's a small world. Still no news?"

"Nothing," Laure replies.

"What happened?" Elin says, still watching Lucas Caron.

"Daniel was the principal architect for the hotel. He went missing in the final stages of planning. Didn't make it home one night. Left the site in the afternoon, and that was it. His car was here, in the car park, but they found no sign of him. Gone." Isaac snaps his fingers. "No footprints. Nothing. Never found his bag, his phone . . ."

"It was big news at the time," Laure says. "Cecile and Lucas knew Daniel well. Child-

74

hood friends. Lucas was devastated. It derailed the project for a while. The hotel was meant to open in 2017, but it was delayed by a year."

"No one knows what happened to Daniel?" Will says.

"There were theories. People said he had issues with his business." Isaac shrugs. "Something to do with expanding too quickly, money problems."

"People thought he'd bolted?"

"Either that, or —"

"Isaac, stop. Enough. He'll hear." Laure flips the conversation. "I think that's everything tour-wise."

"Thanks, I —" Elin stops, her eyes alighting on the door next to Laure. It's nothing like the others in the hotel; ornate, intricately decorated with carvings of fir trees, mountain peaks circling the perimeter.

"What's this?"

Laure tugs at the scarf around her neck. "It used to be a consultation room. It's closed now. Not for use by guests."

"It's empty?"

"Not exactly." Again the hand goes up to her scarf — pulling, adjusting. "It's an archive of sorts. Artifacts stored from when it was a sanatorium. They originally planned to make a feature of it, so guests could learn about the history of the hotel."

"They haven't completed it?"

"It's been postponed." Laure hesitates. Elin senses her weighing something up in her mind. Finally, she speaks. "If you're interested, you can take a look."

Isaac frowns. "Laure, not now. They probably want to unpack."

"Of course," Laure demurs. "Another time."

"No. I'd like to see it. I love anything historical." It's true, but Elin can hear the note of challenge in her voice. This is what Isaac brings out in her. Makes her prickly, combative.

Will tenses. "Elin, we've only just arrived. I want to find our room, get settled."

"Well, you go then, with Isaac. We won't be long."

"Fine," he says tightly. "I'll see you upstairs."

Elin watches them leave, uneasy. *Is this really a good idea? Poking around somewhere private?* "Look, don't worry, really . . ."

"It's fine." Laure smiles. "But I'm warning you, it's a mess. Everything they cleared out before the refurb — it's been dumped in here." Pushing a key into the lock, she opens the door.

"You weren't joking," Elin murmurs.

The room is piled high with medical equipment: aspirators, bottles, an old-fashioned invalid chair, strange glass contraptions. Everything's covered with a thin film of dust.

There's no semblance of order; some things are boxed, others lie heaped on the floor. Office detritus is dotted about in between — cardboard boxes, filing cabinets.

"I did warn you." Laure raises an eyebrow.

"It's not that bad. I've seen worse." *Like my place.* Disorder had crept up on her — bulging cupboards, books in piles. Clothes still hanging on a flimsy metal rail that intermittently collapses under too much weight. She can't seem to summon the will or the energy to do something about it.

"It's interesting, isn't it?" Laure meets her eye. "All this. What this place used to be." Something shifts in her demeanor, composure slipping slightly, revealing a familiar energy and eagerness — a glimpse of the old Laure that wasn't there before.

Elin nods, suddenly aware of not just the mess but the room itself. The air feels dense, stifling. Thick with dust. She imagines it; tiny, filthy particles hovering. Forcing her gaze to the shelf on her right, she picks up a folder. A stack of papers plummets to the floor.

"I'll get them." Laure steps toward her, but slips, her foot sliding out from beneath her.

Elin lurches forward, grabbing Laure's arm to steady her.

"That was close." Laure rights herself.

"You okay?"

"Thanks to your quick reaction."

"Practice." Elin smiles. "Mum, last year,

she kept falling. She used to joke she needed a crash mat, not a carpet." Her voice catches. She turns away, horrified at the tears springing up in her eyes. Will her grief always be like this? Embarrassingly raw?

Laure studies her. "You looked after her?"

"Yes. More or less full time the last few months. I was on a break from work anyway, so . . ." She can hear herself, explaining it away, making less of it, and corrects herself. "I wanted to do it. We had carers, too, but Mum liked me being there."

"I didn't know," Laure says quietly.

Elin shrugs. "I'm glad I did it." It's the truth. She can't explain it any better. Until it happened, she didn't know she had the capacity — the patience, the selflessness — but it came easily.

A reflex. Caring for her mother. Giving back. She'd found something intensely rewarding in the fixed nature of the tasks. There was none of the unpredictability of police work, the nagging sense of leaving something unfinished.

"I think it's amazing. Doing that for someone." Laure hesitates, voice wobbling slightly. "I'm sorry, you know. Your mum . . . she was a lovely person."

Elin blinks, taken aback. Another glimpse of the old Laure: easy emotion, both given and received. Nothing wanted in return.

She opens her mouth, about to reply, but

the words catch in her throat. Their eyes meet and Elin looks away.

Bending, she gathers the fallen papers into a pile. She realizes it's not only papers, but photographs too. The image on top is haunting — a row of women sitting outside on the veranda. They're thin, sickly looking, their eyes turned to the camera. Looking right into hers.

Patients, Elin thinks, shivering at this tangible intrusion of the hotel's past into its present, suddenly acutely aware of how little separates her from what came before.

All at once, she feels a tightening in her throat. One breath is not following the other as it should, instead hiding, elusive, impossible to grasp. Her chest is heaving, her lungs feeling like they're filled with something liquid.

Don't panic. Don't let it take over. Not here. Not in front of Laure.

Laure looks at her closely. "Is something wrong?"

Elin fumbles in her pocket, clamping her hand around her inhaler. "I'm fine." Taking a heavy pull on it, she draws the gas deep into her lungs. "Asthma. It's been worse the last year or so. I don't think the altitude helps. Or the dust in here."

Laure nods, still watching her.

It's a lie. It's nothing to do with the asthma. She's been at altitude before, and she can't remember this feeling.

It's this place. This building.

Her body is reacting to something here; something living, breathing, woven into the DNA of the building, as much a part of it as its walls and floors.

11

"They're not coming, are they?" Will churns his spoon through the smeared remains of his lemon mousse, and looks at her.

Elin pretends she can't hear, pushes a forkful of chocolate tart into her mouth. The pastry is crumbly, the chocolate bitter, but the texture is a disappointment — thick and cloying. She slides her plate aside.

"Elin?" Will tries to catch her eye.

She looks at the table. Two squat candles dribbling wax sit in ceramic dishes between them, the flickering flame highlighting the looping grain of the wood. The table holds the dregs of the meal — half-empty wineglasses, a jug of iced water, slick with condensation, the obligatory bread basket that Will always refuses to relinquish.

"El? Are you listening?"

"We said seven thirtyish."

"Yes" — Will inspects his watch — "and it's after nine now. I don't think . . ." He trails off.

Elin picks up her phone. No missed calls. No messages.

Laure and Isaac simply haven't turned up. Shot through with anger, she reprimands herself: *He hasn't changed. He never will. Why did you think he would?*

Tears of frustration and embarrassment pricking her eyes, she turns away, pretending to study the room. It's busy, nearly all the tables full, humming with chatter. It's less stark at night, the luminous white of the walls softened by the fire, the candlelight, yet still, *the glass.* Elin hates it. Hates how vulnerable it makes her feel.

Because of her police training, she prefers environments she can feel in control of, fully aware of any risks, inherent dangers. With this expanse of glass, she hasn't got that. Even at night, the windows dominate everything. They run the length of the room, a gaping stage set, the darkness outside merging with lurid, staccato reflections of the people inside.

Anything could be out there.

Will laces his fingers in hers. "You're upset, aren't you? You expected something" — he hesitates — "different."

Elin reaches for the jug of water, sloshes some into her glass. "Yes, but I shouldn't have. This is what he does. It's a power thing, he gets some weird kick out of knowing I'll be pissed off. That's what he wants. A re-action."

"I noticed another reaction too," Will says lightly. "Laure. You never said you knew her."

"I didn't think it was important." Elin watches the candle, the liquid flicker of the flame. "It was ages ago. We were only kids."

He waits for her to continue.

"My mum and hers were friends from school. She married a Swiss guy she met teaching English in Japan. They moved here when Laure was born." Elin shrugs. "They didn't visit much. I only saw her, what, three, four times?"

She's playing it down. From the moment Laure and her mother, Coralie, arrived every August, laden down with bags, Elin and Laure were inseparable. They'd spend hours swimming, kayaking, eating picnics in the woods behind the beach — baguettes stuffed with soft cheese, fat, sticky slices of ginger cake.

When Laure went home, for Elin, summer was over. She spent hours writing to her friend, phone calls every Saturday.

But Elin knows why she's diluting it — the memories of Laure dredge up memories of herself before Sam, and she can't help but confront the difference between the old her and who she's become.

But there's something else, too, something she's tried to ignore since she arrived: *guilt.* Guilt for how she left it with Laure, how suddenly the friendship had withered and died.

83

"Did you ever visit her here?"

She shakes her head. "Mum wanted to, but money was tight."

"You didn't keep in touch?"

"No," she says abruptly. "After Sam died, everything stopped."

Elin remembers the letters Laure sent. Then later on, text messages. But Elin only halfheartedly replied — once, twice, then it petered out. It was easier somehow, not staying in touch. Not only because of the memories, but because part of her had been jealous. Life for Laure hadn't changed. She was able to move on.

"Do you know how she and Isaac got together?"

"Social media, I think. He came out here to work. The university in Lausanne isn't far from Sierre; that's where Laure lives. She helped him settle in." She shakes her head. "Part of me thinks it was deliberate, that he knew it would piss me off."

"So ignore it. Have fun. Don't give him what he wants. Relax." Will leans back in his chair. "This, the holiday, it'll only work if you don't let things get to you."

She scans the room. "I'm trying, but this place . . . there's something weird about it, isn't there? Something creepy."

"Creepy?" Will smiles. "You just don't like it because it's out of your comfort zone."

He's only half joking. He's never said it,

84

but she knows her inflexibility pisses him off. He can't understand it, come to grips with it, so he turns it into something funny.

Elin forces a smile. "Comfort zone? Come on, I'm Miss Spontaneous . . . take off at a whim . . ."

"You used to be," Will says seriously, meeting her gaze. "When we first met."

Her hand clenches around the glass. "You know what happened." Her voice is shaky. "You know what I've been through this past year."

"I know that, but you can't let it destroy you. The Hayler case, your mum, Sam, whatever this thing is with Isaac, you've let it all build up into something so huge it's swallowing the rest of your life. Your world, it's getting smaller and smaller." He smiles, but he's forcing it, she can tell. "I'm still waiting on that camping trip you promised. I bought a tent and everything."

"Stop." Elin pushes back her chair, horrified to find her chest heaving. She's going to cry again. Here, in the restaurant with Will. What he's saying, it feels like a warning. That he, like her job, isn't going to wait around forever.

She stands up. She can't face this: losing something else.

"Elin, come on, I was teasing."

"No." Heat chases up her back, her neck. "I can't do this, Will. Not now. Not here."

12

Her attacker is back: Adele can hear the rhythmic shuffle of footsteps, the heavy, sucking pull of breath.

She doesn't move from her seated position, back against the wall. She hasn't moved since she got here.

Listen. Learn. Don't waste any energy.

There's a sudden pressure on her arm. A push — sideways. Adele slams against the floor. The movement jars, sends juddering shock waves of pain through her shoulder and neck.

Crying out, she curls up on her side, legs tucked underneath her.

Her eyes are fastened shut.

Keep your eyes closed. Whatever happens, keep your eyes closed.

This is the mantra she keeps repeating in her head. She's got no idea who this person is or what they want with her, but she knows that the monstrous thing on their face is there to make her scared. She knows that if she's scared, she's weak, has no chance of getting back to Gabriel.

Her father had told her once about what fear did to the brain, a primitive reaction you can't control.

What was it called? That particular part of the brain? *Think . . .*

All she remembers is that when this tiny part of the brain senses a threat, it overrides conscious thought so the body can divert all its energy to facing the threat.

The problem with that is that the rest of the brain more or less shuts down. The cerebral cortex, the brain's center for reasoning and judgment, becomes impaired, so thinking about the best move in a crisis is impossible.

Another sound.

A zip, she thinks. Rustling.

Adele swallows hard. What are they doing?

Think, she tells herself again, *think. There's still time. . . . As long as you don't look, you can get yourself out of this.*

It's only when she feels hands on her that Adele realizes that closing her eyes is a miscalculation, that already, without her conscious knowledge, her reasoning has been impaired. By closing her eyes, she has thrown away any chance, however small, to escape.

Yes. Fear has done its damage.

Adele doesn't feel it at first. The cold, the exertion — it's numbed her skin.

All she feels is pressure. A fingertip pressure on her right thigh.

It's only when the sharp metal point of a needle slides from the subcutaneous tissue through to the muscle that it registers.

A dull, heavy pain.

Adele tries to kick, scream. She opens her eyes but she can't see anything. A blackness is already engulfing her. An impenetrable darkness that smothers everything.

13

"Please." Catching up with her, Will grabs her hand. "Come back."

"I can't." Rocking back on her heels, Elin feels the tug of it again; the tipping over into panic.

"Elin." He strengthens his grip on her hand. "If you keep walking away every time we discuss things, there's no point in being together, is there? If we can't share things, there's nothing linking us. No proper ties."

She looks at him. His face is flushed, angry, but his eyes are warm behind his glasses. Elin feels a surge of guilt: he cares, that's all. He wants to talk, which is normal, isn't it? In a couple. *Normal* is what she has to be, try to be, for Will.

She nods, following him back to the table.

When they've sat down again, Will lightly touches her arm. "Do you want to talk about it?"

"Yes." Elin hesitates. She doesn't want to start the conflict again, but the words are out before she can stop them. "Will, what you were saying then, you're wrong. I have moved on. Look at us . . ."

"You had, but it's stopped, the last few months. The past, it's like a roadblock. You're reluctant to leave the house unless it's to run, and you don't like socializing anymore." He pauses. "I heard you, you know, the other night, in bed. You called out Sam's name. I thought you were dealing with it, Elin. The grief. That it was better."

Elin absorbs his words. *Better?* How would it ever get better? Her grief for Sam is locked inside her, in every cell.

She doesn't know how to resolve it. How do you go about unpicking someone from your life when they're the thread tying every part of you together?

She knows it's hard for Will — he wants to see progress, some kind of sign that she'll be over it, if not now, then soon. Sometimes she wonders if he saw her as a bit of a project when they first got together, like one of his old buildings that needed renovating. A small redesign, one more push, the final fix, and she'll be shiny and new. Except she isn't, not yet — she's falling behind schedule — his schedule, and he doesn't like it.

"It scares me, Elin. How far this could go." Will looks at her. "Your job . . . they won't hold it forever, you know that, don't you?"

I know that, she wants to say, *but I'm not*

sure I can be a detective anymore.

She keeps telling herself that finding out the truth about what happened the day Sam died will fix everything, that she'll be able to move on, but what if it doesn't? What if this is the new status quo?

A sob backs up in her throat, comes out as a squashed, hiccupy gulp.

Will puts a hand across hers, squeezes. "Look, I shouldn't have said anything. We're both tired." He reaches for his glass. "You've been going through all of your mum's stuff, we've been traveling all day, and now this —"

He has a point. The last two evenings she'd been going through her mother's things late into the night. Every item — books, clothes, the faded photographs still in their frames — had brought memories flooding back, left her feeling strangely isolated, adrift. It's been more than six months since she died, but the grief is still raw.

Draining his wineglass, Will lowers his voice. "That's what pisses me off the most, you know. The fact that Isaac left you to deal with caring for your mum, her estate, the crappy admin, the personal stuff, and now you've come out here, for him, and he's playing games."

"I know," Elin says tightly. "But I thought it might be different this time."

Will raises an eyebrow.

"Come on, he should *want* to be here, Will.

91

It shouldn't be this hard . . . and he said, didn't he? He said we should meet for dinner."

"Stop." Will cuts across her. "We're falling for it. What we're doing — getting wound up, questioning, overanalyzing — you said that's what he wants. Let's just enjoy the night." He picks up the drinks menu, scans it. "Cocktail?"

Elin hesitates, steadies herself. "You're right. Let's make the most of being here."

Will summons the waiter over. "One of these." He stabs the menu with his finger. "And this one."

When the cocktails arrive, he laughs. "Minimalist like everything else."

He's right. The drinks are pared back, restrained. No lurid blues or pinks, no gaudy decoration. Her lychee martini is a soft blush color, a whole lychee straddling the rim of the glass. His is almost colorless.

Elin sips. The sweet tang hits her right away. The vodka burns the back of her throat: a sudden heat. It's strong.

"Try mine?" Will pushes his glass toward her. He looks at her and smiles, but it's stretched thin at the edges. He's pretending now, but a few drinks in and it'll be real.

Closing her hand around the stem of the glass, Elin feels the tension slipping from her shoulders. *Will's right.* She can't let Isaac get to her. Besides, she thinks, she isn't here to build bridges.

This is about getting him to admit what he did, once and for all.

14

Will pushes open the door and stumbles into the room. Hand jerking out, he clumsily jams the keycard into the slot on the wall.

A fail: the plastic card bends back, slides past the target. "Give it to me." Laughing, Elin takes it from him, slides it carefully into the narrow slot. The room illuminates, the bright spotlights dotted above her head sending the room into sharp relief.

Instantly, she reacts: a bitter chill moving through her. Everything about this room jars, putting her nerves on edge.

It isn't that the room's empty — there's a bed, a sofa, a table and chairs, but there's none of the usual decorative stuff for the eye to hook on to: cushions, curtains, vases.

The bed is built into the wall, jutting out in one uninterrupted line, the wardrobe, too, a strange gap beneath it. A long, low sofa fits seamlessly against the wall, the white linen cover almost an exact match to the wall itself.

Perhaps her discomfort says something

about her. She remembers her last review at work: *Elin struggles to accommodate change. This may hamper her career prospects.*

"What's wrong?" Will kicks off his shoes, mouth relaxing into a lopsided grin. His eyes are heavy lidded, loose. He's drunk. Worse than she's seen him in a while.

His phone is in his hand. A loud ping sounds out.

Elin knows what it is immediately — his WhatsApp group. Joke sharing to the extreme. Some of the members are friends, others are acquaintances, friends of friends.

Will's group communicates in a totally different way from her and her friends — no interaction is allowed beyond the actual sharing of the joke and a brief response. No pleasantries or chat, just a bombardment of jokes.

He's staring at the screen, smiling. "Look." He holds up his phone.

Elin scans the screen. *Making a belt out of watches, it's a waist of time.*

She can't help laughing. Though she'd never admit it, most of the jokes are actually pretty good. It's a puerile, basic humor — a humor that neither she nor Will has ever moved on from.

She looks down at her own phone and sighs. "Isaac still hasn't called. No message either."

She tosses the phone onto the bed, puts her fingers to her temple. Her head is starting to throb: a dull beat at the base of her neck.

Reaching for a glass, she pours mineral water into it, takes a long swig.

It doesn't get rid of the taste of the cocktails: the tang of the alcohol turning sour, metallic at the back of her throat.

"Forget it." Will smiles. "Don't ruin the night now. Not now you've relaxed."

Elin stiffens. The effects of the alcohol are starting to fade. She feels pissed off all over again.

Arm dropping to her waist, Will pulls her to him, cups her hips. "We could have a romantic first night . . ."

She shrugs him off. "Maybe." It isn't going to happen. The more she tries not to think about Isaac, the forgotten meal, the more the frustration piles up inside her.

Elin's full with it: *Their first night and he's left them high and dry. No normal person would do that. It shouldn't be this hard, surely? Equal effort from both sides. Communication.*

Weaving an unsteady path across the room, Elin pulls open the door, steps out onto the balcony. Swirls of milky ice frost the wooden slats.

She takes a breath of pure, icy air.

Another.

Her head starts to clear, the alcohol fug

96

dissolving, slipping away.

"Will, look," she calls. "You can see the view at last." The clouds are breaking up, revealing pale streaks of sky. The hazy semi-circle of moon is casting a soft light across the mountain peaks opposite.

At first glance, it's magnificent, yet the more she looks, the more she realizes how sinister the mountains appear: raw, jagged spikes. The highest is hooked, like a claw.

Elin shudders. She thinks about what Isaac told her about Daniel Lemaitre, the missing architect. *No body. No evidence.*

It's not hard to imagine, she thinks, looking out; *this place somehow consuming someone, swallowing them whole.*

"It's stunning," Will says from the doorway, "but you'd better come in. That top is thin. I've heard stories about drunk people not feeling the cold. Someone finds them the next day, semiclothed, dead from hypothermia." He looks, starstruck style, at the wooden chair beside her. "That recliner — it's the same as they'd have used back then."

"Geek." Elin smiles, then freezes, putting her finger to her lips. She can hear something: footsteps, the crisp squeak of snow. A lighter clicking. A voice, speaking in melodic French.

Peering over the balcony, she glimpses choppy black hair, a scarf.

Elin sucks in her breath.

Laure.

She's walking out of reception, slowly picking through the snow near the front of the hotel. She's wearing a thick black puffer coat, unzipped. The gray scarf is still around her neck, but loose, ends now dangling to her waist.

Laure comes to a stop just below their balcony. There's a cigarette in her hand, thin plumes of smoke eddying into the air. She's talking loudly, rapidly, into a phone, gesticulating, the tiny glowing light from the tip of her cigarette dancing against the night sky like a firefly.

Elin stays still, scared to make a move, draw attention to herself.

Laure turns, ever so slightly. The glow from the outside lights catches her face, highlighting the acute angles; the slice of jaw, the bold nose, her brows.

Her expression is fierce, her eyes narrowed, lip slightly curled.

Elin can't understand the French, but the feeling in Laure's voice is clear. Sharp edged. Angry. Nothing like the person she'd seen earlier.

Elin stares, transfixed. This new Laure is alien to her.

15

Day Two

The smell hits her first: freshly baked bread, bitter coffee, the savory tang of cheese.

Elin scans the table: baskets of shiny croissants, baguettes, tiny rolls studded with salt flakes. A dark-haired waiter, brandishing wooden tongs, is transferring pains au chocolat to an empty basket. He moves aside, revealing ham, salamis, smoked salmon, ceramic bowls of creamy yogurt.

Her stomach turns.

"Now this is what I call a breakfast." Will rubs his hands together.

Elin laughs. "Sure you'll cope?" His appetite is the stuff of legend. Post-surf, he's been known to eat not one but two twelve-inch pizzas, and then finish off with an industrial quantity of ice cream. Breakfast is his favorite meal — the big refuel.

Grinning, he nudges her. "So what are you going for?"

"I'm not really hungry." She reaches for the

jug of orange juice, and pours some into a glass. Midpour, her hand falters. "Shit." She watches the juice pool on the tablecloth, liquid sunshine, before being absorbed.

"Lightweight," Will whispers, trying not to laugh.

Elin smiles, tries to ignore the dull ache in her temple. This is why she doesn't drink. She'd tried too hard, she thinks, conscious of the moment, four cocktails in, when it became less about fun and more about obliteration.

Dangerous echoes, she thinks. Her mother did the same thing when Sam died. Drank to block it out.

Elin remembers days when her mother hardly left the house. Spent hours staring out at the beach, endless cups of tea growing cold in her hand.

Her father took the opposite approach. Accelerating, he sprang into a relentless kind of action. Cleared Sam's room. Removed all newspapers from the house. Resolutely switched off the TV whenever the news came on.

She always thinks that his leaving, only a few years after Sam's death, was the natural continuation of that. Starting another life in Wales, a new wife and family: the ultimate way to move forward. Closure by deletion of the past.

Elin couldn't escape them, though — the

100

words he'd tried so hard to outrun.

They were everywhere: at the kiosk on the seafront, in the news playing loud on TV in the restaurant.

LOCAL BOY DROWNED. THE TOWN IS STILL IN MOURNING AFTER THE TRAGIC DEATH OF SAM WARNER, AGE EIGHT.

Elin shrugs the thought away. "Are they here?" Taking a plate, she glances across the room. However positively she tries to position it in her head, it's going to be awkward — the missed meal, the memory of seeing Laure from the balcony, angry and exposed.

Will looks over her shoulder. "No. All clear." Stabbing a piece of salami, he levers it onto his plate.

Nausea sweeps over her. The thick slices of sausage are slick with oil, tiny orbs of white fat studding the interior. "I'll try some bread." Picking up a plain roll, she spoons a single, scarlet blob of jam onto her plate.

She finds a table by the window, sips her orange juice. The liquid is thick, fresh, the pulp fibrous on her tongue.

Head starting to clear, she looks outside. Fresh snow is piled high against the windows, impossibly white against the blue-sky backdrop. For the first time, it looks inviting rather than sinister. Perhaps Will's suggestion to go for a walk wasn't such a bad idea.

101

Will strides toward her, plate piled high. "Don't look now, but Isaac's just walked in. He's on his own." Sitting down, he lowers his voice. "He's coming over."

Elin looks up as her brother approaches. "Hey." She keeps her tone neutral, already preparing words, clever sentences spooling through her head, but stops when she sees his face.

Something's wrong, Elin thinks, looking at his mussed-up hair, the wild expression in his eyes.

"Laure's gone missing," he says quietly, looking around to check that no one's in earshot.

"What?" Her pulse quickens.

"She's missing," Isaac repeats. "Something's happened to her."

16

Jeremie Bisset powers up the narrow path behind Le Sommet into the forest. Instantly, his surroundings darken, the open trail giving way to a mass of dense-growing pines.

In summer, the path is a rocky trail, used by hikers to access the glacier beyond, but now it's choked with snow. Smothered.

He tilts his head upward. Overnight, the sky has cleared. It's now a pale, milky blue, streaked with fragmented wisps of cloud. It won't last. The forecast for the next week is grim.

Within minutes, he finds a rhythm; a steady metronome of pole and ski. A surge of euphoria: he loves this, the uphill slog. In the winter, he tours every morning before work. Sets the alarm before dawn, follows the trail up toward Aminona.

It's the only thing he does with any kind of regularity. Usually, he hates routine of any kind. It reminds him of the hospital. The final days with his father. Every day a grim loop of brittle regularity — ward rounds, medication, lights out.

Jeremie forces the thought away. His breath is coming hard now, fast. His hamstrings and quads are already burning.

Not an easy ascent, but that's why he likes it. Part of him wonders if it's psychological — the repetitive climb his way of dispelling the feeling that he's constantly falling. Last night, again, he'd woken in the predawn under damp sheets. Grief. Work. The ongoing custody battle.

He pictures his ex's face; the disdain clearly visible as she bundled Sebastien into the car.

Jeremie pushes the thought away, powers on.

Within minutes, he's through the forest.

A sudden light, dazzling off the snow. The dim gloom of the forest canopy has given way to an open bowl above the tree line. No vegetation can grow here. The only thing between him and the glacier above is a wall of gray pleated limestone, its serrated undulations crusted with snow.

Jeremie stops, listens to his breath, exhalations coming in short, ragged puffs.

Sweat is trickling down his back beneath his thermals. Waiting for his breathing to settle, he looks out. He can see right down to the valley floor. Jutting cranes bisect the town, giant right angles looming over the cuboid shapes of the industrial heartland. A blocky, manmade geometry, nothing like the raw of the wilderness here.

The wind gusts, tugging at his jacket. He shivers, thinking about the impending forecast, the storm closing in.

Moving rapidly, he tears the skins from his skis, thin strips that stick to the base of the skis for ascending slopes, which he removes for skiing downhill. The special surface allows him to slide forward on the snow, but not backward.

He deftly winds up the skins, and folds them against the netting so they don't stick together. He returns them to their bag. As he zips it shut, he stops.

A noise. Footsteps?

Jeremie pivots, scans his surroundings.

Nothing. No signs of life.

Again.

The sound is muted, indistinguishable.

Turning his head, he examines the landscape around him more slowly this time. There's no one there. He holds his breath, ears ringing in the silence.

Another sound.

Perhaps it's coming from above . . .

Jeremie rakes his eyes over the sheer face of rock above him.

He startles, heart racing.

The more he looks, the more the mountains above seem to be moving toward him. With a thicker covering of snow than in decades, the towering cornices and ridges of the mountains no longer look familiar, but something sinister, alien.

Jeremie drags his eyes away. He's tired, he thinks. Four hours' sleep — it screws with your mind.

He crouches down, pulling his boots tighter, and flicks his bindings into downhill mode. Skating forward, he reaches the trail running parallel to the forest.

With no lift system in this half of the valley, the snow is thick, untouched, an unbroken expanse of white.

As he starts to turn, adrenaline surges through him. His skis throw thick, gauzy clouds of powder into the air.

Halfway down, he slows. He can see something ahead; a glinting, a reflection in the snow that shouldn't be there.

A piece of metal? It's hard to tell . . .

He waits until he's parallel with it and then stops.

A bracelet.

A smooth arc of bronzed metal. Copper.

It's then he sees something else, stuck to some kind of material. A faded blue cotton. His breath catches in his throat, his eyes finding the button on the underside. The fabric — it's clothing.

Jeremie clicks out of his skis, a chill moving through him.

He stumbles in the deep, powdery snow,

each step burying his legs up to the knee.

When he reaches the bracelet, he kneels down. Closing his fingers around the top of the metal, he tugs. It isn't going to come easily.

It's wedged in, snow and ice set like cement around it. As he digs his hand into the snow, he pushes as much of it away as he can, trying to gain enough room to get his fingers around the top of the bracelet.

It won't budge. He'll have to go farther, loosen the snowpack around the sides as well. Pulling off his glove, he uses his fingers to scrabble, lever the snow away.

Useless.

Within seconds, his fingers are red, numb. Pulling off his rucksack, he reaches for his pocketknife. He flicks it open and starts hacking at the snow, jabbing the hard surface with the blade, hooking dense, crystalline clumps away.

Better.

A few inches in, he can see more of the bracelet, more of the fabric.

Pinching his fingers around the top of the bracelet, Jeremie yanks hard. He jerks backward, the material and bracelet coming with him, together with something else.

Jeremie stares, frozen.

Bile fills the back of his throat. Dropping the knife and the bracelet, he gags, vomiting over and over into the snow.

17

"Isaac," Elin starts, her words puncturing the strange silence. "If this is some weird joke . . ." He'd done things like this as a child. Nothing was off-limits. Anything to get a reaction.

"It's not." Isaac's eyes lock on to hers. "When I woke up, she was gone." His face is pale, purple shadows under his eyes.

"Maybe she's gone for a swim, or to the gym?" Elin suggests. "The hotel's enormous. There must be loads of places she could be."

"I've checked. No one's seen her. Taking off like this, it's not like her." He sits down. "I found this, too, near our door." Pulling something from his pocket, he places it on the table in front of her.

A necklace.

The fine loops of the chain spill over the table; a liquid, sinuous gold. Elin stares, her eyes finding the small gold *L* in the center. "That could have just fallen off."

"Look at it," Isaac urges. "The chain's

broken. Something's happened."

"Like what?" A familiar surge of frustration: she's forgotten this. The relentless attention seeking, the endless pivots from one drama to another.

"I don't know, but she'd have felt it break. Stopped to pick it up if she could. Coralie gave it to her. It's special." He hesitates. "Like Sam's necklace is to you."

Elin's hand comes up on autopilot, clamps around the chain. Her mother had the necklace made a few years after Sam died: his lucky crabbing hook, cast in silver.

"So what are you trying to say?"

"It's like she left in such a hurry, she didn't have time to pick it up, or couldn't . . ."

"Maybe."

A waiter appears next to Isaac. "Coffee?"

Isaac gives a brusque nod. "Black, please."

"Perhaps she went for a walk?" Will says, still chewing. "The weather's better."

"Maybe, but why wouldn't she leave a note? Something's wrong. I know it. She wouldn't just go off without telling me."

His anxiety is contagious. Elin can't help but feel panicked, even though what he's saying is surely an overreaction. Why assume she's missing? She hasn't been gone long. There are many possible explanations for where she might be.

Then she pictures the scene she'd glimpsed last night. Laure, on the phone outside, the violent, angry expression on her face.

"When did you last see her?"

"Last night. We were in bed, reading. Turned off the light about eleven."

"You didn't hear anything in the night? No disturbances?"

Will looks at her, surprise marking his features. He's never seen her like this, Elin thinks. *In work mode.* It surprises her, too: a year out of the force yet it's still there — a reflex, throwing out questions, gathering information.

"Nothing," Isaac replies.

The waiter returns with a jug of coffee, places it on the table in front of them. Steam swirls in a ragged line to the ceiling.

"Look," Elin says, "at work we see stuff like this all the time. People panic because someone's gone off, they worry because it's out of character, but usually there's an explanation, some kind of emergency, a friend needing help . . ."

"Without leaving a note? Without calling?" Isaac scoffs, a sharpness to his tone. "Come on, you'd only just arrived. We had plans for today. The spa . . ."

Again, Elin thinks about Laure pacing outside on the phone, glowing cigarette tip dancing wildly against the night. "So you've got no idea where she could be?"

Isaac's face darkens. "No." He pours coffee into his cup. The steaming liquid sloshes over the sides, pooling on the table.

"Has her phone gone, any of her stuff?" If this was a missing persons case, Elin thinks, this is the first thing she'd ascertain. *Was this spontaneous or planned?*

"Nothing. Not her phone, her bag." Isaac picks up a napkin, rubs it over the liquid. "Elin, her clothes are there, her toiletries . . . she hasn't taken anything. You'd hardly leave everything if you'd planned to take off, would you?"

"Look," she says, treading carefully, "sometimes people do take off. Leave their stuff behind. It's not unheard of." She hesitates, unsure of how to phrase it right. "Isaac, did anything happen last night?"

"No."

Something in his inflection makes her tense. *He's keeping something from me.*

"Isaac, please. You've got to be honest."

The last corner of the napkin turns sodden; a pale, murky brown.

Isaac nods. "Last night, Laure was upset. Edgy. I assumed she was stressed, about seeing you again, but now I think it was something else." He frowns. "She was off, preoccupied. I was getting ready for dinner, and she came out of the shower, announced she wasn't coming. Said something had come up. I got angry, said whatever it was, she should put it off, because we'd agreed to meet you."

"So you were planning on coming?" Keep-

111

ing her voice level, she notes his lack of apology.

"Yes, but I wanted Laure to come too." He rubs his eyes. "I don't know, perhaps I should have said forget it, I'd go on my own, but it was your first night here. We started arguing. It escalated. Laure's stubborn. Once she digs her heels in . . ."

"Did she tell you what she was planning on doing instead?"

"No. That's what pissed me off. All she said was that it had to do with the hotel."

"Work?"

"Yes. The last few months, it's been nonstop for her." Draining his coffee, he stands up. His body is tense, coiled. "I'm going to ring around to her friends, family, the neighbors in Sierre. If it's possible she might have taken off without her stuff, it's worth a try."

"You're sure you don't want something to eat first?"

No reply; he's already walking away.

Will waits until Isaac is out of earshot, then looks at her. "You did say this trip wasn't going to be straightforward." His words are light but she can hear the tension in them. He hacks at the slice of salmon on his plate.

Elin forces a smile. "Chances are she's in the hotel. They had a fight, she's probably drinking coffee in some dark corner of the lounge, hiding."

"Is that what you'd do to me?" Will forks a

ragged, pinkish sliver of salmon into his mouth, face deadpan. "Punish me by hiding away?"

"Will, don't joke."

He smiles. "Sorry. I just think it's too early, isn't it? For him to be pronouncing something bad has happened."

"But what about last night? Laure. On the phone. Outside our room. If she's missing, then it could be relevant."

The words hang in the air. Elin reprimands herself. This is supposition. They don't know anything. Yet again, she's reminded why she shouldn't be working. She isn't ready, is she? This guesswork, the jumping to conclusions — it's wrong.

"Elin, already he's got you on edge."

"So what do you propose I do? Ignore what he's saying?" Elin's grip tightens on the glass, fingertips turning white from the pressure.

"No, but for what it's worth, I think it's bullshit. They've had some tiff, and you're bearing the brunt of it."

Elin doesn't reply. Looking up, she sees Isaac walking down the corridor. She absorbs his silhouette, the loping, slightly bowlegged walk. It's so familiar it stings. She blinks. Memories rise up, like bubbles coming to the surface.

Sky. Running clouds. The black dart of birds.

Then blood, always blood.

113

Will glances at her. "I don't know if you realize it, but you always look a certain way when you see him."

"A certain way?" Elin can hear her heart, pulsing in her ears.

"Scared." Will pushes his plate away. "Every time you see him you look scared."

18

Wiping his mouth with the back of his hand, Jeremie turns, forces his gaze back to the snow, the grim discovery. The bile stings, acidic in his throat.

Beneath the bracelet is bone. Bone contorted in an inhuman angle.

He shifts position, barely able to catch his breath. He can feel sweat beading up on his forehead.

There have been a few discoveries like this over the past few years; global warming forcing glaciers to retreat, revealing corpses missing for decades.

Not far from here, a married couple was found on a glacier near Chandolin, over seventy-five years after their disappearance. They'd fallen into a deep crevasse.

Photos appeared for days in the newspapers, online: graphic and intrusive, despite the passing of the years. A battered leather bag, a wine bottle. Black heeled boots with old-fashioned, crudely nailed soles.

Jeremie had been transfixed — not only by what the pictures revealed of a forgotten way of life, but by the magnitude of what they represented: closure. He imagined the family, their descendants, their grief no longer suspended.

He moves his gaze lower. Below the bracelet, a watch. It's expensive, he can tell: wide, gold strap, a large, flashy face, bezel studded with tiny diamonds.

There are words on the inside of the strap — an engraving. He peers closer.

Daniel Lemaitre.

Jeremie recoils. *The missing architect.*

Opening his pocket, he pulls out his phone and dials 117, a fresh band of sweat breaking out across his forehead.

19

"Isaac." Elin raps on the door. "Isaac, it's me." Her chest is prickling with heat, the technical merino layer she's wearing designed for outside, not in.

The door swings open. Isaac's face is flushed, blotchy.

"Sorry I didn't call before," Elin says, hesitant. "Will wanted to go for a walk after breakfast." She forces a smile. "We didn't get far. The snow's so deep."

Isaac nods, something shifting across his face: a flash of emotion, gone so fast she can't make it out. It was the same when they were children. Elin floundering, at a disadvantage, wondering what was going through his mind.

He turns and walks back into the room.

"Isaac, is it all right to come in?" It's ridiculous that she needs to ask, but it's impossible to tell if he wants her there.

"It's fine," he says abruptly.

Walking in, she clocks his hiking boots on the floor. They're wet; the black laces splayed,

117

sodden, encrusted with fragments of ice. "You've been outside too?"

Isaac nods, pacing past the window. "Just got back."

Elin doesn't reply, taken aback by how rapidly he's speaking. He's wired, she can tell. This frenetic movement, the flushed face.

He's panicking.

"What were you doing?"

"Looking for her. Up toward the forest. I thought maybe she'd gone outside, fallen." His features are tense. "I've tried everything else. Searched the hotel, the rest of the grounds. Called friends, family . . ."

Elin looks at him, a crushing feeling enveloping her, as if she's being held too tight. Isaac's movements, the pacing to and fro, suddenly seem exaggerated.

"And?"

"No luck. There's no sign of her. No one's heard from her either. I've just called the police."

"Already?" She tries to keep her expression neutral.

He nods. "Useless. Said she hasn't been missing long enough to warrant them investigating. They said that if there's no sign she's gone out hiking or skiing, and isn't in trouble, then we should leave it for now." He shakes his head. "I know she hasn't been gone long, but I don't like it. If she's okay, why hasn't she called by now?"

118

"I don't know." Elin walks farther into his room. "There could be . . ." She stops.

The glass.

Once again, it overwhelms her. Isaac's room faces out toward the forest. The terrain is wild: a dense mass of snow-covered firs lifting up toward the mountains.

Her eyes dart between the trees. Even though the branches are covered in snow, the overall impression is of something dark, impenetrable.

She can feel her heart beating faster. Swallowing hard, she's conscious of not being able to control her response.

Why is she reacting like this? This visceral response, every cell in her body repelled by what's in front of her.

Isaac follows her gaze, face impassive. "Laure hates the forest. She always says it's the perfect cover for someone looking in. We can't see them, but they can see us. These windows, lights . . . they've got the perfect view."

"Enough." The more she looks, the more distorted the image becomes, like the trees are replicating in front of her.

"You okay?" Isaac's still studying her.

"Fine."

"You don't still get panic —"

"No," she says abruptly, cutting him off. "I don't." She overcompensates with a loud, exaggerated yawn before forcing her gaze onto the room itself.

The same layout as hers, but a larger, busier artwork hangs on the wall, the soft furnishings a milkier shade of gray. Her eyes lock on detail: laptop, TV, unopened bottles of water. Clothes and shoes are scattered across the floor. Laure's shoes — a pair of navy New Balance trainers, scuffed hiking boots, suede slip-ons.

In fact, most of the stuff is Laure's. The jewelry on the side, a mossy-colored scarf slung over the wardrobe door, a tub of face cream, lid off.

Elin looks at the bed. Here is Isaac's influence — the faint imprint of his body against the sheets, duvet snarled into a loose knot. He slept like that as a child. They both had. Like the bed was unable to contain their energy. She doesn't sleep like that anymore. That energy had left her months ago.

Her gaze moves to a lopsided stack of books on one of the bedside tables. French. One is open facedown, splayed wide, spine bent at the middle. Isaac's right, she realizes. There's a sense of suspended animation, like Laure's simply gone down for breakfast. It doesn't look like a deliberate decision to leave. "Where's her phone?"

"Phone?" Isaac's gaze snaps back to her.

Elin stiffens, something in his tone prickling her. "I'm just trying to help."

He nods, forces a smile, but there it is

again; a shadow of an expression, gone before she can make sense of it.

"Here." Pulling a phone from his pocket, he taps in a code, passes it to her. "I've been through it. There's nothing odd."

Elin looks at the screen. It's almost fully charged, connected to the same network that her phone had found when she landed in Geneva — Swisscom. She scrolls through the call log. The last call was yesterday morning. Someone called Joseph.

How was that possible? She heard Laure on the phone after dinner — surely that call should be logged here?

Isaac looks over her shoulder, his breath uncomfortably hot against her neck. "That's her cousin."

"And you know everyone else on here?"

"Of course. Friends, like I said. There's nothing on her e-mail either." Stepping back, his face colors. "I didn't want to look, but —"

"What about her laptop?"

"Nothing." He grabs it from the desk, passes it to her. "It's synced to her phone. The e-mail is the same. Everything else looks like work stuff."

Elin perches on the end of the bed, flicking through the desktop, the saved documents, internet history. He's right — it all looks work related. Nothing obviously concerning.

Putting the laptop back on the desk, she

heads into the bathroom, Isaac right behind her. Makeup is scattered around the sink — compacts, moisturizer. Several towels are curled in wonky S's on the floor. A white canvas toiletry bag is open on the shelf above the sink.

Delving through the contents, she finds pink fat-bellied tweezers, wax strips, a blusher brush and compact, tinted moisturizer, mascara. Tampons are zipped into a side pocket along with antihistamines and a foil strip of ibuprofen.

As she zips the bag back up, Elin feels a creeping sense of uneasiness. *She wouldn't leave this behind.* If Laure were planning on going somewhere, if she was anything like her, this toiletry bag was a safety blanket. Part of her daily armor.

She turns, about to speak, and it's then she sees it — in the reflection of the mirror, Isaac grabbing something from the other side of the shelf, sliding it into his pocket.

Elin watches, motionless. He turns, smiles — he hasn't noticed she's seen him.

Quick, but not quick enough: *He took something. Hid something from me. He's meant to be upset about his missing girlfriend, but he's already being deceitful.*

Her fingers clench, disgust thickening in her throat, a solid mass. How could she be so stupid? She'd nearly fallen for it, the words,

122

the feigned emotion, but people don't change, do they? The ability to lie, deceive, it's woven so deep, it's impossible to pick out, remove.

When they were children, Isaac lied all the time. He hated his middle status — two years younger than Elin, two years older than Sam — so lying became his default: a way to grab attention, to take advantage, to put them in their place.

She remembers Sam proudly bringing home his first swimming trophy, Isaac's barely concealed expression of agony as their parents effusively praised him. Two weeks later, a deep groove appeared in the wooden stand; more than a scratch — a slash. Something that could never be passed off as accidental.

Isaac denied it, but they all knew it was him. Knew what he was capable of.

"This must be like being back at work for you." Picking up one of the towels from the floor, he feeds it through the rail. "You know, I'd never have thought it. You, in the police, all this time."

"I know."

"You never did say," he continues, "why you decided on it. When we were kids, you wanted to be an engineer."

Elin looks at him, feels the words coming, backing up inside her. She could just come out with it, couldn't she?

I chose to do it because of you, Isaac. Because of what you did.

20

"What are you working on at the moment?" Isaac breaks her reverie.

It would be easy to lie, but Elin can't. Can't add another layer onto something already far too complex. "I'm not working. I'm on a break," she replies, walking back into the bedroom.

"A break?" Isaac follows, stops beside the window.

"Yes. There was this case, a big one." She's gabbling, heat chasing up her neck. "I screwed up."

Images come, spooling: *Splayed fingers across her face. Striations of rock: variegated streaks of gray and black. The water. Always the water.*

"What happened?"

"I can't really say."

"Elin, come on, I'm hardly going to tell anyone."

She nods. "The case was high profile. My first one as a DS. A murder, two girls, both fifteen. The guy had tied their bodies to a boat, let the propeller do the work." Elin tenses, remembering. "We had nothing to go on. The boat was stolen. No prints. No CCTV footage at the harbor thanks to blown-out cameras. We ended up putting out an appeal. Online, papers. A press conference with the parents." She clears her throat. "A month in, we had a breakthrough. An anonymous tip-off gave us a name — Mark Hayler. We found him on the database. Previous arrests for possession of Class As, a conviction for grievous bodily harm."

"A proper lead." Isaac scratches the corner of his eye, the skin sore and angry looking.

"It was. We went to his home address, but he'd got wind we were searching for him. We found him at his ex's. He surprised us, ran toward the seafront. We split up. I caught sight of him, tried to call it in, but my radio was bust. I didn't think, just followed. Across the beach, into the caves. I went in, but I lost him. By the time I came back out, the tide was in, up to my neck. I started swimming, but he was in the water, waiting. He hit me with a rock." She touches her lip. "That's how I got the scar."

"I noticed."

"He kept pushing me under. I . . . I froze. It was like my body . . . it stopped working. Eventually, I went under, didn't come back up." She gives a funny, brittle laugh. "I think

126

he assumed I'd had it then, left me there."

Elin doesn't tell him how when she was under, part of her had almost let go. It had felt so strong. The desire to give in. Stop fighting. But her will to live came out stronger. The will to know the truth about what happened to Sam.

The thought, once again, pulls her up sharp. Reminds her why she's here. "I took some sick leave that turned into a career break, and here I am. Unofficially unemployed."

"You don't want to go back?"

"It's not that I don't want to; I feel like I can't. Haven't got it in me. The mistakes I made, not stopping to think, not waiting for backup, it made me question my judgment, my ability . . . the fact that I froze like that in the water, it made me realize that I hadn't dealt with stuff like I thought I had."

Isaac looks at her steadily. "I didn't know. I'm sorry."

Elin finally meets his gaze. Wary at first, then all at once it's replaced by an anger that's more comfortable, more familiar. Easier to control.

"We haven't spoken, Isaac. That's why you don't know. We've hardly talked since you left."

"I know." His voice cracks. "But I didn't know then what would happen."

"You mean Mum's cancer." Her words are cold.

Isaac's head dips. "Yes. I didn't know how to come back, even if I should. I didn't want to upset things. Rock the boat." His face is sullen.

Elin stares at him in disbelief, a white-hot fury pushing through her.

He doesn't get it.

Even now, he doesn't get it. Doesn't understand what his absence had done, how it had torn their mother apart.

"Upset things? Mum wanted to see you, Isaac. Not just phone calls, or your bullshit e-mails." She feels herself shaking. "You didn't even come to her funeral. Do you know how that felt? How it looked to other people?"

"That's what it's all about for you, isn't it?" He stiffens. "How it *looks.*"

Elin balks. *There it is again, surfacing: the real him.* Sharp little words like poisonous darts. "Stop trying to turn it on me. This is about you."

"I couldn't get off work. I told you."

"Rubbish. That's just an excuse."

Isaac's hand goes back up to his eye, tugging at his lid.

"You're not even going to try to justify it?"

Silence, then: "Fine. You want the truth? I felt like shit, Elin. Guilty. Guilty I hadn't been back, that I didn't call enough. Guilty of how

128

I left it."

Her thoughts skitter. "So you did think about it?"

Isaac nods. "I kept wondering if I should come back, to visit, but part of me knew me being around would have the opposite effect. That it would hurt her."

"Hurt? Mum had been hurt for years. Ever since Sam."

Isaac visibly flinches at his name. She's seized by a sudden desire to ask him: *Do you think about Sam, Isaac? Do you?*

Because she does. She thinks about him all the time; Sam jumping off the kayak, skinny body making shapes in the air. Sam on the Downs, his kite cutting the sky into pieces of blue. Sam holding her hand when Isaac shouted. Sweet-hot whispers in her ear: *I won't let go.*

"Sam, what happened, it destroyed Mum. You know that. That day, the day we found him . . ." Her words are coming rapidly, too rapidly. She's scared she can't control them, won't be able to stop herself from asking him outright.

Did you do it, Isaac? Was it you?

Panic flares in his eyes. "Let's not go into that now. You wanted to know the reason I didn't come back."

Elin wavers. She could still do it, ask him, but what if she scares him off? She'll be left with nothing.

Finally, she nods.

"Mum . . . she was better," Isaac falters. "With you, later on, she found an . . . equilibrium. You were always so much better with her than I was. When she got ill, I knew seeing me would make it worse. She'd have stressed about me living here, taking so long to find a job . . ."

Elin looks at him, her cheeks prickling with heat, unable to believe what he's doing: trying to justify his selfishness. Opening her mouth, she's about to retaliate, when her attention is pulled toward the window. There's a helicopter hovering in the sky. It's painted red and white, a spray of shooting stars branding the side.

"What's that?" She can hear it now: the rhythmic *whump-whump* of the blades.

"An Air Zermatt helicopter." His eyes follow its movement toward the forest.

"Why would it be here?" Elin squints upward. The propellers are moving so fast they're invisible. A blur.

"I don't know. Usually they're used for transporting things — building supplies, avalanche defenses. It's the cheapest way of getting things around the mountain."

She catches another movement: two 4×4s, driving up the winding road toward the hotel, tires sending a fine dusting of snow into the air.

The first vehicle has emergency lights on the roof. Lurid, fluorescent orange streaks mark the bonnet. White and orange stars form the shape of a flag on the side. Next to that, a single word in black, in lowercase: "police."

The cars stop near the entrance to the hotel. Elin watches two groups climb out. Six people, seven. The two from the first car are wearing navy trousers, a two-tone blue jacket, "police" emblazoned on the back. The second group are in more technical clothing — softshells with thin sleeveless jackets over the top.

There's an urgency to their movements as they rush to the boot of the 4×4, start pulling out various pieces of equipment. Leaning on the tailgate, they tug off their shoes, replacing them with ski boots. As if in unison, they slip on black harnesses. Various carabiners, pulleys, and slings are attached to each, swinging against their chests as they work.

A shiver shoots down Elin's spine: a cold prickle of fear. "Who are they?"

"The Groupe d'Intervention." Isaac's voice is tight. "Like police special forces. They're trained to deal with similar situations. Hostage. Terror. Some, like these, work in the high mountains."

"Why would they be here?"

Jaw twitching, his gaze moves to the helicopter, swooping low over the mountain. "I don't know."

The group on the ground hoist large rucksacks onto their backs. Elin and Isaac watch as they put on helmets, lift skis out of the car. They walk quickly toward the path leading to the forest. For the first time, Elin notices a familiar man in a gray fleece talking to the first group of police, pointing at the forest.

"Lucas Caron," Isaac murmurs.

Elin nods. It's then she sees it: on the rug beneath her feet.

Blood.

Barely visible unless you knew what you were looking at, had seen it before.

A hazy splatter pattern, blooming out in tiny, ragged circles.

21

Adele is shivering. Her limbs are numb, prickling.

How long has she been asleep? Hours? The whole night? It's impossible to tell: the real world seems to have dissolved around her. Wherever she is, it's dark. *No,* she corrects, pulse quickening — not dark. Something's fastened around her eyes — a rough, scratchy fabric, catching on her eyelashes as she tries to open them.

Panic pulls through her. Seized with a sudden, overwhelming claustrophobia, she kicks out, tries jerking her arms and legs, but they won't move.

Stop. Calm down. Work out what's going on.

Adele slows down this time, isolating the movements. She wriggles her hands, her fingers, realizes that they're bound, fastened behind her back. Ankles too.

She's still sitting on the floor, back propped against a wall.

Keep going, she tells herself. If she's alone,

which she thinks she is, she needs to orient herself. Work out where she is.

Adele listens. All she can hear is dripping, a steady trickle. Is she in the hotel somewhere? They can't have moved her far, surely? Not without someone noticing.

What if she shouts? Tries to get someone's attention?

It's then she tastes something in her mouth: coppery, salty. It takes a moment to realize what it is.

Blood.

Adele tries to run her tongue around her teeth, work out where it's coming from, but she can't. There's something in her mouth . . . a gag. Her mouth is so numb, she hadn't noticed.

Fear flaring in her stomach, her thoughts run full pelt: *You're going to die here, aren't you? You're never going to make it out of this. You can't move, can't shout. No one will find you.*

She takes a deep breath. *Stop.* She has to get through this. For Gabriel.

Think.

She's fit, strong from the physical demands of her job. She can figure something out.

An idea starts to form: she can take advantage of the fact that, whoever this person is, he or she might not come back for a while. That might be enough time to get a sense of

134

the space, what she might be able to use to get free . . .

There won't be another way, she thinks, panic rising up inside her. No one will miss her.

Gabriel isn't due back from his dad's for a week. He won't think it unusual she hasn't called for a few days. Stephane likes his week to be his and his alone. Truth be told, it's always suited her. Adele didn't want to hear the high, overenthusing tones of Lise, Stephane's girlfriend, in the background.

Work won't raise the alarm either. She's not on shift for several days.

Adele tenses. She can hear footsteps.

Her plans . . . they're too late.

Her captor is back, close. Adele can smell them: something chemical, caustic, the starched, bleached odor of a hospital.

Something else, too, hanging heavy in the air. It's the scent of something primal — excitement, anticipation.

Whoever this is . . . they want to hurt you.

Another noise: breathing, labored and heavy. *They're right beside you.*

Terror mounting, she tries to move, but her wrists are throbbing, the rope burning into her flesh.

All at once there are fingers on her face, touching and probing. The blindfold is ripped away with such force it yanks the flesh on her cheeks, leaving them throbbing. Tears sting her eyes, but she forces them back.

A flashlight beam, swinging wildly, ricochets from floor to ceiling and back again.

It settles on her face, the fierce glare blinding her. Adele blinks, wants to put her hand up, shield her eyes from the searing ferocity of the light, but she can't.

The flashlight beam dips momentarily and scuds along the floor.

Taking her chance, she looks up, adrenaline coursing through her body. Adele can't see much; her eyes are still adjusting to the light. Every time she moves her head, the dim scene in front of her seems to rotate, but she can see one thing, above anything else: the outline of a mask.

The figure, blurred and amorphous, crouches down. With the loose clothing and the mask, it's still impossible to tell whether it's a man or a woman.

Her captor positions the flashlight on the floor, beam focused on the back wall. They start rooting through a bag on the floor.

What are they doing?

She waits: silence.

There's a strange moment of suspension, a lag. Adele feels a sudden rush of fury. If they want to hurt her, kill her, then be done with it. Not this . . . not this *delay.*

She makes a decision. If her captor comes near, she'll use the only weapon she has: the force of her body. She'll jerk forward, strike them with the full weight of her head. Inflict whatever damage she can. She isn't going to make it easy.

But they don't move any closer. Instead, they reach out a hand, a piece of paper held between two fingers. The paper is only inches from her face, so close the image on it blurs.

Her captor moves it backward. The photograph resolves.

Adele instantly recognizes it — a male body. Lifeless. Mutilated. Bloody.

She now knows that this is no mistaken identity. No random assault. This is planned, meticulously planned.

Revenge.

Her stomach turns. She wants to retch, but she knows she can't. With the gag in her mouth, she'll choke. Instead, she tries to control her breathing. Pull air deep into her lungs.

Don't move a muscle. Don't react. Don't let them know they're getting to you.

She forces herself to think about Gabriel. Supplant the blunt force of the image with happy ones: his baby toes curling up when he fed. Fat, starfish hands clutching soggy batons of cucumber. The green-blue of his irises.

But the vision of Gabriel dissolves: the image in front of her is replaced with another.

A close-up.

The photograph plummets to the floor. She

can sense movement, behind her. A hand at the back of her head, in her hair. There's a slackening around her mouth.

Her captor has removed the gag. *Perhaps this is it,* she thinks. Perhaps the photos were the point of all this. They wanted her to see the photos, and now they'll let her go. It's then she sees it: another mask, directly in front of her, thin cracks in the rubber like sores.

Adele wonders if she's seeing double. If there's another person in the room.

But as the mask moves, gets closer, she realizes it isn't another person at all.

The mask is for her.

22

Isaac follows her gaze, eyes widening. "Shit, I hadn't noticed."

"You hadn't noticed," Elin says evenly, her pulse pounding in her ears, "that there's blood on the rug?"

"No, but it's hardly anything, is it?" Crouching down, Isaac rocks forward on his haunches. "Besides, how do you even know it's blood? It could be anything, a stain . . ."

"It's blood." Her fingers curl into a fist.

"Well, if it is, it's probably been there ages." Tiny beads of moisture are breaking out on his upper lip.

Elin shakes her head. "I don't think so. The standard of cleaning is really high in a hotel like this. Marks like this — the rug would be cleaned, or replaced."

Her tone is brisk, matter-of-fact, but internally, she's raging: *He has answers for everything, doesn't he? Never fazed.*

Isaac straightens, pushes his hair away from his face. "You think it's Laure's?"

139

"It looks recent, so I'm guessing it's from you or her. Has either of you hurt yourself since you got here? A cut, or . . ."

Relief floods Isaac's features. "I know what it is. Laure cut herself shaving the other night. It was deep, wouldn't stop bleeding. I had to get her a Band-Aid, from downstairs. She must have walked across the rug."

Elin processes it: *Laure cut herself shaving.* It's the most likely explanation.

But another thought is there, beating through her head:

He's done it before. He's capable.

Elin's eyes fix on the vase in the corner, the glass reflecting a tiny prism of the room, swimming in front of her. Her head feels like it's going to explode. She doesn't know what to feel.

Already, she thinks, she's being sucked in, turned this way and that, no idea what's up or down. She's forgotten this — how mercurial it is, being with Isaac.

Trying to gauge him . . . it was like looking through water. One minute you have the perfect view, can see right to the bottom, but within seconds, the water's shifted, and all you can see is something hazy and unclear.

Isaac touches her arm. "Elin, are you all right?"

She hesitates, a beat too long. "Fine." She gives a tight smile, but her eyes find more blood.

More rust-colored specks dotting the soft fibers of the rug.

Back in her room, Elin closes the door and leans against it, waits for the churning nausea to subside.

There's a note from Will.

Gone for a swim. Join me?

She kicks off her shoes, walks over to the window. The weather has committed, set in — the pale blue skies of only a few hours ago now consumed by thick gray cloud. Snow is falling furiously. Everything is a perfect, pristine white: the cars parked around this side of the building, the hotel signage, the outside lights.

Yet every time she blinks, she sees not white, but red. Bloodred.

Blood on the rug. Tiny droplets.

Her thoughts jump to what Isaac did while she was in the bathroom: hid something from her. Slipped something into his pocket.

Questions ricochet through her head.

What could it be? How is it connected to Laure?

Elin pulls open the French doors. As cold air floods the room, she tries to get her thoughts in order. Logic says that Isaac's explanation for the blood made sense; that whatever he pocketed was private, unconnected with Laure's supposed disappearance, but it still gnaws away at her: *If he'd deceive me like this, then what else is he capable of?*

The truth is, she has no idea. Elin knows nothing about him, his relationship with Laure. She's only skimmed the surface of his life these past few years — filtered scraps of information he'd thrown their way.

His life before he left the UK is clearer — his degree from Exeter in computer sciences, the year off training to be a ski instructor. He came back to the UK, did a postgrad the following year. After completing his research, he worked at the university, taught for a few years, and then moved to Switzerland in 2016.

Since then?

A blank. Whole chunks missing.

Elin pulls her MacBook from her bag. She places it on the desk, flips it open.

Sitting down, she types some key words into Google. *Isaac Warner. Switzerland.*

The results appear. A few lines down, something interesting: a ski school in Crans-Montana. Isaac's name, listed under "Staff."

Elin clicks on the link. In the seconds that follow, a thumbnail image of him appears. It's a headshot, all tan and wraparound sunglasses. A few lines of information: Part-Time Instructor, graded as BASI Level 2. Specializes in teaching children, beginners.

Fine, a part-time job, but what about the

lecturing?

Going back to the main search page, she types more specific key words: *Isaac Warner, computer sciences, University of Lausanne.*

Elin skims the first few results. Still nothing referencing the university.

Has she got the name wrong? She doesn't think so; he mentioned it several times. *So why isn't it showing up?*

Alarm bells are sounding in her head, but she silences them. She mustn't judge. Mustn't jump to conclusions.

Elin tries again. This time, she goes straight to the university website. Clicking through link after link, she finally finds the departmental page for computer sciences.

Under "Staff": a list of names; more thumbnail photographs.

None of them is of Isaac.

She forces her eyes to focus, looks again. *Nothing.*

Lifting her eyes from the screen, Elin picks up her phone with a sense of dread, aware of something spiraling: one thing leading to another, picking up momentum.

What she's doing . . . this probing, it's wrong, an invasion of his privacy because of some unsubstantiated idea, but she has to know. Know if what he did in the room just then was an aberration, a one-off, or if Isaac still ran true to form.

If Isaac still lied.

As the university switchboard connects her to the computer sciences department, nerves are prickling her stomach. She's put on hold. Tinny music plays, a foreign, unfamiliar tune. Midbar, the music breaks. "Bonjour, Marianne Pavet."

Elin's unprepared, scrabbling for the right words. "Hello, this is . . . Rachel Marshall. I have the résumé of a Mr. Isaac Warner. I was wondering if someone from the department could give me a reference?"

Marianne cuts her off in heavily accented English. "No, no reference. I'm not able to give a reference." There's an awkward pause.

"Please. He's listed your department."

A sigh. "Look, I'm not sure why Mr. Warner would give our name as a suitable reference. He was dismissed last year."

Elin sucks in her breath. "Dismissed? Are you sure we're talking about the same person? Isaac Warner?"

"Yes, he was dismissed." The voice is brusque now, impatient.

"Can I ask what for?" Her heart is pounding.

Another lie: his job was the excuse for not coming to their mother's funeral, wasn't it?

There's a weighty silence.

"Intimidating other members of staff. I'm sorry. That's all I'm prepared to say."

There's a click. The line goes dead.

Elin puts the phone on the desk. *What should I do next?*

She has to work out if there's more to this, and if Isaac won't tell her the truth, she'll have to ask someone else.

But who? Who here knew both Isaac and Laure?

Her thoughts flicker to the murmured conversation and laughter that Laure had shared with Margot, the receptionist at the spa. They'd seemed friendly enough . . .

But the thought of speaking to her behind Isaac's back triggers a cold stab of fear.

She closes her eyes and hears echoed threats.

Only babies tell and you're a baby.
Tell tell tit your tongue will split.
Her head is throbbing.
Do that again and I'll kill you.

23

"Come for a proper tour? Your partner's already had it." Margot smiles, her face half concealed by the large computer screen in front of her. "He's got the pool to himself."

"Not exactly," Elin replies, the door to the spa closing behind her with a soft thunk. "I wanted to have a quick chat."

Margot's eyes flicker over, her mouth stretching into a little O of surprise.

She reminds Elin of Laure; edgy in that pared-back, European way that always makes her feel slightly inadequate. Cropped hair, gray-painted fingernails, minimal makeup — artful sole flick of eyeliner, dark streak of matte lipstick. Silver hair grips, decorated with tiny stars, stud the front sections of hair.

Yet the closer Elin gets, the more the illusion is shattered. Margot's nails are chipped, bitten down, the lipstick bleeding into fine lines etched around her mouth.

Coming level with the desk, Elin spots a half-eaten croissant on the shelf below.

146

"Is this about Laure?" Small flakes of pastry are still stuck to her lips. "Is she still not back?" Margot tugs at her dark top, pulling it loose over her stomach.

She's not at ease. The hasty removal of the pastry, this masking of her body . . . she's softer than she'd like, and conscious of it. She's tall, too, Elin observes, looking at her long legs folded beneath the desk.

"No, I . . ." Hesitating, Elin feels a flash of panic. Is this a mistake? Is she letting her mind run away with her? Laure's only been gone a few hours.

Too late. She's here now.

"She definitely hasn't been here at any point this morning?"

"No. I've been here since the spa opened." Margot's eyes flicker to the door as if she half expects her to suddenly appear. "You really think she's missing? That it's something serious?"

Margot's face darkens. Elin catches a flash of silver in her ears, tiny, striated arrows pointing to the floor.

"We don't know, but this was meant to be their engagement celebration, so her taking off . . . Isaac thinks it's out of character."

"He's right. Laure wouldn't want to worry anyone. Not deliberately."

Elin considers this. She has to tread carefully now. "Laure hasn't mentioned anything to you? Any concerns that might explain why

147

she'd leave so suddenly?" She forces a smile. "I've tried to ask Isaac, but . . ."

An awkward pause. Again, Margot's hand comes up to her waist, loosening the folds of fabric over her stomach. "Look, this is awkward." Her cheeks are flushed. "He's your brother."

"It's fine." Elin softens her tone. "I just want to make sure everything's okay."

Margot nods. "I think they've been having problems. Laure . . ." She bites her lip. "Recently, she's felt a bit . . . how do I say? Claustrophobic . . . in the relationship."

Elin notices the curious rhythm to her speech. It isn't just the German inflection to her English, it's staccato; a beat too long between each word.

"Since they've been engaged?"

"No. Before too." Margot hunches over the desk, picking at her fingers. Tiny fragments of gray nail polish flutter to the desk.

"Why get engaged if she's having doubts?"

"Laure thought making a commitment would help, that if they were engaged, Isaac would feel more secure." Margot sweeps the flakes of nail varnish away, knocking her bag over in the process.

It tumbles to the floor, contents flying. Loose hair grips scatter, together with nail varnish, a book, an envelope. Margot bends down, scrabbling to pick them up.

"Has it worked?"

148

Margot shrugs, flushing. "I . . . I don't quite know how to put this. She said recently, Isaac's been . . . aggressive. Not himself."

"Aggressive?" Elin tries to keep her expression neutral.

Margot nods. "She didn't go into it. Look, speaking about it like this makes it sound like they're not happy. They're fine. Laure worries . . . that's normal, surely? When you're about to commit." She hesitates. "I'm not sure she meant it."

Elin tries to quell the growing sense of unease gnawing at her stomach. "Has she mentioned anything else she's worried about? Friends, family?"

Margot shakes her head.

"What about work? Isaac said she's been working a lot lately."

Something flickers across Margot's face, so fleeting that Elin isn't sure if she's imagined it. "Yes, but there hasn't been any pressure. Laure loves her job."

Elin nods.

"Look, I've probably said too much. They've got their issues, but like I said, I don't think it means anything."

So why mention it? Why reference any of this if her mind hasn't automatically made the connection? Margot might not consciously want to implicate their relationship worries in Laure going missing, but she has.

"I understand. There's one more thing . . .

I wondered if you knew why the police are here?"

"It's nothing to do with Laure," Margot says hastily. "If that's what you're wondering."

"So what is it, then?"

The flush on her cheeks darkens. "I don't think I'm meant to know."

"Please."

A pause. Elin holds her breath. *Tell me. Tell me.*

"They've found some remains. A body." Margot lowers her voice. "Behind the forest. They think it's the architect who designed the hotel. He's been missing."

Daniel Lemaitre. Relief floods her body. *It isn't Laure.*

"Isaac told us about him yesterday. People thought he had business troubles, didn't they?"

"That's one theory."

"There were more?"

Margot nods. "Look, I'll be honest. The renovation, it stirred up . . . how do you say it? Bad feeling." Her voice pitches higher. "I think people believe that his disappearance was connected to that."

"Bad feeling? In what sense?"

"Some of the locals didn't want a hotel here. There were demonstrations, petitions. It took years to get through planning because

150

there were so many objections."

"Why?"

"The usual variety of reasons." Margot shrugs. "Design too modern, environmental concerns, enough hotels in the area already . . ." She hesitates. "To be honest, I think some were excuses for something people didn't want to voice."

"And what's that?"

"For the fact people didn't want anything built here." Her voice is barely a whisper. "I don't think it mattered what they'd proposed. Hotel, park, factory, people wouldn't have liked it."

"Why?" Elin asks the question, but she knows what's coming, because she feels it too. Ever since she stepped out of the transfer bus, she's felt it — that creeping sense of something dark, threatening.

"This place . . . people don't like it. The fact that it used to be a sanatorium. Superstition, I suppose." Margot's face closes. "I think Daniel bore the brunt of that."

Elin falters. What she's implying is that Daniel's death wasn't an accident. "You think someone hurt him because of his involvement in the hotel?"

"It wouldn't surprise me. As much as I like my job, sometimes this place . . . it just feels wrong."

"In what way?" Elin's stomach pitches.

"I can't describe it any other way. Just wrong."

Elin forces a smile, but a chill pushes through her as she processes Margot's words. The logical part of her brain is saying it's simply an old event. Potentially a past crime, unconnected with Laure going missing, but something's niggling at her.

As she goes to find Will in the pool area, she feels another flicker of unease: Laure's disappearance coming at the same time as the discovery of Daniel's body. The two events colliding . . . it feels like an omen.

24

Will's doing laps; arms slicing through the shimmering water in quick, clean strokes. This is no performance; he's at home in the water. At ease.

Elin fixes her eyes on him, follows the rhythmic motion. At the end of the pool, he flips, changes direction. She turns her head, blinks.

Too bright.

The spotlights on the ceiling are reflecting off the glass, the water, fine slices of light ricocheting off it like blades.

Dizzied, she takes a deep breath. *Control it. Don't let it control you.* Keep breathing. In and out. Repeat.

"Will," she calls, walking to the edge of the pool.

He doesn't hear her.

"Will," she repeats, louder.

This time he notices her and slows; the easy motion becoming staccato. Swimming to the side, he levers himself out of the pool with his arms. "Watching me, were you?" Will grins. "I wouldn't have put you as a voyeur." Exaggerating the word "voyeur," he raises an eyebrow.

"Nothing wrong with a bit of leching." Elin smiles, but it's fleeting, her mind pulling to Isaac, what she's learned.

"What's up?" Fat droplets of water fall off Will's shoulders, hitting the tiles. "As much as I'd like to believe you've come to admire my superior swimming skills, something's wrong . . . I can tell."

"It's Isaac." Bringing her hand to her mouth, Elin bites at her thumbnail. "I've been to see him."

He hauls himself to standing, still dripping, his breathing labored. "Let me guess . . . Laure's back?"

Elin observes the taut muscle in his arms, the broad chest, the strong shoulders splattered with tiny freckles. At thirty-four he isn't boy-lean, but he's still at his peak: no softening, no paunch.

This fitness was one of the things that had attracted her when they'd first met. It reassured her: visible proof that he was self-motivated, disciplined, strong — mentally and physically. He wouldn't need to be propped up by her.

"No . . ." Elin's finding it hard to form the words. "I found blood. Blood on the rug in their room. It looked fresh."

154

Will smiles, the whites of his eyes laced with red from the chlorine. "Elin, come on, you can't think —"

"No, of course not." Elin keeps her voice light. "He said she cut herself shaving."

"So she probably did."

"It isn't just that, though. When I was looking around in the bathroom, Isaac pocketed something."

"Pocketed something?" Will repeats, his eyes fixed on her. Without his glasses, his irises seem more vivid.

"Yes. Before I could see what it was."

"It could have been anything. Something private. Condoms, pills . . ."

"Maybe."

Lacing his fingers together, he stretches out his arms. The gesture is relaxed, easy, but she knows it's masking something else: he's pissed off. Frustrated.

He doesn't know why she's dwelling on this. Will doesn't overthink. It's a family thing. Elin's even heard his sister say as much — the informal family motto. Deal with it. Move on.

She's never quite known a family like Will's before. He's the middle child — older brother, younger sister, and all of them, parents included, are the hale-and-hearty type, never making a fuss about anything.

It's not in a stiff-upper-lip way, brushing things under the carpet — they're simply forensic in their approach. If an issue comes up, they'll talk it through, endlessly, exhaustively, and then deal with it. A plan is made and then executed. Job done. No looking back. No regrets.

This is only possible because they're all so open, in touch with their emotions and each other — lunch every Sunday, cozy chats and in-jokes. Holidays together each year. Elin sometimes wonders whether Will takes it for granted, all that love and affection.

She can't help but be a little jealous, not only of how close they are, but how easy it seems — no weird silences or secrets, no game playing. A family life that's completely opposite to anything she's ever known.

"You know," Will starts. "You're overthinking this whole thing. It's . . . weird. She's only been gone for a morning. Like I said, I think it's a massive overreaction on Isaac's part. Don't get sucked in. All this drama, it's deliberate. She'll turn up, and you'll have wasted the first day of what was meant to be a holiday . . . ."

He trails off. Elin knows what he wants to say, but he stopped himself. Even now, he's tiptoeing around her. Struggling to tell her how it is.

"Thinking all this stuff," Will finishes. "Let's just enjoy this. You and me." He smiles. "We managed it last night, didn't we?"

Elin hesitates. "But there's something else

too. I've just spoken to the receptionist, Margot. She said that Laure and Isaac had been arguing, that she was worried about the engagement."

Will shrugs. "That's normal, surely? Making a commitment, it's a big step."

"But I think Isaac's been lying. I found out he's been sacked from his job at the university. Harassment. He told me he was still working there."

"And how do you know all this?" His voice is dangerously calm.

"I" — she falters, cringing, knowing how her words will come across — "I rang the university in Lausanne."

Will steps back, despair crossing his features. "You've been digging around for information about him?" A pulse is ticking in his cheek. "Elin, this was meant to be a chance for you to get away from all the shit haunting you at home, but this . . . you're putting yourself back to square one."

"But what if something's happened to Laure?" Her eyes are smarting.

"For Christ's sake." Will's voice rises an octave. "Nothing's happened to her."

"That's not the only thing. When I was with Isaac, the police arrived." She knows she's gabbling, but why can't he see what she sees? How it pieces together? "They've found a body, behind the forest. Margot said they think it might be the architect who went missing."

"Daniel Lemaitre?"

"Yes."

"And you think that's to do with Laure?"

"I don't know, but it just doesn't feel right. Laure disappearing, now this."

"Elin, look, even if something's wrong, if something's happened to Laure, it's not your responsibility." Will's talking too slowly, too carefully. "I know it's hard, in a situation like this, but you're not a detective any —" He stops, flushing.

She blinks. She knows what he was about to say.

You're not a detective anymore. The words hurt, but he's right. She isn't a detective and this isn't her case. Isn't a case at all. But still, it stings. The first time anyone's said it out loud.

I'm not a detective anymore.

At what point had she stopped being that? Had other people stopped believing that? When the three-month break turned into six? Nine? It feels horrible, unnatural. Her job had always defined her. After Sam died, she knew it was all she wanted to do. Find the truth. Get answers. If she can't do that anymore, what is she? *Who* is she?

She can't keep the tremor from her voice. "He's my brother. I'm trying to help."

"You're going above and beyond help, and

if I'm being honest, I'm not sure why. Where was he when you needed him? When your mum was ill?" Will looks at her steadily. "The way I see it, you're willing to put yourself out more for him than you are for us."

"Will, come on. It's not a competition, you versus Isaac —"

"It's nothing to do with that. I'm serious, Elin." His voice is soft. "I've seen more emotion from you about this, about Isaac, than I have about us moving forward."

"Moving forward?" Elin repeats. Delay tactics. She knows what he's talking about. Last month, he'd dumped a pile of magazines on the coffee table. Designery home ones. Talked about paint colors, storage solutions. Asked her opinion on terrace versus apartment.

"You know what I'm saying. Moving in together. Nearly three years, and we're still living in separate apartments." He swallows hard. "I want us to be together, Elin, all the time. Share the day-to-day stuff. Be a proper couple."

"I know, but it's hard, taking that step, while I'm still dealing with everything."

Will shakes his head. "I don't think that's it. I know I probably sound like an idiot, unsympathetic, but I think you have a choice in this. You can be brave, Elin, choose not to let the past take over your life."

"A choice?" Her voice is shaky. "I'd hardly

choose my life like it is now . . ."

"You do have a choice. Look at my father. The macular degeneration. He's had to change his whole way of life to accommodate it, but he's never complained." Will looks at her. "He made a choice, Elin. Not to let it get him down, ruin his life. You can do the same."

"Not everyone can be like you and your family," she says tightly. "So bloody strong. You're lucky, Will, that you're all so close. It helps to have that support network, people to talk to without judgment. When you have that as a base, it's easier to take risks, make decisions."

"I know." He sounds tired. "But we have the chance to build the same kind of family, our family. The only way we'll get there is if you break down those walls you've built between us. I just don't get how with this, with Isaac, you're giving it your all, but with us . . ." He shakes his head.

Elin's instinct is to come back, defend herself, but he's right. She has put up walls between them. She doesn't want to, but she has.

"It's just, Isaac, he —" She stops. Part of her wants to just tell him, tell him the one thing that might make him understand what she's really doing here. Explain that while she's desperate to move on, she can't until she knows the truth about what happened to

160

Sam that day. But the words are stuck.

It's always the same — on the verge of telling him but stopping short. It feels a step too far, that she's not just exposing part of herself but a part of her family, too — an intimacy that scares her.

Will looks at her. "You know, if you keep all this up, when Laure's back later — and I've no doubt she will come back — I think we should talk about whether staying . . . if it's a good idea."

"You want to leave?" Elin repeats, blindsided, panic surging through her, little pricking darts jagging at her nerves.

We can't leave. Not yet. We leave now, and this whole trip will have been for nothing. I'm not even close to getting answers.

"Yes. I don't want to keep seeing you like this. Your reaction, I don't like it. You're stressed, Elin. I don't think it's good for you, being here, around him. You're . . . You're not being yourself."

Elin wants to protest, but he's right. She's not being herself. Her thoughts aren't calm; they're acrobatic, wheeling thoughts she can't make sense of.

Will's mouth is poised to say something else, but he thinks better of it. Slowly, carefully, he lowers himself back into the pool using the heels of his hands.

25

As Elin pushes through the doors into the changing area, Will's words beat out in her head: *You're not being yourself.*

Tears stinging the back of her eyes, she slips her feet into her shoes, bends down, picks up her bag. As she straightens up, she pauses.

A sound: a door, swinging open and shut.

Elin turns, expecting to see someone emerge from one of the cubicles, wet hair, swim bag in hand.

Silence.

No one's that quiet, surely? Changing necessitates noise: the scratchy rub of clothing on damp skin, the little grunts of frustration as buttons get tangled in wet hair, straps are turned inside out.

Yet there it is again — the click and swing of a door.

Elin waits, still expecting someone to emerge, but there's nothing.

The silence stretches out, amplifying the hammering of the pulse in her ears. Every sense is heightened as she turns, scans the space.

Everything's still. Quiet.

Pushing forward, she starts walking toward the door leading back to reception. *Don't be stupid,* she tells herself, *it's nothing.*

But that's not true.

She heard something. She isn't imagining it.

Elin walks slowly down the length of the changing cubicles.

The experience is a strange one; she hadn't realized how peculiar the changing room design was before, each door seamlessly melding into the next. The effect is of an internal corridor bisecting the space. A stark, sterile tunnel.

Not only that: there aren't any handles on any of the doors.

How do they open?

Elin tentatively pushes the one closest to her. The pressure of her hand does something; the door swings inward with a click.

She surveys the space inside. A narrow bench runs along the left-hand wall of the cubicle. It has a flap at either end, folded up to allow the door to open. When lowered, it would both be a bench of normal width and lock the door closed.

Walking the length of the cubicles, she pushes at each door.

Click.

Click.

Click.

But there's no one there.

As the last door starts to swing back on itself, she steps inside.

She works through it: *Could they have gone out another way?*

Putting her hand on the opposite door, she gently presses.

Yes: the cubicle opens out onto the other side of the changing room so people can go in and out from either side.

A growing sense of uneasiness builds inside her. It's possible: someone had been there, slipped out the other side.

They definitely haven't gone through to reception. She's been facing that way the whole time. But they could have gone to the pool . . .

So where are they now?

There's only one way to check. Slipping her shoes off, she pads back out to the pool, scans the space.

A lurch, deep in her gut.

Only Will is there, striking out through the water. Elin stands, frozen for a minute, then makes her way back through the changing room to the spa reception.

Someone was there. Someone was definitely in there. Watching.

Looking up, Margot smiles. "He's still swimming?"

164

"Yes. Going for a record by the looks of it." Elin forces a breeziness into her voice that wasn't there before. "Did anyone else come in after me?"

"No, it's quiet. I think people went out earlier because of the break in the weather. It'll get busy again soon, now that the snow has started up again."

Elin nods, fingers tightening around the strap of her bag.

Part of her wants to dismiss what she heard as a figment of her imagination, a different sound altogether, but another part of her is sure: Whoever was in there was watching her.

Waiting.

26

Needing to clear her head, Elin leaves the hotel via the back entrance, hikes the short path up toward the forest, the opposite route to the one she'd taken earlier with Will.

Her mind keeps circling over what happened in the changing room.

Is she letting her imagination get the better of her?

I'm not sure.

But despite the confusion, with every step, she feels stronger, more in control.

It's always the way: she does her best problem solving while exercising — churning through unresolved questions about cases, thoughts about Sam, Isaac, her mother.

But the snow is hard work. Underneath the thick layer of soft powder that's just fallen, there's an older, more compacted layer.

Elin stops at the top of the path, just before the entrance to the forest, breathing heavily. Snow is settling on her jacket, caught in the creases of the fabric.

She exhales slowly, her frosted breath clouding the air. The snow has stopped but the sky is still leaden, heavy. She can tell there's more to come.

Even though she's no longer moving, her heart is pounding, sweat starting to soak her thermals. It's the altitude — the air is viscous, sticky. Her body hasn't yet acclimatized.

She closes her hand around the inhaler inside her jacket pocket, her fingers grazing the blocky edge of the mouthpiece. The cold air doesn't help. At home when she exercises, the air is warm, moist. As long as she takes her preventive inhaler, starts slowly, paces herself, she's fine. But up here, the air cooler, thinner, she has to be careful. On her guard.

She closes her eyes, takes one, two deep breaths, and in that moment, off her guard, her mind trips, catches.

A rapid-fire series of snapshots:

A breeze cutting the surface of the rock pool, making a blur of the rocks below.

A hand grabbing her arm.

Blood dispersing like smoke through the water.

Fear ties itself into an ugly knot in her stomach. She's never had this before.

The intrusion of the flashbacks into consciousness, this merging into real life. They usually came in the gray time, when she's drifting off to sleep, or awakening. They've never crossed the line before.

Disconcerted, she takes a long breath, walks higher. Snow is smothering everything: the ground, the trees, branches bowing under the weight of it.

Her boots are rubbing at the backs of her heels. Despite the thick socks, her feet are sliding around with each step. The shop assistant had warned her that they were too big, but she'd ignored him.

Elin's never liked anything too tight. The legacy of asthma.

It's strange, she thinks, how for her, claustrophobia doesn't only exist in spaces outside herself, but within her too.

That horrible sense of being trapped inside your own body.

One of the first things she did when she bought her apartment was to knock down the dividing wall separating the two main rooms.

As the last section came down in a cloud of dust and plaster, sending light flooding through the space, her sense of relief was palpable.

Elin turns, taking in the landscape opposite. The gray weight of the sky stretches out endlessly, only broken by the jagged horizon of mountain peaks. Clusters of chalets are dotted across their flanks, impossibly small.

On this side of the valley, the winding strip of the road leading to the town on her right is barely visible between the snowdrifts banked up on either side.

The town itself is hidden by a small ridge. Elin can just make out the metal spine of the chairlift infrastructure, pylons heading upward into the mist.

On her left is the hotel below. The weak rays of sunlight pushing through a break in the cloud are reflecting off the vast expanse of glass, the snow piled up high around it.

This is the view she wanted to see, the perspective she's needed, but the more she looks, the more confused she becomes.

One question keeps beating out inside her head: *If Laure did take off of her own accord, where could she go from here?*

The hotel is isolated, its own entity. There's nowhere nearby that Laure could plausibly be. Nowhere she can keep safe, stay warm.

She can't have gone up, surely, Elin thinks, glancing toward the forest. Isaac had told her there were no huts up there, no shelter. Beyond the trees there's only high mountain, the glacier. Looking up, she can see both are shrouded in a thick mist. It's swirling, tendrils crawling like fingers over the rock.

The sight makes her flesh creep. She turns away.

There's a definite possibility Laure's gone down, either to the town or to the valley, to Sierre, but that's more than twelve miles away.

So how?

169

Walking was almost impossible in these conditions, and she can't have got a taxi; she had no phone, no purse, no bag.

Elin knows that the only way she'll get answers is by finding out *why* Laure felt she'd had to go. What motive she had for leaving.

Personal, professional, there have to be clues, she's sure of it.

She needs to know more — find out what makes Laure tick. Pulling out her phone, she starts flicking through various social media accounts. Though she's registered on most of them, Elin's never posted anything. She's always felt too self-conscious, foisting her random thoughts on the world.

Most of Laure's accounts are set to private, bar one: Instagram.

Elin clicks into Laure's feed. She's not sure what she'll find, but it's unlikely to be the real Laure. One of the first things she learned in the police was the extent to which people curate their lives: CVs, diaries. Conversations with friends. E-mails.

The most easily manipulated? Social media. The extrovert colleague, having a meal with her "squad," could in fact be eating alone, reading a book. The artsy shot of the prize-winning book? Discarded after the first page.

Yet the fact that it doesn't tell you everything is in itself revealing. The curation, the person they're *pretending* to be, can say a lot:

an insight into someone's desires, their inse-curities.

Elin starts scrolling. Laure's grid reminds her of Will's: considered, filtered to look subtly overexposed. Landscapes. Architec-ture. Interspersed are shots of her with Isaac, friends. A cocktail bar. Book club in a trendy apartment. Mocking poses for the camera.

She glances at Laure's self-deprecating comments. *Trying not to try too hard.*

There are no mundane day-to-day shots. No "motivational" quotes, older family members reluctantly posing for the camera. Nothing about the images reveals a softer side, any vulnerabilities. She wants to be seen as serious, creative, in control.

This is revealing: the complete lack of flaws, of being able to show herself as anything other than living a perfect life, indicates an insecurity. Laure wasn't quite confident enough that people would like the real her, so she's having to posture.

All in all, someone trying very hard.

But still, no sign of any instability, anything seriously awry. To find that, Elin will have to look somewhere real. Somewhere Laure wouldn't be so aware of, somewhere her friends wouldn't be able to see, to judge.

Her office.

As Elin starts to walk back down the path toward the hotel, her gaze is once again dragged to the immense white expanse

171

stretching out below her.

A thought strikes her:

What if Laure wanted to get lost in this? What if all this is planned?

She can almost understand it, she thinks, wanting to step out into this nothingness.

A perfect, endless oblivion.

Then an image of the blood spatter on the rug appears in her mind.

Tiny, rusty dots. A constellation.

172

27

Her captor has moved her off the floor.

Adele's now lying flat, on a bed of some kind. It's a softer surface, more forgiving.

Blinking, she opens her eyes, but the shapes and colors around her are out of focus. It takes a few minutes for the scene in front of her to resolve.

A wall: bumpy, striated, the surface slick with moisture.

Adele tries to analyze this, work out where she might be, but she's distracted: her face is burning. With a lurch, she remembers: *the mask.* Panic bubbles up inside her, sweat building between her flesh and the thick layer of rubber.

Frantic, she tries to reach up, claw it off, but her hands won't move.

What's happened?

Adele tips her head forward to try to get a better look, but the movement makes her dizzy, as if her brain is on catch-up, three steps behind her skull.

She tries again, twisting her torso to the right, but as her head follows, the C-shape of tubing attached to the mask blocks her vision; a grotesque black curve.

Adele tries craning her neck, angling her head far enough to the right so she can see past the tube.

It works: she gets a glimpse of her right hand. It's fastened at the wrist to the bed. A table sits a few feet away. It's made of metal, similar to one used for camping — foldable, portable.

In the center is a small metal tray. Surgical instruments are lined up on the surface in a neat row — scalpels, a knife, a fine pair of scissors.

Adele's heart falters, trips.

It's then she hears it, the sound that cuts right through her: the strange wet suck of air being inhaled, the high-pitched whistle of the exhale.

The sound of their mask. Different from hers, louder.

Despite herself, she tilts her head again, farther, catches a glimpse of them.

Her captor is holding something — a phone. *Your phone,* she thinks, recognizing the battered blue case.

Their fingers are moving rapidly across the screen.

Several beats pass and then Adele hears a familiar whooshing sound. It takes her a moment to process the significance: *They've sent a message. A message from your phone.*

A few seconds later, another sound. A low beep.

Someone's replied.

It's then it hits her: *They've sent a message pretending to be you.*

She feels her stomach plummet: no one will know she's missing now. Whoever gets the message will assume she's fine.

No one will look for you. No one will know that anything's wrong.

Adele tries to scream, but the sound behind the mask is muted, pathetic.

The figure turns, staring at her for a few minutes as if considering something.

Then comes the voice. "Ready?"

A delay: her ears absorbing sound before her brain registers it. Adele flinches, reeling.

The voice. She knows that voice.

Adele's mouth opens, but no sound comes out. A quake inside her: the last bit of hope, gone.

There would be no getting out of this.

In a way, she's always known this moment was coming. What happened has never gone away. She's forced it to the furthest reaches of her mind, but the knowledge has always been there — like a clot, sitting benign inside your vein, just waiting for the moment to come unstuck and wreak havoc.

Adele lies perfectly still, waiting. All she can hear is her captor's breathing.

Any moment. Any moment.

The flashlight beam jolts, moves again. Bending at the waist, the person fumbles in the small black bag on the floor. They rummage in the bag, withdraw a syringe.

A sharp scratch on her arm before everything goes dark, but not fast enough for her to miss the sound of the small metal table being dragged across the floor toward her, the clank and jolt of the metal instruments as it moves.

28

"She still isn't back?" The hotel manager tenses, the papers clasped in her hand creasing between her fingers under the pressure.

Elin examines the name badge pinned to her dark shirt: CECILE CARON. GENERAL MANAGER. The woman she saw in the pool yesterday; the developer's sister.

There's definitely a resemblance: the same rangy height, muscular frame, similar sandy-blond hair, although Cecile's is shorter, even shorter than Elin's. It's cropped close around her face, revealing sharp, angular cheekbones.

Her features are strong, defined. She's isn't wearing any makeup, but she doesn't need it. Any adornment would look silly somehow. Superfluous.

Elin shakes her head. "Isaac hasn't heard from her. No one has."

A shadow crosses Cecile's face. "Are you sure he's spoken to everyone?"

Elin nods. "Everyone. Friends, family, neighbors. They thought she was here, with

Isaac." She pauses. "I don't know if Laure mentioned it, but this was meant to be their engagement celebration."

"She told me." Cecile emerges from behind the reception desk, papers still grasped tightly in her hand. "She also said you're a police officer in the UK?" Her expression is unreadable. It immediately makes Elin feel uncomfortable.

"I am." As soon as the words are out, Elin flushes. She should have corrected her: *Why not tell the truth? Why give myself an authority I don't deserve?* "Isaac is my brother. He's called the police. They've made a note of it, to follow up, but they think it's too early to warrant investigating. I said I'd ask a few questions in the meantime."

Giving a brusque nod, Cecile murmurs something to the receptionist. She turns back to Elin. "Let's go to my office. It's better if we speak there."

Following her out of the lobby, into the main corridor, Elin struggles to keep up with Cecile's efficient stride.

Her trousers pull up slightly as she walks, as if they're catching on her legs, the visible muscle in her thighs. She's the first member of staff that Elin's seen who looks somehow *wrong* in the uniform; a fish out of water.

The pared-back Scandinavian style — black shirt, slim-fit tapered trousers, gray pumps, don't suit her body. Her broad shoulders, solid limbs, are pulling at the fabric, subtly altering the cut of the clothes. Like Elin, she's probably more comfortable in workout clothes.

Cecile takes the first door on the right. They walk down another short corridor. The offices are at the end, on the left. Pushing at the door, she holds it open.

"Please, go in. Take a seat."

For the first time, Elin picks up on the American inflection in Cecile's English. Either educated there, or lived there long enough for it to become the default.

In Cecile's office, she's once again faced with a wall of glass, but any view of the mountains is now obscured by a bank of thick, black cloud. The snow has started up again, dizzying in its intensity, large, fat flakes plummeting to the ground.

Cecile's desk is positioned centrally, directly in front of the glass. Like a target, Elin observes, shoulders stiffening. In full view.

As she takes a seat, her gaze roams around the rest of the space: two computer screens side by side on the desk, a pile of papers, a reusable coffee cup.

Directly facing her are several photographs, nestled together on the desk.

Elin recognizes a younger Cecile right away: clasping a trophy, a medal slung at an angle around her neck. In the other she's in a pool, swimming cap peeled off, dangling from her hand, the other clenched in a fist pump.

Cecile follows Elin's gaze. "I used to swim competitively." A short, hard laugh. "Back in the day."

She flushes, embarrassed at being caught staring. "Bit of a career change."

"Didn't quite make the grade." Cecile smiles. "You know how it is. The competition's fierce the higher you go."

A dream unfulfilled, thinks Elin, watching Cecile's eyes flicker toward the photograph, then away. A dream that meant enough for her to keep a photograph on her desk, however painful it is to remember.

But then, who doesn't have dreams like that? Who doesn't wonder: *What if life had taken a different path?*

She changes the subject. "So you haven't seen Laure?"

"Not since yesterday. She was having lunch in the lounge." Her forehead creases into a frown. "Are you sure she hasn't rung anyone else?"

"No."

"No one's picked her up from here? Someone Isaac doesn't know?"

"It's possible, but it still doesn't explain why she hasn't been in contact, why she didn't take her things. Her phone, bag, purse . . . they're still here."

"She definitely hasn't gone home?"

"No. The neighbor's got a key, let himself

180

in. No one was there."

"But it's possible, surely, that she's gone of her own accord, didn't want people to know. Had cold feet about the engagement? People get anxious right before making that final commitment." Cecile shrugs. "I know I did."

Elin looks down at Cecile's hand. *No wedding ring.*

Cecile clocks the glance. "Divorced."

Catching the note of defiance in her voice, Elin immediately empathizes with the implicit pushback in it. People asking, having to await the clichéd platitudes that followed: *You'll find the right one. Don't worry, it's not too late.*

Elin's only thirty-two, but before she'd met Will, she'd heard them all. Hit your late twenties and people felt the need to box you up, categorize you.

If they couldn't, they saw you as a threat. *An indefinable.*

"Yes," Elin concedes, turning the conversation back to Laure. "People going off, it happens more often than you'd think. The family starts panicking, only to find out it's planned. Sometimes people don't like having to explain, so they bolt." She leans forward. "So you're not aware of any problems? Reasons for her to take off?"

"No. Laure's always been an exceptional employee. Punctual. Bright." Cecile fiddles with a pen on the desk. "Look, I'm probably not the best person to speak to. We had a good relationship, but a professional one. Laure . . . she's a private person. She wouldn't share personal things. Not unless it was necessary."

"Would you mind if I take a look at her desk? See if she's left something here. Travel details, anything like that." Elin keeps her voice deliberately light.

"Why?" Something flickers across Cecile's features that Elin can't decipher.

"You can stay," Elin adds. "I'm not interested in anything work related."

Cecile relaxes. "Of course. It's through here." She pushes on the smoked glass of the right-hand wall. The door opens outward with a soft click.

Inside, it's the same layout as Cecile's, but half the size. Hovering near the door, Cecile's already staring down at her phone.

Elin scans the surface of the desk. It's neat: laptop, pencil holder, phone, a small succulent in a lime-green pot. The end of a phone charger dangles aimlessly off the side of the surface. It's innocuous. Impersonal. Revealing nothing.

Reaching below the desk, she tugs at the right-hand drawer. It's unlocked, easily opened. There isn't much inside: a presentation, notes from meetings, a folder. She flicks through, then discards them, picking up the blue manila folder. Several folded pieces of paper are inside. An article printed from a website. The headline is in French: *Dépression*. Clipped to the top right of the page is a business card.

AMELIE FRANCES
PSYCHOTHERAPIE | PSYCHOLOGIE
24, RUE DE LAUSANNE

Elin steals a sideways glance at Cecile. She's on the phone.

Quickly slipping the card into her pocket, she turns to the drawer on the left.

It's empty but for a purple folder. She opens it and leafs through: mobile-phone bills going back every month for over a year. They're in Laure's name, but addressed to the hotel.

"Found something?" Cecile looks up.

"I don't know." Elin hesitates. "Do you use work mobiles here?"

"No. Any calls that are for work they expense from their personal mobiles, but we mainly use the phones here." She gestures at the landline on the desk.

This must be her personal mobile, surely? But why keep her personal mobile statements here? Then Elin notices something. The network: Orange.ch. Wasn't the mobile Isaac showed her Swisscom?

That means Laure has another phone.

When she picks up the most recent bill, her

183

eyes leap the page. One number appears repeatedly on the call log.

Texts too. It must be Isaac's, she thinks, pulling out her own phone to check.

It isn't. Whoever she's been repeatedly calling, it isn't Isaac. In fact, Elin thinks, looking down the log, Isaac's number doesn't appear on here anywhere. Her body tenses. There's something about this she doesn't like.

Why keep the statements here?

But Elin knows the answer: *She doesn't want Isaac to see them.* Her mind immediately makes the next leap: Is Laure seeing someone else? Has Isaac found out?

Her mind draws back to the call she witnessed last night: Laure could have been using this phone. This could be the number of the person she was speaking to, the number she'd been unable to find on Laure's other phone.

Elin's mobile vibrates.

A message from Will.

Weather all over the news. They're evacuating hotels on the other side of the valley.

"Got everything you need?"

Dragging her eyes from the screen, Elin notices the impatience on Cecile's face. She's had enough. Wants to get back to work.

"Yes." She gestures to the folder containing the bills. "Is it okay if I take these?"

"Of course, and if there's anything else I can do, please let me know." Her voice is earnest, but her expression is curiously opaque. Elin's finding it hard to tell if the words are genuine or simply a cool professionalism.

"Really," Cecile adds, as if sensing her thoughts, "anything at all. Laure's a valued member of the team —" She breaks off, her eyes fixed on the window.

Elin follows her gaze to the car park outside. One of the police 4×4s she saw earlier is pulling away. It's moving quickly, wheels churning up snow.

Looking back to Cecile, she stops, noticing her tense expression.

Elin's about to ask her about it but pulls back.

Don't overstep the mark. If something has happened to Laure, she needs to approach this situation, the people here, very carefully.

29

"A printout?" Isaac's voice is too loud, strained, but it doesn't matter. The lounge is packed, his words lost amid the hum of conversation, the clink and clang of cutlery. Music is playing on low: a contemporary jazz track, suitable for daytime.

No one's venturing out in this, Elin thinks, looking outside. The sky is black, huge snowflakes being pulled in all directions by the wind.

She nods. "It was in Laure's desk."

"So that's why you sent Will off. So you could confront me with it."

Elin bristles. "I hardly *sent* him. He'd finished lunch and wanted to check his e-mails."

Isaac sets down his fork with a clatter and pushes his plate aside. The chicken salad has barely been touched, lettuce leaves, slick with oil, heaped up on the side of his plate.

He's a mess, Elin thinks, looking at the

stubble grazing his cheeks, the crumpled clothes.

"So what's it about?" he says abruptly.

"Depression. There was a business card attached to it, for a psychologist."

Running a finger over the rim of her glass, her eyes lock on the fireplace behind him. The flames are leaping high, curling against the glass.

"A psychologist?" Isaac's eyes widen before he collects himself. "It would . . . make sense." He looks at her, assessing, as if trying to pregauge a reaction. "Laure has been struggling with depression recently. It's been worse the past few months. Her medication . . . that's what I took from the shelf. I wasn't certain you saw."

"I did." She meets his gaze. "Why did you hide it?"

"I didn't want to go into something private, without her permission. I thought she'd be back and I wouldn't have to . . ." Shaking his head, he looks down to the floor. "But that's all gone to shit, hasn't it?" He clears his throat. "I've canceled everyone, you know. Laure's friends. Mine. Even if the weather doesn't come in as they're forecasting, there's no point in them coming now."

"You're sure?"

"Not much of an engagement party without the bride-to-be, is it?"

Hearing the anger flaring in his tone, she

changes the subject. "So how long has she been depressed?"

"On and off for years, since Coralie died. It didn't help that her father didn't stick around. When Laure hit eighteen, he pissed off back to Japan."

"Coralie's *dead*?" Elin falters, picturing her, the narrow face, the slanted, feline eyes. Coralie was a one-off, a no-bullshit firebrand, so full of energy that it's hard to imagine that she's gone.

"A hit-and-run in Geneva. Near the lake."

"Laure didn't say." Why hadn't she mentioned it, Elin wonders, stung, but deep down, she knows: Why would Laure trust her with that after Elin had ghosted her?

"She's good at putting on a brave face, but underneath, she's fighting to hold it together. Here especially. She can't afford to lose another job."

"Another?"

"Her last role, they more or less asked her to go. They gave her a good reference, because she went quietly, but even so."

"What happened?"

"The hours, the workload . . . it got to her. She wasn't sleeping properly, kept calling in sick, started lashing out at staff, guests."

Elin tries to splice the information together with what she knows about Laure. It's impossible, like he's speaking about two different people. She stumbles over what she's about

188

to say next. "I . . . I also found a mobile-phone statement, Isaac. It's not the phone you've got. I think she's got another one."

"Wait, what? I think I'd know if . . ." Isaac trails off, heat flaring up his neck.

"She did. It's in her name. The bills were sent to the hotel." Elin picks up a piece of bread, puts it down again. Her soup, the quivering drops of oil suspended in the steaming liquid . . . it's unappetizing. Too much.

"Well, if she has, she can't have used it much."

"There's lots of calls, Isaac. Texts too. There's a number she rang repeatedly the past few months. A Swiss mobile."

Isaac passes his tongue over his teeth, agitated. "Have you got the bills?"

She nods. Reaching into her bag, she passes him the most recent one. His eyes scour the page with an aching slowness. *He doesn't recognize the number.*

"I'm going to ring it now." Isaac pulls his phone from his pocket; his hair falls across his forehead, sending his face into shadow.

"Ring what?"

"Laure's other phone. The number's at the top of the page."

As he dials, Elin chews the edge of her fingernail, a horrible sense of trepidation settling over her. Her eyes alight on the huge chandelier above them. It's an abstract design

189

— made up of hundreds of sharp-edged fragments of glass suspended at varying heights. It's eye-catching, but the complexity, the lack of symmetry, is too much. It's too harsh a centerpiece.

Isaac pulls the phone from his ear. "It's going straight to voice mail. An automated voice." He picks up the bill again, grasping it so tightly the paper puckers. "I'll try the number she kept calling."

It's a few seconds before someone picks up. "Hello?" A hesitation. "Hello?" Isaac repeats. "Are you there?" Slowly, he drags the phone from his ear, puts it on the table. All Elin can see is the confusion in his eyes. Not anger. A quiet devastation.

Laure's lied to him and he had no idea.

Touched, Elin looks down at her hands. He won't want her pity. Never has.

"They picked up, then hung up after I spoke."

"Try again."

But this time, almost as soon he brings the phone to his ear, he puts it back down. "This time it's not even ringing."

"They must've switched it off. Isaac, it doesn't matter. If something has happened, we can get the police to go further back. On her other one too. The phone provider can produce a list of any numbers dialed or received in the past six months."

Isaac drums his fingers on the table, silent.

She's not sure if he's even heard her.

A waitress, a brunette, runs a cloth over the table next to them. When she finishes wiping, she turns, smiles.

"Would you like anything else?"

Elin is about to reply, but Isaac gets there before her. "No," he says tightly. "The food's crap anyway."

"Isaac . . ." She smiles apologetically at the waitress.

"What? I'm saying it how it is."

The waitress straightens, flushes. "Sir, I can get you something different if you'd prefer, and I can, of course, pass on any feedback to the team."

"No, it's fine." Elin shoots Isaac a warning look. "Really, we're fine."

As the waitress moves away, Elin frowns. "Why do you always have to do that? Lash out? It's not her fault Laure's missing."

It's always been his default: taking things out on other people. She remembers the time he lost a toy their father bought him for acing his exams at school, a leggy metal robot that spoke when you pressed its antennae: *I am at your command but treat me with caution!* Sam bore the brunt of his anger — room torn apart, his Playmobil pirate abducted in retaliation.

Sam stuck close to Elin for weeks afterward. They became each other's human shield: every time Isaac got angry, they'd seek each other out for protection.

The awkward silence continues; Isaac rubs the back of his neck. "You're right," he says finally, "but I don't like this. It feels . . . wrong. If she's not back tonight, I'm calling the police again."

"She might be back by then," Elin replies without conviction. "All this . . . it could be for nothing."

"You might change your mind after seeing these." Delving into his bag, he withdraws a pile of photographs, drops it on the table. "Look at these, then tell me it's nothing."

Elin slides the pile toward her. Her breathing quickens: the photographs are all different, but they're of the same person.

Lucas Caron. "Where did you get these?" A cold bead of fear moves through her. *This doesn't look right. They don't look like normal photographs.*

Isaac looks at her intently, his face pale, bloodless. His foot is tapping the floor. "I found them hidden in Laure's ski bag. Look at them."

Lucas walking toward the hotel, beanie pulled down over his head, looking down at his phone. Lucas talking to a member of staff at the entrance to the lounge. Lucas sitting on the terrace with a group, sipping wine.

It looks like surveillance. Like Laure's been following him. Staking him out.

"It's weird, isn't it?" Isaac demands. His

foot is moving faster now, his knee hitting the tabletop. "Tell me you don't think it's weird. They're not holiday snaps, are they? It doesn't look like he knows they're being taken."

"We don't know enough to form any firm conclusions. There might be an explanation." Elin tries to keep her voice on an even keel, but it's hard. She knows her words sound lame.

What explanation could there be? Why would Laure have these?

"Like what?" Isaac's eyes are hard, shiny. He scratches furiously at his eyelid.

Elin pulls his hand away, her palm on his. The gesture's automatic, instinctive. His hand flattens, relaxing beneath hers.

Time folds back on itself. She's a child again, Isaac helping her back to sleep after a nightmare. They shared a room for years because of it. He used to stretch across, hold her hand in his. He did the same for Sam when he was a toddler.

For a while, Sam had even worse nightmares than she did, and it was her fault. They had a phase of playing dress-up. Sam would be a soldier, a knight, and sometimes, if Elin persuaded him, a sheep, in a homemade white woolly costume — her creative interpretation of the Nativity.

But then Sam started having bad dreams about the costumes — imagined them coming to life at the end of his bed, dancing head-less around the room. Elin remembers her mother's tactful removal of the costumes, the murmured words about "not playing this game for a while."

Sam.

The thought pulls her up sharply. Elin withdraws her hand with a horrible sense of disquiet. She's rushing in again, isn't she? Taking this at face value.

Everything he's shown her, everything he's said — it's just words, nothing more. Reach-ing for her water glass, Elin blinks, angry at herself. Despite everything, she's let down her guard. She should know better.

She's forgotten how easy it is to lose track of someone; the sum of their parts.

30

The fatigue doesn't hit until she's back in the room. Elin rubs at her eyes. She can feel the beginnings of a headache; a dull, persistent throb at the base of her neck.

She picks up the water bottle, opens it. It fizzes, a rapid hiss, bubbles chasing up through the neck. Pouring herself a glass, she takes a long swig. She needs to rest, but she can't take her mind off what Isaac showed her.

What does it mean?

Lowering herself onto the leather chair by the window, Elin picks up her phone, types Lucas Caron's name into Google. But before she can check the results, she sees an e-mail from Anna, her DCI.

Elin, just checking in as you didn't reply to my last e-mail. Don't want to hassle you, but we do need a decision by the end of the month. Call me if you need to talk.

Her eyes chase the words around the screen

several times before she minimizes the e-mail, goes back to Safari, to Lucas Caron.

A slew of articles has appeared in the search results: a Wiki biography, numerous articles in the business and hospitality press. Elin scrolls to the next page. More articles. Among these are sports results, listing his times in marathons, cross-country ski races.

Clearly as enthusiastic about sport as he was about his career, Elin thinks, which, looking at the headlines, is most definitely soaring:

Behind the Brand: Over the Past Decade, Lucas Caron Has Emerged as the Man to Watch When It Comes to Swiss Hospitality

The Beginnings of an Empire: How Lucas Caron's Reinvention of Minimalism Is Transforming the Luxury Hotel Landscape

The Hippie Hotelier: How Daily Yoga Helps Lucas Caron Stay on Top of His Game

More recently:

Le Sommet: Saying Good-bye to Chalet Style. A Study in New Minimalism

The Beginnings of an Empire. Why Lucas Caron Likes to Look to the Past for Inspiration

Elin clicks on the second article. A photograph dominates the screen: Lucas sitting cross-legged on one of the sofas in Le Sommet's lounge. There's no hint of discomfort — his smile is wide, natural.

But even in this, a more formal shot, he looks more like someone you'd see on the cover of a climbing or hiking magazine than a property developer. He's dressed in a pair of faded jeans, a gray zip-up technical top that emphasizes his muscular frame. His dark-blond hair is falling messily about his face, his beard barely trimmed.

Elin's foot jigs beneath her. It doesn't add up, does it? The laid-back vibe doesn't jibe with the hotel, its design. Scanning the text below, her eyes leap to several quotes:

I've always chosen to work with buildings that have a history, buildings that ask me to continue telling their story. The fact that Le Sommet's story started with my great-grandfather's vision for a sanatorium makes this development special to me. It's always been my dream to reinvent the building; as a child, I used to look at the structure, imagine it born again, something new.

The article continues:

Lucas started making buildings at the age of nine from anything he could find. "Lego,

197

sticks, the food they brought to me in the hospital. In fact, I think that hospital was where my love of buildings, architecture, began. I vowed that when I was better I'd build something of my own, something important. Squeeze the life from every day."

Hospital? She scans the rest of the article, finds a paragraph of explanation:

Lucas was born with a congenital heart condition called ASD (atrial septal defect), a hole in the heart. It was treated successfully via surgical closure, but the operation and various complications meant he had several long hospital stays as a child.

He's starting to make sense to Elin now: Lucas Caron is someone with something to prove, mentally, physically. He's also someone who wants to break the mold. One phrase in particular reflects that: *squeeze the life from every day.*

She can see why Laure might be intrigued — the mix of businessman and bohemian — but it still doesn't explain the photographs, why she took them.

Going back to the search, she casts her eyes down the rest of the results. At the bottom of the page she notices a blog story. It's in English, the title provocative: "How Switzerland's Property Developers Are Ruining

Their Own Towns."

Elin clicks on it. The content reflects the title — commentary on various property developers, including Lucas. The comments section at the bottom catches her eye: vitriolic remarks about Lucas Caron and Le Sommet, insults about the proposed design, his personality.

There's talk about Daniel Lemaitre's disappearance, his personal and professional relationship with Lucas. Gossip mainly; accusations of nepotism, rumors that Lucas was about to pull him from the project.

Still intrigued, she types Lucas's name into Twitter. She frowns: his name appears in hundreds of tweets, the majority of them negative.

She hears the click of the door. *Will.*

"What are you doing?" He walks toward her, puts his phone down on the side.

"Reading an article about Lucas Caron. Isaac just showed me some photos Laure had of him."

"And?"

"It looks like he didn't know the photos were being taken."

"Elin, this isn't any of your business. I think if she isn't back by tonight, you should let Isaac call the police again. Leave it to them."

There's an odd note in his voice: a cool kind of resignation. Not only that, his eyes . . . they're empty, she thinks, panicking. Hollow.

He's pulling away and it's her fault. The worst thing is, she knows she can fix it, tell him what he wants to hear — that she's ready to take the steps she's meant to take — but it would be a lie.

I'm not ready.

Her life is on hold until she gets answers about what happened to Sam. Something inside her, some important part, is stuck. Snagged on the day he died, like a stitch of a jumper caught on a branch, forever pulling her backward.

Reaching into the wardrobe, Will pulls a sweater over his head. "You know, when I was getting changed, I was thinking, what I said before . . . Please, Elin. I want to go."

"But —"

"As soon as we can," Will interrupts. "And there's this." He holds out his phone. "I don't want to be stuck here any longer than we have to. A massive storm is coming in."

Elin scans the screen.

Unprecedented storm closing in on the Alps. The Italian resort of Cervinia has closed all lifts after high winds force cable cars to swing out of control. More than 6 feet of snow is forecast in the next 48 hours.

"I can't leave, Will. Not now."

"Can't? Or won't?" Will sits on the bed. He looks at her, eyes narrowed, disbelieving.

"Elin, I don't think you're listening to what I'm saying."

Panic spools through her. She has to tell him, doesn't she? Tell him what she really came here for, or she's at risk of losing him. "I can't. Me being here, it's not just about reconnecting with Isaac. It's about getting the truth."

"Truth? What's this all about?"

"It's about Isaac." Her voice wavers. "I think he killed Sam. That's why I'm worried about Laure. I know what he's capable of."

31

"Killed?" Will repeats, his eyes locked on hers. "You said it was an accident."

Elin sits down on the bed beside him, her mouth dry. "That was the official verdict. Their assumption was that he fell into the pool, hit his head on a rock, drowned. It fit with what I remembered, but then, a few months later, I started getting these flash-backs."

"Of what happened?"

"No, that's the point. I told my parents and the police what I thought I had remembered." Those memories are still clear, pared back to the most important images. For years, she has mined these images for accuracy, turning them this way or that to probe them for truth, but the bones of them are always there. "But those memories — they're different from what I see in these flashbacks."

"So what had you told the police?"

Elin closes her eyes. "We were rock pool-ing, the three of us." She can picture it so clearly: the fierce June sun, angled high, throbbing against their skin. Sam's red, peeling neck, Isaac's gray T-shirt, splattered with saltwater stains. "We had this competition, who could catch the most crabs. A chart, pinned to the beach-hut wall." She scuffs her feet together. "The boys took it so seriously. Everything was a competition between them."

"I was like that with my brother too."

"But this . . . it was odd. The intensity. Taking pleasure in each other's failures. It never made sense . . . it wasn't even like they were similar. Sam was the opposite of Isaac. An open book. Mum always said he was like her, the easy child." He even looked like her, she thinks — pale skin, blond hair so fine that if it got wet you could see the bone-white of his scalp beneath.

"So you weren't easy, then?" Will raises an eyebrow.

"No, not like Sam. Everyone says the youngest is the happiest, and it's true. He was always the one who made us laugh, smoothed things over when we argued. Looking back now, I think he had the best bits of me and Isaac combined. High energy like me, but with Isaac's laser focus. He could sit down, concentrate in a way I never could — Lego, homework, reading. Nothing seemed to faze him . . . except Isaac. He knew how to push Sam's buttons."

"He did it a lot?"

"Yes. He was different to me and Sam. There's a wild streak there. Mum was usually unflappable, but Isaac made her nervous sometimes." Elin pinches the bedspread between her fingers. "I felt it too. He was unpredictable. I think part of it was because he was extraordinarily clever. He liked to toy with people, with situations, understand why they reacted like they did."

"That sounds quite cold."

"Yes, he could be. Sometimes he didn't seem to have the same response to things that other people had. As though a part of him had worked out that emotions didn't get you anywhere in the long run, so he put himself above them."

Will looks at her. "Or perhaps he sensed that Sam was your mother's favorite? Perhaps he closed off. Self-preservation."

"But I never said that." Her voice is sharp, surprising herself. "I never said Sam was her favorite."

"But how you said it, it sounded like . . ." Will shrugs. "Forget it. What happened next?"

"Isaac was angry because Sam was winning. I'd had enough, left them to it, went over to another rock pool. I'd only been gone a few minutes when I heard shouting. I turned, saw Sam's bucket knocked over." Elin blinks. "His crabs were slipping back into the water. Sam was screaming, battering Isaac with his fists. It was getting out of hand, so I went over, told them to stop."

"The peacemaker."

Elin nods. "They made up. Isaac apologized. Everything seemed fine, so I wandered farther, toward the cliff. I thought they'd sorted it out." She falters, even now, the memory knife sharp in her head. "I don't know how long it was exactly, maybe fifteen minutes, twenty. I could hear Isaac. He was screaming. I ran back."

She can feel it now; panic triggering inside her, like a siren. "I found Isaac in the rock pool. Up to his shoulders. Beside —" The words catch in her throat. "Beside Sam. He had him under the arms, trying to drag him out, but he couldn't get his footing. He kept shouting, 'We can help him, we can help him,' but I knew he was dead. His color . . ." Her voice splinters. "We tried, kept going until the paramedics got there, but he was gone."

Will takes her hand in his, squeezes. "So where was Isaac when it happened?"

"He said he'd gone to the loo. When he came back he found Sam in the water. He assumed he'd slipped, hit his head on a rock."

"Without anyone noticing?"

"The rock pools were isolated, at the end of the beach. Unless someone happened to be there, they wouldn't have seen."

Will's forehead is creased in concentration. "So why do you think Isaac was responsible?" He runs his thumb over the back of her hand.

"A few months after, I started getting these flashbacks. The only way I can describe it is like when you're dreaming. At that one moment, it's clear, but then once you're properly awake, you can't hold on to it. A snapshot, the outline of something I haven't yet filled in. Most of it goes until the next one."

The psychotherapist she saw last year told her that this isn't unusual, that it's her conscious mind's way of protecting itself. Protecting her.

"Can you recall anything from the flashbacks clearly?"

"Only one thing. One image I can't get out of my head. Isaac's by the cliff. His hands . . ." The words are sticky in her throat. "They're covered in blood."

"But surely that's impossible. You found him in the pool, trying to pull Sam out. Was there blood on him then?"

"No. That's what I can't work out."

"Have you talked to anyone about this?" Will reaches behind him, grabs the bottle of water from the table. "What you remember?"

"Apart from the psychotherapist, no. Mum, Dad . . . they'd lost Sam. This . . . it would have been like losing Isaac too. I couldn't do it to them."

"And you haven't said anything to Isaac?"

"No. I know what would happen. He'd go on the defensive, think I was accusing him of hurting Sam."

"Well, you are, aren't you?" Will opens the water, slugs some back. His gaze is fixed on her. Intent, unblinking.

She balks at that. "But . . ."

"Elin, come on. That's what you're implying."

She's silent. *It is, so why is it so hard to admit it to someone else?*

"The one thing I don't understand is why you didn't tell me about this." He forces a smile but the hurt in his eyes is obvious. "It's pretty big, keeping it from me."

Elin bites down on her lip. "Be honest, would you have wanted to get involved if you knew? If I'd said on our first date, Will, I think my older brother might have killed my little brother, and I might have seen it, but my brain has somehow repressed the memory. That's pretty heavy stuff."

"You should have told me. I wouldn't have judged."

"I couldn't take the risk. I liked you, Will. From the minute we met, I saw a future with you." Her voice cracks. He *has* to understand, know she hasn't deceived him deliberately. "You haven't got anything like this going on. You're normal, have a normal family." She smiles, attempts to lighten the mood. "Your sister can be a bit of a cow, but apart from that . . ."

Will returns her smile. "But why are you so convinced that you're going to get the truth if you confront him now?"

"Now Mum's gone, it's the right time. It can't go on forever."

"Are you going to tell him what you remember?"

"I don't know. I don't really have a plan. I thought if we were talking about Sam, Mum, he might let something slip."

Will rubs his knuckle. "You know, if you're right, if these flashbacks stem from an actual memory, then Laure going missing —"

Elin nods. Neither of them needs to say it out loud. "That's why I can't leave now." She pictures Laure yesterday, the empathetic words about her mother. With it comes another pang of guilt. *I owe Laure this.*

Turning away from the laptop screen, she presses at her forehead.

"Is something wrong?" Will looks at her closely, his expression worried.

"Just tired. I think I'm getting a headache."

He rummages in his bag, then tosses a small packet toward her. Ibuprofen. "Take these, and then we're going to the spa. Dinner's not for an hour."

Elin acquiesces, compliant. Anything to loosen the knots inside her head.

She can feel them, the thoughts, the unanswered questions, like rocks, weighing heavy in her head.

32

"Els, come on."

"Just . . . give me a minute." Elin shifts from foot to foot. The decking is freezing, the wooden slats coated in a fine layer of snow. The wind gusts, flattening the thin fabric of her swimsuit against her body. She shivers.

Snow is hammering from the sky, drifts building around the two outdoor pools, the assortment of chairs and loungers. Rolls of vapor barrel off the largest pool, closest to her, melding with the snow to create a warm, wet fog. Only small squares of the water itself are visible, islands of a shadowy, shimmering cerulean.

Will takes her hand, tugs her past the main pool. "You've done it before. It's only a hot tub, it's not deep." His skin is puckered with goose bumps.

He slips behind an enclosure of slatted wooden panels. Elin follows, staring at the circle of blond wood.

Will climbs up then submerges his body

beneath the water. He looks at her, his expression challenging. "Coming?" Without his glasses, his eyes are darker.

Elin stares. Even more steam is being thrown off the surface of the water, making the darkness shift and sway. Images come, unwanted: *A shadowy face. Water, battering the sides of the caves. The sharp jag of panic in her chest.*

Blinking, she blocks it out, clambers up the steps to the tub. As she slides her body into the water next to Will, she's conscious of the sharp angle of her hips butting up against him, but he doesn't seem to notice. He snakes an arm around her waist, lightly squeezes. "Okay?"

She nods. The water is so hot it's almost painful, but she can already feel the warmth tugging at the tension in her limbs, pulling it loose.

Will's right. She should relax. Unwind. "This is what I needed," she says, leaning into him.

"Told you." He presses a button behind her. There's a low rumbling, then the water starts to pulse, ripple. Within seconds, it's churning, coiling, pummeling her back and thighs. "You've got to learn to relax. Everyone needs downtime."

Elin studies his face. His dark eyes are warm as he looks at her, his tanned skin dotted with tiny water droplets. *I'm lucky,* she thinks, *he cares, and isn't scared to show me that he does. I shouldn't take it for granted.*

"Want to get closer?" Will does his usual comedy leer, drawing his hand up her thigh. Tipping his face down to hers, he kisses her. His mouth is warm, soft, but she breaks away, a sound catching her attention.

It's hard to make out what it is above the wind, the water. A thud? Footsteps?

With a sudden sense of disquiet, she turns, looks around. Once again, the darkness seems to shift, mutate; a quiet, watchful darkness.

An uneasy feeling creeps over her. Just like in the changing room earlier, she has the horrible sensation that she's being observed.

She briefly looks the other way. The wooden paneling stares back at her: blank, featureless, dusted in snow.

There's no one there.

"Did you hear that?" Elin turns back to Will. "It sounded like someone was behind us."

"No."

Detecting a tightness in his tone, she doesn't say anything else. They sit in uncomfortable silence, bubbles beating against her body.

Tension is now emanating from Will, his body rigid against hers.

She reprimands herself. She's ruined it, hasn't she? *Again.* This was meant to be fun, relaxing, and she's already made it into something awkward. She's always had this ability. To spoil things.

Her mother said it was a fear of letting go, losing control of emotions she wasn't comfortable expressing. "You did it on people's birthdays. I don't think you ever set out to ruin them, but something always went wrong. You'd fall over or spill a drink. Once, on Isaac's birthday, you ate too much cake. Sick all down your dress."

After a few minutes, Will stands up, tiny bubbles stuck to his skin. "Look, you were right," he says stiffly. "This probably wasn't a good idea." He doesn't meet her eyes. "I'm going to try the other pool. Do you want me to walk you back first?"

"No, it's fine. I'll meet you in the room." Her voice is small. She doesn't like this: the unusual coolness in his speech, his tone.

Will climbs out. Elin follows, heading toward the indoor pool. Within seconds, she's shivering again, the sharp wind peeling off any residual heat from the water.

A few yards on, she hesitates. She's come to a junction. The decking leads in two directions: straight ahead back to the spa, the way she and Will came, or left, toward a small square of water.

It's the only section of water that isn't steaming, Elin thinks, curious. Instead, the surface is reflecting the lights overhead — a black, frosted glimmer.

Ice.

Walking toward it, she stops, just a few steps from the edge. It's only about a few yards wide, a narrow ladder running up the side.

A plunge pool.

She hasn't seen one of these for years. The last time was on a weekend trip to Cornwall with Laure and her mother; a shabby sea-front hotel near Newquay. That one was even smaller, like a well. They'd dared themselves, she and Laure. *I'll do it if you will.*

Elin stares into the water, a knot of fear opening up inside her, the very same fear as back then: the narrow dimensions, that you'd scrape skin on the way in unless your arms were tucked in tight.

There's one big difference, though: back then, she'd done it. Done it because Laure dared her. Because she wanted to prove to herself that she could.

But that was before Sam. Before everything changed.

She's about to walk away, when she feels a presence behind her. *Will.*

"I've looked, but I'm wimping out. You can do it for me —"

There's no response. No laugh. No hand on her arm. Instead, she can hear breathing, the soft thud of feet on the decking. Elin freezes.

It's not Will, she realizes with a sickening lurch. She turns, but all at once, there's a pressure on her back, a sudden, jutting force just above the base of her spine.

Elin's heart stutters.

She jerks forward, toes clamping, contracting, trying to get purchase, but the decking is slippery with compacted snow and ice.

Hauling her weight backward, she tries to grab hold of something, anything, but there's nothing there. Instead, her arms wheel uselessly in the air.

It's over in seconds. Elin plummets forward, the thin layer of ice on the surface giving way with a crack.

33

There's no time to scream; she's swallowed by the freezing water, lungs balling into two tight fists. Her ears burn, mouth and eyes fill with water.

She's sinking.

Lower, lower.

Elin forces herself to open her eyes, but the water is black, impenetrable. Her lungs are seizing, red-hot with shock.

Start moving. Do something.

She starts cycling her feet, pedaling against the water. Almost instantly, the downward movement reverses; she starts moving up.

When her head finally punctures the surface, she's gasping for breath.

As she scrambles to the ladder, Elin clamps her hand around the freezing metal, hauling herself onto the closest rung. Her feet are numb, sliding with each step.

There's no time to look up, see if whoever had pushed her is still there, what they might do next. Her instincts have kicked in: *I have to get out.*

The refrain is familiar: the words she said over and over a year ago as she fought to get out of the cave after Hayler grabbed her, hit her, as she made the decision to escape the rising tide.

I have to get out. I have to get out.

When she reaches the top, she runs, on autopilot, toward the main pool. "Will," she shouts, stopping on the walkway beside the pool.

She can't see a thing. The water is barely visible, hot vapor gusting across the surface in ragged clouds. "Will, are you there?"

In one gust, the wind clears the steam. A young couple is standing at the end of the pool, looking up at her, but she barely registers them.

She can see him: skirting the top of the steps leading out of the pool, striding toward her.

"What's wrong?"

"Someone pushed me into the plunge pool." Her voice sounds detached. Odd. "I thought it was you, then" — the words catch in her throat — "someone pushed me in."

Will frowns, rocks back on his heels. "Are you sure? The decking's slippery, from the snow. You might have caught your foot."

Elin blinks, his words bouncing off her, each one a betrayal. *Is he actually doing this? Questioning me? Questioning what happened?*

"No," she says stiffly, tears hot at the back of her eyes. "Someone deliberately pushed me in, tried to scare me."

And it had worked. In that water, every fear she's never been able to label took over: a fear of being submerged, slipping below the surface to somewhere unreachable. Alone.

Alone like Sam is now.

That's what this all comes back to, doesn't it? Always Sam.

Will's watching her, mouth poised to say something, but instead he takes her hand. Several beats later, the words finally come, but they're different, she can tell. They're neutral words, sharp edges sanded off inside his head. "Let's not jump to conclusions. We need to get you inside. You're shivering."

They don't linger in the changing rooms. Elin hurriedly pulls on dry clothes, meets Will in reception shortly after.

Back in the room, Will bundles her into bed, piling throws on top of the duvet. Elin lies back against the pillow, but the sudden inactivity, the absolute stillness, only emphasizes the erratic hammering in her chest.

He passes her a steaming cup of coffee, sits on the bed beside her. "Decaf. I didn't think you needed any extra stimulation before dinner. How are you feeling now?"

"Better." Elin sips the coffee. It's too hot, but she likes the distraction. "It was the shock . . . I know it sounds stupid, but I honestly thought I wasn't going to come back up." Her voice cracks. "Part of me thought, the same thing that happened last year . . ."

Will puts his hand over hers, squeezes.

"It's not only that." Elin pinches the throw between her fingers. "Earlier, when you were swimming, someone was watching me in the changing room. I heard a door being opened and closed, but no one came out."

He stiffens. "Watching you? You think it's the same person?"

"Maybe."

A shadow passes across his face. He's thinking it, too, isn't he? After what she told him. *Isaac.*

Will clears his throat. "Elin, I really think we should leave. I understand about Sam, why you're here, but after what just happened in the spa, it's too much of a risk. You can't carry on."

He's right. Being here, around Isaac, being pulled into whatever's going on . . . she isn't ready. What she's come here for, it'll have to wait.

"I think you're —" She stops, picking up a sudden movement near the door. "Will, something's being pushed under the door."

Walking over, he crouches down, picks something up — a piece of paper.

He unfolds it and starts reading.

"What is it?"

218

"They're evacuating the hotel. We've got to leave tomorrow."

34

Day Three

Eleven a.m. The third and penultimate bus is ready to leave.

Sitting in the lounge, Elin watches the staff swarm the lobby, dragging suitcases and bags, shouting instructions.

The majority of the guests are already down the mountain, but there are a few left, standing quietly in small groups, looking overwhelmed by the noise and chaos.

Will catches her eye. "We've got to get the next bus, Elin. We can't leave it any longer."

"I know, but I wanted to speak to Isaac first." Pouring a coffee, she tips in some milk, watches the liquid swirl. "We can't just go, not without seeing him."

They're the last ones to have breakfast. The buffet table is depleted — all that's left are a few croissants in a basket, some slices of local ham, teas, coffees, half-empty jugs of juice.

"Look at it out there." Will sits down, eyes

fixed on the windows. "It's worse."

She follows his gaze toward the terrace. You can barely tell it's daytime; the sky is overcast, blackened, reception filled with a silvery light. The windows are gilded with ice but you can still see the snow — frozen pellets plummeting from the sky. The car park, the trees beyond, are choked — soft beds of powder deepening by the minute.

It's like the hotel is being invaded; the mountain itself on the attack.

As she sips her coffee, a silence settles over the room. Elin looks over to the lobby. The majority of the staff have gone. The bus must have left. They haven't seen it go because the car park is out of view on the right. Elin's glad: watching the packed bus crawl through the heavy snow would make her dread the journey ahead.

Will passes her his phone. "We've made the news."

She scans the article.

AVALANCHE PROMPTS
SWISS HOTEL EVACUATION

Buses are today evacuating over 200 tourists and hotel staff from a five-star mountainside hotel in Switzerland as heavy snow causes widespread disruption across the Alps.

Le Sommet, located at 2,200 meters, is in an area of extremely high risk for avalanches, said Katherine Leon from Valais Police in Sion.

"The avalanche risk is now at a maximum of 5 out of 5 with the main part of the storm still due to arrive. While some guests didn't want to go, the mayor, in conjunction with the Communes, has now ordered the mandatory evacuation," Leon said. "The avalanche risk is immense."

The evacuation will be taking place on Sunday morning, with each bus ferrying up to 50 people at a time to hotels in nearby Crans-Montana.

Cecile Caron, the hotel's manager, said the evacuees remained calm.

"Thought I'd find you here."
Elin looks up.
Isaac.
He looks disheveled. His hair is greasy, curls lying flat, matted against his scalp. The skin above his left eye is raw, shiny red, inflamed.
He studies their bags. "Ready to go?" His voice is flat, icy.
"We have to, Isaac. We don't have a choice." Elin exchanges a glance with Will. "Even if it wasn't for the evacuation, there's nothing I

can do now."

"I'm not going," he says abruptly. "I called the police first thing. They said they'd come up today. I'm waiting for them."

"You're sure they're still coming? After the evacuation order?"

"I don't know, but I can't leave." Isaac looks at her, unblinking. "What if she's out in this? Hurt? If I go, it could be days before anyone gets back up here."

"They won't let you stay indefinitely. You've got to leave it to the police."

"Police?" Isaac laughs hollowly. "What do you think they're going to do? If the storm gets worse, they're not going to risk their lives to find her. That's how it works in situations like this, Elin — you know that. They make a call, weigh up the risks."

"Look, chances are things will have calmed down in a few days. You can come back up . . ." She trails off. They both know how unlikely this is. If the storm progresses as forecast, the roads might take days to clear. By then it would be too late. "Isaac, we're not going far. We'll stay in town. As soon as the weather improves we'll come back up."

"You're really going." His face constricts. "You're no better than Dad, are you? When the going gets tough, you run."

Elin blinks, flinching at the force of his words. Without saying anything else, he turns, walks away, doesn't look back.

Anger sparks inside her — at him, at herself. She roughly pushes back her chair.

Will puts a hand on her arm. "Let him calm down. He just needs —"

But he doesn't get to finish his sentence.

Screams. Screams, then a shout.

The sound is muffled, muted, like it's coming down a tunnel.

Then a face appears at the window, twisted in an expression of absolute terror.

35

Elin's cup falls from her hand, clattering against her plate. Coffee streaks across the table: a thin, dark slash.

A man — staff, Elin thinks, taking in the uniform, the gray puffer coat branded with the same lowercased le sommet.

He's hammering on the window, fists pounding so hard the glass is vibrating. Snow is being blown sideways, blurring his face. All she can make out is dark, closely cropped hair, heavyset features.

Thud. Thud.

Her heart accelerates, tripping double time.

Standing up, Will stumbles toward the window, Elin following close behind.

The man's face becomes clearer, his features contorted; his eyes are wide, staring, pupils enlarged.

He's mouthing something. *"La piscine . . ."* The rest of his words are lost to the wind, the thick wall of glass. *"La piscine . . ."* the man repeats, louder this time, so she can hear it through the glass. *The pool.*

"I'll get someone," Will says, his voice tremulous.

She nods wordlessly. Adrenaline coursing through her, she gropes for the handle of the door leading onto the terrace. She finds it, pushing down hard.

It doesn't open.

Elin pushes again. Harder.

Finally, it gives, freezing air hitting her cheeks along with powdery flakes of snow.

The man moves toward her, his body trembling. *"La piscine . . ."* His voice is high, gabbled, tipping into hysteria. He says the words over and over, final syllable merging with the first. He points toward the spa.

Stepping out onto the terrace, Elin looks where he's pointing, but she can't see anything. The spa sits to the left, but it's screened off by a complex structure of fencing and planting.

"Please, let me —"

Elin recognizes Cecile Caron's voice straightaway. Will is behind her.

"Let me through." Cecile's already pulling on a jacket. Her tone is calm, authoritative, but Elin can hear the flayed undertones: fear, panic.

"Axel, show me." Following him, Cecile turns to Elin. "Please, go back inside."

Elin stays put, watches Axel start walking back along the terrace. His movements are uncontrolled, jerky, feet giving way on the ice, compacted snow.

"I've got to go with them."

"No." Will puts a hand on her arm. "You don't know what this is."

She hears his words, but they don't register. *What if it's Laure?*

Going back inside, Elin picks up her tote and snatches her coat from the chair. She pulls it on, heads outside. Cecile and the man disappear down a set of steps at the end of the terrace.

Elin strides toward them. Despite her thick fleece, the wind cuts through the fabric, biting into her chest, her throat.

When she reaches the steps, she finds that they're steep, the treads icy. Clinging to the handrail, she moves carefully, precisely.

At the bottom, there's a wooden fence separating the grounds from the spa.

As Axel pushes the gate open, the spa comes into view. Steam is billowing off the pools, twisting, coiling, as it rises to meet the falling snow.

She increases her pace until she's right behind them, feels the wooden slats vibrate beneath her feet.

Axel speeds up, circling the larger pool until they reach the smaller one, set a level lower. He stops. *"Ici."* His arm shakes as he points toward the pool. *Here.*

With Axel's silhouette blocking her view of

the water, Elin has to step to one side. A light is flickering overhead.

A sudden gust of wind whips through the vapor, teasing it apart, pulling it to nothing. The pool comes into view, the cover about a third of the way across, snow collecting unevenly across the surface.

It's then she sees it: the lifeless form of a body at the bottom of the pool. The uplighters cast a dull glow upward, highlighting her hair drifting about in the water.

It's shoulder length. Dark.

A woman, Elin thinks, bile rising in her throat. A refrain is beating out in her head: *Is it her? Is it her?*

Elin takes a step closer. Looks again. It is her. She recognizes her immediately. Black puffer jacket. Dark jeans.

Laure.

36

Elin's muscles seize, the scene around her becoming strangely distant, dropping in and out of focus.

"We need to get her out of the water. Try CPR."

It takes her a moment to realize it's her own voice. On autopilot. Calm. In control. Nothing like how she's feeling inside.

But before she's able to move, a hand yanks at her arm. Someone's pushing roughly between her and Cecile. Their footsteps kick up snow.

"It's her, isn't it?" The voice is thin, high. Panicked.

Isaac.

"Move . . . just move." His hand is still on her arm, shoving. "I want to see if it's her."

He's past her now, his expression wild, cheeks patchy blotches of red.

Elin puts her bag down, lurches forward, tries to reach for him. "Isaac, no —"

But it's too late. Her hand barely grazes his

jacket, uselessly groping the air. Pounding past her, he's already skirting the pool, slipping every few steps on the snow. He's only yards from the water.

"Isaac, please!"

Isaac ignores her, ripping off his coat. He clumsily kicks his shoes off and away. Diving into the pool, he breaks the surface with a thundering splash. Water arches into a sloppy spray.

Above, the lights are still flickering.

Elin catches only glimpses: Isaac blurred, luridly magnified in the distortion of the water as he propels himself to the bottom of the pool.

She can barely breathe, panic clawing at her throat, threatening to take control.

In what seems like seconds, Isaac's pulling back to the surface, on his back, his arms wrapped around the shadowy shape of Laure's body.

Let her be okay. Please let her be okay.

Isaac reaches the surface of the pool. His hair is plastered over his forehead in dark, ragged streaks. He's gasping for breath, chest heaving.

"I'll help." Will's voice, from behind her. She hadn't even noticed he was there.

He drops to his knees at the edge of the water. Leaning over, he hauls Laure from Isaac's grasp, hoisting her up onto the decking beside Elin.

It's the first time that she sees the body faceup.

Elin recoils: a visceral, full-body reaction.

There's a black gas mask strapped around Laure's face.

No: not a gas mask. There's no filter. In its place is a thick, ribbed tube, running from nose to mouth.

Squatting next to the body, Will's already pulling the mask away, moving Laure onto her side. There's a precision to his movements, a desperate urgency.

The mask is gone.

Elin stares at the exposed face, water running in fine droplets over the pale skin. Her breath catches in her throat with a sharp jag.

It's not her.

The woman, whoever she is, has similar hair, frame, clothes, but it's not Laure.

Will starts tipping her forehead back, positioning her body for CPR, but Elin knows without doubt that it's too late.

The woman's skin is bluish, her green eyes open in a hazy death stare, mouth slightly parted.

Still, Elin bends down, feels for a pulse in the woman's neck. There isn't one.

"Will," she says softly. "She's dead." She's sure it hasn't been long, though — rigor mortis usually occurs around two to six hours after death, and it hasn't set in yet. Elin's no expert but she knows that the warm tempera-

231

ture of the water would possibly shorten that timeline even further — her guess is that the woman's been dead for one to two hours at most.

Isaac hasn't moved. Still soaking wet, he's crouched beside the lifeless body.

Elin absorbs the reaction. He really thought it was Laure, didn't he? You couldn't fake that response.

The implication is clear: he genuinely didn't know where Laure was. He can't have been involved in her disappearance.

Her gaze moves to the woman's wrists. They're tightly bound with a thin, woven rope.

She's been restrained.

Then her eyes catch something else: several of the woman's fingers are missing. One on the first hand. Two on the second. An involuntary shiver passes through her.

Will follows her gaze, eyes glazed. "I'm going to take Isaac inside. Get him dried off."

Elin is about to reply when she hears a voice.

"It's Adele." Cecile's voice, from behind her. Flat. Expressionless. "One of the housekeeping staff."

Turning, Elin sees the group behind her has swelled to four, five staff. One of them is sobbing, the rest talking in muffled voices, eyes darting toward the body.

I have to do something — take control.

This is probably a crime scene, and it's already a mess. The snow surrounding the pool is pocked with footprints, some smeared, some already covered in a fresh layer of snow.

Elin turns back to the body. Snow is collecting on the woman's face, clothes, the mask beside her. The sight, once again, pulls the breath from her body. It's like she's on pause, every fiber in her body in stasis.

Part of her wants to run, block it out, but she knows: this moment, it's a pivot point. *Now or never.* If she can't help now, in such a desperate situation, when no one else is qualified to do so, then she'll probably never be able to.

Turning properly, she faces the small group behind her.

"I can help. I'm a police officer," she says, hesitantly at first.

The group doesn't look up.

Elin allows herself a moment, collects her thoughts.

Clearing her throat, she raises her voice. "I'm a police officer. Please step back. This might be a crime scene. We don't want to destroy any evidence."

37

"I've called the police. They're on their way. I . . ." Cecile stops, eyes pulled toward the body. Her face crumples. "I can't help thinking, perhaps we should have tried to resuscitate her. It feels wrong, not even —"

"There was nothing anybody could do," Elin says softly. It's even more obvious now, she thinks, looking at Adele's body, the stiffening neck, the bluish hue to her features.

Bending down, she takes a closer look. The woman is about the same age as Laure, perhaps a little younger. Her black puffer jacket is unzipped, her T-shirt ridden up, revealing a thin, muscular torso.

Her initial theory is right: rigor mortis definitely hasn't developed in her body, so she hasn't been in the water long.

Her dark hair is matted, the water on the surface already freezing into translucent shards, the very top flecked with snow. A whitish foam is seeping from her mouth. It's cooling at the corners, solidifying.

Elin knows what this means: the froth is a mix of mucus, air, and water that combines during respiration. Its presence is enough to indicate that she became immersed while she was still breathing, though it isn't enough to prove conclusively that she drowned.

As Elin glances at her eyes, she can see that they're lifelike, glistening. No lines to indicate exposure to air postdeath.

Her gaze tracks sideways to the mask on the snow. Her skin prickles. The black rubber is already dusted with snow, but it doesn't take away from its grotesque shape, form.

What is it?

Elin's always hated masks, of any kind: Halloween, surgical. The concealment, it horrifies her. Not knowing what lurks beneath.

"That mask" — Cecile follows her gaze — "I recognize it from the archive. It was used here, in the sanatorium. A breathing aid." She brings a hand up to her mouth, starts chewing at her nails.

Elin nods. *What did it mean? Some kind of game gone wrong? Something sexual?*

She looks again at Adele's hands. The rope around her wrists suggests she's been restrained, possibly held somewhere for a while. Enough time to amputate the fingers, she thinks grimly, her gaze moving to the small stubs remaining, about half a centimeter above the knuckle.

But there's still no indication of how she

Lucas Caron.

The angry words of warning slip away under the scrutiny of his gaze.

He's taller than in the photographs; his black technical jacket is pulled taut over broad shoulders, but he isn't bulky. This is a functional fitness, from hours spent outside actually doing a sport rather than pumping iron in a gym. Once again, she imagines him halfway up a mountain. Hanging off a cliff.

Through a messy curtain of hair, he looks toward the body, his features tightening. He rubs a hand across his beard, flecked with snow. This close, there's no doubting his connection to Cecile. The physical resemblance is unnerving.

"Lucas Caron." He holds his hand out.

Elin shakes it. His palm feels calloused. Rough.

"Elin Warner." She gestures down at the snow-covered decking. "I'm sorry, but you shouldn't really be walking here. I'm trying to preserve the scene for the police."

Lucas's gray eyes lock on hers. "That's what I need to tell you. The police . . . they aren't coming." His voice is low, urgent. "There's been an avalanche. The road is blocked. They can't get through."

238

38

"The avalanche is about half a mile down. One of the drivers has been there to take a look, says it's about fifteen feet high. They'll be able to clear it, but it could take a few days." Lucas tugs up the hood of his jacket. The movement momentarily obscures his face, but Elin's already seen the flare of panic in his eyes.

"They can't clear it any quicker?"

"Not easily." His expression is grim. "It's a dry avalanche. Not just snow. It's literally stripped the mountain — trees, rocks, vegetation. It's a monster."

"Why is it so hard to clear?"

"These avalanches . . . they're incredibly violent. The force of the fall acts like a grinder, dividing the snow into finer and finer particles. By the time it comes to a stop, the snow is so densely packed that you can't use a blower, as the debris gets caught in the machine." He clears his throat. "It's the movement too. The avalanche warms a tiny layer of the snow, creating a liquid that freezes, so the avalanche isn't just compacted, but set like concrete."

"And there's no other way to get to town?"

"No. The only other way is by helicopter, but the wind's too strong. They won't take one up in this. It's not safe."

Elin digests his words, the impact of what he's saying finally hitting home. *They're on their own.*

Glancing back down at the body, a steady beat of trepidation sounds out in her gut.

"Are you able to help? Until they get here?" Lucas shifts from foot to foot. "There are only a few guests left, but we have a lot of staff too. I can't take any risks."

Elin senses him taking stock of the situation, of *her.* For the first time she can see the innate confidence of a businessman, a shrewdness at odds with the laid-back appearance. He's used to being in control, she thinks, watching him. Giving orders.

"I can't. I don't have any jurisdiction here." Nor at home, Elin thinks, biting down on her bottom lip, already regretting the lie she'd told.

"But you can help, surely? While we wait for them?" Lucas glances around him, his expression set — too set, as if he's masking his panic. "This, it's not something anyone here could . . ." He trails off, as if the magnitude of what he's facing is overwhelming him.

Elin feels a sharp pang of sympathy; he's in over his head. A possible murder on his premises, when they hadn't been open long . . . The hotel's reputation is at stake. He wants to do things the right way. Damage limitation.

"I honestly don't know what I can do. Switzerland has different procedures, protocol."

"It can't be that different, surely?" His voice has an edge. "The basics."

Elin wavers. "Let me call the police," she says finally. "If they're happy for me to be involved, then I'll see what I'm allowed to do in these circumstances."

Lucas pulls his phone from his pocket. "You need to call 117, the main police switchboard number. Every call goes through there first."

She does as he says. The call is answered almost instantly.

"*Bonjour, Police. Comment vous appelez-vous? Grüezi Polizei, Wie isch Ihre name bitte?*" The voice is male, formal.

Heat rushes to her cheeks, her juvenile fear of speaking another language kicking in. "Hello, I —"

"Yes, I speak English," the man interrupts. "How may I help?"

"My name is Elin Warner. I'm at the hotel Le Sommet near Crans-Montana. I think you've already spoken to the owner of the hotel about the situation. I wanted to see if I could help."

"Help?" he repeats, his voice clipped, wary.

"Yes. I'm a detective, in the UK police force. Mr. Caron has asked me to assist as the police can't reach us. I'm concerned because the scene is quickly deteriorating. I don't know how much evidence I'll be able to salvage, but I'd like to try."

A pause before he speaks again. "Okay, one moment. I will put you on hold."

Frowning, Lucas looks at her. "What are they saying?"

Elin moves the phone away. "Nothing yet. I'm on hold."

"Madame Warner, are you there?" The police officer is back on the line.

She brings the phone back to her ear. "Yes."

"I have asked the question about your assistance to my sergeant. We need to discuss, and then I'll call you back."

Elin says good-bye and hands the phone back to Lucas. "They'll let me know. Either way, my instinct is that we need to do something immediately. It shouldn't interfere with the police work." Time is of the essence, even when the victim is dead — snow washes away evidence, fibers, hairs. Memories start to fade. "The first priority is to preserve as much of the scene as possible. It's vital we protect any evidence. No matter how small."

Her words sound more confident than she

feels. Elin stares into the choppy depths of the pool with a feeling of despair. This is going to be an uphill struggle, the worst crime scene you could probably get: in constant flux, wind and snow collecting on top of other snow, eclipsing potential evidence, people already trampled over the scene, around the pool.

"What do you need?" Lucas clears his throat.

Elin steals a sideways glance at him, watching as his gaze, once again, moves to the woman's body. This time she notices a new emotion flicker across his features, an emotion she can't decipher.

Embarrassment?

It's possible. The grim reality of a death affects people in myriad ways.

"We need rope to put up a rough cordon around the pool. I know most of the guests have gone, but it's a reminder to the staff." Elin's mind starts churning over protocol. "I can use my phone to take photographs, then I need to scour the pool area, bag any evidence." She hesitates. "If you have any plastic gloves, sealable bags, sterile equipment, like tweezers, it would be helpful."

"I'm sure we've got most of what you need. It might be rudimentary, but . . ." Breaking off, Lucas beckons over several members of staff.

"I'll also need a full list of everyone who is

still in the hotel. Guests, staff."

"No problem," Lucas replies. "It's all written down."

Elin reaches into her pocket, and pulls out her phone. Where should she start with the photographs?

Adele's body.

The gusting wind is already changing the scene; depositing snow on Adele's features, tugging at her clothes. But before Elin can start, a voice: barely audible against the sound of the wind.

"I've found something."

39

Turning in the direction of the voice, Elin can see a female member of staff a few feet ahead, her hand trembling in the air.

Elin carefully skirts the side of the pool, walking toward her. As she gets closer, she can see that the woman's young — early twenties at the most. Her hair's scraped back from her face, revealing brown, haunted eyes.

When Elin stops beside her, the woman's hand lowers, finger pointing toward the decking.

Elin's gaze pulls downward. She instantly notices the glass box beside her, half concealed by the legs of a chair.

A sudden, liquid feeling of dread. She knows, from the woman's expression, that whatever this is . . . it isn't good.

"I saw it, when I started walking back." The woman's voice cracks, a hand coming up to her mouth.

Elin nods and crouches down to examine the box. It's not dissimilar to the display boxes all around the hotel: made entirely of glass, not more than a foot and a half in length.

A fine layer of snow is covering the surface, but a section of the glass has already been cleared, presumably by the woman — finger-tip marks streaked through the fine-powder snow.

Elin starts at the half-revealed contents, her stomach contracting.

Fingers. Three fingers.

The flesh is a horrible grayish white, marked with dark smears of blood.

These must be Adele's.

Elin's hands start trembling, her stomach still churning.

Deep breaths, she tells herself, feeling the eyes of the others on her. Steeling herself, she crouches lower, carefully blowing the rest of the snow away.

Elin can see everything now: the minutiae, the detail. Just as it was designed, she thinks, repulsed. This glass is meant for prying eyes.

Each finger is attached to the bottom of the box with a fine nail. Surrounding each one is a thin copper bracelet.

Three fingers. Three bracelets.

She tips her head. She can just about make out something engraved on the inside of the first bracelet. *Numbers?*

Moving closer to the glass, she can see that she's right: there is a row of five tiny numbers.

87499. Her gaze flickers to the next bracelet: the same thing again. 87534.

As Elin takes a photograph, her brain is trying to process what she's seeing: someone's amputated Adele's fingers, then fixed them to this box with the bracelets around them.

It means that this wasn't a spur-of-the-moment thing. It was planned. Premeditated. Every element — the restraint, amputation, the sandbag, *this* . . .

All carefully thought out, part of a narrative. Because that's what it is, she thinks, nausea sweeping over her: *a story.* They're trying to communicate something. Which, in turn, implies an organized crime. An organized killer.

This is someone intelligent, savvy about how the police work. Which probably means there'll be little evidence to go on. Someone harder to find.

Elin feels the prickle of sweat under her arms. *I'm out of my depth.* This isn't her country and half of what she's doing now isn't her area of expertise.

When she looks back to the box, her own inadequacy taunts her, flashes of her past mistakes looming large.

She feels her chest tighten, her vision blur, and when she blinks, she realizes the contents of the box have changed. The fingers are swelling; becoming bigger, bloodier. The blood is no longer dry; it's seeping from the tips of the fingers, leaching through the edges of the box onto the snow.

Blood.

So much blood it's carving channels in the snow, already reaching the tip of her boot . . .

Staring in horror, Elin stumbles backward. She's struggling to get her breath.

She wrenches her gaze from the box, and pulls her inhaler from her pocket, takes two, three puffs.

"Is everything all right?"

Elin looks up. Lucas Caron is standing above her, his face expressionless. The wind is tugging at his jacket, creasing the fabric into thin folds.

"Fine." She pushes her inhaler back into her pocket, takes several deep breaths until she feels her breathing settle.

"I've got some of the things you asked for." Lucas passes her a small cardboard box. "The gloves and bags. The rest of the equipment is coming. One of the staff is making sure everything is sterile."

"Thank you." Elin takes out a pair of gloves and a bag. She reaches for her tote, puts the rest inside.

Casting a sidelong glance at the box, she can see that the blood, the oversized fingers, they're gone. It's as it was the first time she looked at it.

But the terror remains, a terror unique to a situation like this.

What's happened here, it isn't logical, rational, something that can be explained. Elin knows it has its roots in something dark, something so dark it feels almost tangible, a presence in itself.

40

Elin tugs off her plastic gloves as she walks into the spa changing rooms. She vigorously rubs her hands together. They're cold, her fingertips red, but not freezing.

It's the one benefit of all her running, the hours spent pounding the coast road, the Dartmoor hills in bitter conditions — her body's strong, accustomed to being out of its comfort zone.

She looks at her watch. It's 4:30 p.m. Over five hours since they found Adele's body. It's now pitch black outside, the conditions deteriorating further — snow whirling madly, as if being turned in a centrifuge, fat white flakes illuminated by the lights against the dark sky above.

Every now and then, the wind picks up snow from the ground, sending it in a terrifying dance before dumping it somewhere else. If this had been in the UK, the CSIs would have been wild. Elin pictures her colleague Tim's pinched face and furrowed brow, the expletive-laden muttering under his breath.

She can't do much more — she's taken hundreds of photographs, noted down the bracelets' numbers, and methodically collected any possible evidence, which was few and far between. Her initial instinct was right: whoever did this was organized.

There's next to nothing in the makeshift evidence bags; some hairs, several empty sugar sachets, a few cigarette butts. A pair of blue bikini bottoms, snarled into a knot, half buried in the snow. She's collected them all, but she isn't hopeful.

As she starts to gather up her things, Elin feels her phone vibrate in her pocket. When she pulls it out, she doesn't recognize the number — it looks foreign. "Hello . . ."

"Good afternoon, may I speak with Elin Warner?" A man's voice, the English heavily accented. Not a French lilt, but German. Clipped, guttural.

"Speaking."

"This is Inspecteur Ueli Berndt, from the Police Judiciaire, Valais." He clears his throat. "I understand you wanted to speak to someone about assisting with the ongoing situation at Le Sommet."

Elin hesitates, momentarily taken aback at his directness, the formality of his tone. "That's right. Would you like me to take you through the details of the scene?"

"Monsieur Caron told my officer what happened, but I'd like to hear it again, from your perspective."

He listens quietly as Elin haltingly talks him through the facts, her observations. She can hear pen on paper in the background, his slow, rhythmic breaths, and she can't help but be acutely aware of her rustiness in relaying the information — her imprecise language, the lack of conviction in her tone.

She finishes, but he doesn't speak right away. She can still hear the rough scratch of pen on paper, murmured voices in the background.

When he finally does reply, his tone is measured. "Okay, so this situation, it's unusual. Normally, we'd need to be present, to come to the scene, see proof of the incident before we formally open an investigation with the prosecutor."

"I understand." Phone pressed to her ear, Elin starts moving, walks the length of the changing room. "And there's no way you can get anyone up here?"

"No." Berndt's tone is matter-of-fact. "I've spoken with the gendarmerie, the local police in Crans-Montana, but they're not able to get anyone to you either."

"So where does that leave us?" Elin paces back the other way. She can feel herself growing hot, not from the movement, but from the steady pulse of fear in her stomach as the reality of his words hit home.

We really are on our own. Totally isolated.

"That's what we've been discussing. This situation . . . it is delicate, something we've not had to consider before. We've set up a task force to decide next steps. Myself as investigating officer, the gendarmerie representing Crans-Montana, a prosecutor, and the Groupe d'Intervention."

"Have you come to any conclusions?" Elin listens to the howl of the wind outside, a deafening clap of thunder.

"Yes. The Swiss Constitution is clear that you have no authority here as a UK officer; however, after discussion, the prosecutor has advised that he's happy if you carry out specific instructions." Berndt's voice softens slightly. "I think we would be stupid in this circumstance not to use your expertise." He hesitates. "There is one thing we need to check first, though. Is Mr. Caron happy for you to be involved?"

"He is. He's the one who asked me to help out. You can contact him, ask him to confirm—"

"Okay," Berndt replies. "Could you please tell me how many people are left in the hotel?"

"Forty-five altogether. Mr. Caron has already shared a log."

"The breakdown into staff and guests?"

"There are eight guests and thirty-seven staff. The majority had already been evacuated by the time the avalanche struck. The last bus, which never left, was meant to take everyone remaining in the hotel."

"That's better than I thought. The number is manageable. So, as I'm sure you're aware, the first priority is safety. Please use standard procedure to try to contain the situation. I need you to keep everyone together, as much as possible. If that isn't viable, you'll need to make sure you know where they are."

"Fine." So far, as she expected.

"Then we'll need any photographs you have taken of the scene and of evidence. You can send these to me directly." He clears his throat. "The next priority is to get a full list of names, dates of birth, and addresses of everyone present and ascertain their whereabouts this morning."

"That's fine. Would you like me to speak to the person who found her, or any of the other witnesses?" Elin takes a seat on the bench behind her, feeling suddenly drained, the past few hours starting to take their toll.

Berndt pauses. "Yes. Obviously these won't be classified as formal interviews, admissible in the investigation, but they'll still be helpful."

"That makes sense," Elin replies, but she knows that in terms of content, they'll have to be. They can't afford to be anything but thorough, not at this stage. She hesitates, another thought striking her: *Laure.* She has to make him aware she's missing.

"There's one more thing," she starts. "Someone's missing from the hotel. She's actually a member of staff, but was staying here for her engagement party. My brother, Isaac, reported it to the police yesterday."

"I've been briefed." Berndt's voice is clipped. "Her name is Laure Strehl, is that right?"

"Yes."

"Can you run me through the circumstances again?"

Elin lists what she knows, realizing that it's very little. No one saw her go, and she only has Isaac's word on her last movements.

"Is it possible she left of her own accord?" Berndt asks as she finishes.

"Yes, but I think it's unlikely given the conditions, and the fact that she didn't take her purse. She hasn't been home. I've checked."

"We can check CCTV at the station in Crans, Sierre" — Berndt murmurs something to someone in the background — "see if she got there somehow." He pauses. "And there's definitely no signs of any violence, an abduction?"

"No, but after finding Adele, I'm concerned."

"That's understandable." He takes a breath. "And is there anything you've learned so far that might help us ascertain what's happened to her?"

"Nothing definitive, but there are a few things that might be worth your looking into. I found a card for a psychologist in her office. My brother said she'd had depression. They might be able to give some insight into her recent state of mind."

"Anything else?"

"I've found out that she has a second phone. It's not connected to work, and my brother didn't know anything about it. The night before she disappeared I overheard her outside, making a call. I couldn't understand, because she was speaking French, but it was obvious that she was agitated. Angry."

"You think she might have been using this second phone to make the call?"

"Yes."

"I'll request records from both the providers and we'll also contact the psychologist. If you send me the details —"

Elin flips the call to speaker mode as he spells out his e-mail address. She taps it into her phone.

"Thank you," Berndt says, "and please keep us informed if the situation changes. We'll update you regarding the weather, if we can get anyone out to you, and if we get anything back from the information you've provided."

They talk for a few more minutes and then Elin says good-bye. Despite her utter exhaustion, she feels a flicker of pride: *I did it.*

Several times, she'd felt it, like a shadow behind her — the claustrophobia of an attack closing in, but she'd overcome it, put the fear behind her.

But the flicker of euphoria is short-lived.

What's happened to Adele has made finding Laure even more urgent. If the two are linked, and the killer is holding Laure like they had Adele, then it's only a matter of time before something happens to her.

Like Adele, Laure's abduction would be premeditated, and looking at Adele's body, she's got a good idea of what's coming next.

41

Elin finds Axel in the lounge. He's sitting apart from the group of staff at the table next to him, looking out at the dark sky, the falling flakes of snow illuminated by the outside lights. The coffee in front of him looks untouched, a milky skin lying on the surface.

His face is pale, expressionless, seemingly oblivious to the sense of suppressed panic in the room, the low murmur of chatter, but Elin's seen that look enough times to know what it is. *Shock.*

Elin gently touches his arm. "Axel?"

"Oui?" he replies, barely looking up. When his gaze finally drags around to meet hers, she notices his eyes are bloodshot, the skin around them swollen.

"My name's Elin Warner," she starts, her words drowned out by another clap of thunder, a jagged bolt of lightning splitting the darkness.

She tries again. "Axel, I'm a guest here, in the hotel, but I'm also a police officer in the

258

UK. Mr. Caron has asked me to make some inquiries about Adele's death while we're waiting for the police to arrive."

He nods.

"Are you happy to speak in English?"

"It's fine." His hands are bunched up in his lap, fingers knotted together.

"I was wondering if you could tell me what happened before you found Adele. It's important we record the details while your memories are fresh, so we're able to share them with the police when they arrive."

"I'll try," he says haltingly, pulling out the chair beside him.

Taking the seat he's offered, Elin withdraws her notebook from her bag. "If you can begin with the moments before, what you were doing outside —"

"I was going to check the pools," he starts, eyes still glued to the scene outside. "Make sure they were covered. The evacuation was nearly complete . . . management wanted the pool area secured."

Elin nods encouragingly.

"I'd just done the main pool, was starting on the second. That's when I saw her." His voice is shaky. "I'd just set the cover going. It's electronic, automatic. It was about a third of the way across when the wind gusted, stripped the steam from the pool." His fingers twitch. "I didn't even think it was a person at first, but then I could see her hair. Moving in the water."

There's a heavy silence.

"That's when I ran." Axel stops, puts his hand to his face. "I know what you're going to say: Why didn't I jump in, pull her out? I keep asking myself that, replaying it. If I'd just jumped in then, she might have had a chance."

Elin puts a hand on his arm, ignoring the looks coming from the neighboring table. "Axel, people don't always react in the same way," she says gently, lowering her voice. "There's no right way of dealing with something like this, and regardless, I really don't think there was anything you could have done. I'm sure she was gone by the time you found her."

From the look on his face, Elin knows he doesn't believe her. He'll live with this forever. Go over it in his head a thousand times a day. *What if, what if, what if.*

"And in the moments before you found her, you didn't see anything suspicious around the pool area?"

"No, but then I wasn't out there for long. I was helping with the buses. They were having problems in the car park because of the snow."

"You didn't see anyone else? Another member of staff? Guests?"

"No. There were only a few guests left, and the staff who were left were helping with the evacuation."

Elin feels a surge of despondency. *No witnesses.* It's unlikely anyone saw anything. The killer probably took advantage of the fact that the hotel was being evacuated. No guests would be out there, and with only a skeleton staff. The perfect moment.

She flips her notebook to the next page. "How well did you know Adele?"

"Not very. To say hello to, maybe." Axel shrugs. "I've got a family. Three children. I don't really socialize with anyone here outside of work."

"So you probably wouldn't be aware of any issues she might have had?"

"No, but she'll know more." He gestures at a dark-haired woman at the next table. "That's Felisa, the director of housekeeping. Adele worked for her."

"Okay, thank you." Elin stands, and gathers up her bag. "Do let me know if you think of anything else, even something small."

"Wait." Axel frowns. "There is something. It's probably not relevant, but Adele . . . I saw her arguing with someone."

Curiosity piqued, she sits back down. "Recently?"

"Last week. I'd been to the spa, the main pool, clearing up a spillage. Adele was at the back of the building. When I came around the corner, I heard raised voices. It was . . . heated. I remember thinking they were so caught up, they barely noticed me."

"Did you hear what it was about?"

"I didn't catch it. I carried on inside." He gives a humorless smile. "I always say, don't get involved in work things. Keep your head down."

Elin digests his words. "Did you recognize who she was arguing with?"

"Yes. The assistant manager here. Her name's Laure. Laure Strehl."

42

A *connection,* Elin thinks, walking toward Felisa. A connection between Laure and Adele. They clearly knew each other well enough to argue about something.

Could it link to what's happened?

Pushing the thought aside, she stops beside the table, a few feet away. "Felisa?"

The woman nods, studying Elin, the notebook in her hand. She's slight with delicate features, perfectly arched brows tapering to two thin points. Her dark hair is arranged in a complex plait. Her skin is olive in tone. Spanish, perhaps? Portuguese?

"This is about Adele?"

Elin nods. "Is it okay if we move, for some privacy?" She gestures to an empty table nearby.

"Of course." Felisa looks at Elin properly again, assessing. Her eyes move to the blond straggle of hair tucked behind her ears, the helix piercing. She's heard she's a police officer, hasn't she? Expects something . . . different.

Elin's used to this — she's well aware what people say behind her back. *Blokey. Too focused on her career to make the "best of herself." Whatever that meant.*

She doesn't care; she's always found it hard, the whole "feminine" thing.

Ever since she was little she knew that there was a world out there beyond her — a tribe of women with glossy hair and dexterous fingers that knew how to twist and tease hair into complex styles. Women who watched videos on YouTube about mastering the exact right shading technique to make their cheekbones "pop."

Her friend Helen, a detective constable, was one of them. She'd shown Elin once, over wine and curry. A video about "contouring." Repeated it, as if seeing it several times would make Elin understand it better, but it still felt like a foreign language. An instrument she'd never master.

She moves to the seat opposite Felisa, but before she can sit down, a guest approaches her. She's in her late thirties, small and curvy, her dark hair wound into a loose knot. Her expression is pinched, anxious. Elin eyes her warily.

The woman steps forward; too close. She's in Elin's personal space.

"Excuse me, you are the police officer,

yes?" Her words are strongly accented: Italian, possibly.

"Yes, I —"

"We're worried," the woman interrupts, throwing a glance behind her to the table on the left. "My parents . . . are older, they're . . ." She hesitates, forehead creasing in concentration as if she can't find the right words. "They're struggling with this. Frightened. I think we need more information."

Elin clears her throat. "Please, I understand the situation is a little scary, but we have things under control. There have been a lot of discussions already with local police and a plan is in place. I . . ." She senses she's rambling, so stops.

The woman frowns, something new in her expression. *Anger,* Elin thinks. A normal response when someone feels scared, impotent, but it always worries her.

Anger is often unpredictable, a barrier to keeping things in check.

"Under control," the woman repeats, clasping her hands together. Her voice is high, thin. "I'm not sure you have. People are scared. It's not just the guests, it's staff too. I heard a group of them talking, over there." She jerks her arm in their direction. "About how long it will take to get people out to us. If they work here and they're scared, how are we, the guests, meant to feel?"

Elin exchanges a glance with Felisa. "I'm

going to brief everyone fully in a few minutes," she replies evenly. "We're putting clear protocols in place to contain the situation. This evening, we'll be moving everyone into rooms on the lower floors, rooms that are usually reserved for employees. Members of staff will be used as security in all of the public spaces."

"Security?"

"Yes. In every corridor. We're doing everything we can to keep people safe."

There's what seems to be an interminable silence as the woman absorbs Elin's words.

Finally, her shoulders relax. To Elin's relief, she says, "I'll tell them." She gestures again to the table where her parents are sitting. "But I still think you need to communicate more effectively. Keep everyone informed if anything changes."

"Of course."

Elin waits for the woman to leave, then takes a seat. "Sorry," she murmurs.

"It's fine," Felisa replies. "It's to be expected, isn't it? People are worried."

Elin nods, putting her notebook on the table. "So, I'm trying to get a sense of Adele's last few days, work out what might have provoked the attack."

Sipping her glass of water, Felisa nods. "She finished her shift on Friday, wasn't due back in until Tuesday of next week."

"And you saw her on Friday, before she

left?" Elin scribbles furiously. Her writing is loose, a scrawl, but she can't do any better. The fatigue she felt in the changing room is now all-consuming, every movement slow, lackluster, like wading through mud.

I need to eat something.

"Briefly. She was hurrying, wanted to get back to her son before he left with his father for the week."

"They're not together?"

Felisa shakes her head. "It's not a recent thing, though. They were never really together. I think they tried for a while, for the sake of the boy, but . . ."

"And how did she seem to you?"

"Fine. Stressed, because she didn't want to be late, but —" She breaks off. "Do you think she even made it home?"

"I don't know. I'm sure the police will check."

Privately, Elin's sure she didn't. Because she knows Adele was tied up, Elin's hypothesized that she had been held somewhere at the hotel or nearby until she was killed.

Felisa's hand clamps around her glass, knuckles turning white with the pressure. "Who would do this? It doesn't make sense."

Elin presses on. "Were you aware of any issues Adele had? Personally? Professionally?"

"No, but Adele's Swiss. I know it sounds strange, but there really is a Swiss . . . reserve." She gives a weak smile. "When I lived in Geneva, it took two years for my neighbor to progress from *'Bonjour'* to *'Bonjour, ça va?'* " Felisa hesitates, as if debating whether to say something else. "It wasn't only that; Adele, as a person, she could be . . . distant."

"In what way?"

"She was unusual, for one of the housekeeping team. Staff turnover in jobs like this, it's high. Lots of foreign staff. The fact that Adele's Swiss, it's rare. I think she liked the job, but I always got the feeling that she thought she was beyond it, so didn't really want to engage. Kept to herself." Felisa smiles. "I think she was probably right. She's a clever girl. I was surprised she was even doing a job like this."

"So why was she?"

"I asked her once. She said she didn't have a choice. No qualifications, had her little boy to look after."

Elin nods, mulling over what Felisa's said. *Something's not right about Adele's situation. Something doesn't fit.*

"One more thing. I wanted to ask you about Laure Strehl. Are you aware she's missing?"

"Yes." Felisa rests her elbows against the table. "Do you think . . . that whoever did this to Adele . . ." She trails off, swallowing hard.

"We don't know. That's why we need to understand if there's any connection between

268

them. Would you say that Adele and Laure were friends?"

"Yes," she replies, something flickering across her face that Elin can't decipher.

She knows something, doesn't she? Knows something and isn't sure if she should repeat it.

"Were they close?" Elin probes.

Felisa audibly exhales. "Up until a few months ago, yes. I used to always see them together, then it stopped. I assumed it was just a disagreement, then a few weeks ago, I was with Adele, and Laure walked right past her without saying hello." She frowns. "It was strange. Adele's face, afterward, her expression . . . she looked frightened, that's the only way I can describe it."

"Of Laure?"

"Yes. It didn't surprise me. Laure . . . Don't take this the wrong way, but she could be intense. Takes herself too seriously. At meetings, she's the one who doesn't crack a smile, writes every tiny detail down." She lowers her voice. "Cecile, the manager, she's the same." She frowns. "But then, I think that's for a different reason. She doesn't have a family, a partner, so she puts everything into this place. Too much, I think."

Elin nods, turning Felisa's words over in her head, one thing in particular troubling her: the disagreement between Laure and Adele.

When she speaks to Cecile, she needs to

269

ask her if she was aware of it, if other people had picked up on it.

Her only concern is that it will confuse things further. Each time someone speaks about Laure, the picture Elin has of her in her head shifts ever so slightly. It had started off clear, but now it's muddied.

Impossible to resolve.

43

"None of the staff saw anything?" Lucas tugs off his fleece, hangs it over the back of his chair. Rolled-up sleeves reveal tanned, sinewy forearms, two battered cotton bracelets on his right wrist. Lime green, blue.

"No. I've spoken with everyone. They were helping with the evacuation, the remaining guests in the lobby, getting ready to leave. They all have an . . ." Elin hesitates, not wanting to use the word "alibi." "They're all accounted for." Every single one, she thinks, replaying the conversations in her head. All plausible, verifiable alibis. The guests too.

How is it possible?

Reaching for her coffee, she swigs, hard. The hot, bitter liquid scours her throat, but it feels good, the caffeine punching through the fog in her head.

"They chose exactly the right moment." Cecile rubs at her nose with a frayed tissue. Her face looks drawn, her eyes sunken.

Elin nods. "Now we've established that no

one saw anything, we need to check CCTV. Are there cameras for the pool, the surrounding area?"

"Yes. I'll speak to the director of security. It won't take long." Cecile pauses, as if she's about to say something else, but changes her mind.

Lucas walks toward the window. "Anything else you need, please ask. Whoever did this, I want them caught, quickly. What happened to her . . ." Elin sees his jaw twitch. An absolute revulsion.

Tension is radiating off him. Half-moons of damp mark his underarms, his lower back. He's obviously stressed, but despite that, Elin is able to pull the final pieces of him together. What she's read, glimpsed . . . it's genuine.

This, his private space, reflects both sides of him, the contradictions she's picked up on before — the businessman and the laid-back athlete.

The room is understated: pale walls, a highly polished wooden desk. A chrome coffee machine sits in the corner. Above it, a shelf houses a single row of books — climbing and alpinist titles on one side, glossy design and architecture on the other.

Artwork takes up the right-hand wall: old-fashioned anatomical drawings of the heart framed in white. Precise, graphic etchings.

Her mind jumps to the article she read — his childhood stay in the hospital.

It all fits, but despite that, Elin feels a slight sense of discord at the visible contradiction. In a way, he'd be easier to explain if one of the sides *wasn't* real. The thought is disconcerting.

Cecile fiddles with her empty coffee cup, running her finger over the rim.

"Can you tell exactly when Adele was killed?" The words spill out fast, laced with panic. "So we can understand if whoever did this is still here, or if it's possible it was someone on the buses."

"I can't say definitively," Elin says evenly. "We need to wait for the postmortem."

"You must have an idea." Cecile's voice pitches higher. "You must know, from your job, when someone died."

"Cecile . . ." Walking toward her, Lucas's tone is sharp.

"What?" Cecile's voice tips into hysteria. "She must, mustn't she? At least have an idea?"

Lucas looks at his sister, lips drawn into a tight line. He's embarrassed, Elin can tell, by this show of emotion. "Please." A hand on Cecile's arm. Another warning look. "We have to be calm."

Elin notices the intimacy of the gesture, and also the slight condescension in his tone. She can tell that this exchange is a familiar pattern of behavior; they're used to these roles, how the conversation will play out.

Lucas's demeanor reminds her of Isaac's in moments like this: deliberately benign, which only ever serves to amplify the situation rather than defuse it.

"Calm?" Cecile looks at him, chin lifted. "Lucas, one of your staff has been killed. In your hotel. I wouldn't be calm if I were in your position, I'd be terrified. They're probably here now, waiting to pick off somebody else."

Elin clears her throat. "Look, we have no proof that the killer, if they are among us, wants to hurt someone else. We don't know Adele's personal circumstances. Something like this, it's usually done by someone close to the victim, with a definite motive. Partner. Friends. Family."

"But what about Laure?" Cecile's foot is tapping the floor. An erratic rhythm. "She's still missing. Whoever did this to Adele could have her, couldn't they?"

"She's still missing?" Lucas's features tense before he rearranges them into a neutral expression.

Watching his reaction, Elin's curiosity is immediately piqued. "Do you know Laure well?"

Lucas sits down, shifting uncomfortably in his chair. He shuffles some papers on his desk, as if he's using the time to compose himself.

He's hiding something.

274

"As well as I know any member of staff," he replies finally.

Elin decides to cut straight to the chase. "The reason I'm asking is because we've found some pictures of you among Laure's things."

"Pictures?" Lucas repeats, his voice hesitant. His hand finds the pen on his desk, and he starts twisting it between his fingers.

"Yes. Photographs. I don't think you'd have been aware they were being taken. Would you have any idea why she'd have photographs like that?"

Lucas is silent for a minute, then looks up at her, his expression resigned. "Laure and I . . . we were involved."

"A relationship?" Elin's aware of the sudden pull of her breath, a shock she shouldn't rightly be feeling. It was the only rational explanation for the photographs, but she'd been hoping it wasn't the case.

"I wouldn't describe it as that. It wasn't serious."

Cecile gives a small, brittle laugh. "I didn't think you'd be so predictable."

Elin looks at her, curious at her tone. "When was this?" she says, looking back to Lucas.

He's still turning the pen between his fingers. "It was just after we opened. It was stupid. I know better than to mess around with staff, but it happened. There was an

275

event, we hooked up. . . . Look, I carried it on when I shouldn't have. We slept together a few times, then I ended it. She was pissed off, but" — he drops the pen with a clatter against the desk — "that was it as far as I was concerned. I'm pretty sure for her too."

Just after they opened. Elin turns his words over in her head. That was when Laure was with Isaac, so it had to be an affair. Her mind shifts to Isaac — what she'll tell him, how he'll react.

"You said Laure was annoyed when it ended?"

"Yes. She came to the office a few weeks later, confronted me. Said I'd used her, given her the wrong idea." His expression is contrite. "It was a mess, but I didn't want her to feel awkward, have to give up her job over it, so I apologized, told her I was sorry if I'd led her on."

"And that was it? The last contact you had?"

"Apart from work, yes." Lucas's face tightens. "Look, I don't think that this, what happened between us . . . it can't be connected to her going missing. It was a while ago. She's obviously moved on, with your brother."

Sensing his discomfort, she changes the subject. "The other thing I want to ask you about is Laure and Adele. Both Axel and Felisa mentioned that they were friends, but recently had fallen out. Were you aware of any issues there?"

276

"No."

She turns to Cecile. "And you?"

"Nothing."

"And there haven't been any other issues with the hotel? No recent conflict with the staff or any other complaints?"

Neither replies. The silence stretches out, thinning until it becomes awkward.

Elin catches Lucas's almost imperceptible glance in Cecile's direction.

What aren't they telling me?

44

"There is something," Lucas starts. Reaching down, he opens the drawer below his desk. He pulls out a piece of paper and slides it across the desk toward her. "I started getting these a few months ago."

Il faut bonne mémoire après qu'on a menti.

"A liar should have a good memory," Lucas translates aloud, his voice shaking slightly. "I dismissed it at first, but now, after what's happened . . ."

"Do you know what it refers to?" Elin examines the note, her mouth dry. The words are typed in a large font, covering most of the page.

This is a threat, isn't it? There's no other way of reading it.

"I presumed it had to do with the hotel. We had a huge number of complaints before the build started. Locals initially, then environmental groups. It started small, then it exploded online. We started getting bigger groups coming. Not only Swiss, but French too."

"Protesters for hire?"

Lucas nods. "Something like that. It started to get personal." He looks down at his hands, flushing. "Vindictive. It seemed to be more than the hotel. An excuse to hate, cause trouble."

"And the others?" Elin prompts, still studying the paper. The type isn't particularly clear, crisp, which implies an inkjet rather than a laser printer. That means it was almost certainly done on a regular home printer, so the chances of working out who sent it are minimal. It'll have to wait for the police.

"I only have this one, I'm sorry." He reaches into the drawer again, pushes another piece of paper toward her. "There was another one, the first, but I threw it away. Thought it was a one-off. Something about revenge . . . more of the same."

Elin examines the paper.

Chassez le naturel, il revient au galop.

This time it's Cecile who translates. "Chase away the natural and it returns at a gallop."

"What does that mean?"

Lucas rubs his hand over the back of his hair. "I suppose the expression in English would be . . . a leopard can't change its spots."

Elin nods. "How did you receive them?"

"They were sent directly to me." Behind him, snow hits the window in an angry splatter, making them all turn to look at the glass.

"And apart from the protesters, you have no idea who might have sent them?"

"No." Lucas looks genuinely bewildered. He gestures to the letters. "Do you think these are linked to what's happened?"

"It's too early to say." Elin's still working it through in her mind.

If they are linked — how? What could Adele's death have to do with this?

"Do you mind if I take them?"

He shakes his head, hair coming loose from behind his ear, briefly concealing his features.

Putting the letters inside her bag, Elin stands up. "One final thing. I was told yesterday about the remains of a body being recovered from the mountain." She deliberately pauses, waiting for their reactions.

"Yes." Lucas stiffens. "But we don't yet know who it is. From what the police said, it doesn't sound recent."

The hairs on her arms stand up on end. "So they don't have any idea who it is?" Elin makes sure not to mention what she's heard. She wants to know how far he'll take it.

The question hangs in the air. Lucas hesitates, mouth opening then closing. "No."

Elin absorbs his words. *Why would Margot know, but not Lucas? Surely the police would have told him?*

He has to be lying. This is his childhood friend who's been found, a friend he was professionally involved with, a friend so close, his disappearance derailed the opening of the hotel.

Why lie? What exactly is he trying to hide?

Her phone rings as she's leaving Lucas's office.

"Miss Warner, it's Berndt. Are you free to talk?"

"Yes, it's fine. I'm alone." Elin walks down the corridor toward the lifts. "Have you found something?" She cringes at the hesitation in her tone; it's as if she's questioning herself.

What's wrong with me?

But she knows what the answer is: Lucas's lie — it's shaken her. She can't get her head around what it might mean, the implications.

"Not exactly." He sounds tired. "We've completed a search on the names you've provided using RIPOL, our database, but nothing of particular interest has come up, not for Valais, in any case."

"What does 'particular interest' mean?" Elin shifts from foot to foot, confused: Is he referring to background information? Any active or closed investigations?

"I can't say more because of data protection, but so you're aware, we've found nothing that makes me think that you or anyone

281

else is in any danger from someone on site currently. However" — there's a brief pause — "I have a further request. In Switzerland, procedure for searching for people on our databases is more complex than in the UK. There's a central database, but we can only access it by canton."

"By canton?" *What does he mean?* Confused, she flushes, her palm sweaty around the phone. She can feel self-doubt chipping away at her — a negative, taunting voice inside her head. *Amateur. Out of the game too long. Impostor.*

"Yes," Berndt replies. "It means someone could have a criminal record in a neighboring canton, or county, such as Vaud, but it wouldn't show here, in the canton of Valais." He hesitates. She can hear a phone ringing in the background. "I can make a request for each canton, but it must be for specific information about a person of interest."

Processing what he's said, she stops a few steps before the lift. "So I need to flag up any people who might be significant to the inquiry and then you can request more information?"

"Yes, but so you're aware, each request needs to be approved by the prosecutor. I'll try to hurry it through, but it might take a little time."

"Okay. And Laure? The CCTV? Phone records?" Elin tries to keep the impatience from her tone. She doesn't like this feeling of impotence — not being the one in control, knowing exactly what's going on.

"We've checked the CCTV for the station. No one matching Laure's description got off a bus or boarded the funicular, either late that night or at any time during the following day. We've checked local taxi firms, too, and no one's picked her up from the hotel in over a month. We're still waiting on the phone providers."

"And the psychologist?"

"We've left messages. It shouldn't take long."

"Okay," Elin replies as confidently as she can, but part of her feels like she's floundering. At the moment she doesn't have anything relating to Laure's disappearance or Adele's death.

No evidence. No eyewitnesses. No motive. She's in the dark.

As she says good-bye, a text comes through from Will, telling her that he and Isaac are having dinner in the lounge.

Staring into space, her vision clouds, and clearer, more defined images take its place.

Images of Adele.

All she can think about is the look of horror in her eyes. What it must have felt like to sink below that water and know that you were never coming back up.

45

"Laure and Lucas?" Isaac's eyes darken. "They were together?"

"Yes. A little while after the hotel opened." Shifting position in her chair, Elin picks up her fork, pushes a small piece of potato into her mouth. Although it's dinnertime and she should be hungry, she's having to force herself to eat. Her appetite is gone.

Elin sweeps her gaze around the lounge. The few remaining guests are huddled around tables, drinking, talking. *They're nervous,* she thinks, noting the big gestures, the forced, too-loud laughter. She knows from work that it's a common reaction: *Pretend nothing's happened. If we pretend hard enough it just might be true.*

But the illusion is soon shattered: she clocks a member of staff standing by the door, looking around. Security, keeping watch as she'd advised.

Relief relaxes Isaac's features. "That was when we were on a break. We were arguing, stupid things . . ." Taking a long drink of his beer, he pushes his plate aside. It's a pasta dish, untouched, the pale, creamy sauce sitting sticky and congealed.

Despite the confidence in his words, Elin notices the visible swallow. *He's shaken by what I've told him. He didn't know.*

"A break?" she repeats, catching Will's eye, unable to stop the pit opening up in her stomach. Not quite the happy couple she'd assumed.

Would he ever have told me about the break if this hadn't happened?

It's impossible to say and the thought stings: there was a time when she knew everything about him.

Exactly which toy car was his favorite. The precise shape of the fragmented birthmark between his toes. How many loaded spoonfuls of chocolate Nesquik he liked in his milk.

Elin feels a sudden, sharp pang of longing for what might have been: a life, connected. They used to talk about it as kids — buying houses in a row, boisterous family meals, their children playing together, being friends.

But that was a long time ago. Feeling a catch in her throat, she has to clear it with a sharp cough. She reaches for her water and sips it.

Isaac rubs at his eyelid. The eczema has spread. A small continent, reaching for his eye. "But what if there's something more to it?"

"In what way?"

"Those pictures she's got of him. That's not normal, is it?" He drums his fingers on the table, his expression grim. "What if something went on between them that we don't know about?"

"Like what?" Will pulls the bread basket toward him, removes a slice of brown, seeded baguette.

"I don't know. Maybe it got nasty, or . . ."

Elin clears her throat. "Isaac, we can't presume anything. Not yet. Jumping to conclusions is the worst thing we can do. We have to stick to facts. Adele's been killed, and Laure's missing. That's all we know."

"Isaac, mate, she's right," Will says, tearing the bread into pieces. "Don't go thinking the worst yet. Not when you don't have the information."

Elin looks at him, smiles, grateful for the backup — another thing Will excels at. *Bridging.* Smoothing things over.

"Christ, I feel so bloody useless. Finding that woman, like that —" Isaac's voice splinters. "Elin, Laure's at risk, isn't she? Every minute we're not doing something, there's every chance she . . ."

She immediately feels the pressure of his words; a weight, pulling her down.

"What if the police can't get up tonight?

286

Tomorrow? You've got to do something. Find her." He looks toward the window, at the heavy snowfall illuminated by the outside lights. "Look at it out there."

"Isaac, I'm doing as much as I can. I'm speaking with the police, but it's limited, what I can do without a full team. It's not safe to —"

He cuts her off. "What if this were Will?" He jerks his head toward him. "You'd want to find him, wouldn't you? Knowing what's just happened?" His eyes are narrowed, fixed on her, like he's testing her.

Elin blinks, taken aback at the force of his reaction. "Like I said, we don't even know if they're linked."

Isaac stares at her, his expression incredulous. "You really think that what's happened to Adele is a one-off? Isn't connected to Laure? It can't be a coincidence. They both worked here, they were friends."

Elin hesitates before replying. She agrees with him. After speaking to Lucas, she's even more convinced the two are connected.

"Look. I —"

"What is it?" Isaac leans over the table, eyes flashing. "You know something, don't you?"

Elin recoils slightly, smelling beer on his breath, the faint sourness of sweat. The look in his eye — it scares her.

Reminds her of the moments just before he'd flip. Let loose. Throw things, confetti-

287

style, around the room. Even now, she can remember her mother's expression when it happened — the barely suppressed flinch, the disappointment, bizarrely not at Isaac but at herself, as though she were somehow to blame for his behavior.

A few months after their mother died, Elin found a dusty cardboard box in her mother's loft, stuffed full of pop-psychology books, torn-out articles, all on the same theme: *How your parenting style affects your children. How to get your child to open up.*

The discovery made her indescribably sad: their mother had chosen to blame herself over Isaac. The ultimate excuse for a boy gone wrong.

"I was just about to tell you," she says, chasing the thought away. "I spoke to Adele's boss, Felisa. She said that Adele and Laure had fallen out. Did Laure mention anything to you about it?"

Isaac shakes his head, dark curls slipping across his face. "No. As far as I knew, they were still friends."

Elin bites down on her lip, frustrated. How is she going to be able to find out what's gone on between them? Her mind hooks on an idea — Laure's laptop.

It hadn't yielded much on first look, but she hadn't been very thorough as she wasn't really convinced at the time that Laure was actually missing.

"Let's take another look at her laptop." She turns to Isaac. "There might be something we dismissed that might be relevant in light of what we know now."

Nodding, he stands up. "I'll get it."

Once he's out of earshot, Will looks at her. "You really think there'll be something on there?"

"I don't know, but it's got to be worth a try. I'm going to take another look at her social media, too, see if I've missed anything."

"You know, I think all this, it's made your decision for you, hasn't it?"

"What do you mean?"

"Going back to work. For someone who wasn't sure, you seem pretty well decided now." His expression is serious. "You've come alive, Elin. Doing this."

"They asked me to help."

"And you could easily have said no. Explained."

Elin shrugs. "Maybe." She doesn't know how to reply because he's right — some part of her *has* come alive, but she knows there's still a big difference between helping here and going back to work. Her decision isn't made yet. She thinks about Anna's e-mails. The e-mails she's steadfastly ignored.

Leaning back in her chair, Elin picks up her phone, flicking again through Laure's Instagram.

This time, given what she's found out, she's

looking for any evidence of Laure with Adele.

She starts scrolling. There's nothing, tallying with Felisa's theory of a falling out. It's two or three months back before she finds her, fitting with the idea that the issue between them was fairly recent.

The first image of them together: Laure in a bar, dressed in a flimsy, strappy top, arm loosely slung around Adele's bare shoulder. The second is in a dimly lit restaurant, part of a larger group. Someone's standing back from the table, taking a group shot.

Elin keeps scrolling, goes further back: over four months ago. One image in particular catches her eye. It was taken here, in the hotel lounge. She recognizes the large, futuristic chandelier in the center of the image, the abstract slivers of glass catching the light, bleaching out the image in places.

"Look at this." She holds up the phone to Will.

Laure's in the foreground with a man. She's holding up a glass of pink-hued wine to the camera, head thrown back in laughter. The glass is smeared, dappled with condensation. In the background, sitting at one of the tables, Elin can make out two people, heads bent, not more than a few inches apart.

They're deep in conversation, their expressions somber.

Although they're out of focus, she can still

make out exactly who they are.

Adele and Lucas.

46

The intimate body language, their postures — it looks like more than polite conversation.

"Adele and Lucas knew each other socially," Will says slowly.

Elin feels a creeping sense of unease: they definitely knew each other, certainly more than Lucas had implied.

Could the falling out have been over him?

The thought, its depressing predictability, disappoints her.

"What are you looking at?" Isaac asks. He peers over her shoulder. Once again, she catches the bitter scent of beer on his breath.

"I found this." She tilts the screen of the mobile toward him. "Lucas and Adele, together."

Isaac sits down beside her. Grabbing the phone from her hand, he pinches the screen, zooming in. "Looks pretty cozy, doesn't it?" He gives a brittle laugh, eyes igniting with a familiar intensity. "Maybe he was at it with her too?"

"We can't say that," Elin replies, her tone carefully neutral.

Isaac continues flicking through Laure's Instagram. The speed of his movements, the erratic gestures, they bother Elin. She reaches for his hand. "Isaac, stop. We were going to go through the laptop."

He opens his mouth, about to protest, then closes it.

Elin pulls the laptop toward her, flips it open. This time she decides to work more methodically, starting with the desktop, the folders stacked in neat rows across the screen.

She stares glassily at the sheer number of them, the similarities in labeling — date, names. Most look like work files — *Health & Safety, Trainings, Travel.* She clicks into them regardless.

Halfway through the list of folders she finds one with a more generic name: *Work.*

Clicking on it, rather than a series of files, she finds another folder with the same name. Elin's finger hovers over the file, clicks again.

Another folder, but this time, it yields something.

Her pulse is racing.

A list of files.

She can tell right away from the file names that they're encrypted.

Why? Why encrypt files on her personal laptop?

"What have you found?" Will leans over the table.

"Some of the files on her desktop, they're encrypted."

"Can you open them?" Isaac peers at the screen.

"No, but I know someone who can, an old colleague, Noah."

The head of the Digital Forensics team, Noah had been a key part of several big cases Elin had worked on, first as a DC, then the last case as a DS, after her promotion.

"I'll message him, see if he can do it quickly." Reaching for her phone, she types:

Encrypted files . . . can you do your thing?
Caveat: need it fairly soon.

Three little dots appear on the bottom left of the screen. He's replying.

Assume it's not an official request?

No, but any chance . . . ?

There's a delay. She stares down at the screen, wondering if it's an ask too far: would he want to help given they hadn't spoken in months?

Finally, a reply:

Okay, I trust you, but curious. Working

again? Abandoned us for pastures new?

Long story. Sending to your personal e-mail now.

I'll see what I can do.

Elin forwards the files to Noah, then turns to Isaac. "Once we have these —" She pauses, noticing Cecile walking toward them. Her short hair is tousled, her eyes red, the skin below them puffy. She looks tired.

"Sorry to disturb, but the security footage, it's ready, if you want to look."

Elin flashes Isaac an apologetic look. "Do you mind?"

His eyes narrow, but he rallies. "It's fine."

Standing up, Elin squeezes Will's hand. "See you later, okay?"

He nods, smiles, but his expression is uneasy. He casts a worried look around the room, toward the open door.

Elin knows she should probably be feeling the same, but following Cecile, she feels her heart thudding.

It isn't fear causing the reaction, but something just as primal.

Excitement: a sudden bolt of adrenaline.

Will's right, about her coming alive. She's forgotten this — life not just happening to her, but being *part* of it. Changing the path of something. Taking action.

47

"Before we go through the footage" — Cecile gestures at the tablet on the desk — "I wanted to talk to you about Lucas. What he said earlier, about Laure, I don't want you to get the wrong idea." She looks embarrassed as she catches Elin's eye.

"About what?" Cecile's perfume is lingering in the air: light, citrusy, surprisingly feminine.

"What happened between them." Cecile tucks a loose section of hair behind her ear. "I don't know if you're aware, but Lucas . . . he's my brother."

"I guessed. The name was a bit of a clue."

"Of course." Smiling, Cecile pulls her chair from her side of the desk, moves it until she's next to Elin. "What he said, how it sounded, it's a veneer he has up, a way of protecting himself." The words tumble out. "Lucas hasn't had an easy time of it. His marriage — it ended badly. He hasn't had a proper relationship since. These short-term things,

296

they're because he's scared."

"Of what?"

"Opening himself up. Being vulnerable." Cecile toys with the hem of her shirt. Her words are matter-of-fact, but the emotion is obvious in her voice. "Because he was in and out of the hospital as a child, other people, our parents in particular, treated him like he was something . . . fragile. I think he's always had this sense that he's got something to prove. When Odette, his wife, left him, those feelings of inferiority . . . they intensified."

"A breakup can be destabilizing," Elin replies, thinking about her last relationship before Will, how absolutely it had thrown her. Made her question everything.

"I was the same after my divorce. You keep going over things in your head. Blaming yourself." Cecile's eyes are distant, glazed. "I had all these plans, like Lucas. Children. Family life . . . None of it happened. It takes time to mentally readjust."

"I suppose what happened with Daniel Lemaitre didn't help, the fact that he went missing before the hotel even opened. It must have been tough."

"It was. It put pressure on things. Finances. PR. Everything. Delayed the build by nearly a year." She hesitates. "But the stress for Lucas, it wasn't only financial. Daniel and Lucas, they were close."

"You knew him, too, didn't you?" Elin

297

prompts.

"Not as well as Lucas, but yes. Our parents were good friends. We used to ski together almost every weekend, and when we got older, dinners, parties . . ." A look Elin can't decipher crosses Cecile's face before she smiles. "But he was better friends with Lucas. He tended to dominate any friendships we had as a group. You've got a brother; you probably know how it is."

Elin nods, thinking about the similarities between them. Two strong women still defined by sibling dynamics, fighting for oxygen against alpha brothers.

Cecile picks up the tablet, gives a short laugh. "Anyway, Lucas probably wouldn't appreciate my speaking about his private life." She flushes, embarrassed. Elin's touched. Not only by her protectiveness of her brother, but by her awkwardness. Something else of herself she recognizes in Cecile — the struggle to verbalize difficult topics, to emote.

Cecile ducks away from her gaze, and there's a flurry of movement as she taps the screen of the tablet, inputting a code. "Our security system is state of the art. A commercial IP system. It means you can livestream to any of our devices." The overhead lights catch the faint smear of fingerprints along the bottom of the screen. "This home screen shows each camera, its feed. All you do is select one, then find the relevant time slot. There's sound too."

"Okay." Elin drops her arm to the table. "You do the first one, show me how it's done."

"Where do you want to start?"

"What about the spa? Is there one outside?"

Cecile grimaces. "There is, but I'm not sure how good the picture's going to be with the steam, the storm . . ." Starting to scroll, she abruptly stops, selecting one from farther down the screen. "Here. This is it in real time."

She's right, Elin thinks with dismay, looking at the image. The camera shows the rough outline of the pool area, but the steam and snow scudding past the lens is obscuring most of the scene. The picture has a liquid, ethereal feel.

"It's not ideal," Cecile says, "but the picture might be better earlier in the day. When exactly are we looking for?"

"Everything from this morning until Axel found the body."

Cecile scrolls back, the image remaining visible on the screen as she rewinds.

"Okay, back to nine a.m." But before she can finish her sentence, the screen goes black, just before five p.m. "There must be a mistake," she murmurs. Frowning, she repeats the action. "It's blank. The entire morning, afternoon, it's gone."

"Are you sure?" A ripple of disquiet rolls

through Elin.

Cecile tries again, more slowly this time, but the result is the same: the footage is gone. She catches Elin's eye. "Someone's wiped it."

"Wiped it, or made sure it never filmed in the first place," Elin says, with the gut-propelling realization that this is part of a plan.

It isn't a coincidence, is it?

Someone knew they had to wipe this so they couldn't be identified.

They're one step ahead, she thinks, looking out the window into the darkness. Her theory, that this is an organized killer — it's holding up, and that scares her.

Elin moves forward in her chair. "Is it possible to wipe it without the system sending notifications?"

"It's possible, I'm sure. Most things can be hacked, can't they?"

"Who has access to the system?"

"The security director, a few staff who work under him . . ."

All of whom have alibis, Elin thinks, disconcerted, mentally running through her notes. "Let's try another camera. Is there one for the entrance to the spa?"

"Yes. It's in the corridor, I think." Cecile jabs at the screen again, her hands making a nervy, panicked movement. "This is it."

The camera is positioned facing straight down the corridor. All of it is in shot —

polished concrete floor, the stark white of the walls.

This time, Elin skims through the recording — slowly rewinding from the present toward midday. But once again, just before five p.m., the screen goes black.

The next piece of recorded footage is from the day before. Sitting in silence for a moment, a seed of an idea unfurls in her mind. "Can I check the footage from another day?"

"Of course."

Elin scrolls backward, easily finds the right day, the approximate time. It takes only a few minutes before she finds herself in the footage; walking down the corridor toward the spa to find Will in the pool.

Continuing to scroll, she tries to work it out: how long did she take in there?

Five, ten minutes speaking to Margot? The same with Will?

She works through the footage until she leaves the spa, heading back up the corridor toward the lobby. Scanning the screen, she realizes that Margot was right — no one had entered the spa until she came out. If someone had been in the changing rooms with her, they must have gone out another way.

Elin turns to Cecile. "Is there another way into the spa? Through the changing rooms?"

"Yes. There's a door at the back. It's used to access the maintenance area, the generators, pumps. It does open out into the changing area, but it's only used by maintenance staff." She hesitates. "You need the right access pass."

"Does CCTV cover that door?"

Biting her lip, Cecile flushes again, heat chasing up her neck, cheeks. "There's a camera, outside, on the roof opposite the door. The staff . . . they don't know it's there." She falters. "Look, there are cameras all over. Lucas had thefts among the staff at one of his hotels in Zurich."

"Can you find the feed?" Elin interrupts. She doesn't care about the morals of hidden cameras. She simply wants to see the footage.

"Only a few of us have access, so it's on a different system." Taking the tablet, Cecile moves off the home screen and opens another one, tapping in a passcode. She hands it back to Elin. "Here."

Elin already knows the rough time window from the other camera: it was about half past three when she finished speaking to Will.

When she finds the right time, she presses play. Nothing happens for the first few minutes. The image is static, fixed on the door. The only movement is from the snow drifting past the screen. Any sounds are muffled by the wind.

Holding her breath, Elin drums her fingers on the table, willing her hunch to be correct.

Beside her, Cecile is watching the screen intently.

Still no movement.

Elin exhales heavily, frustrated. Whoever it was, they had to have used this door to access the changing room, surely? Unless they'd gone in before her . . .

"Is there —" she starts, then freezes.

A movement.

A person in the bottom left of the frame.

The figure is tall, well built, dressed in a black waterproof coat, hood pulled up around the face. They're wearing dark, shapeless trousers.

Elin feels winded. She was right all along.

Someone had been in there. Someone had been watching me.

She focuses on the figure; he or she is clearly not aware of the camera. Not even a glance in its direction. They're walking purposefully toward the door.

So who is it? Who was watching me?

It's impossible to tell. Unless the figure turns, she doesn't stand a chance of identifying them. The formless clothes, the hood — it's the perfect disguise. She can't even tell if they're male or female.

Staring at the screen, she watches as the figure puts a key fob to the electronic pad on the door, starts pushing it open.

Turn, Elin wills, *turn.*

Then, as if the person has heard her: the figure glances around, toward the camera, clearly looking to see if anyone behind is watching them enter.

Elin's looking so intently at the screen, her eyes start to water. The image blurs. She blinks once, twice, but the picture remains the same.

She reaches out a hand, hits pause. The image is freeze-framed.

Elin pinches the screen, spreading her fingers wide. The image zooms in, the picture quality so clear she can almost make out the pores on the person's face.

The blood pounds in her ears with a deafening roar.

She knows who it is. She knows exactly who was watching her.

48

"It's Laure," Elin says, her mouth dry. "It's definitely her." Clearing her throat, she turns to Cecile. "When I was in the spa yesterday, in the changing room, I felt someone watching me. I heard one of the cubicle doors being opened and closed, but no one came out. I checked all the doors. . . . No one was there. Now it makes sense. Someone could have come through this side door."

Cecile's hand hovers over the screen. "You think she was watching you?"

"If there's no CCTV in the changing room, I can't say definitively, but why else would she be going in there?" Elin scrolls forward another few minutes, her stomach filling with a gnawing dread.

As she expects, it's Laure who reemerges.

The image is like another punch to her gut.

An instinctive sense of relief that Laure's alive, unhurt, which is immediately punctured by an immense hurt. Disappointment.

Why? Why would she do something like that?

305

Then Elin's mind makes the next leap. "There's something else I need to check. Yesterday, someone pushed me into the plunge pool."

Cecile's face darkens. "You're thinking it's her?"

"I don't know." Elin looks back at the screen. "Is there a camera near there?"

"Not officially, but yes. It's on the fencing to the left." Cecile finds the feed.

Thanks to the moisture on the lens, it's hard to make out faces, only fleeting glimpses of bodies — seminaked forms, arms wrapped around themselves.

Elin can't see either of the main pools, only the plunge pool and a small section of wooden walkway above it. For a few minutes, the footage is still: no more movement. Then a group of people appear; five, six, walking out of shot back to the indoor pool.

There's no sign of her.

The image on the screen is motionless again — only clouds of steam pulling up in pockets through the air.

Two more minutes.

Elin finally comes into view; walking from the bottom of the frame, up the wooden walkway. She watches herself turn left, her hair a pale arrow, pointing down the nape of her neck.

A chill comes over her; it feels strange, seeing herself like that, half naked, vulnerable.

In her mind, she's as strong, as physically infallible, as any man, yet in this image she seems anything but.

She sees herself stop beside the plunge pool. The camera is too low to catch her head; all she can see is a segmented profile of her torso.

There's no sign of anyone else. No one walking near the pool.

Elin bites her lip with frustration. *I can't be wrong. Surely . . .*

But then she catches a sudden movement behind her.

A shadowed figure at her back.

Elin holds her breath. She wants to shout to herself — *Move, turn, run!*

But there's nothing she can do apart from watching the scene play out.

She watches herself fall forward. Though it felt impossibly quick at the time, here it feels almost hideously slow.

Individual frames of movement.

She flinches as she sees herself crash into the pool, sending water surging into the air.

It's only then that she has a view of who pushed her; she feels a sickening drop in her stomach.

Laure.

Check again, she tells herself. She has to be sure.

Elin skips back through the footage, this time zooming in on the figure.

307

She's wearing exactly the same clothes; the same hood with the floppy peak. The face isn't as clear as it was in the image by the generator room, but she's certain it's Laure.

Glancing at Cecile, her hand shaking against the desk, she says, "It's Laure." Her mouth is thick, claggy. "Laure pushed me."

She knows that this is one of those moments when there's no going back.

One of the moments when the knowledge is so powerful, it sweeps away everything else that came before.

Elin can't believe it — doesn't want to believe it — but she knows it's true.

It was Laure watching me. Laure who pushed me.

The thought — cold, disturbing — leads to another: that Laure might not be a victim at all. She might be involved in this. The predator.

49

The lift to their floor shudders to a halt, doors sliding open.

Elin walks out into the corridor, legs like jelly. She can't think straight — she'd imagined everything but this: Laure wasn't being held by Adele's killer; Laure had pushed her. Pushed her into that pool.

Her thoughts, raw, questioning, keep circling back to the same point: *Why push me? Why cause Isaac the pain of going missing if it wasn't for a sinister motive?*

Though she wants to ignore it, the most obvious conclusion is that Laure's involved in this.

That she's capable of killing someone.

It's where everything's pointing, isn't it? Everything she's learned so far, this new information . . .

Images flit through her mind: Laure striding across the beach, skimboard under her arm. Laure reading, bottom lip stuck out in concentration. Laure diving off the cliff steps into the sea.

It's impossible, surely?

Has Isaac missed the signs? Laure's colleagues, friends?

It's not beyond the realm of possibility. Elin's thoughts lurch to a case from three years ago: a woman in her forties, convicted of murdering her ex's new partner.

A brutal, vicious stabbing: seventeen times in her head, neck, chest. A neighbor found her bleeding out beside her son's playhouse in the garden.

The suspect had worked in a bank in Exeter selling mortgages. Colleagues, friends, they'd all described her the same way: *Quiet. Unassuming. Kind.*

Elin and the team found out that she'd planned the murder for over two years. The Digital Forensics team dug up pages and pages of research on her laptop about methods of killing someone, how to avoid detection.

What had chilled her the most was the fact that no one had a clue: the killer was on good terms with the victim, had even been on holiday with her a few months before.

From sipping sundowners together to a murder in cold blood.

Have we misjudged Laure in the same way?

As Elin opens the door to their room, her mind flips back the other way.

Maybe I'm jumping to conclusions. Does

310

pushing her into the plunge pool automatically mean Laure's involved in Adele's death?

But still the thought nags: *Why else would she do it?*

Sitting down at the desk, Elin pulls out her notebook. The only way she's going to get this clear in her head is if she writes it out. With a tentative hand, she notes down a summary of what she's learned so far.

Laure's mental health issues, the article, the psychologist's card.

Relationship with Lucas/photographs of him.

Laure's second phone/repeated phone calls to unknown number.

The angry phone call the night Laure went missing.

Laure's argument with Adele.

Possible blackmail letters to Lucas — linked in some way?

Elin absorbs the words, unable to avoid the obvious picture her notes build: everything here, it all points to someone unpredictable. Unstable.

But is it enough to conclude that she's capable of being involved in killing someone?

311

An even bigger question is gnawing away at her: *Why?*

Why would Laure want to hurt Adele?

Elin's thoughts move to *how* Adele was killed; the sandbag, the mask, the presence of the glass box, the fingers. All of it extreme, none of it necessary to kill her, which surely implied it wasn't random. It meant something, perhaps something deeply personal.

But what? She knows Laure and Adele had argued — was it possible that the argument, whatever caused it, was enough of a motive for Laure to kill her?

She's not sure.

It also doesn't explain Daniel Lemaitre's body. Are the two deaths connected, and if so, how?

Her phone starts to ring. When she pulls it from her pocket, she can see that it's Noah.

The files.

50

"When I said quick," Elin says, surprised to find her hand shaking around the phone, "I didn't expect . . . especially this late —" She checks her watch. *Ten past eight.*

"I always work late. You know that."

"I used to," she says. It feels strange, speaking to Noah again, and she knows that it's her fault, this awkwardness. During her break she hasn't seen any of the team in person, only exchanged messages. She's blocked them out, compartmentalized them.

Noah laughs. A familiar sound: deep, slightly husky. A few beats pass. "Warner, I've missed your dulcet tones."

"Same," Elin replies with a sharp, sudden tug of homesickness. No, she corrects, not homesickness — *work* sickness. However hard she's denied it to Will, she's missed this: not just communicating, but the hustle and bustle of the office, the incident room. Meetings. Interviews. Living beyond the space in her head.

"You sure?" Noah replies. "From what I've heard you're pretty happy in retirement." The words are light, but Elin notices the intake of breath, the move from jokey to serious.

"It's not easy, Noah." Her voice wobbles. "Deciding whether to come back. I don't want to let people down."

"But you know we're all behind you, right? With what happened. None of us thinks it was your fault. You acted on instinct. Gut. We'd all do the same."

A long pause.

Elin realizes her foot is tapping the floor, her hand still trembling around the phone. Her throat feels thick suddenly, and she has to force herself to speak. "I know."

Noah moves the conversation on. "So the files . . . I'll let you take a proper look, but they're mainly copies of e-mails, some letters. I've already sent them through."

"The encryption wasn't up to much, then?"

"Nope. Pretty basic. A sixteen-bit key. In fact, I'd say demeaning for someone of my expertise."

She laughs. "Noah, look, thanks for doing this on such short notice."

"I'm used to it. You've always been pretty demanding."

"Any reward required?"

"Only curry on your return."

"Deal." As she says good-bye, Elin's already opening her laptop.

The first of the files he's sent is a Word document, information copied and pasted in both French and English. An article printed out, similar to what she found in Laure's drawer yesterday.

The headline is in French, *Dépression psychotique.*

Easily translatable: psychotic depression. Her eyes flit over the English text:

Read about psychotic depression, a severe form of depression that causes people to experience the usual symptoms of depression, plus delusions and hallucinations.

Elin churns it over: *Did this refer to Laure?* Was she concerned, aware of something wrong, a decline in her mental state? Perhaps researching it?

The next file is another Word document. On the first page is a row of text. The words are in French, but Elin recognizes it straightaway.

It's the anonymous letter that was sent to Lucas. Elin falters, eyes falling away from the screen.

It was Laure who sent the letters.

It's one thing hypothesizing, but this is proof. Proof that Laure had some kind of disturbing preoccupation with Lucas Caron.

She pulls her eyes back up to the screen, opens another file.

Again, a Word document; it spans several pages and contains copies of e-mails.

They're between Laure and a woman named Claire. No addresses are shown, just the body of the messages.

Elin scans through:

Laure,

As requested, please find attached draft copy of article. It's important that the information isn't traceable back to me.

Claire

A HOTEL BUILT ON CORRUPTION?

The first foundations are being dug for the extensive renovation program and expansion of what was Sanatorium du Plumachit into a luxury hotel named Le Sommet.

Lucas Caron, great-grandson of the original owner, has poured millions into the renovation. A result of nine years of planning, when complete, the resort will incorporate a new conference center and a 7,000 sq m Alpine spa.

Yet the renovation has been dogged with issues; the original plans attracted fierce opposition from environmental groups concerned about development in what is a national park. Laws on building in such areas are especially strict in Switzerland

and formal opposition has continued for years.

An online campaign and petition saw more than 20,000 signatures, and environmental groups have staged several protests on-site.

Local doctor Pierre Delane has opposed the project from the start. "It doesn't fit with the landscape. The façade is too modern, a brutal change to the original building."

Most significantly, there have been fears regarding the safety of guests. Stefan Schmid, a mountain guide, warned municipal officials in 2013 that the area above the hotel's main access road was susceptible to avalanches.

Examining the area, geology professors from the University of Lausanne noted a fact that the original builder never flagged: the hotel's main access road is located at the base of a canyon, in the direct path of a natural channel for snow falling from Mont Bella Lui.

These concerns have led to accusations of bribery and questions arising over how Mr. Caron was able to obtain the zoning variance for the hotel expansion given all of the safety concerns, but the charges were dismissed due to lack of evidence.

Another local resident commented, "There's the stench of corruption surrounding this project."

Elin stares at the screen, foot tapping the floor.

This "Claire" is clearly a journalist, but why would Laure want copies of this article? The fact that the journalist mentions it's a draft, and is asking Laure to ensure that the information isn't traceable back to her, implies that the article was never published. So why would it be pasted into a Word document and encrypted?

Shifting in her seat, she reads on. Another e-mail.

Laure,
Further files & research. Sources didn't want to be identified, but we believed them to be reliable.

Claire

The first attachment contains a shorter article, referring to a protest held at the site, the second a copy of a planning document, a file from the local council.

Her French isn't perfect, but it looks like a list of the objections to the planning notice.

Elin racks her brain for an explanation.
What was Laure planning on doing with this information?

Her mind flickers to the letters Lucas received. Is this what they're referring to? Were the letters some kind of blackmail?

The article is troubling — the accusations

318

of bribery, corruption. It's the first she's heard of it and that bothers her. Something like that . . . surely it would have appeared when she'd searched for information about Lucas online?

But not in English, she thinks. Any articles — they were more likely to be in French. Using Google Translate, she searches using the specific French terms: *Le Sommet. La corruption.*

Nothing comes up. Not a single article. She was right — either the article was never online, so there's no record of it, or it was never published. Whatever the story was, it's been squashed.

But it's one more thing linking Laure to the hotel, to Lucas Caron.

Did Laure have some kind of obsession? Did it connect to Adele's death?

Either way, however hard it is to acknowledge, Laure's become a person of interest. Elin's going to have to tell Berndt that she thinks Laure's involved.

51

"Laure Strehl?" Berndt repeats. "The woman who is missing?"

"Yes." Elin fiddles with the corner of her notebook, almost willing him to mishear so she doesn't have to be the one to do this; to implicate Laure.

"Okay, let me put you on speakerphone — the rest of the task force is here. We're working late." She can hear buttons being pushed, a staticky fizz and hum as it switches to speakerphone. "Can you hear me okay?"

"Yes, it's fine." *Deep breaths,* she tells herself, leaning back in her chair. *However hard, however wrong it seems, I have to do this. Find out the truth.*

"Elin, I'd like you to explain what you need" — Berndt speaks slowly, deliberately — "whether you have any particular questions relating to Miss Strehl you'd like us to look at."

She feels her cheeks grow hot at the official way he says Laure's name.

Clearing her throat, she forces the words out. "The main point I'd like to clarify is whether there's anything in her records that might be relevant to the case."

"That's fine, but first, we have an update relating to the psychologist." There's a shuffle of paper. "Laure wasn't a patient with her. There's no record of her ever having visited there."

Elin processes his words. *If that's the case, why have the business card in her drawer? The article on the laptop?* She mulls it over: it's possible Laure decided to go to another therapist, or simply hadn't got around to calling.

"So next, I think we should look in her records. Criminal, clinical."

Muted voices sound out in the background.

"Elin, it's the prosecutor, Hugo Tapparel. There is a certain threshold of evidence that is required for accessing the database to find out this information." His voice has a cool authority that unsettles her. "Could you please detail what you have, so we can decide if it meets that threshold?"

Fumbling over her words, Elin lists what she's found, acutely self-conscious, aware that she's probably overstepped the mark in what she's done and said to get the information about Laure. But what choice does she have?

There's silence, and it's Berndt who speaks first. "So let me be clear . . . the encrypted files imply Laure's involvement in the attempted blackmail of Lucas Caron, and also contain e-mails to a journalist relating to an associated exposé."

"Yes, I —"

She's interrupted by the prosecutor: "Elin, can you confirm which officer instructed you to search the laptop? I don't believe that this was an order from the task force . . ." He trails off, the implication clear: he thinks she's gone too far.

She stiffens. Surely they were making this harder than it needed to be. Why put up barriers?

Berndt cuts across him, his tone more emollient. "I think to follow up on Hugo's point, please send us the files. We'll let you know what we find."

"Thank you." Elin hangs up, takes a long drink of water from the glass beside her. Every step of this feels like she's pulling teeth. But she knows that none of that compares to what she has to do next: Tell Isaac about Laure. Her suspicions.

Elin rubs at her eyes; they feel gritty, sore, her lids heavy. Leaning back in her chair, she closes them. She can hear the wind outside, the blunt force of it pounding the building.

Then something else: a voice, echoing. So clear it's like it's in the room with her.

Isaac's voice.

Urgent, shouting:

322

"We've got to get him out. We've got to get him out."

Then a scream: primal, raw, a low, guttural keening.

The sound of water, frantic splashing.

Her vision narrows to a tiny point: Sam. The edge of his T-shirt being tugged by the water.

The shirt no longer looks like a part of him, but something other, like Sam had already gone, had no right to lay claim to it.

52

Elin opens her eyes with a start, her body jerking awake to a loud knocking at the door.

Had I drifted off?

Glancing at the time on her phone, she can see that she has: she's been asleep for over half an hour.

The knocking comes again: louder now, more insistent.

Will? *No.* Why would he knock? He had a key.

"Elin?"

Walking to the door, she opens it to find Margot standing outside in dark jeans, a shapeless, boat-neck white top. Once again, Elin's struck by her self-consciousness, her stooped posture, the rounded curve of her shoulders.

No one's ever told her to be proud of her height, she thinks with a pang of sympathy, imagining the teasing at school — the name-calling and mockery.

"Is everything okay?"

"I was wondering if you've heard anything about Laure." Margot smooths her hair back. It's greasy, sitting flat against her scalp, several of the starred grips holding it tightly in place. It makes her features look hawkish. More pronounced.

Elin hesitates, but realizes her mistake.

Margot steps back, her expression frozen. "Oh, my god." Her voice is high. "She's dead, isn't she?"

"No." Elin struggles to get the words out, her tongue stuck to the roof of her mouth. "She's not, she's still missing. We don't know anything yet."

Margot's eyes are bright, glittering. "I thought . . ." Her voice cracks. "She's been gone so long."

"Come in." Elin's tone is soft. "We can't talk here."

Margot follows her into the room, her face white and pinched. She checks the screen of her phone before turning it between her fingers.

There are a few moments of silence.

Elin takes a deep breath, looks through the window. More snow, climbing up the glass. It's nearly to the top of the frame.

When she turns back, Margot's looking at her. "I'm sorry about that."

"It's fine. I know things are scary. It's easy to jump to conclusions."

Margot nods, still turning the phone in her hand.

Another heavy silence.

When Margot finally puts the phone down on the desk, the movement doesn't stop; she starts picking at her nails. Tiny flakes of gray varnish flicker to the floor.

Something's up, Elin thinks, watching her. *Not just Laure. Something else.*

"Margot. Is something wrong?"

A pause, then she nods. "Something's been on my mind. Before, when we spoke, I wasn't entirely honest."

"About what?"

"Laure and Isaac's relationship. After what's happened to Adele, I think there's something you should know." Her foot is tapping the floor. "The reason I didn't want to mention it before is because of who it involves." Her gaze slips past Elin, then back again.

"Go on," Elin says slowly.

"Lucas Caron. He and Laure, they . . . had something, a while back."

"I know. Lucas told me."

Margot looks at her in surprise. "Did he say anything about it starting up again?"

"No. He said it was over. A short-term thing when she and Isaac were on a break. You don't think it was?"

"I don't. I saw them a few weeks ago in the corridor to the spa. On the CCTV. Laure was coming to meet me for lunch."

"And something happened?" Elin prompts.

"Yes. It looked like Laure was going to walk past him, but he stopped her, grabbed her arm." Margot leans against the desk, her mouth twitching. "Her face — it was like she was scared. She was trying to get away, but he wouldn't let her."

"What happened then?"

"They spoke for a few more minutes, then Lucas walked off."

Elin tries to keep her expression neutral, but her mind is racing.

Lucas hadn't said anything about this.

"Did Laure carry on into the spa?"

"Yes, but it was strange. She didn't mention what had happened. That's what made me think something might have started up again — that she didn't want to tell me because this time she was with Isaac, engaged . . ."

"Did she seem worried, though?" Elin probes. "Anxious?"

"Not particularly." Margot bites down on her lip. "I wish I'd said something, asked her about it."

"But she was open with you about their relationship initially?"

"The first time, yes, but she was single then, had split from Isaac. To be honest, at first I thought it was a rebound thing, but when it ended, I wasn't so sure. She was really upset."

Margot shrugs, the gesture at odds with the intensity in her eyes. "But that's reasonable, right? If someone tosses you aside like you're rubbish. No one likes that, do they? Feeling used."

"Is that what she said happened?" Elin says, aware of her uneven breathing. All this, what it implied . . . she didn't like it.

"Yes. Lucas more or less dropped her. I think she had the impression it was something more than it was, you know?"

Elin nods, thinking about what this means. It lends weight to her picture of Lucas: he's a liar. Denying that he knew the body on the mountain was Daniel, the photograph of him with Adele implying he knew her better than he'd said, and now this.

In a situation like this, that bothers her — he'd explicitly told her that he hadn't really been in contact with Laure since the fling.

Why lie?

But Elin knows the answer: he'd only lie if he's got something to hide.

53

Elin finds Isaac sitting with Will in the lounge at a small table by the window.

They're not talking. Head bent, Will's looking down at his phone, and Isaac's staring out through the glass into the darkness.

Pulling out a chair, she takes a seat between them.

Her heart is thumping. What she's about to do — it's horrible. She's never been any good at delivering bad news, softening the blow. Her words always come out clumsy, wrong.

Will looks up, his expression stony. "You've been gone awhile. It's late, Elin. Half past nine."

"Not that long."

"I messaged you, went back to the room. When you weren't there, I came back and found Isaac." His tone is accusing, unusually judgmental. "Thought he might need some company."

"I must have just missed you," she replies, ignoring his comment. "I went through the

CCTV footage with Cecile, and then I went back to the room and spoke to Noah. He sent the encrypted files."

"So quickly?" Isaac looks up for the first time.

"Yes." Haltingly, she tells them what she's discovered. When she finishes talking, she's acutely aware of Isaac's gaze fixed on her. Unblinking.

There's an awful, loaded silence.

Elin can't meet his eye. Instead, she glances around the room at the other occupied tables. One group eating; another, a group of staff, playing cards.

Finally, Isaac speaks, leaning across the table, forearms pressed to the wood. "Are you trying to say you think Laure's involved in this? Are you out of your mind?"

The sharp edge to his voice makes her falter. "Well, she's not locked up, is she? Being held somewhere, like you thought. We know from the CCTV footage that she's been here the whole time. If she has, why hasn't she been in touch? Let you know she's okay?"

Isaac stiffens. "I don't know, but there has to be another explanation, doesn't there?"

Several beats pass. She can hear the rapid pull of his breath.

Elin hesitates, struggling with what she's about to say next. "Did Laure speak to you much about her depression?"

"Bits and pieces." Isaac's expression is

closed. Defensive.

"Laure's laptop, the encrypted files . . . there was something on there about psychotic depression." She fumbles over her words. "It's when the depression gets so severe, it can result in psychotic episodes."

He flushes; his face is growing angry, livid. "Did you know?"

"No." His voice is clipped. "She never told me."

Elin reaches out, puts a hand on his arm, but he pulls away. "Isaac, she might not have wanted to. Might not have known how you'd take it . . ."

"How I'd take it? Elin, we're engaged." He clenches his fist. "It doesn't make sense, these lies . . . not now."

"But it won't, that's the point. If you're experiencing one of these episodes, you lose contact with reality. False perceptions, false beliefs, they can lead to paranoid, delusional behavior."

Isaac shakes his head, eyes narrowing to slits. "All this," he says quietly. "You're trying to tee me up, aren't you? You really think she's got something to do with what's happened."

She can feel her face growing hot. "We don't know for certain, not yet, I just wanted to —"

"No. You're digging away at the wrong thing, some theory, when we should be out there looking for her. She isn't involved, Elin. I know she isn't." Staring down at his hands, he pushes his knuckles together. "Look at what happened to Adele. You think Laure could be capable of that?" He bites down on his lip. "Christ, Elin. She was your *friend.*"

Will gives her a worried glance, his foot nudging hers beneath the table. He wants her to stop, she can tell, but she can't. Isaac has to confront this. If Laure's involved, he needs to be aware.

"Isaac, no one's saying anything definitively, but I think you should be prepared. Laure's lied. Repeatedly."

He shakes his head. "It's not as easy as that, is it, Elin? We all lie. That's what people do. The unpalatable bits, the ugly bits, the bits that make you look bad. Look at you — you've not been honest, have you? About what's going on with your life, this break from work." He tenses. "You haven't even told Lucas and Cecile you're not actually working at the moment, have you?"

Elin takes a breath, about to speak, but no words come out. She can't say why she hasn't told them. It's too complex to tease apart, even in her own head.

A tangle of reasons. A reflex, a refusal to admit, even to herself, that she's no longer a detective, might never be one again, and, most embarrassingly of all: pride. Wanting to still be seen as someone important.

Isaac looks at her, something triumphant in his gaze. "It doesn't mean you've done something bad."

Bracing her hands against the table, Elin feels it snap: an invisible thread that's been pulled taut inside her for so long. "Fine. I'll tell them. Is that what you want? For me to spill every detail?"

"No." Isaac's voice is hard. "Not if you don't want to. All I want is for you to understand that nobody's perfect. Everyone's got flaws. Even you. Laure, she's probably screwed up, done some stupid bloody things, but it doesn't mean she's involved in killing someone."

"I know that, but —"

"But what?" Isaac stands up, scraping back his chair. His cheeks are blotchy. "Have you heard yourself, Elin? You're like Mum, blinders on. You think that the world's black and white, that there's this bloody perfect answer for everything. Just because Laure's done one thing, it doesn't automatically lead to another. Things are messy, there aren't always explanations."

"I've never said that." Her voice sounds thick, muffled. She's aware that she's sweating, the skin under her arms prickling with heat.

"I know you haven't said it, but we've all felt it." He turns to Will. "Don't tell me you haven't? Haven't felt her *disapproval*."

She blinks, taken aback by the vitriol in his words.

"Someone's got to say it, Elin. Why do you think I haven't been in touch? It's because it's exhausting being around you. You want everything done exactly right, all the ducks in a row. It makes me sad. That's one of the reasons why I left, why I left Mum too."

"Isaac, please —"

"No, it's true. This is meant to be about finding Laure, but it's become something else entirely." His eyes flash. "I knew from the minute you came out here that this wasn't just going to be some fun trip. You had some point to prove."

She bristles. "What do you mean?"

"You've always been like this. Always on this . . . mission."

"Mission?"

"Yes. To save people. Be the hero. Over and over again. This, your job, it's the same pattern. Every time."

Will stands, puts a hand on Isaac's arm, his jaw tensed. "Look, mate, don't you think you should stop? Everyone's tired . . ."

Isaac jerks his hand away. "No. She needs to know."

Elin's neck starts to burn, hot coils of anger pulling up inside her.

What's wrong with him? Can't he see?

The only reason she's like this is because of what happened to Sam.

Because of what *he* did.

"Isaac," she starts, her voice tremulous, "no matter what you say, answers . . . they are important. The truth matters. How can you move on without it? Look at what happened to Sam. My mind is on loop because of it. Going over that day again and again, and that's because we don't *have* the answers. We don't know what happened."

Isaac freezes, a ragged trail of red creeping up his cheeks. Swallowing hard, he opens his mouth to speak and then closes it again.

A weighty silence stretches out between them, telling her everything that she needs to know.

Elin can feel her hand jiggling in her lap. "You don't want to talk about it?"

He studies the floor, refusing to meet her gaze.

"Come on, Isaac. I want to know what you've got to say. You've spent years avoiding talking about it. I want answers."

"Elin, stop." Will reaches out, placing his hand on hers.

Isaac drags his gaze up to meet hers, his eyes clouded with emotion.

Guilt, Elin thinks, looking at him. He's riddled with it.

Isaac turns away. "I'm going to bed. I don't want to do this here. Not now." He still won't meet her gaze.

"That's right," she says as he walks away.

you won't be seen. Don't tell anyone or bring anyone. I'm sorry. Laure

Laure.

Her breath catches in her throat. This has to be her other phone, surely? Elin leans over the side of the bed and drags her bag toward her. Bringing it up onto the covers, she pulls out the mobile phone bill, checks it against the number on the message.

It is: it's Laure's second phone.

But it was switched off when Isaac tried it. She must have turned it on again.

Elin stares at the screen, her eyes pulling each word apart before putting them back together.

Two phrases come to the fore:

I want to explain. I'm sorry.

She works through it in her mind. *Explain:* that inherently implies she has something *to* explain. The apology, the inference — the same.

A cold bead of confirmation in her chest: *Laure really is involved in this.*

There's no doubt now.

Lying back against the pillow, Elin tries to piece things together — facts, supposition — but she's agitated, twitchy. Her brain isn't working like it should.

She drags herself out of bed, pacing toward the window.

Her mind is churning, every twist and turn

340

of thought coming back to the same conclusion: She has two options.

The first is that she tells Cecile and Lucas, and goes to meet Laure with backup. The other is that she goes on her own — slips out and meets Laure one-on-one.

Neither option is ideal.

With the first, she risks scaring Laure off, perhaps compelling her to do something else. If Laure is being genuine, she might see Elin bringing someone else as a betrayal, proof that Elin doesn't trust her. If she's in the grip of some kind of delusion, already feeling in some way wronged, then this could be dangerous.

The other option, one she's finding hard to consider, is that this is some kind of trap. The risk is there, isn't it? Impossible to ignore. Laure pushed her, after all. Tried to scare her.

But surely, if she'd wanted to hurt her, she'd have done it then, at the spa?

Brain flip-flopping between the different scenarios, Elin keeps pacing. Outside, the wind is tugging at the snow, teasing it this way and that. It's now laid unevenly across the terrace in random, windblown piles.

She knows she should wake Will, get his point of view, but after their last conversation, she knows what his answer will be:

Leave it alone. Don't go near it.

Her eyes trace the small peaks of snow by

the window.

A memory rises up: Laure's letters.

The letters Laure sent her, arriving every week after Sam died. Letters reaching out — full of sympathy at first, then fun. Anecdotes about school, boys, her mother, Coralie. Trying to draw Elin out, reconnect.

Letters that Elin chose to ignore because she was jealous, couldn't cope with the fact that Laure hadn't been dealt the same shitty hand as she had.

She blinks, eyes smarting. She has to meet her, doesn't she? Give her the benefit of the doubt.

This time, she has to listen.

55

It's 8:48 a.m. Elin rereads the name etched on the glass plate on the wall. *Suite Plaine Morte.* It has to be this room — from the hotel website, she knows it's the only penthouse in the hotel.

But as she looks through the glass door, it's clear that the suite itself isn't on the other side of it. Instead, there's another small corridor leading to a set of lift doors on the far left-hand side. Laure was right: the suite has its own access corridor as well as its own lift.

As she puts her hand up to the door, her phone pulses in her side pocket. Relieved she's put it on vibrate mode, Elin pulls it out, scans the screen.

Laure?

No: a different number. Berndt.

RIPOL search shows we do have intelligence on Laure Strehl — reference canton of Vaud. Seeking permission to share detail with you ASAP.

Intelligence? What did that mean? Elin wonders if she should call him back. She looks down at the screen again. It's 8:50. She doesn't have time. It'll have to wait.

Putting the phone back in her pocket, she slips through the door.

She's beginning to feel nervous; she's walking too fast. Despite her thin sweater, she can feel the prickle of sweat between her shoulder blades.

The corridor space is unnerving, one of the few in the hotel that doesn't feature glass. Instead, the walls are a cream-colored marble, pinkish veins dancing across the surface.

Despite the privacy the marble gives, it makes the space feel compact. Suffocating.

Halfway to the lift, she notices something: small, square pictures lining the walls.

They're sketches, framed in black — a messy tangle of loose, inked lines. It takes a moment for her eyes to resolve the confusion of shapes, but when they finally do, Elin steps back.

People, she thinks, a hand coming up to her mouth.

Parts of people: face, leg, knee.

The effect is brutal. They look like images of amputation. Dismemberment.

As she walks past them, the silence is excruciating; she's aware of every sound she's making.

Every breath. Every footstep.

How will I justify my presence if I run into someone? What should I say? Then there's the CCTV. What if someone sees me going up? Cecile, or Lucas?

A vast mirror makes up the end wall. Elin can't avoid seeing herself approach — limp hair, jeans hanging baggy over her legs. Sam's necklace hugs the base of her throat, echoing the line of her sweater. The scar above her upper lip catches the overhead light, drawing a faint, silvery line from her mouth to her nose.

A few steps on. She's nearly at the lift that must go directly up to the suite.

From the corner of her eye, she notices a movement in the mirror — a flicker of shadow.

Elin freezes, convinced she can see a silhouette, but when she looks back, it's gone. She knows it's only a reflection — a distortion of the overhead lights, reverberating glimpses of her own movement, but it doesn't stop the cold jag of fear in her chest.

Am I mad doing this alone? Taking the risk?

Walking the final few steps to the lift, she takes a deep breath, reprimands herself: *Don't lose it now. I'm about to get answers.*

A few moments later, Elin steps out of the lift into the entrance of the penthouse. Her eyes graze the larger space beyond: living area, fireplace, huge glass windows.

She checks her watch. It's 8:52 a.m. Eight minutes early.

Is Laure here already?

Elin glances around. She can't see anyone, but she can't rule out that Laure might already be lying in wait, making sure that Elin hasn't brought anyone with her.

Walking farther in, she stops. She's not sure what she was expecting, but it wasn't this scale. The views. Glass wraps the entire space, revealing exactly how much snow had fallen — the landscape now a perfect, pristine white, every landmark smothered.

After putting her bag down by the sofa, Elin moves around, getting her bearings. The living and dining area of the suite is open plan, but divided into areas. On her far right, a small kitchen, and opposite, another seating area. A corridor leads off to the right, which she's guessing is where the bedrooms are.

The main living space, where she's standing, houses a fireplace and three vast architectural sofas set around a coffee table.

A dining room is positioned slightly lower, down several steps. A large oak table is the centerpiece, a huge artwork dominating the right-hand wall. It's one of those strange, dismembered images again — vivid blues through to black segments of limb.

Everything's simple, almost abrupt in its starkness, with none of the usual ostentation found in suites like these. There's no blingy ornamentation: kitschy fabrics, gold-plating, huge vases filled with flowers. Instead, the lines are clean, the colors muted, tasteful.

The luxury is in the finish, the detail — the marble walls, statement leather chair, various expensive-looking pieces of furniture, the vast white sheepskin covering the floor.

Elin stops, pulling herself up sharply. *Don't get distracted.*

Laure could be here, in one of the other rooms. Keeping her voice low, she calls out, "Laure?"

She stands perfectly still, but there's no return call: only silence, her own voice echoing back in her head.

Elin walks toward the corridor on her right, every sense on high alert for movement or sound. The first room she enters is a library-cum-games room; the second, opposite, is a snug den. Terraces wrap each space.

She swiftly surveys each room, but there's no sign anyone's here. Everything is neat, untouched.

Despite that, as she walks toward what must be the bedrooms, her top is now damp from sweat, the fabric chafing uncomfortably against the flesh of her back.

She could still be here somewhere. Hiding.

Elin cautiously makes her way into the first bedroom. *The master,* she thinks, taking in the large bed jutting out from the wall, the private pool on the terrace, the hot tub.

No one's there.

Scanning the other three bedrooms and finding them empty, she walks back to the living space, a knotted, pulsing tension in her limbs. All she wants is to get this over with.

She peers down at her watch again: 8:57. *Three minutes left.*

It's then she hears a noise: a scuffed, scraping sound, like something's being shoved, shifted somehow.

Elin turns around, her own breath loud in her ears. In the windows she glimpses her reflection and something else.

A silhouette?

Just like in the pool's changing room, she has the unmistakable sense that someone's watching her, eyes crawling over her.

With a mounting sense of panic, she scans the room again.

Nothing.

Another look at her watch: two minutes. Time is dragging, painfully slowly.

Finally, a sound.

Something more familiar: the metallic whirr of the lift, quickly swallowed by the shuffle of the doors as they part. Feeling her breathing rate increase, she clamps her elbows to her ribs: an automatic, defensive gesture.

Keep calm. Deep breaths. Don't panic.

The lift doors are fully open now, but no one steps out.

It's empty.

All she can hear is the dull, mechanical hum of the lift as it settles into position.

Elin falters, her eyes pulling downward. Something there, on the floor.

She feels her legs soften, then buckle.

56

It's Laure. She's dead.

The words roll about inside her head, a realization that's being batted back and forth,
back and forth, her mind not wanting to take
it in, absorb it.

The lift is making noises, horrible noises.
The doors, sensing her presence, are repeatedly opening and closing, almost in time with
the pulse beating in her head.

A mechanical horror, reflecting the scene in
front of her.

It's as if the lift itself has inflicted the damage, the doors as incisors, chewing her up,
spitting her back out.

Laure's slumped in the left-hand corner of
the lift, head tilted sideways, to the right, at
an unnatural angle, dark hair spilling over
her face.

She's wearing a mask.

The same black rubber mask Adele wore.
It's concealing her face, her features, but Elin
can tell it's her. The hair, the lean frame. The

same pumps she was wearing the other day. Blood is soaking her gray T-shirt, concentrated around the neck.

Elin's gaze tracks downward.

Just below the mask, there's a deep incision in Laure's neck. It looks like it's been cut from behind; her head pulled back, the knife drawn across it from left to right.

Her throat slit, like an animal.

Elin steps forward to examine it. The wound is deeper on the left, trailing off toward the right. It starts below the ear, running obliquely downward, straight across the midline of the neck.

Someone right-handed.

Most likely, the carotid artery and the jugular vein had been cut. The loss of blood would have been huge. Fatal, but enough time for Laure to realize what was going on, to feel the blood, her life, pumping out of her.

Elin swallows hard, feels bile rising up the back of her throat.

How could someone do something like this?

Despite the obvious trauma, with a trembling hand Elin brings her fingers to the other side of Laure's neck, feels for a pulse.

There isn't one: her skin is cool. She's been dead a little while, but not long. There's no stiffening, no signs of rigor.

Her head starts to spin as she absorbs the implication: whoever killed her can't be far away, can they?

Breathe, she tells herself. *Breathe.*

Elin forces herself to turn, focus on the wooden chair beside the lift. Detail: the hollowed curve of the backrest, the looping pattern of the wood grain. Tracking it with her eyes, she gulps in air, breathing through the adrenaline, waiting for the swimming of her head to subside.

As her breathing returns to normal, she looks back. Every cell in her body is willing this not to be real, for this to be some twisted projection of her imagination. But it's not: Laure's body, the inhuman brutality, they're real.

Elin knows that this time, she can't let fear get the better of her. She needs to look properly, get the crucial first impressions.

But the lift doors are still moving, pulsing backward and forward as she moves between the sensors. She needs something heavy to wedge them open.

Frantically scanning the space outside the lift, her eyes alight on the chair. She takes it, weighs it in her hands. It's solid: it'll do the job. She places it in the doorway against the left-hand side. The doors stop moving.

Stepping back inside the lift, Elin squats down beside Laure's body.

She tilts her head sideways, looking at Laure's hands.

Parts of her fingers have been removed: the

forefinger of her right hand, the index. She can't see the left, not without moving the body.

It looks like they've been severed with a sharp instrument: pliers, or shears of some type. Unlike Adele's amputations, there's blood around the wounds, streaked up the back of her hand.

Her gaze moves upward to the blood soaking Laure's shirt. A lot of blood, but not enough . . .

Elin looks around the lift. Apart from transfer from the body, a smear across the wall, it's clean — nothing on the floor, no spatter on the walls or ceiling.

This isn't where she was killed.

Laure's body has been moved from the primary scene. Placed in the lift only minutes after Elin had taken it.

Whoever killed her had pushed the button for this floor, then quickly left the lift.

As she stands back up, her head is spinning — not from revulsion, but because of her own naivete, inadequacy.

All my theories, my ideas, were wrong. Laure was either trying to warn me or this was a trap set by the killer.

Pulling her phone from her pocket, she taps out a message to Will.

Found Laure in penthouse suite. She's

Her hand is shaking, sliding over her screen, the jerking movement spelling out an unintelligible word.

She takes a deep breath, composing herself, then deletes several letters before continuing: She's dead.

Pressing send, she steps out of the lift.

This time, her heel strikes something. The sound — a hollow knock, the slight jolt — pulls her sideways. Elin stumbles, grabbing at the wall for balance. As she rights herself, she inspects the floor to see what her foot hit.

A glass box.

A sudden stab of trepidation, but it's not the contents of the box catching her off guard, it's the realization that it wasn't there a few minutes ago.

When she propped the door to the lift open, the floor was clear.

That meant only one thing. The killer had been in the suite while she was examining Laure's body. Only a few steps behind her.

Somehow the killer had gotten into the penthouse and placed the box there.

It's then she hears a noise: something strange, unfamiliar. Not a breath, but more of a whistle, then a heavy, labored pull of air.

Elin whirls around, and glimpses someone beside her.

She can't tell who it is because the figure doesn't have a face. All she can see is the mask.

57

Elin blinks, fear spiking the base of her stomach.

Her first, dizzy impression is that she's imagining it — some hallucination triggered by the shock of finding Laure's body — but the sound coming from the mask flips that thought on its head.

The distorted breathing is magnified, grotesque.

She freezes, thoughts spiraling through her mind: about what might come next; the horrific injuries inflicted on Laure and Adele.

What would they do to me?

The horrible, lurid workings of her brain paralyze her.

She tries to move her limbs into a defensive position, but it's like she's wading through mud. Every motion is thick, gluey.

It's only when adrenaline starts to kick in that her body does something definitive: a sudden jerk, her right leg kicking up, out.

She can do this, can't she? She's tired, yes,

but she's strong — her body is in shape. She's primed.

But it's too late.

Her attacker is stronger. Faster. And they have the benefit of knowing what they're going to do next.

A plan.

The figure grabs her, turns her so her back is to them. Her right wrist is ripped backward, rotated until her arm is wrenched behind her back. A hand is clamped over her mouth, her neck yanked backward.

With a sideways glance, Elin glimpses the mask — it's only inches from her face. Heightened detail: microtears in the rubber, fine white streaks.

It's now that she feels an absolute sense of terror set in — something so primal she's only ever felt it once before: the Hayler case, with him, that day, in the water. The memory makes her angry, gives her a sudden spike of energy.

Digging her heels into the wooden floor, she wrenches herself forward, left leg kicking back, jabbing her attacker in the thigh.

It seems to work: their grip slackens. Elin senses a hesitation.

Then: a distant sound — the thud of a door slamming.

Someone's coming.

Will?

All at once, they let go, pushing her back, away.

Elin falls, her head slamming hard against the floor, the impact pulsing through her body. She cries out. The pain is excruciating; it's violent enough to make her vision cloud, white stars flickering against the blackness.

Within seconds, she feels hands on her face, fingers clutching, grinding her cheek into the wooden floor. This close, she can smell them: sweat, something soapy mixed with something else. Something familiar she can't quite grasp.

An object grazes her cheek. It's rough, plasticky.

The mask.

Panicked, she reaches up her hand to try to push it away, but instead she just claws at air.

Another thud. She hears her name being called.

Will.

Silence: a longer hesitation. The hand on her face is roughly removed.

Elin waits, staring in revulsion at the glass box only a few feet away, the bracelets catching the spotlight overhead. Her body is tensed for whatever's coming next, but all she feels is movement: a rush of air.

Her attacker is no longer holding her down.

Tipping her head sideways, she tries to see if the masked person is still there, but there's no one.

Heavy footsteps, running. Dull rhythmic thuds.

They've gone.

Elin draws herself up to a sitting position. Her head and back are still throbbing from the fall. Her heartbeat is thick in her chest, the sound reverberating in her ears.

Tears prick her eyes — shameful tears, her naivete taunting her once again.

How could I have got this so wrong? How could I have imagined that Laure could have been responsible?

This isn't a crime of passion, of revenge over a fling gone wrong.

It's bigger than Laure. Something far bigger, and now she's back to square one.

58

"You're sure you're not in pain?" Leaning forward, Will takes her hand in his. His forehead is damp with sweat, his eyes thick with emotion.

"I'm fine. Whoever it was . . . they didn't have a chance to do . . ." She stops, reconfigures the sentence. "They must have heard you coming." But her words sound shaky, untethered. She can't stop her eyes from flickering across the room. Despite Will's presence, the vast space still seems full of danger.

Hiding places everywhere.

It isn't helped by the frenetic movement of the snow outside — sharp, white arrows targeting the glass, eclipsed only by murky swirls of fog.

Catching the look of fear flashing across Will's features, Elin squeezes his hand, enjoying the warmth of it around hers. She can't help thinking what might have been: *I could have lost all of this, couldn't I? Me and Will . . .*

if the killer got their way . . .

"Honestly, I'm okay." But as she leans back against the sofa, she can feel the rapid pumping of her heart. Her eyes briefly close.

Once again, she sees it — the mask, the rubber hose running from nose to mouth.

No. She can't let her mind go there. Can't let it take over. Not now that Laure is dead. She has to find out who did this and stop them.

"Drink this." Will passes her a bottle of water, nudges his glasses up his nose with his forefinger.

Elin sips from it, hands shaking, the rim of the bottle wobbling against her lips, bumping against her teeth. Her gaze darts involuntarily toward the lift.

Glimpsing Laure's body, there's another sharp jolt of realization: *Laure has died. This is real.*

This time when she looks, she doesn't see Laure's slumped, broken body, but the old Laure. Child Laure.

Memories of her rear up: the tiny creases that bisected her forearms, the colored beads Coralie plaited into her hair, her gangly-legged walk across the sand.

Tears sting the back of her eyes.

"Elin, it's okay, you know. To feel . . ." Will's words drop away.

Neither of them speaks for a moment.

"It's a shock, that's all," she says finally.

360

She forces herself to meet his gaze, but the tears haven't gone away, they've simply moved. She's swallowed them, a sticky mass in her throat, sitting heavy.

Still watching her, Will bites down hard on his lower lip. "Elin, I don't want to say it now, but you coming up here alone like that, it was dangerous. Reckless."

Heat chases up her throat. She thumbs the rim of the bottle. "I wanted to give her a chance to explain. I thought . . ." She falters. "I thought it was genuine, okay? My mistake."

There's an awkward pause. Elin takes another swig of water.

"Didn't you think about the risk? What that might have done to us, especially after what we discussed last night."

"I know, but I kept thinking that if she'd wanted to hurt me, she had the opportunity before, and she didn't."

His face is tight, hands clenched in his lap.

She leans over, lightly kisses him. "I'm sorry," she whispers into his cheek. "I shouldn't make excuses. I put myself at risk. I shouldn't have."

He resists for a moment, before kissing her back. Pulling away, he runs a hand over her cheek, gives her a small, grudging smile. "That's probably the first time you've admitted you were wrong about something." His voice breaks. "Honestly, if you hadn't messaged me then, I don't know what I'd . . ."

But she doesn't hear the rest of his words. A thought snags around the first half of his sentence.

The message.

She shouldn't have had the chance to send it. The killer had wanted to catch her unawares, not give her time to contact someone, raise the alarm.

That means timing-wise, something had gone wrong. Had something, or someone, stopped her attacker on the way up to the penthouse?

"Will," she starts, "how did you get up here?"

"When the lift didn't work, I asked one of the staff if there was another way up. They showed me the staircase. It opens into the den."

"That must be how they got in," she murmurs, putting the bottle of water onto the table next to her. "They put Laure in the lift, then came up the stairs."

This was the potential delay, wasn't it?

For some reason, they'd been delayed in or around the stairs.

Because of that, the killer had needed to improvise, and in doing so had made a mistake. Given her time to send the message.

Elin thinks it through: if the killer had made one mistake, there might be another. She casts a glance toward the lift. She needs to take another look.

Examine Laure's body properly.

Will follows her gaze. Eyes falling on Laure, he flinches. "Don't." His voice is unsteady. "Whatever you're thinking of doing, don't. The police might only be a day out. Leave it for them." He looks at her. "And you need to tell Isaac, Elin, before you do anything else." His eyes once again involuntarily flicker to Laure. "He needs to know what's happened."

Elin shifts position. What he's saying makes sense, but the stakes have been raised. She can't leave it here. This setup is about killing Laure, but it's also about *her*.

The fact that the killer went after her tells her something vital: They wanted her out of the way. The only reason for that is because they're planning something else.

59

Crouching down, Elin starts photographing Laure's body.

With every click and freeze-frame of her phone, her eyes find something new; a blood-stain, a mark, a feature of Laure's face she hadn't noticed before.

Elin takes a deep breath, batting away memories, glad of the screen between them, the slight distance it provides.

Hands shaking, she focuses on the neck incision: photographing it from several angles, making sure she captures the detail of the wound. Yet again, its depth, precision, pulls her up short.

Ruthless. There's no doubt. No indecision as blade met flesh.

An execution.

Her gaze moves over the visible parts of Laure's body — hands, wrists, forearms. Like Adele, there's no sign of a struggle — no cuts, abrasions, or bruising.

No visible marks at all.

The killer had to have used a sedative to restrain her. If they'd used force there would be some bruising, at least.

Elin puts her phone down and reaches for her bag. She pulls out her notebook, starts scribbling down her thoughts, but as her head tips forward it throbs.

There's a strange flashing behind her eyes — not lights, but scenes, fragments of moments. Melting into one another, lucid, bright.

A flashback. Another one.

Elin blinks, tries to stop them from coming, but it doesn't work. They're continuous, unstoppable:

Isaac's face that day, his mouth parted. Fear, freezing his features into something eerily precise, alien.

The burning sun on the back of her neck.

A fishing net, drifting across the surface of the water.

She reaches for the bottle of water Will gave her, and takes a long drink. In seconds, the detail, the essence of the images, dissolves, leaving a void: something vital trickling through her fingers.

"So it's the same." Will walks up behind her. "As Adele."

Elin notices his mouth involuntarily contract in revulsion as he takes in the scene close-up. He stares glassy-eyed before turning away.

"Not exactly," she replies, pretending not to notice his reaction. "The method of killing, it's different. With Adele, it was most likely drowning, but this . . ." She coughs. "The killer has cut her throat. You can't see, not from this angle, but her fingers . . . they're also different. The wounds aren't sutured like Adele's were."

But what do the differences mean?

She doesn't know definitively, but it points to the possibility of Laure's killing being more hurried, and also more frenzied. Yet, she thinks, other elements are the same: the mask, the digit removal, the glass box, the bracelets . . . identical. None of these were essential to the killing itself, so she's certain they're symbolic: the killer trying to communicate something.

But what?

Elin pulls the elements apart one by one. First, the mask. There are two factors: if it was only on the killer's face, you could assume it was simply a way of trying to conceal his or her identity, but the fact that it's on the victim's as well, it has to mean something, doesn't it? Have some significance.

It's impossible to say what that could be: not unless she has more information. It's the same with the finger removal. There could be multiple explanations as to why, but at the moment she's in the dark.

The glass box is the only thing she's certain

of. Like the ones in the hotel — containing the spittoon, the clias helmet, it's a deliberate ploy to draw attention to the contents.

Why?

The overarching motive is key, but now that her previous theory about Laure has been disproved, she's back to the beginning. Trying to link disparate, seemingly unconnected elements together.

Turning back to Laure, she starts taking photographs again when her phone rings, buzzing against her palm. She scans the screen.

Berndt.

His tone is urgent. "Elin, I don't know if you got my message, but we have an update on Laure Strehl. The prosecutor has agreed I can give you the information."

"Go on." Elin's voice is thick, tears pricking the back of her eyes as she realizes her mistake.

He's talking about Laure in the present tense, as if she were still alive, and Elin hasn't corrected him.

"I don't think Laure is a risk to anyone, or at risk herself. The information we found on her file relates to charges filed after some kind of altercation with her . . . how do you say in English? Apartment mate —"

"Yes, that's right." Her voice is small.

"Laure pushed her apartment mate up against a glass door. The glass shattered, the

367

"A memory stick." Will stares.

Elin is unable to stop her hand from shaking. She can't believe the killer meant to leave this on the body. Either her attacker didn't know it was there, or — and she thinks this is the more likely option — they'd only realized or remembered it was there when it was too late.

Perhaps this is what had caused the delay in coming up to the penthouse. It's possible that her attacker had only worked out Laure had it on her *after* they'd put her body in the lift. Then they had gone back, but the lift had already left.

Either way, this is the mistake, isn't it? *This.*

60

"You think it was recent?" Cecile's voice splinters, and like Will before her, her eyes dart involuntarily toward the lift, to Laure's body, the dark rubber mask skewed across her face. Although everyone is trying to avoid it, the open mouth of the lift keeps pulling at their gazes.

"Yes. After examining the body, I'd say she was killed early this morning. I'm not an expert, but I think it's a good assumption. I had a text from her at sixish, which would work, timing-wise, but it's hard to say at the moment if it was from her or the killer . . . a trap . . ."

Cecile's eyes are glassy, wet with tears. "I'm sorry." Pulling a tissue from her pocket, she wipes her eyes. "After Adele, I knew there was a chance, but it's hard to take in."

Elin reaches over, touches her arm. "I understand."

"And you really don't have any idea who's doing this?"

"After this, no." Elin shifts on the sofa. The movement jars: a dull ache crawling up her spine from where the killer had knocked her to the floor. Her one lead is the memory stick, but she doesn't want to mention it to either Lucas or Cecile until she's had a chance to look at it.

At this point, she hasn't questioned anyone about their alibis, so everyone's still a suspect, including them.

Her eyes slide to Lucas, a few feet away. He's standing by the kitchen area, talking intently on his cell phone. His hair is scraped away from his face, twisted into a loose knot behind his head. For the first time she can see his face clearly, and with it his expression.

Elin doesn't like it. It's closed. Opaque.

As if sensing her eyes on him, he looks up, but gives no nod of recognition, just continues talking, phone pressed against his ear.

Cecile wraps her arms around herself. "It's got to be someone here, hasn't it?" Her voice is strained. "You've got to speak to everyone again. The staff, guests. See if they have alibis for this morning."

"Of course," Elin says evenly. "You'll obviously need to provide information about your whereabouts too."

Her words hang for a few moments unanswered, before Cecile finally replies. "That's fine," she says stiffly. "It's not very exciting. I

374

was alone in my room first thing, and then with a member of staff."

Elin nods. "I'll take the details later. First, I need to ask about CCTV. Is there a camera in the corridor to the lift?"

"No. There should be, but it's gone down."

"The camera?"

"The whole system. Overnight. We're trying to get someone to work on it remotely, but there's a problem with the software. It looks like it's corrupted. The external technician said it could take several days." Her features tense. "Before this, I thought it was a fault, but now . . ."

Elin absorbs her words, a heavy weight settling in her stomach.

The killer's done this.

They've taken out the CCTV: the only thing she could use to try to identify them. Without it, Elin is blind.

She's about to reply when she notices Lucas striding toward them. Holding out the phone, his expression is serious. "It's the police. They want to speak to you."

She takes it from him. "Hello?"

It's Berndt. His voice is muffled. "Elin, I'm sorry, but we're not going to be able to get anyone up to the hotel today. The Groupe d'Intervention has just received an update from the pilot, the METAR —"

"METAR?"

"The radar information for the next few

375

hours. Visibility is below one hundred sixty feet and sustained wind speeds are at sixty knots, gusting to eighty-plus."

As if on cue, the wind howls. It feels like it's pulling at the building, tugging at the foundations. "So you can't come?"

"No," Berndt says awkwardly. "Elin, it's not a choice, it's against regulations. The conditions are so bad they've had to pull the aircraft back into the hangar to prevent damage from any flying objects. It's not looking good down here."

"What about the road?"

"The area around the avalanche is still impassable. We've got people working it on foot, but it'll take several days."

"And there's really no other way?" she persists, the tension she's feeling cutting her words short.

Several beats pass. "Not safely, no." Berndt sounds embarrassed. "The Groupe d'Intervention are highly trained, but they're not qualified high-mountain guides. The best-case scenario is that we get to you tomorrow, unless the weather forecast changes."

"So we're on our own." Her voice falters. Once again, self-doubt taunts her: *I can't do this. I'm not capable.*

"I'm afraid so." There's a hesitation before he speaks again, his voice low. "Elin, please listen. Now that someone else has been killed, the protocol we've advised is extremely important. Everyone needs to stay together. No exceptions."

"Okay." Elin's voice wobbles. She wants to cry — proper tears. This isn't how it's meant to be. She wanted to have this under control.

"I'll call you when I know more about the forecast." Berndt clears his throat. As he says good-bye, Elin's eyes are drawn once again to the lift, to Laure.

Reality hits like a door slamming in her face.

No one's coming. Not now, not in a few hours.

Laure's dead and they're stuck here — no way in, no way out, no idea what's coming next.

She's often thought about this, the risks of a crime in a remote location. How vulnerable people would be, how much damage could be inflicted in a short period of time.

Her mind flickers to the terror attacks in Norway in 2011. Anders Breivik, a right-winger on a rampage, shot at teenagers gathered on the island of Utoya during an annual summer camp. The island's remote location meant that by the time police had reached them, sixty-nine people had already been massacred.

She can't help wondering: *What would the killer here be capable of given the chance?*

Her chain of thought is broken. Lucas's voice: "Hey, look at this."

She glances up, and sees Lucas by the lift,

crouching down beside the glass box.

"What is it?" Walking over to him, Elin is tense, acutely aware of him accidentally touching anything, compromising any evidence. "Please," she says, getting closer, "don't touch the box directly."

"This bracelet here . . . there's something on it. It's faint, but I think they're numbers." Lucas tips his head sideways. "Engraved. Like the bracelets by Adele's body."

Elin kneels down beside him.

"This one." Lucas points to the bracelet on the left. "Look."

He's right.

Five numbers, lightly etched into the metal, so faint you might miss them at first glance.

Elin stares; a lurch of realization.

This means these numbers are significant, surely?

"You think they're important?"

"Yes." Elin's gaze moves back to the box, the next bracelet.

She needs to photograph the numbers, write them down, compare them to the ones she found on the three bracelets near Adele's body.

Positioning her phone, she's about to take a photo when, in the corner of her vision, she catches a movement: Lucas looking over her head toward Cecile.

They exchange a glance before Lucas turns away, his expression troubled.

61

"Sure you've got everything?" Will pushes at the door leading from the penthouse into the stairwell.

"I think so." Elin hesitates, casts one final look toward the lift, to Laure. "I don't think there's anything else I can do."

Before they'd left, she'd taken some final photographs of the scene and of the glass box containing the bracelets, made sure the power was switched off for the lift, but she'd found herself lingering longer than she needed to.

It was instinctive: she hadn't wanted to leave Laure alone in there, isolated.

As Will closes the door behind them, she's stricken again with guilt. She can't shake the feeling that she's failed Laure somehow — missed something vital that might have prevented this.

"I'll get some tape up there later. Cordon it off. Cecile's going to block access through the corridor." Elin stops, registering the expression on Will's face. He's looking at her, but his eyes are distant, like he's thinking about something else. "What's wrong?"

"What do you make of those two? Lucas and Cecile?" He lowers his voice. "There's a funny vibe there."

"In what way?"

"I don't know. I'm probably reading into it, but how they were speaking to each other — it felt strained." He starts down the first step, hand grazing the metal railing. "Must be weird, brother and sister, working together —"

He doesn't get a chance to finish his sentence.

Elin can hear voices. The concrete walls of the stairwell are acting like an echo chamber, funneling the sound upward so it's impossible to tell where exactly they're coming from: it could be two floors down or four.

She peers over the rail. The stairway is dark and the concrete steps dappled in shadow. Two people are standing at the very bottom of the staircase. Only the tops of their heads are visible, but Elin recognizes them immediately.

She freezes, a shiver moving through her spine. *Lucas and Cecile.* They'd been gone for over twenty minutes. *Have they been here all this time?*

Moving swiftly, she motions to Will, puts a finger to her lips.

She steps away from the rail, presses her

back against the wall. Without the sound of their movements, Cecile's and Lucas's voices are more distinct.

They're speaking in French. Short, rapid-fire sentences. Incomprehensible.

Turning to Will, she lowers her voice. "Your French is better than mine. What are they saying?"

"There's some slang," he whispers, "but Cecile's telling him something is serious, and he should tell, and that what happened to Laure . . . it isn't a coincidence."

"And Lucas?"

"He's not happy. He said, 'They don't know anything for sure.' "

What's she missing here? What's going on between the two of them?

Elin's barely breathing.

"Vous devez lui dire."

"Non, non. Je n'ai rien à faire, Cecile. Ne pas oublier, je ne suis pas l'un des equipe ici. Je suis le chef, votre patron."

Elin balks at Lucas's tone. Gone is the laid-back intonation. The words sound aggressive, dominant. She looks at Will.

"Cecile's saying again that he should tell someone, but he's getting pissed off, reminding her that he's the boss."

Stepping out, Elin peers down into the stairwell again. They've changed position, moved from the bottom of the stairs. Lucas's hand is resting on Cecile's arm.

More angry words. Two, three sentences, back and forth.

Silence. The click of footsteps on the floor as they leave.

Will looks at her, his expression troubled. "Cecile just said that she'd tell someone if he didn't."

"Tell what?"

"She didn't say." Will exhales heavily. "What do you make of that?"

"I don't know." She pictures Lucas's hand grasping Cecile's arm, the anger in his voice. She needs time to think and get everything straight in her head.

But before that, she's got to do what she's been dreading the most: speak to Isaac, tell him what's happened to Laure.

"I'm going to tell Isaac alone, if that's okay," Elin says, voicing her thoughts aloud.

"It's fine." Will nods his assent. "I'll do some work."

They make their way down the stairs.

On the final step, the trace of something — vague, ill defined. It nags at the edge of her senses, gone before she can identify it.

She opens the first. A document appears. It's been scanned in — the paper slightly yellowed at the corners, the words typewritten rather than computer generated.

Her eyes dart to the words at the very top of the page: GOTTERDORF KLINIK. There's a date to the left of it: 1923.

Below that are several boxes. The words are in German. *Namen, Geburtsdatum, Krankengeschichte.*

The first two are just within her realm of comprehension — name, date of birth — but the third is beyond her.

Opening another screen, she taps the word into Google Translate — *Krankengeschichte.*
Clinical History.

Her initial instinct is correct — it's a medical file.

But there's a problem: apart from the headers, the rest of the document is redacted. The word itself is marked across a text box in black: REDACTED.

She tries another: *the same thing.*
REDACTED.

The pattern continues. A prickle of frustration: not one of the files contains any actual information — no hint at who the files refer to, their contents.

Then her eyes flicker to the top right of one document, just below where the patient name should be.

ID Nr.

Next to it is a number. Intact. How had she missed it before?

Her heart starts to beat a little faster. The numbers, they're in the same format as those on the bracelets.

A five-digit number.

Elin jumps up, scrabbles in her bag for her notebook. Withdrawing it, she finds the page where she's written down the bracelet numbers they found near Adele's body.

She then looks on her phone for the images of the bracelets found near Laure's. None of the numbers from the photographs match, so she looks back to the notebook.

Four lines down, she finds it: 87534.

Elin stares at the number until the digits cross over one another, trying to take it in: this file, the bracelet, they link. That means this clinic is connected in some way to the killings.

But how?

Opening up another screen, Elin Googles the clinic. The website for it appears at the top of the search.

The short blurb above the link is in German:

Die Klinik Gotterdorf beschäftigt sich mit der Diagnose, Behandlung und Erforschung psychiatrischer Erkrankungen.

Even her nonexistent German tells her that

it's likely to be a psychiatric facility.

But where?

Elin clicks on the contact page. The clinic's address is in Germany.

Going back to the home page, she can see it houses several paragraphs of text. Swiping over it, she plugs it into Google Translate.

We investigate the causes of psychiatric disorders to develop better, personalized therapies as well as preventative approaches. The present clinic, focusing on the treatment of mental illness, grew out of the hospital founded in 1872.

Immediate confirmation: it was, and still is, a psychiatric facility.

Why would Laure be carrying around redacted files from a German psychiatric clinic?

Elin knows there's only one way to find out. Scrolling down to find the clinic's contact details, she picks up her phone, dials. It rings only a few times before a woman picks up.

"Guten Tag, Gotterdorf Klinik." Her voice is clipped, professional.

Again, Elin curses her inability with languages. It's always been her nemesis. She took both French and German in high school, could read it adequately enough, but struggled to speak more than a few words.

"Do you speak English?"

"Of course." The woman switched with

ease. "How may I help?"

"My name is Elin Warner, I'm a police officer in the UK. I'm working on a case and I've found some redacted files that appear to be from your clinic, dating back to the 1920s. I was wondering how I could go about finding out more."

A long pause. "I'm sorry, I would like to help, but any request for file information has to be done formally. As you're probably aware, patient confidentiality precludes us from sharing any information."

She'd been expecting this. "I understand, but could you give me an idea of what the records might contain?"

"Wait one moment, please." Elin can hear the rustling of paper, murmured voices in the background.

"Yes," the woman says finally. "There is no problem telling you this. For each patient we have records of everything from the very first signs of the pathology and initial diagnosis, leading through to the hospital treatment they received before being admitted to the clinic. Once they're at the clinic, we start our own records — medication, treatments, the patient's responses."

Elin exhales. "These files we've found, as they date from the 1920s, would they be paper or electronic files?"

"Both. We've made electronic copies of everything that was filed on paper."

She decides to push her luck. "Would it be possible to check if you definitively do still have these on file? I have what I assume is a patient number." She keeps her voice neutral. "I don't need any information regarding their contents, just confirmation they do belong to the clinic and are authentic."

A hesitation, then: "Okay. Can I please have the number?"

Pulling the file back up on the screen, she spells it out. "87534."

"Thank you. Please wait a moment. I'll see if I can find it."

She can hear the woman's fingers lightly tapping the keyboard.

There's a sudden, sharp intake of breath.

Elin stiffens. *She's found something.*

Several beats pass before the woman speaks again. "There is a file with a number matching the one you've given me, but I'm sorry, it's been" — her voice catches — "it's been removed."

"The record's gone?" Elin's unable to keep the surprise from her voice.

"Yes, but I'm sure there's been a mistake, that's all." The woman clears her throat. "I'm sorry I couldn't be of any more assistance."

A sharp click.

She's hung up, but not before Elin caught the alarm in her tone. Her hand clenches around her mobile. *This is no coincidence.*

Whatever is recorded in these files is clearly significant enough for someone to go to great efforts to make sure the information doesn't get into the wrong hands.

But what is it? And how did Laure get hold of the files in the first place?

Elin puts her fingers to her temple. However she positions it, it all comes back to one thing: She's at a disadvantage, scrabbling around for answers to questions she isn't even sure are the right ones to be asking.

It doesn't help, she knows, that she's doing this on her own with no one to bounce ideas off. While she has Berndt over the phone, it's not the same. With her team, there's not only a shorthand but a vital chemistry that can ignite a spark of investigative brilliance that's often key to cracking a case. One of the team's seemingly simple questions or observations can set off a chain of thought that can spin a case in a completely new direction.

Scrolling through her phone, she finds the e-mail Berndt sent containing Laure's mobile phone records.

She opens the first file and pores over the screen. Laure called more or less the same numbers regularly: Isaac, her mother, sister, cousin, several others that have been identified as friends. There are no unusual call patterns in the lead-up to her disappearance.

Elin opens the next file, records from Laure's second phone, but soon puts it down, frustrated. The call pattern is interesting — clusters of calls to the same number over the past few weeks, including one that was likely to be the call in French Elin overheard the day they arrived, but it's next to useless. If there's no way to track the phone Laure had been calling, there's nothing she can do about it.

Sliding her notebook toward her, she reads through the brief statements she'd got from the staff and guests after Adele's murder.

Have I missed anything vital? Some other

*connection between someone I'd spoken to and
Laure and Adele?*

But as she sifts through her notes, she's
struck, once again, by how straightforward
the statements are. Everyone's alibis are in
order, nothing flagged as suspicious or note-
worthy leading up to Adele's death.

The only thing she can go on is what she's
deduced so far. She needs to write it down,
get it straight in her head. She starts with the
crimes:

— Two female victims, both working in the
hotel, similar ages

Listing everything she's found out about
both Laure and Adele, she starts with Adele:

— No issues with friends, family, her ex. No
current partner. (NO OBVIOUS MOTIVE)

— No problems at work apart from the
broken friendship with Laure (Axel overheard argument between them, Felisa
confirmed issues between them)

Next, she thinks through everything she
knows about Laure. A longer list:

— The argument on the phone the first night
(possibly to burner phone)

— Laure's second phone — who did the

396

He's right; she did need something: the hot, bitter liquid immediately pushes through the fog in her head.

"Have you told Berndt about the files?"

"No. I haven't even told him about the memory stick. I meant to, but . . ." She trails off, hearing the flimsy excuse. She hadn't meant to, not really. She wanted to follow it up herself — lead, take action. "I don't think I can now. If he knows I've called the clinic without asking them . . ."

Will frowns. "You think he'd stop you investigating?"

"It's possible. They've only authorized me to carry out the most basic investigation." She hesitates. "I honestly don't think I can cross-check every action I take with them. We haven't got time."

"And you've got no other way of finding out what's on the files?"

"No, but I did find something significant." Raising a finger to the file on the screen, she points to the patient number. "There's a number on the file, one of the only things that isn't redacted."

"A patient number?"

"Yes. It matches the number on one of the bracelets in the display box from Adele's murder."

"So these files" — he raises an eyebrow — "they connect with the killings?"

"Yes." She's unable to keep the excitement

403

from her voice. "I think they tell us something. Bring everything together."

"But if you don't know what's in them . . ."

"It doesn't matter. What's important is that we know they connect to the killings, and that we know *what* they are."

He frowns. "You're losing me."

"The fact that they're medical files, it's got to be important. Until now, I've been thinking in terms of the hotel, the relationships among the people here as a potential motive for the murders, but I think that's wrong. I don't think it's about the hotel at all. I think it's about what it *used* to be."

"The sanatorium?" Will pulls up a chair. She's got his attention now.

"Yes. Think about how the murders were staged, the props. The mask, the display box, the bracelets . . . it's like the killer is trying to draw our attention to something." She jabs at the screen again. "It's the hotel's past, isn't it? Its *clinical* past, the sanatorium. These medical files, when they're dated, they connect it."

"That makes sense," Will says carefully, "but where do you go from here?"

"I need to check everyone's alibi. See if there are any inconsistencies. I can't check CCTV as it's down."

"But what if everyone has an alibi? You still don't have any other concrete leads."

Elin picks up her coffee, takes a long drink.

if they were connected?

"Why didn't Lucas want you to tell me this?"

"The official answer would be that the information hasn't been made public yet, but I'll be honest, he isn't thinking straight. He's trying to contain this, but it's impossible." Cecile's voice is thin with frustration. "It's gone too far."

"Contain it?" Elin repeats, incredulous.

"Yes. What's happened here, it could be disastrous for him, not only professionally, but personally too. This place is more than work for him. Building this hotel has been his dream since he was young. His illness, being in and out of the hospital . . . it gave him this *drive.*"

"His heart troubles?"

"Like I said before, there were several operations, complications, long recovery times. He didn't have a normal childhood. When he did go back to school, he had a hard time."

"Bullying?"

"Yes. He didn't look right, you know?" Her tone is bitter. "Weak, thin. Half the children teased him and the rest pitied him."

"That's stayed with him?"

"I think so. This place . . . he's never said it, but I think it's about exorcising those ghosts. It was the impossible project. Someplace everyone said could never be resurrected." Cecile shrugs. "Like him. No one thought he'd become what he has."

"A point to prove," Elin replies. "It's the same with Isaac. He's always had that need to be the best. The one on top." She frowns. "It probably stems from an insecurity too."

"I don't think it's exclusive to them. That desire to prove yourself. Be something." A smile plays on Cecile's lips. "You know, I read somewhere once that most men want to build a monument to themselves. My ex did. When he met his new wife, he moved to Australia, built his own house in the middle of no-where." She turns, gestures around her. "This is it, isn't it? Lucas's monument. A giant, beautiful, glass fuck-you monument to all those people who said he couldn't."

Elin doesn't reply, taken aback by the strength of Cecile's emotion, her protective-ness. It flips what she saw in the stairwell on its head. She can't help seeing Lucas in a different light. A more favorable light.

Yet something's nagging at her about how Cecile's talking about him. The same feeling she has when she examines her own feelings for Isaac: that while protecting them, they're also excusing them, finding answers for their shitty behavior when perhaps there shouldn't be any.

"I think that's why he's been holding back." Cecile glances around the room. "The idea that this place could fail — I don't think he

412

can even contemplate it."

Elin considers what she's said, and while the reasoning makes sense, it still feels unconvincing. Even if he wants to protect the hotel, surely his first instinct would be to share what he knew?

There has to be something more to this.

"You said before, that Lucas and Daniel were close."

The statement seems to throw Cecile. Her face closes momentarily before she shrugs. "Yes. Look, you should probably speak to him about it."

Elin picks up on the way Cecile's closed down the conversation. Up until this point, she's been open. Forthcoming.

There's something here.

"They were still good friends, though?"

A hesitation. Cecile flushes. "No," she says finally. "I wouldn't describe them as good friends. The relationship in the past few years was more professional than anything else. Daniel's firm had worked on several of Lucas's hotels."

"But you said they *were* close?"

"As children, yes, but when Lucas got ill . . . it changed. Daniel got close to my father. He was a talented skier and my parents used to watch him race. I think Lucas always felt there was a comparison there. Something he had to live up to. It was one of

413

those things. As they got older, they grew apart."

"But the relationship must have been solid enough for them to want to work together?"

"Yes, but to be honest, I think they were both regretting it."

"What do you mean?"

"There were some arguments, the last few months before Daniel went missing. The strain on them both was immense — the opposition to the build, the complaints . . ." Her face looks pinched. "A couple of days before he went missing, he and Lucas had a fight."

"About what?"

"I don't know. Lucas has never gone into detail about it."

Elin thinks about what she's said. Despite the story behind it, her empathy for what Lucas went through as a child, it would be stupid to ignore the fact that he had a possible motive, however tenuous, for not only Laure's death but Daniel's too.

"So what was it you were looking for?" Cecile changes the subject. "I —"

There's a loud rap on the door, then another.

Cecile opens it. A woman in her late twenties is standing outside. She's wearing a staff uniform, her fair hair twisted into a loose bun, strands falling messily over her face.

"I'm sorry," she starts, her words emerging

414

with a strong French accent. "I don't want to disturb, but . . ." Her lip trembles.

"It's fine, Sara." Stepping forward, Cecile gently touches her arm.

Elin looks at her, a horrible feeling of trepidation weighing heavy in her stomach.

Something's happened.

"It's just, just —" Sara's face is flushed, blotchy. "Margot. I can't find her." Any pretense at holding it together is lost as she starts to cry, a throaty sob that makes her chest heave. "I think she's missing. I haven't seen her since last night."

68

"Missing?" Cecile repeats, catching Elin's eye.

Still crying, Sara gives a tight nod. "I've checked everywhere. I can't find her." She folds, refolds her hands. "After what's happened . . ."

Cecile steps forward, out into the corridor, her movements jerky. Elin senses she's struggling to keep it together. "Sara, I know it's hard, but please tell us what you know."

"I'll try," she says. "Margot and I, we're sharing a room. When I woke up this morning, she was gone. I thought right away that something was wrong, but I told myself I was being stupid, imagining things, that she just got up early —" She stops; takes a hiccupy gulp of air. "I'm not sure, but her side of the room . . . it looks like there's been a struggle."

"You've asked other people if they've seen her?"

"Yes, that's what I've being doing this morning. No one has. There's only a few of us left; if she was about, someone would have seen her."

"What about her phone?" Cecile asks.

"It's gone, but she's not answering."

"But there are staff in the corridor to the rooms." Cecile sounds hesitant, uncertain. "No one can go in and out without them seeing."

"I know." Sara's eyes are dark. "But she's gone. I know she has." Her voice is now high-pitched, panicky. "I've looked everywhere."

Elin stands very still, absorbing her words. *It's another one. It has to be.*

She doesn't like it. This timing, so soon after Laure . . . it seems like it's becoming something frenzied, spiraling out of control.

Fear uncoiling in her stomach, she looks at Sara. "We need to take a look at your room. Right away."

Sara's bedroom is only three down from hers. It's an identical layout, but with twin beds.

"This is hers." Sara gestures to the bed closest to the door.

Elin follows her gaze, exchanges a look with Cecile.

Sara's right — there's clear evidence of a struggle. Ivory sheets, snarled in a tangled knot, have been ripped from the bed. A glass tumbler is lying on its side on the floor, the dribbled remains of water pooled next to it together with a book — a *Livre de Poche,* rent at the spine.

It's as if she's been dragged from the bed, Elin thinks.

"This is my fault." Sara puts a hand to her lip, picks at the dry skin around the edges. "I have problems sleeping. I take pills, wear an eye mask and earplugs." She shakes her head. "Anyone else, they would have heard."

"It's not your fault," Elin replies, eyes still traveling around the room, finding more things near Margot's bed — a creased bookmark several feet away from the sheet, a shoulder bag tipped on its side. "We don't know what's happened, not yet."

Sara rubs at her swollen eyes. "But that's not true, is it?" Her voice is brittle, accusing. "Whoever killed Adele has Margot, too, haven't they?"

Elin keeps her tone neutral. "Like I said, we can't assume anything."

But even to her ears, her words sound weak. Hollow. Looking at the scene in front of her, she's pretty certain about what's happened.

Either the killer took Margot in the night, before they abducted Laure, or just after. Either way, it doesn't look good.

Sara turns away, shoulders heaving.

Elin reaches out, lightly touches her arm. "Sara, I know it's hard, but I'd like to go through your movements yesterday, before you went to bed."

Taking a deep breath, composing herself,

418

Sara says: "We had dinner with everyone else, in the dining room. Sat for a while, chatted." She gives a weak smile. "It's all everyone's doing at the moment. Talking. Drinking. No one wants to go to bed."

"And then?" Elin prompts.

"We came upstairs, back to the room. I watched something on Netflix, Margot was reading." Her words come out rapidly, still heavily accented. Elin has to listen carefully to understand her. "We switched the light off at about eleven thirty."

"And this is what you found when you woke up?"

Sara nods. "I haven't touched anything. I got dressed, came straight downstairs, started looking for her."

"And when was that?"

"Close to ten. I slept in."

Elin works it through in her mind. *Ten.* That meant it was possible that Margot was abducted *after* the incident with Laure in the penthouse. A slim possibility given the fact that more people would have been around at that time, but not impossible.

The more likely option, however, was that she was abducted overnight. Yet one thing about that theory doesn't stack up: there was a member of staff acting as security, outside the rooms all night.

How would the killer have got past him?

Opening the door, Elin walks down the cor-

419

ridor toward him. He's young; his face still chubby, faint pockmarks scarring his nose, his cheeks.

"Is everything okay?" he asks, but the ignorance implied by his question is belied by the nervous glance toward Sara's room.

He knows what's going on. He knows and he's scared.

"Were you here all last night?"

"Most of it." He moistens his lips with his tongue. "I came on just after eleven. No one came down the corridor while I was here." He gestures at the silver flask next to him. "That stuff, it's like rocket fuel."

"You're sure? You didn't hear anything?"

"Nothing. Only guests, staff, coming back to their rooms."

Elin presses her forefinger into her palm. *Think, Elin, think. How could the attacker get into the room without being seen?*

Could the killer be someone Margot or Sara knew? Perhaps Margot let them in unawares, meaning the attacker was able to get into the room without raising suspicion.

Elin thanks him and goes back to Sara's room, scans the space again.

Am I missing anything?

Her gaze settles on the French doors.

She carefully makes her way toward them and stops just short of the doors themselves, bends down. Tipping her head at an angle, she looks at the floor.

Her pulse quickens. She can see the faint, smeared ghost of a footprint, where the wet sole print has dried, leaving a residue.

She straightens to examine the doorframe. There are small marks in the wood — they'd jimmied it open.

That's how they got in.

Shaking her head, she feels a surge of frustration. The precautions they'd taken to keep people safe had made it easier for the killer, hadn't they? By moving everyone onto the lower floors, it was easier to climb up. Easier to escape.

"Found something?" Cecile calls from the other side of the room.

Elin gives a sharp nod. "I think they came in through these doors."

As she opens them, freezing air fills the room. With it comes the high-pitched whistle of the wind, a bitter blast of snow.

All she can see is white; the trees in the distance are bleached by snow.

When she scans the terrace, she can see straightaway that the snow has been disturbed — it's compacted, a bumpy, uneven layer. Even though fresh snow has fallen on top, started to fill in some of the marks, she can still see definite compressions.

It's hard to make out what it is — not footprints. Something bigger, wider.

Analyzing the blurred outline, she takes in the shape.

The marks start to resolve.

It's the imprint of something big, heavy: a body.

Margot was dragged.

Elin processes it: if she was dragged out of the room, this implies she was sedated too.

A sharp jab of realization: *They didn't have long.*

If they wanted to find her, they had to be quick. Based on the last two killings, the potential escalation, the killer would probably act fast. Ruthlessly.

She takes a deep breath, turns back to face Cecile and Sara. Before she even starts to speak, Sara shakes her head, a strangled noise coming from her throat.

"You think they've taken her, don't you?" She buries her face in her hands. "The person who . . ." Sobs pull at her chest, shoulders.

Cecile puts an arm around her. "Look, let's go down to the lounge, sit for a while. You've had a shock." Glancing at Elin, she mouths: "Is that all right?"

Elin nods, her gaze already snapping back to the snow outside, and the curious flattened pattern of compressions.

If they'd gone out this way, the marks wouldn't stop there, would they?

But the thought — obvious, too obvious — bothers her.

Surely the killer wouldn't have been so stupid as to leave a trail? A way of tracking them down?

Unless they didn't have a choice.

Perhaps the killer had needed to improvise, like they had in the penthouse. It's possible they'd planned to get Margot out through the corridor, but something had gone wrong.

The other explanation, one that's more likely, is that the killer is getting careless. Either way, it's a lead. Something that might direct them to Margot.

69

It takes longer than she thinks to make her way back to her room, pull on her coat. Her fingers fumble over the room pass, her zipper, while her mind churns.

Is this a good idea? Should I even consider going out alone? Should I speak to Berndt first?

Elin immediately discounts the thought: contacting Berndt, talking him through it, will not only waste precious time but risk him forbidding her to look for Margot altogether. She knows that if she doesn't contact him, she can't be accused of explicitly defying any instructions.

Picking up some gloves together with several of the plastic bags Lucas provided, she pulls open the French doors, making her way out onto the terrace.

The outside world grabs her: her boots immediately sinking into the thick powder snow, the wind pulling her hair around her face.

She examines the glass balustrade in front of her.

Can I get over it?

It's not particularly high, but it won't be easy.

She lifts up her leg, and tries to scramble over it, but immediately gets caught, one leg hanging over, the other left behind.

Elin tries again. She does it this time, but hoisting herself up and over takes effort — the strength of both her arms and her thighs.

How would the killer have got Margot over this? Sedated, she'd have been a dead weight.

Safely on the other side, Elin exhales hard from the exertion. She's made one deduction, however small: the killer has to be strong, she thinks, watching her breath emerge as white vapor, quickly being dissolved to nothing by the wind. Capable of lifting someone quickly and easily.

Snow is falling heavily. It's claustrophobic. Suffocating. She can barely see more than a few feet ahead, nothing visible in the whiteness except the outline of the frosted trees, the geometrical shapes of Le Sommet's signage beyond.

The weather forecast was right — the storm is getting worse.

Steeling herself, she steps forward, then pauses, hearing a low rumble.

A rumble that's followed by an enormous boom, reverberating through the air.

There's a roar, a sudden, arctic breeze.

Her mind immediately lurches to what Will

had told her earlier: *an avalanche.*

She's read that you hear one before you see it. As the snow and ice fall down the mountain, they exert a huge force on the air, compressing it into a terrifying low whistle.

Elin can hear that now, a deafening piercing sound, cutting right through her.

Panic biting, she surges forward toward the hotel, starts to retrace her steps, but it's a futile decision: she has no idea whether she's heading into the path of the avalanche or leaving it behind.

But within seconds Elin knows she made the right call.

It's just missed me. I'm still standing.

But she's swallowed by what can only be the aftermath: a white cloud of snow that's been kicked into the air from the force of the fall.

Tiny, glittering particles hit her face. It's bitter, stinging.

Blinking, she wipes the snow away, but she can't see a thing; only more snow.

It'll take a few minutes to settle, for her to see exactly where the avalanche fell.

Heart pounding, she waits, terrified, for the next ominous sound, the next rumble that might come even closer.

But nothing comes — only the cloud of snow, glimmering particles still suspended and falling slowly through the air. Elin breathes slowly in and out, but she's shaky, it. I'm pretty sure she keeps her passwords in her diary."

"Not exactly security conscious, then?"

"No." Sara smiles weakly. "We were joking about it the other day. Her Apple account got hacked so she needed to change her password, but the new one was too hard to remember, so she wrote it down."

"Do you know where her diary is?"

"Whose diary?" Cecile takes a seat beside them.

Sara hesitates. Her eyes lock on Elin's, a flicker of understanding passing between them.

"Margot's," she says clearly. "She keeps it in her bag. I'll show you."

"This feels weird —" Sara puts Margot's bag on the bed, starts rummaging through it. "Like I'm invading her privacy."

"I know," Elin says softly. "But we need to do everything we can to find her." She watches Sara pull the contents from the bag — purse, hair grips, a half-empty bottle of water, chewing gum. The final thing to emerge is a leather-bound notebook.

"This is it. She doesn't use an actual diary." After flicking through the pages, Sara stops near the front of the book. "There." She points to the top of the page. "I think this is the password."

Elin reaches for her phone, and finds the

Elin shrugs, tensing. She knows she's not doing a very good job at hiding her annoyance, but she'd never been any good at diplomacy. She always let things pick away at her, fester, took them so deep inside, they imprinted themselves on her face.

Blueprints of emotion.

Cecile's speaking into the phone in rapid French. A few moments later, she turns back, slips her phone into her pocket, her expression troubled.

"Lucas doesn't think you should do this on your own." Her mouth is tight. "Put yourself in a vulnerable situation."

"What do you mean?" Elin falters.

"He thinks it's too risky." Cecile's speaking slowly, as if she's speaking to someone stupid. "I —" She breaks off, flushing. "Look, it's hard to say this, but I agree with him. You've been a huge help, but after what's happened to Laure, to you, you're probably not in the right frame of mind to take on anything now. I think we should wait for the police."

"The police?" Elin repeats, incredulous. "But we know they're not coming, not soon, anyway." She curls up her hand under the table, squeezes hard so that she can feel her nails nudging against her palm. A warning: *Don't lose it. Don't say something you might regret.*

"So you've called Berndt? Told him about Margot?"

436

Elin shakes her head. "Not yet."

Cecile looks back at her, her gaze steadfast, neutral. Something loaded is carried in the glance. "I'm sorry." Her palms are raised, apologetic. "I'm going to have to be honest. I didn't want to be the one to say this, but Lucas . . . he's found out about your job."

"My job?" Her mouth is dry. *They know.*

Cecile nods. "Lucas found out earlier that you're on extended leave. He's uncomfortable with you carrying on in the circumstances. You didn't mention it. If you'd have told us, explained . . ."

"But that doesn't affect my ability to help you." Elin's heart is lunging in her chest: hard, knocking thuds.

They've found me out, exposed me as a fraud.

"I'm sorry," Cecile repeats, dropping her gaze. "It's Lucas's call." There's a grim finality to her tone.

Elin glances down at the floor, trying to tamp her anger down. Familiar doubts start crowding her head, jostling for position.

Are they right? Is my judgment flawed?

She stands up. "I'm going to my room."

She walks away, concentrating carefully on each step, as if any break in rhythm would shatter her self-control, force her back to the room full of angry recriminations.

72

"Calm down," Will murmurs. "Just tell me
exactly what she said."

Pacing, she walks down the length of their
room toward the window and back again.
"That she didn't think I should carry on, look
for Margot. That I'm 'not in the right frame
of mind.' " She fumbles, the memory of Cecile's words making her face burn. "They
found out, Will. That I'm on leave . . ."

Will reaches for her arm. "Perhaps they're
right. Maybe it's better to wait for the police."

"The police? There's been another avalanche, Will. They aren't going to get to us
anytime soon, not unless the wind drops and
they can get a helicopter up."

His words are slow, careful. "What did
Berndt say?"

"I haven't called him." Elin doesn't meet
his eye. "He probably won't approve of me
trying to find Margot, not without backup,
and I don't know how much he knows about
my job. He could pull me from the whole

438

thing." She hesitates. "In any case, it doesn't work, waiting for them to arrive. The killer might have hurt Margot by then, and it's a risk — the killer might see the police arrive. We'll lose the element of surprise."

"You're right." Will pinches the bridge of his nose, pushing up his glasses. "I just keep thinking about what happened in the penthouse. The close call with the avalanche earlier." His voice wobbles. "If anything were to happen to you . . ."

"I'll be fine. Careful." Elin pulls him toward her. "Will, I wouldn't do this if I didn't think it was right. This situation's gone beyond anything I imagined. I won't take any unnecessary risks."

"Fine," he says abruptly, making her look up in surprise. "Look for her, but whatever it is you're planning, you're not going alone. You haven't stopped since this morning. You're tired, haven't eaten anything."

She pulls away, taken aback. Is he doubting her? Like Cecile and Lucas?

"Will, I'm trained for situations like this. What happened before was different. I wasn't expecting it, my judgment was skewed because of my relationship with Laure, but with this, I'm on the offensive. I know the precautions to take."

"Elin, there isn't any more to it, okay? I just don't want you doing it on your own."

She doesn't speak for several seconds. When

flicks the screen with an upward motion to find the flashlight function.

It comes on, but the light is pitiful: hardly enough to illuminate her hand.

Will pulls her back. "Elin, we can't do this. We can't see a thing." His voice is strained. "Someone's done this deliberately. I don't like it."

Elin moves the flashlight to his face. The narrow pocket of light picks up the shadows under his eyes, the slick sheen of sweat on his forehead.

I shouldn't have brought him. He's panicking.

"You go back. I'm going to keep searching." She lowers her voice to a whisper. "If someone has done this on purpose, it means we're close."

The muscles in his neck visibly tighten. "Not without you."

They inch forward, stepping lightly, carefully, following the line of the wall, but the huge bulk of the machinery makes it hard to navigate. They have to keep alert, constantly adjusting their path.

Each machine seems to make a different noise: some churning, whirring, others like an insect flying, the humming of frantic wings.

A few steps on and the space widens, but not by much. Elin can make out several narrow corridors weaving between the machinery.

thighs, butto
crashes to the
but it stays on
dimly light the

Elin cries out
jags of pain m
are making her

When her ga
standing over
The ties are ha
ankles.

For a momel
going on.

Has Margot n
Her attacker?

Then it hits I

Elin raises her arm, moves the phone around in a circle. The light illuminates the metal boxing around the machinery.

There's nothing here.

She's about to start moving again when, somewhere in front of her, there's a noise. The sound startles her, sends her phone crashing to the floor.

Bending down, she fumbles, picks it up. It's intact; the light is still glowing.

She pivots, about to speak to Will when she hears another sound: a soft scrape.

Elin turns the phone so the beam is positioned in front of her. In the weak, dull glow of the light, she can make out a shape on the floor — a figure.

Steadying the beam, she sucks in her breath.

Margot.

She's lying on the floor, huddled in a semi-fetal position, legs curled up beneath her. Her head is tipped away from Elin so she can't make out her face.

There are no other sounds, no movement, but even so, she keeps moving the flashlight in a circle, walking a few yards past Margot to see if anyone's there, in the shadows beyond.

No one.

Elin exhales slowly, heavily, relieved.

It's possible this is simply a holding place. If so, there might be a chance to get Margot away before the killer returns.

Crossing the
yards, she keep
This close, she
are bound. A r
taut between h
Will stays b:
around.
Elin sets the
the light facing
Margot so she
Elin.”
Margot look
vacant. Her f;
patchy black :
cheeks.
“Margot, you
get you out.”
But she make
Margot’s hear
stare, with thos
She’s in sho
sedated.
Elin picks up
got’s feet, glan
ankles. “I’m g(
get you back u]
But all at on
ment that’s imp
Margot strike
Elin’s legs co]
Unable to rij
hard, a shock

74

Elin scrambles to her feet. Panicked, she rears up, takes several steps back.

I’ve got this wrong, again. All my theories, ideas, about Lucas, Isaac, they’re wrong.

Her eyes shift toward the ties hanging limp around Margot’s wrists and ankles. She wasn’t properly tied: the knots were loose enough for her to simply pull them free.

This whole thing . . . it was a setup.

“You. You did this.” Elin can hardly get the words out. Her head feels leaden, unbalanced.

Margot doesn’t reply. She simply looks at Elin, her eyes empty, unreadable.

Dread swells in Elin’s chest: there’s no trace of the awkward, unsure person she met just a few days ago: hunched, ashamed of her body. Margot’s standing tall — her full height, over six feet. Her strength, her musculature, is clearly visible.

It’s possible, isn’t it? She could have done this. Abducted people. Killed them.

Margot reaches down, grabs the phone. She points it at Elin's face. The light is blinding, dazzling her.

Where's Will?

Elin blinks, tries to shake the searing bright spot away.

"Yes," Margot finally replies. "It was me." Her voice is cold, emotionless, all warmth stripped out of it.

"No one abducted you, did they? This was a trap, like the message from Laure. You planned the whole thing." Elin's mind gropes backward, spooling through the events of the past few days, trying to find connections.

Was any of what Margot told me true?

Isaac and Laure's relationship? Laure's altercation with Lucas? She'd been so gullible. Swallowed Margot's anecdotes whole, without question.

Margot reads her hesitation correctly, a cold half smile playing on her lips. "Don't worry. You made the same mistakes anyone would, human mistakes. The ego always wins. It's a weakness in everyone, the desire to know the most, be the hero, the one to save the day. It's why you did the job you did."

Despite her shock, her fear, Elin feels a surge of anger.

How dare Margot judge her?

Margot takes another step toward her.

For the first time, Elin can see a knife in her hand, the blade glinting in the flashlight.

She feels sweat prickling her back, a slow trickle between her shoulder blades.

Her mind races: *Where's Will? What's he doing?*

"I don't understand," she says, playing for time. "What's all this about?"

"The truth." Margot's voice is robotic. "This place is poison. It shouldn't have opened again." She takes another step forward, now only inches away from Elin. "I'm sorry. You weren't meant to be involved."

Elin stiffens. It's chilling how matter-of-fact Margot is, even in her heightened state. She's cold, mechanical. Elin is an obstacle, so she needs to be removed.

"Margot, it doesn't have to be like this. You don't have to hurt me, or anyone else. We can end this here."

But it's as if Margot can't hear her. In one smooth motion, she raises her hand, draws the knife high, her features blank, expressionless. She's like an automaton: nothing's going to stop her now.

Elin recoils, her breathing shallow. Her head starts to spin.

"Please, Margot, no . . ."

Margot lurches forward. The action is sharp, decisive, the blade cutting cleanly through the air.

Elin twists to the side, the knife only narrowly missing her face.

But the movement doesn't throw Margot

— she springs forward, making easy work of the space that's opened up between them.

It's now that Will makes his move: a blur of motion.

Leaping forward, he shoves Margot sideways. The phone ricochets from her hand, hitting the floor.

This time, they're plunged into total darkness.

Silence, then Elin hears a sickening crack, the dull thud of something striking the floor.

There's a struggle: movement, scuffling, grunts, the sound of fabric ripping, tearing. A low moan. Another, softer thud; something sliding across the floor.

Only a few moments later, another sound: footsteps, heavy thuds in the darkness, labored breaths.

Elin's heart lurches, a slick, oily dread loosening her stomach.

She knows right away that the footsteps aren't Will's.

Will wouldn't run away. Will wouldn't leave me.

Whatever it is that's been holding her together until that point fractures. She's seized by a sudden, bottomless fear.

"Will!" Her voice is high, untethered. "Can you hear me?"

He doesn't reply.

Elin knows instantly that it's not because he doesn't want to.

staunch the flow of blood. "I'll be okay, Will. It'll be okay."

75

Elin can't equate the pale figure in the bed with the Will she knows. There's no sparkle, none of his usual zest for life — the uncoiled energy always threatening to spring free. She's not sure if her mind's playing tricks on her, but his breathing sounds staccato, unsteady.

Inching forward, she reaches out a hand, laying it across his. It doesn't move; he doesn't register the weight of her fingers.

Her breath catches as she watches him. His head is tilted to the left, the dark blond of his hair limp against the pillow. His face is drained of color, the familiar lines between his features flattened, lain smooth. There's purple bruising to his face, in addition to multiple small contusions.

A blanket is pulled high over his waist, covering the wound. It's deep, but it had missed major organs and arteries.

Once they'd got him up to the room, Sara, a trained nurse, had dealt with it efficiently, thoroughly. She'd cleaned the wound, dressed it, administered basic painkillers and sedation, but he'll need proper treatment soon — antibiotics and monitoring.

Elin freezes. His breathing's changed again: a heavy rasp before settling back into the unsteady rhythm of before. The animalistic noise triggers something inside her — panic. *This is my fault. I'm responsible.*

Stepping back from the bed, she narrows her eyes, hopes to change the perspective, make the scene something different.

It works: time tips, folds back on itself. Not to Will, but to Sam.

She can picture him like this, laid out beside the rock pool. He looked the same as always: pale, skinny body, matted white hair, but there was something blank about him, as if something hungry had found its way inside him, scraped him clean.

She remembers feeling hot, then angry. In her childish selfishness, she'd expected *more,* an expression on his face — some kind of sign that he was sad to have gone, to have left her, but there was nothing. Only a void. It's the same now, with Will.

Her shoulders start to heave.

"He'll be okay." Isaac grasps her hand. "We got him out in time."

Only just, Elin thinks, images flickering through her head: the smeared blood on her hands, the floor. Calling Isaac, slippery fingers fumbling over her phone.

Details of what followed escape her. Fragmented pictures: Sara treating him on the filthy floor, staff moving around him — a continuous loop of bodies, shouted instructions.

"Elin, as soon as the medics get here, they'll take him to the hospital. He'll be fine." Isaac tries to meet her gaze, but she looks away.

She can't stop thinking it over, the same words on loop:

Will's in that bed because of me. Because of what I did.

He'd wanted to go with her, protect her, and she'd failed him. "I did this to him, Isaac. I rushed into it. He warned me —"

"Elin, don't."

"No. It's true. I pulled him into this. I've been a crap girlfriend. It's not just this, I've been messing up ever since we got together. I've kept him at arm's length, never let him get close . . ." Her voice catches. "What if something happens? He takes a turn for the worse? I've never told him how I feel, not properly."

Elin stops, puts her fingers to her temple.

Something strange is in her head: a blizzard of emotion, feelings crisscrossing, misfiring.

Isaac's looking at her, his face suffused with embarrassment, fear. Isaac, who's never lost for words, is struggling. His own grief mirrors hers; it's too much to handle. He, like her, is coming unstuck.

His mouth moves, starts to make words, but none come out, either that or she can't hear them. There's a strange distance; the world is receding to a pinpoint — a familiar, liquid blackness. A familiarity. The breath in her lungs is being replaced with something denser, heavier — a boulder rolling inside her chest.

"I can't do this, Isaac, I can't." Her breaths are falling over themselves, stunted, half formed. She tries to focus on the picture on the wall: the abstract slashes of paint, but the lines won't resolve.

"Elin? Have you got your inhaler?"

She closes her eyes. Darkness. She senses a burst of movement, a hand in her pockets, then close to her mouth. Blocky plastic against her lips, her teeth.

"Breathe in." There's a sudden rush of gas, cool, dry in her mouth.

It only takes seconds. Her chest starts to loosen, her breathing softening.

Head still swimming, she turns to Isaac. "Sorry, I —"

"It's fine." He takes her arm, propels her backward, onto the sofa. "I had no idea your asthma was this bad."

Elin draws herself upright. For a few, fleeting moments, she considers lying, but she knows she can't. Lies on top of more lies — it can't carry on.

"Isaac, this . . . it isn't asthma now, not entirely. I mean, I still have it, but it's under control. What happened then was a panic attack. They've been worse this past year, since Mum, the case I told you about." She gestures to the inhaler in his hand. "That, it helps, obviously, but in a way it's a prop. A comfort blanket."

He looks at her, his gaze steady, penetrating. "When did this start?"

"With Sam. You were right, what you said before, about me always having to look for answers. It's because of Sam. All this, it goes back to him. Every case I'm working on, I'm looking for answers, but Sam's is the one I keep coming back to. I just want to know what happened. The truth, so I can move on."

The words come out in a rush, a torrent. Words she's wanted to say for so long. Isaac makes a frustrated noise. He looks at her, his eyes red, bloodshot.

"Elin, stop, please. Stop doing this."

"Stop what?"

"Endlessly bringing things back to that day. Even now, with Will like that." He jerks a hand toward the bed. "Sam died, and there's nothing we can do about it. You think I don't go over and over it in my mind all the time as well? I look at photos of him and I want to pull him out, physically reach in, make him real again, but he's never going to be. He's not here. You've got to accept it. Move on."

"Isaac —" She stops, taken aback. *How can he do that?* Take this self-righteous tone when all this comes back to *him*.

"What? It's true. I can't bear seeing you like this. You're a shadow of who you used to be. No one blames you, Elin. No one. I didn't want to have to say it, but I think it's what you need to hear."

Elin stares at him. "Blames me? For what?" Her voice is high. "All this, it's because of you, Isaac. What you did that day to Sam. That's what's been holding me back."

"Me?" Isaac falters.

"I keep getting flashbacks. Flashbacks of what really happened. You, with your hands covered in blood. You did it, didn't you? You killed him. You had that argument, and it went too far." The words are sliding out of her now, easy, ugly, fueled by resentment, anger — everything she's been hiding for so long.

"No." His voice catches. When he meets her gaze, his features are tight. "Like I said, let's not get into this now." He looks at the bed. "Not with Will like this."

"No, it's not going to be that easy. I want to know, Isaac. I want you to tell me exactly what happened."

Silence. Several heavy beats pass. Her throat is throbbing, thick with more words. More questions.

"Come on." Elin roughly grabs his arm.

"You can start with the first lie. You didn't go to the loo, did you? You were there, with Sam."

It's then she notices something strange in his eyes, something that sends a cold drop of fear right through her.

Pity.

This isn't right, she thinks, panicked. He should be sad, sorry, even defensive, but not this . . . he shouldn't be pitying her.

Isaac's eyes pull up to meet hers. They're dimmed, sad.

"Okay," he says finally. "You want the truth? I wasn't there when he died, Elin. It was you with him, not me."

76

Elin falters. "I don't understand what you're saying. I wasn't there. I was by the cliff."

Isaac rubs roughly at his eye. "No. You'd come back. I asked you to watch Sam while I went to the loo. When I came back, he was in the water. You were gabbling, repeating yourself, said you watched him go in, couldn't do anything." He hesitates, swallowing hard. "Look, the doctors, they said you were in shock. That you froze."

"No. No." Rocking forward, she folds her arms tight around her body. The words aren't being absorbed. "That's not right."

Isaac carries on. "They said there wasn't anything you could have done. The postmortem showed that he died instantly, a brain hemorrhage caused by the fall. The impact from the rock . . . it was the wrong place on his skull, that's all. Bad luck."

Elin feels a sudden, sharp wave of nausea, the world as she knew it shattering, becoming something new.

Several beats pass.

She speaks first. "Tell me what happened," she says in a whisper. "The details."

"You're sure?"

She nods.

Isaac shifts his body to face her. "When I left for the loo, you'd put your line in next to his. That's the last thing I saw."

"And then?" Her words are barely audible.

"I came back, saw Sam in the water. I waded in, pulled him out. I —" He stops, and Elin knows why. He doesn't want to say the words. Doesn't want to implicate her. Tell her that he saw her standing there, doing nothing.

The thought causes a sudden pull of breath, a sharp, painful inhalation.

All this time, she's been blaming him. Thinking he hurt Sam, Laure . . .

"What about the blood," she says, "on your hands?"

"That was from when I pulled him out of the water. There was a cut on the side of his head."

Elin's silent, realizes her fingers are moving, almost entirely independently from her brain. Flexing, then retracting around nothing but air.

"So you're saying that I was there and I did nothing to help him." Her voice stutters.

"Yes, but the doctors said it was shock." Isaac puts his hand on hers. "People react differently when something like that happens, you must know that from work. Elin, you were only twelve. I've thought about this a lot, read about what can happen when you experience something traumatic. You saw something horrifying. You froze. It's normal."

"No. No. It didn't happen. It can't have happened. Not like that." Her voice sounds screechy. Something animal, out of control. "Isaac, no. Please say it's not right, what you're saying. It's not right!"

"Elin," Isaac starts, "I didn't want to tell you, not like this, but perhaps now that you know the truth you can accept what happened. Move on. All these fears you've had . . . maybe they've been rooted in you."

"In me?"

"Yes. We should have made you see a therapist, talk it through, but Mum was worried about you blaming yourself. So instead I think your brain put up barriers around that day, against what happened."

Elin shakes her head. She doesn't want his pity, these platitudes. It feels like she's had the guts pulled out of her. Her head is throbbing; she's fit to burst. She can't remember ever feeling this tired. All she wants is to be alone.

"Please, Isaac, just go." Her voice sounds strange. Empty.

He hesitates, opening his mouth as if to say

something before shaking his head, walking away.

Watching him leave, she squeezes her eyes shut tight to block it out, block everything out, but it doesn't stop them from coming — thoughts, sharp, like knives.

She hadn't helped him. Sam. Her Sam. Her little brother. Lover of stories and fables. The soldier.

The knight.

The reluctant sheep in the white woolly costume.

Elin puts her head in her hands. She feels cogs turning, deep within her brain, shifting into place.

It all makes sense now, doesn't it?

Her mother's reticence to talk about Sam — the strained, try-too-hard face whenever she mentioned his name. Her father leaving, his halfhearted attempts to stay in touch.

They'd blamed her, they thought she could have saved him.

Fragments of a memory pull to the surface: the first anniversary of Sam's death. Her mother in Sam's room, sitting on his bed, holding a book: *Peepo*. A toddler-Sam favorite, but he still loved the simple language, the repetition.

Her mother was reading it under her breath, body slightly rocking. Elin went over, lightly squeezed her shoulder, but she'd recoiled at Elin's touch, the action fierce enough to send the book flying out of her hand, careering into Sam's Lego spaceship.

It clattered off its base plate, splintering into fragments. Her mother, still not acknowledging her, dropped to her hands and knees, scrabbling to pick up the pieces.

At the time, Elin thought it strange, how she'd recoiled at her touch, but she never really understood the significance.

Until now.

Leaning back against the pillow, Elin feels hot tears prick the back of her eyes.

It all makes sense now.

Her mother knew.

They all knew.

It was her.

Day Five

When Elin wakes, she has no idea what time it is. As she reaches out a hand to check, she winces; her lower back feels stiff, and she's sore all over. It's not just from the scuffle with Margot — she's in a cot the hotel had provided so Will could have their bed to himself as he recovers. It's narrow and unsubstantial, the thin mattress barely cushioning her against the rigid latticework of springs.

It's 6:01 a.m.

She glances over at Will. There's enough light that she can see he's still pale, but his breathing is rhythmic, steady.

Relieved, she lies back against the pillow. Her head is throbbing; every fiber of her body still craving sleep. As she rolls over onto her stomach, she feels her eyes close.

This time, sleep comes harder, quicker, seizing her, pulling her under. Within minutes, she's drifting. It's dangerous, she knows, because this time, when the flashback comes, it's not fragments like it always has been, but the whole.

Sam, leaning over the rock pool, net thrust deep into the thick of murky seaweed-water. It happens in slow motion; Sam turning, to say something — *no crabs,* maybe, or *my neck's burning,* and as he twists his body back to face the water, he loses his balance.

Elin starts to laugh at his comic expression, which she soon realizes isn't a comic expression at all, it's fear. Fear twisting his features into knots because he's falling backward.

There's nothing worse, is there? No eyes on where you're going. No control.

He breaks the water cleanly.

She knows now that this was the first warning sign: Sam should have splashed. Should have made a noise, cried out as he hit the water, thrashed around, laughing, as he tried to right himself.

But there's none of that: just a single splash followed by a sickening crack.

Then Sam, lying still, the impact only continuing in the water; circles rippling outward.

Part of the rock is stained; deep gloss-red across the white barnacle lace.

Sam's face doesn't look like Sam's face. His eyes are wide open. Staring. Jelly limbs like when he was a toddler.

There's a split on the side of his head. More

than a cut; something open, gaping. Elin wants to move, she remembers that much; she wants to dive in, do something magic to help him, but her feet won't budge.

They're stuck. Glued to the rock and the half dome of limpet that's digging into her left heel.

Move, she tells her feet, *move.*

But they won't. Nor will her eyes. They're stuck too.

Stuck on Sam's body in the rock pool, his T-shirt swollen by the water, the breeze catching it, making it ripple like some obscene balloon.

His legs catch the sway of the water, a ragged flag of seaweed snagging on his ankle. Her bucket falls from her hand: a loud crack on the rock below.

Seaweed-water spools between the clusters of limpets and barnacles. Crabs are on the march, shrimps body-popping against the rock, desperately seeking water.

It's then her mind hooks on something.

Zooms in. Stuck on one action, on loop:

Bucket falling from hand. Bucket falling from hand.

She reaches up, grips the necklace tightly, fingers closing around the curve of the hook, her heart thudding as the memory shakes loose the echo of another.

A similar action.

Something dropping to the floor.

In the scuffle between Will and Margot, something had dropped onto the floor.

She closes her eyes and the memory fleshes out: the two of them grappling, the grunts, heavy breaths, and among that, something more muted.

A soft thud, a scrape of something scudding along the floor.

Elin sits up, reaches for her water. As she takes a long drink, her mind teases the thought apart.

What could it be? What had fallen to the floor?

78

"You're sure about this?" Isaac's voice is light, but his eyes are wary. "After everything that's happened? You weren't in a good way when I left." Turning back to the bedside table, he picks up his coffee and drains it.

His face looks gray in the half-light, his curls matted and flattened.

Behind him, the room is in disarray; the sheets are torn back, cups littering the bedside table. Elin feels a sharp pang of guilt: he's grieving, barely coping, and now she's laying this on him.

"I can't leave it." She pushes the thought away. "I heard something drop, I'm certain of it. We've got to at least go and look."

"But surely, if there was anything there, we'd have seen it when we were helping Will." His eyes track across her face. "A whole group of us were down there. If someone else had found it, they'd have told us."

Elin picks apart his muted reaction, the carefully neutral expression. He thinks she's overtired, clutching at straws.

There's an awkward silence.

She's suddenly aware of how she must look — her face clammy, damp with sweat, her hair mussed from a disturbed sleep.

A flush creeps up her face.

"Not necessarily." She runs a hand through her hair, tries to flatten it. "All we were concentrating on was helping Will. Something could easily have gone unnoticed."

"Either way," Isaac says carefully. "This probably isn't the right call. Margot's most likely here, somewhere in the hotel. She left the room, escaped. It's too risky." He hesitates. "It's not only that. What about Will? Shouldn't you be with him?"

Elin feels her shoulders tighten — another wave of guilt.

He's right.

She *should* be with Will. It's the least she can do after what happened, but the urge to follow her instincts is too strong.

"When I left, he was still asleep. He's been fine all night. Sara's messaged me, said she'll look in on him in a minute, and this . . . it won't take long." She stops, wincing at her own words.

Self-justification of the worst, most selfish kind.

"You're sure?" Isaac reaches for a sweater, pulls it over his head.

"Yes. The fact that Margot went for me . . .

it proves this isn't the end of it. She wanted me out of the way because she's got something else planned."

His eyes flick past her to the window. "I still think you should wait. The forecast says it might break later today. The police might be able to get here."

"It doesn't look like it." Elin glances outside. It's still dark, but the outside lights illuminate the snow plummeting from the sky — thick, oversized flakes. "And we can't afford to wait. How Margot spoke, I can tell that this is something personal. It's revenge."

Isaac's eyes drift then come to rest on the chair a few feet away.

Elin follows his gaze. *Laure's leather jacket, slung across the arm.*

Something shifts in his expression.

He gives a quick, decisive nod. "Okay. Let's do it." His eyes are burning with an emotion that's beyond anger. It's something raw, darker, deeply personal.

79

The lights are now working in the generator room. Under the harsh neon glow, the space is different — sterile, inert, the thrumming machinery blandly functional rather than sinister.

Weaving through the equipment ahead of her, Isaac turns. "She attacked Will toward the back of the room, didn't she?"

She nods. "We're not far from it, though." A few feet on and Elin can see it: blood. Will's blood. Inching toward it, her stomach contracts.

The tiles are streaked with red — messy smears from where the staff had lifted Will. Faint bloody footprints reach outward before trailing to nothing.

Elin forces herself to take a deep breath. "If something was dropped, it must be somewhere here." Her eyes scour the floor, the gaps between the bulky apparatuses.

"See anything?" Isaac moves beside her.

"Nothing so far." She bites her lip in

frustration. Nothing to hint at the sound she heard — that soft thud, the scuffing sound of something sliding across the floor.

Unless, Elin thinks, lowering herself to her knees, the impact was enough that the object traveled farther than she thought. After all, the tiles are smooth, slick . . .

Tipping her head sideways, necklace swinging against her chin, she looks under the machine in front. *Is there enough of a gap for something to slip under?*

There is . . . She turns her head the other way. It's then she sees it: a white corner, just visible and half protruding from beneath a metal cage surrounding the generator.

She reaches for the edge, and tries to pull it toward her. *It doesn't give.*

Changing tack, she clasps the edge between finger and thumb, tugs. This time it slides out easily. She stares: *an envelope, packed tight.*

"Have you found something?"

She stands back up. "An envelope." Hands shaking, she lifts up the flap, withdraws a thick pile of papers, letter size, folded in half.

She examines the first piece of paper, and takes a sudden breath. She recognizes the words, the layout.

Gotterdorf Klinik.

"It's a medical record. The same as the ones on Laure's memory stick." One big differ-

474

ence, though — this one isn't redacted. She scans the page, starting with the name at the top. Bette Massen.

Massen: that's Margot's surname, isn't it? Elin then notices the number below the name: 87534. Her pulse quickens. *It can't be a coincidence.*

Scanning down, she can't read any further. The German medical vocabulary is beyond her. She flicks to the next one. "There's more," she murmurs, then stops.

Something's fallen to the floor. Black-and-white photographs.

Bending down, she gathers them together, picks them up.

Shock surges through her as she examines the first image. Five women, lying side by side on a series of operating tables. A cloth is draped loosely over their lower limbs, but it's been carelessly pulled back, as if it was hastily moved for the photographer.

So the lens could capture the handiwork.

Not that you could call it that, Elin thinks, bile rising at the back of her throat.

Their bodies are mutilated; stomachs splayed open, flesh retracted with some kind of metal tool to reveal the organs beneath.

Her gaze moves to their heads. It's hard to see, as the bodies are prone, but it looks like part of the skull has been removed, the brain matter clearly visible.

Her brain is shouting at her: *Don't look.*

475

Don't look.

But she has to. A shiver moves through her at what her eyes find next: three people standing behind the women, clad in surgical clothes. They're all wearing masks. The masks are concealing their faces, but she's pretty sure they're men. Their frames, their height, the formal, broad-legged stance.

The masks are the same grotesque rubber masks that were attached to Adele's and Laure's faces.

The same mask the killer wore.

Elin feels another wave of revulsion as she draws the conclusion: the only logical reason the doctors would be masked is to conceal their identity. They didn't want people to know who they were, because they were doing something wrong. It certainly looks wrong. Far from being a clinical procedure, it looks like a crime scene. Something inhuman. Barbaric.

Her fingers contract around the photograph, and once again she has to force herself to examine it, her eyes finding new detail.

Elin sucks in her breath: the woman closest to the camera has her arm falling off the side of the table. Several fingers have been removed.

There's something around her wrist too. It's hard to tell what it's made of because the image isn't in color, but it's definitely a bracelet. It looks similar to the copper bracelets she'd seen in the boxes.

"This is it," Elin says slowly, still digesting the knowledge, its implications. "What all this has been about."

Isaac's face is twisted in disgust. "What exactly are they doing?"

"I don't know," she says grimly, "but whatever it is, it doesn't look legal."

After passing the photograph to Isaac, Elin holds up the next one. It shows a scrubby patch of grass and what looks like a solitary grave, the earth recently disturbed, no headstone or marker.

Flipping to the next, she brings her hand to her mouth. While not as graphic, the image is equally disturbing. It shows a woman lying on an operating table, two sandbags strapped tightly to her chest. The weight from the bags has caused her chest to cave, bow. The woman's eyes are closed.

Elin can't tell if she's alive or not. She doubts it: breathing looks impossible. The weight of the sandbags on her chest would have meant her lungs would have struggled to inflate. Once again, three masked men are standing behind her.

Their fixed pose, the masks . . . it's chilling.

With fumbling fingers, she moves to the next one. The image shows two women, again on operating tables. Sheeting is pulled up high over their bodies, but there are long incisions in their necks. Elin stares, shuddering as the scene moves into sharper focus.

Her mind immediately makes the connection to the methods used to kill Adele and Laure — the sandbag with Adele, the neck incision with Laure.

Her theory is right — how they've been killed, the signature . . . the killer is trying to communicate something.

This.

Margot's reenacting what happened in these images. Every little detail, from the method of killing to the masks, the bracelets . . .

Turning to Isaac, she's about to say something when she notices he's still looking intently at the first photograph.

"What is it?"

"Look at this. Something's written on the back." He passes it to her.

He's right: something's written in pencil, in an old-fashioned, looping script you don't see anymore. *Sanatorium du Plumachit, 1927.*

"This was taken here, in the hotel. All of that . . ." Her mouth is dry. "It was done here."

An idea strikes — she goes through the photographs again until she finds the one of the grave. Bringing it closer, she examines the background. Though there's no snow on the ground as there is now, she recognizes the mass of fir trees rising steadily upward, the glimpse of high mountain above.

478

"This was taken near the sanatorium, wasn't it? These women, they were buried near here."

"Looks like it. Unmarked graves."

Elin finds the first photograph, turns it over, her gaze moving lower this time.

Below the name of the sanatorium is a list of five sets of numbers, each set containing five numbers in a row. Her mind makes the leap:

Five women. Five sets of numbers.

The numbers are in the same format as the numbers on the bracelets. She runs her finger over the number at the top: 87534. A slow burn of recognition: the same number she'd found in the medical file on Laure's memory stick, on one of the bracelets by Adele's body . . . it's a match.

One of these women is Margot's relative.

Elin catches Isaac's eye. "It matches with the medical files. The numbers on the back of the photograph, they're patient numbers."

"So the numbers on the bracelets each refer to a patient?"

"Yes. I'm pretty certain, looking at this, that one of these women was a relative of Margot's."

"But these files refer to this German clinic, a psychiatric facility. How did they end up here?"

"I don't know. We need someone to translate them, but my guess is they weren't transferred here for mental health reasons." The more she looks, the more sinister she finds the images.

Several details bother her: the way the masked men behind the women are lined up, in a row. There's a power imbalance implicit in their posture, position — the women lying vulnerable, masked surgeons standing over them, in control.

A threat.

Then the grave — the fact there was no headstone, no sign of any ceremony. *Was it done secretly?*

Elin pushes back her hair. "This is what all this has been about, Isaac. Revenge. Somehow Margot's got hold of the contents of these files, the photographs, and now she's getting payback."

His expression changes; features tensing. "If you're right" — he points at the masked figures — "and she is working from these photographs, there are five people in this one, Elin." He holds it up. "If you include Daniel, she's killed three so far, so that means —"

"There are two people left," Elin finishes.

There's a pause. "But the one thing I don't understand," he starts, "is why she targeted them. Adele and Laure, Daniel . . . What happened in these pictures, it was years ago. It's horrific, traumatic, but there must be something that's happened more recently for her to target them now."

480

"I agree, but it's impossible to say, not until we know more."

"So what next?" Isaac trains his eyes on the envelope in her hand. "We've got this information, but it doesn't tell us where Margot is, what she's planning."

"You're right," she concedes, and it's then she notices something, on the very edge of the envelope. A small dark flake.

Margot's nail varnish.

A sudden, sharp tug at her subconscious. An image: flakes of nail varnish on the desk. Margot reaching to sweep them away, and with it a bag tumbling, its contents spilling across the floor.

The thought that up until now had been shapeless, elusive, resolves into something. Something her conscious mind hadn't picked up on at the time, but her subconscious clearly had.

Fear spikes the base of her stomach. "We need to find the Carons. I think I know where Margot might be, Isaac. I think she's been in the hotel all along."

80

"The archive room?" Lucas says dismissively, sliding his coffee cup along his desk. "There's nothing there."

Elin can feel the tension emanating from him: tight shoulders, jutting jaw.

He's not bothered by my waking him, it's that he doesn't like that I've gone against what he advised. That I'm still investigating.

"Are you sure? There're no other doors? No other way out of the room?"

"No." Lucas's voice is curt. Flipping down the lid of his laptop, he meets her gaze, a challenge in his eyes. "What makes you so sure she's been in there?"

"A hunch." Elin kicks herself.

A hunch. She sounds like an amateur.

"You want to put yourself at risk over a hunch?" Mouth twitching, he exchanges a glance with Cecile. "The police might be up today. The weather is meant to be improving. I'd prefer to sit it out as we've been advised."

He doesn't mention what he now knows

482

about her job, her lie, but he doesn't have to: the knowledge sits between them, weighing heavy.

"Sitting it out could be a problem." Elin takes care with her words, keeping her tone flat, unemotional. "My worry is, she's out of control. What she did to Will was unplanned, spontaneous. There's every chance she could do the same again. Once she knows the police are here, the situation could escalate rapidly." The end of the sentence is drowned out by the sound of the wind.

She feels her mobile buzz in her pocket. Pulling it out, she can see that Isaac's calling. She replaces it; she'll call him back.

"You really think Margot's capable of all this?" Cecile asks.

Elin puts the envelope down, her hands not quite steady.

This is what I've been waiting for — their reaction to the image.

"I think she's capable," Elin says softly, "because of this." Pulling out the first photograph, she places it on the desk. "This is Margot's motive. I can't think of a stronger one."

Cecile recoils, a hand coming up to her mouth. Lucas is harder to read, his expression fixed.

"What is it?" He rubs a hand across his jaw, ruffling his beard.

"This photograph was taken here. We think

483

one of these women is Margot's relative." Elin flips the photograph over. "The numbers on the back match the patient number on the medical file we found in the same envelope, as well as the number on one of the brace-lets."

"But what are they doing to these women?" Cecile reaches for the image, her eyes glassy. "It doesn't look like a normal operation."

"I don't think it is. These women came from a psychiatric clinic in Germany. There's no legitimate medical reason, as far as I can tell, for them to have been transferred here, to a tuberculosis sanatorium." Reaching into the envelope, she pulls out the medical file belonging to Margot's relative. "We'll know more from this. I couldn't understand it all."

"I can translate." Cecile reads in silence, then starts to speak. "It says she was admit-ted to the clinic for psychiatric issues after the birth of her fourth child. The family doc-tor referred her there after counsel from her husband. It details her medications, treat-ments." She frowns. "There's no mention of a transfer here, though."

"I don't think there would be. I think this was done in secret. Off the record." Elin turns the image over. "It's written quite clearly. *Sanatorium du Plumachit.*" Reaching for the envelope again, she pulls out the photograph of the grave, passes it to them. "We found this among the photographs too. It looks to me like it was taken here. Near the hotel."

"A grave," Cecile says slowly. "You think these women were buried here?"

Elin nods. "You didn't know anything like this went on here?"

"No." Cecile's face darkens. "There's nothing in the archive about this."

"Lucas?" Elin waits for his reaction. Any tells, signs of deceit. "You had no information about the graves when you were planning the build?"

Tilting his head away from the image, Lucas shakes his head.

Elin realizes that something feels strange about his reaction; his expression seems *too* neutral, too detached.

Focusing on him, her mind whirring, she doesn't realize that Cecile is saying something to her.

"Sorry?"

"I was saying, it happened so long ago." Cecile frowns. "What's it got to do with Adele and Laure, Daniel? Why kill them?"

"I don't know," Elin admits. "Only Margot can tell us that."

Cecile's eyes are still picking over the photograph. "Seeing this, I think you're right. If this is about what happened in these photographs, who knows what she might do next. I think you should try to find her. Confront her."

Lucas looks uneasy. "I don't know . . ."

485

here before, I saw it on the floor. I didn't make the connection until I saw her nail varnish on the envelope. It triggered something. I remembered her picking her nails on the desk. When she swept the flakes away, her arm knocked over her bag. Some hair grips fell to the floor . . ."

Her eyes find something else: several tiny flakes of gray between the holes in the matting. Licking her finger, she presses it down between one of them. Several of the flakes adhere to her finger. Elin stares, going over the sight in her mind.

It's Margot's nail varnish. That very particular gray color.

"What is it?"

"Nail varnish." If she was in any doubt — not anymore. "Margot's been here. Recently." She looks closer. Several larger flakes are clearly visible between the matting. If she'd been just fiddling with her nails, the flakes would have spread over a larger area, over the matting too. There wouldn't be any underneath, like this. Something has caused the varnish to flake off.

"This floor isn't original, is it?"

Lucas straightens up. "No. The original floors were unworkable. This was only meant to be temporary, but then the plans for the room changed so we left it."

Elin nods, still examining the matting. It's then she notices it: a fine line scored through the surface. Her eyes follow it: the line measures roughly a few square feet.

She runs a hand over the line, fingertips tingling.

This can't be a coincidence.

"What is it?" Lucas gives her a questioning look.

"I don't know yet. Give me a moment." Pulling her penknife from her pocket, she crouches down, hooks the end of the blade into a corner of the scored-out line. She pushes down hard until the corner of rubber matting lifts up.

She tugs at the edge, peeling the section up and away. Beneath the rubber matting is a thin layer of vinyl floor tile. Unremarkable, except that this, too, is dotted with tiny flecks of nail varnish. It also contains the same score mark: a large square in exactly the same shape as the rubber matting.

Elin feels the irregular flicking of her pulse. *I'm onto something.*

Hooking the knife into the line scored into the vinyl, she peels the square away. It comes up smoothly, easily, as if someone's done the action before.

When she's finished, she stops, staring. Beneath the vinyl isn't the solid concrete floor you'd expect, but something else entirely. A wooden door, two metal handles sitting retracted against the top. The surface is thick with dust, but Elin can just make out more dark flakes.

Margot's been here. She's repeatedly lifted this door, the matting above, making her varnish flake off.

Elin looks up at Lucas. "Do you know what this is?"

"No," he replies without hesitation. "I've never seen it before."

"Not during the build?"

"No. When we started the refurbishment, the vinyl flooring was everywhere. It was old, filthy. Uneven. We instructed the builders to level it with the matting until we decided what we were going to do with it." He looks down at the door. "Do you think this is where . . . ?"

"It's possible." Elin's voice is uncertain. If there *is* a room under there, it would be the ideal place to hold someone. Easy access to the hotel, yet with total privacy.

She grips the handles tightly, and heaves the door upward. It gives easily, a waft of stale, musty air rushing toward them.

She peers into the gap. An inky blackness. She can't see a thing.

Pulling the flashlight from her bag, she switches it on. The beam picks out the beginnings of some steps, roughly hewn from stone.

"I'm going down."

"Now?" Lucas looks at her in surprise.

"We can't wait. We've got to stop her before

she hurts anyone else."

"Okay, but I'm coming with you. It's not safe for you to go in there alone."

"Fine." She meets his gaze. "But I'm going first."

scissors, knife.

Blood stains the surface of them, dark, shiny.

She clamps a hand over her mouth. *This is where it happened. This is where Laure was mutilated before her death. Adele too.*

Elin stares, image after image filling her head. Her palms are sweaty, slick around the flashlight.

"This is where . . ." Lucas doesn't finish his sentence. He looks appalled.

"Yes." Her voice wavers. "The perfect location. Enough room, privacy. Easy access to the . . ." She breaks off, noticing something — a different, stronger smell.

The fetid mustiness of the past few yards of the tunnel has been replaced with something else — the smell of decay. Something meaty, metallic.

Elin steps forward, her breathing shallower now.

It must just be the blood from the instruments, the blood Margot's tried to clean; but without any ventilation, it's lingered, caught in the cracks.

She's about to turn back to Lucas when she notices it — tucked into the curve of the tunnel wall at its widest part.

Elin freezes, a sudden, sharp wave of nausea rocking her stomach.

Impossible.

83

Elin clamps a hand over her mouth, bile already rising and filling her throat, her mouth.

Margot.

She's hoisted onto a strange pulley system, fixed to a wooden rack.

The grotesque rubber mask is half hanging off her face so her profile is clear, features livid from where the blood has pooled, settled.

One eye is closed, the other open: vacant, lifeless.

Elin is trembling as she stares, trying to get a handle on what's in front of her.

Has she killed herself? Committed suicide because she knew we were onto her?

But as her eyes track downward, Elin can see that her torso is being pulled taut by a complex system of ropes attached at her wrists and ankles. The rope around her ankles is connected to some kind of crank, a turning wheel.

There's no way she could have done this to herself.

Elin's gaze moves left, to Margot's head. A metal clamp is fastened to her forehead, blood trickling down her face where it has punctured the skin. The surface of the clamp has metal hooks on it, fixed to a length of rope. This, in turn, is affixed to another turning wheel.

The blood flutters in Elin's ears as her eyes move to Margot's neck. There are marks on her skin where it's stretched and torn.

If the metal clamp puncturing her head didn't kill her first, then the force from this medieval-style rack had been enough to detach her head from the spinal cord.

Instant death.

Pictures spool through her head, a ticker tape: Margot as she'd seen her yesterday, and now *this*. This barbarity.

Elin knows with absolute certainty that this will be the one she'll remember, the one that will stick in her head for the rest of her life.

Taking a deep breath, she waits for the familiar panic. But it doesn't come: her head feels sharp, clear, cutting through to what's in front of her, but the thought that comes next almost makes her wish otherwise.

"Margot was working with someone else." Elin turns toward Lucas. "All this time, she's been working with somebody else."

84

There's no reply.

Elin turns in a circle, glances warily around her.

"Lucas?" she repeats, her words echoing out in the darkness of the tunnel.

Still no answer.

A prickle of fear: she turns again, slowly this time, moving the flashlight in a circle.

Flashes: *The metal trolley. Discarded equipment. The streaked concrete of the walls.*

But no Lucas.

Where could he be?

He was right behind her only a few moments ago. Her mind turns over the possibilities: perhaps he saw or heard something, went deeper into the tunnel?

Walking forward, she scans the space in front of her, mouth dry.

No sign of him.

She starts to go back the other way when she hears a distant thud. Her brain scrambles; instantly deciphers the noise.

The hatch.

He's gone. Back the way they came.

A sudden, devastating flash of comprehension; there's only one reason he'd run at this moment.

Her mind hooks onto the next conclusion: *Lucas is the person Margot was working with. He's the killer.*

But if that was the case, why did he not kill her in the tunnel, when he had the chance?

Turning, she starts sprinting back through the tunnel. It's hard work — the slight incline, the altitude. Each stride feels clumsy, useless, like she's not making any headway. A bead of sweat trickles down her forehead. Impatiently, she wipes it away, carries on.

Her thoughts lurch to Margot: *Why would Lucas kill her?*

Had something gone wrong, or was this what he intended all along? Had he groomed Margot to be the perfect fall guy? Wanted it to look like revenge so he could carry out the rest of his plan unhindered?

Thoughts flash through her mind — what Cecile had told her, his relationship with Laure, his passion for the hotel. *His lies.*

It makes sense, doesn't it? His motive could be one she's considered before, perhaps the biggest motive of all: protecting the hotel. She remembers Cecile talking about his passion for the place: *building a monument to himself.*

Is this some deluded attempt to try to protect his legacy? It's possible: the murders an attempt to conceal the truth about the sanatorium's dark past.

Had the people he killed known something about it?

A logical rationale should have told him it could never work, but she knew a killer's logic was never rational. In his mind, his course of action would make total sense: the only viable conclusion. It's that sense of utter conviction that enabled killers to do what they did — a ruthless single-mindedness.

Whatever the answer, she knows she has to act fast.

Finally, she reaches the steps. She walks up the first few, tilts her head upward. It's completely dark: no light from the archive room above.

Her suspicion was right: he's closed the hatch. Clamping the flashlight between her teeth, Elin reaches up, pushes with all her strength on the handle attached to the underside, but it doesn't budge.

She tries again; this time feeling the surface with her fingers, trying to find a weak spot, but there isn't one.

A new tactic: moving backward to the step below, she crouches down, then springs off her feet, propelling herself upward with all of her body weight.

It doesn't work; the wood moves only a fraction, revealing just a thin crack of light.

Stumbling slightly as she lands back on the narrow step, Elin looks all around with a sense of rising panic; there's no other way out.

He's locked her in.

Several minutes tick past as she tries to come up with a plan: no one but Lucas and Cecile knows she's down here. Cecile might not come looking for her yet, and that would give Lucas enough time to execute whatever he has planned.

There's probably no point in attempting to go back through the tunnel to find the exit, since Lucas said it was likely to be blocked.

Think, Elin, think.

A thought flashes into her mind — something basic she hasn't even considered.

My phone.

She pivots on the step and fishes it out of her pocket. The screen comes to life but now Elin doesn't feel so clever — there's only one bar of signal, flickering in and out of range. She moves it slowly backward and forward. Nothing: the flickering goes, replaced by two words: *No Service.*

This time, she moves as high as she can go, until she's crouched on the top step. Glancing at the screen, she sees the Swisscom name has appeared. The flickering bar becomes solid.

A faint signal: it might be enough. Sitting on the step, she taps out a message to Isaac.

Locked in the archive room. There's an opening in the floor in the center — like someone's etched a square in the rubber. Lift it up, and the tile beneath, and you'll find a hatch.

An immediate reply: On my way.

Several minutes later she hears something overhead: rough thuds, scrapes.

A loud creak, and all at once there's an influx of light.

Elin blinks, momentarily blinded. She can make out Isaac directly above her, kneeling over the opening. His face is flushed, sweaty.

Reaching out a hand, he helps her up. "Are you okay?" His voice is gruff, thick with emotion.

"I'm fine." Straightening, she takes a deep breath. "Margot's dead, Isaac."

"Dead?" His voice cracks. "But you thought —"

"I know. But I found her, down in the tunnel." She falters as an image of Margot's broken body fills her head. Horrible, graphic images.

"So it wasn't her?"

Elin hesitates, trying to get her thoughts

straight in her head. "I'm not sure. I'm pretty sure she was involved, but I think she was working with somebody else. The person who locked me down here."

Isaac frowns. "What do you mean?"

"Lucas," she says bluntly. "He came down with me, to find Margot. He was with me the whole way, and then when I was examining Margot's body, I turned around, and he'd gone."

Isaac blows out his cheeks, letting out a slow whistle of air. "But why wouldn't he just kill you? Get you out of the way?"

"I don't know," Elin replies. "I've been thinking about it. I was distracted by Margot. . . . Maybe he didn't think he needed to."

Isaac looks anxiously toward the door. "So what are you going to do now?"

"We've got to find him. Before he gets to anyone else."

85

When Elin walks into the lounge, it's brighter, but only barely — the windows reveal a silvery milkiness to the sky outside that makes it seem more like dawn than late morning.

Two small groups are gathered at the tables next to the bar, but no one's talking. They're on their phones or sipping their drinks.

Elin notices Cecile at the first table; her hands are clasped around a small cup of coffee.

As Elin walks over, nerves dance in her stomach: *How is Cecile going to react when I tell her about Lucas?*

Cecile looks up. Her face looks pinched, drawn. "How's Will?"

"He's stable for now."

"Good."

Elin lowers her voice. "Cecile, we need to talk alone."

"Okay." Cecile stands up, scraping back her chair. They move to a table on the other side of the room, out of earshot of the groups behind.

Taking a seat, Elin pulls at her shirt. It's hot. The fire, only a few feet away, is roaring in the hearth.

In fits and starts, she recounts what's happened, pulled short by the conflicting expressions on Cecile's face — confusion, disbelief, and something else, something unexpected — a sense of resignation.

It's as if something's come loose, cut adrift in her features.

Had she suspected all along?

"You honestly think Lucas is part of this?" Cecile says when Elin finishes. Her eyes look like shadows, hollowed out.

Elin takes a long breath. "He ran, Cecile. Tried to lock me in. There might be another explanation, but I'm not sure what it would be."

Cecile's silent for a moment, her gaze passing over the glass box suspended from the ceiling only a few feet away. Elin's seen it before; it contains an old manometer made from glass and wood. The note inside explains it was used to measure air pressure when the surgeon collapsed the tuberculosis patient's lungs.

Seeing it now, after what she's discovered, Elin feels an absolute revulsion: Lucas knowingly incorporated this into the design. Made it a feature.

"So what do you want to do?" Cecile says finally. In the mirror behind the bar, her reflection seems to distort, her heavy features elongating.

"Two things. We need to keep everyone together, make sure no one leaves this room. Then we need to find Lucas."

"He could be anywhere. The hotel's huge, and it's possible, isn't it, that there's another hidden space like the tunnel?"

"Yes, but if he's planning on doing something else soon, it's more likely he's somewhere in the main building."

Cecile gives a single, abrupt nod, eyes hardening. "Let's start with his office."

The space is unrecognizable; the pristine, designer perfection destroyed.

Lucas's desk is in disarray: papers littered across the sleek wooden surface, several notebooks lying on the floor. Drawers are wrenched open, his chair pushed away from the desk.

It's like it's been raided. A burglary.

A chill moves through Elin, a sickening lurch of realization: *He's been back here. Looking for something.*

She goes over to his desk, begins leafing through the discarded papers. Mainly business documents, copies of presentations.

Among a stack of files, her eyes alight on something familiar.

The letters — the threatening, anonymous notes Lucas had shown her. The letters she now knows were from Laure.

There's what looks to be over a dozen of them, all different. Elin's hands are clumsy as she gathers them into a loose pile.

He'd mentioned only three, hadn't he?

Had this been going on longer than he said? If so, it's possible that these might have had a part to play in triggering the first murder. If he'd felt under threat . . .

"What is it?" Cecile turns toward the desk.

"I've found some more letters . . . the ones Laure sent him."

She frowns. "Why would he be looking for those?"

"I don't know." Shaking her head, Elin looks at them again, and this time something catches, tugging at her consciousness.

Something about the room doesn't look right.

It takes her a moment to work out what it is: the cupboards.

They're the only thing that has been left untouched. There's a long line of them, only a few feet above floor level.

A small locking mechanism sits halfway up each door.

Elin walks over, crouching beside them to examine the lock. "Do you have a key to these?"

"No. He's probably got it on him."

Standing back up, Elin casts her eyes

around the room, looking for something sturdy enough to break the lock.

There's a large glass paperweight on the corner of Lucas's desk. Grabbing it, she drops to her knees. Positioning the paperweight above the lock on the first and largest cupboard, she slams it down hard against the mechanism.

It doesn't work — her palms, damp, sweaty, lose their grip on the glass, and it skims over the surface before thudding to the floor.

She wipes her palms on her trousers, tries again. This time she hits the lock dead in the center: it gives way with a loud click.

Working her finger into the edge of the door, she slides it open.

Elin recoils.

The cupboard's empty, bar one thing: a mask.

The same black rubber mask that's cast its horrifying shadow over the past few days. Without any features to fill it, it's slack, collapsed in on itself.

She can't take her eyes off it. The moment stretches, a cog turning deep within her brain.

There's no doubt now. It's the same mask she saw on Adele's and Laure's bodies. Margot's too.

Lucas is behind this.

Cecile appears by her side. "That was in there?" Her voice wavers.

"Yes." Elin reaches for it, taking in the

detail: the hairline cracks in the rubber, the wide tube connecting nose and mouth.

Turning it between her fingers, an outline of a thought starts to form, but before she can get a grip on it, it fragments, drifts away.

Cecile crouches down next to her. "I know how this looks, but it doesn't make sense." She's gabbling, words running into one another. "Why would he sabotage the hotel, everything he spent so long trying to build? He knows it wouldn't survive this, surely?" Reaching out, she touches the mask. "I'm sure it's a mistake. A misunderstanding."

A pit opens in Elin's stomach. Cecile will give it everything she's got to explain this away. She's still protecting Lucas, even now.

Yet she can't condemn her, because she understands it. It's what Isaac did for her all these years, isn't it? Held back the truth. Protected her.

"Cecile, I —"

"I'll try the other cupboards," Cecile interrupts, reaching for the paperweight. "I'm sure he has all kinds of things like this. Artifacts from the sanatorium." She gestures around her. "Look at the walls, the pictures. He's interested in the history of the place, that's all. It doesn't mean anything more than that."

"Cecile, I know this is hard, but . . ."

Elin doesn't get to finish her sentence. Cecile starts shaking, her hands loosening their grip on the paperweight. Rolling from her lap onto the floor, it lands with a dull thud.

"This . . ." she starts, voice cracking, "it's my fault. All my fault."

Elin can see the resignation in her eyes.

She knows, doesn't she? She knows what he's done.

"It's not your fault, Cecile." She lays a hand on her arm. "None of this is."

"It is." Cecile turns to her. Her eyes are red, bloodshot. "There's something I haven't been honest about. Something you should know."

86

Cecile stands up, and walks over to the window. "It's to do with Daniel. What happened to him." Her eyes slide toward the floor.

More lies, Elin thinks, straightening. *Lie after lie after lie.*

"Before Daniel went missing, he'd been at a meeting at the sanatorium with Lucas and the building contractors. No one knew anything was wrong at that point. His wife had received a message from him, saying he'd gone for dinner in town, had too many drinks to drive home, and was planning on staying with his parents in Crans."

Elin nods, silent.

"The next day, Lucas's building manager came up. Only a kid, checking on the building once a week. It was more or less derelict. People kept breaking in." Cecile stops, eyes drifting away toward the window. "That afternoon, Lucas got a call. The kid had started checking the rooms. In one of the old wards, he found a body." She takes a long breath. "Dismembered, a mask over the face."

"Like this one?" Elin glances at the mask in her hands.

She gives a sharp nod. "Lucas was at the office in Lausanne when the kid called. Told him not to tell anyone, that he'd get there as soon as he could. Lucas said afterward that part of him had hoped it was a stupid prank. One of the protesters, but no . . ." Cecile's face closes. "The boy was right. There was a body. Daniel's body."

"I'm guessing he didn't call the police." Elin bites down on her lip, her mind desperately trying to dissect what Cecile's saying. She has so many questions, she doesn't know which to ask first.

"No. He called me, in a panic, asked what he should do. I was at our parents' house in town. I met him here." Cecile brings a hand up to her mouth, a strange noise coming from her throat: an uneven, gulpy exhalation. "Daniel was stretched out on one of those invalid chairs, that horrible mask still attached to his face." Tears spring to her eyes. She reaches up, wipes them away.

"And you still didn't call the police?" Elin hears the accusatory tone in her voice, but she can't help it. Part of her doesn't want to hear what's coming next, but she forces herself to listen.

"No. Lucas didn't want to. He was in a

panic, said it would kill the project dead in the water." Cecile shrugs. "He was right. There was already so much opposition to the renovation, it wouldn't survive this." She hesitates. "I knew what this meant to him. He'd poured everything into it — not just money, capital, but his life. Marriage. Everything, into this one project."

"So what did you do?"

"Lucas got rid of Daniel's body. Got it away from the scene."

"You didn't ask what he did with him?" Elin's voice is still accusing, brittle.

"No." Cecile's face briefly hardens. "I didn't want to know. I'd done my part. Promised to keep his secret."

"But what about the scene, where he'd been murdered? Surely the police searched it when Daniel was reported missing. From what you've described, there would have been blood, evidence."

"Lucas cleaned it up, made it look like it had never happened. Moved furniture about, shifted some of the filth. It was easy enough. The place was a mess to begin with." She looks down at her hands. "The police weren't very thorough. Their main theory at that time was that he'd gone of his own accord."

"But what about the building manager who found Daniel? Surely he'd have wanted to go to the police?"

"Lucas bribed him." Cecile's voice sounds

hollow, tinny. "Paid him a lot of money in the hope he'd go away. And he did."

Elin tries to shore up her thoughts. "So did you talk to Lucas after Adele's body was found? Discuss the similarities?"

"Yes, but he said if we told you about what happened to Daniel, we'd be arrested. Concealing a body, not reporting it, hiding the evidence." Cecile's voice is small, her shoulders rounded. It makes her look somehow diminished. "Lucas said he hoped that we'd find whoever was doing this, that no one would connect Adele's case to Daniel. I never thought he'd be the one . . ." Her voice splinters.

Elin looks at her, suddenly weary. How many more lies would emerge? People only telling her half the story . . . She's been at a disadvantage this whole time.

Cecile's quiet for a moment before she speaks again. "You know, Lucas said something when he finally came out of the hospital that's always stuck with me. He said he'd had enough of being helpless, people telling him what to do." She stops, stumbling over her words. "He said, 'From now on, I'm going to do what I want. To hell with anyone who stands in my way.' "

Elin watches the snow dance against the glass.

He got his wish. No one could call him helpless now.

She turns back to Cecile. "I'm going to start searching room to room. Can you go back to the lounge, check on everyone?"

"You don't want me to come with you?"

"No. If he sees more than one person, he might get spooked. We've got to play this carefully."

"If you're sure . . . ." Cecile walks toward the door. "Call me if you need anything."

"I will," Elin replies, and as she puts the mask back in the cupboard and picks up her bag, she realizes Cecile's words about what Lucas had said are still rolling about in her mind:

From now on, I'm going to do what I want. To hell with anyone who stands in my way.

Something shifts deep in her brain, a cog turning. Stopping, she stares at the floor, trying to process it.

Could it be right?

Or is her mind exhausted, overworked, imagining things? A scratch across vinyl — her brain jumping to the wrong place, finding the wrong conclusion.

There's one way to check: look for the evidence. Something concrete, irrefutable.

Reaching for her phone, she finds the site she needs in seconds. Her hands are clammy, her finger leaving damp prints on the screen as she scrolls, trying to find the relevant section.

Too fast — she's gone too far.

518

She forces herself to slow down and scroll carefully back up.

The words leap from the screen.

My theory: it's right.

It's then, as she looks, that something else pulls into her consciousness. Something so subtle it might never have found her unless she'd made the other connection.

Elin walks back over to the cupboard and opens the door. Kneeling down, she pulls out the mask, brings it close to her face. She breathes in, a deep, forensic inhalation. The mask slips down onto her lap.

I'm right. I'm right.

Things are finally coming together. Little pieces coalescing: fragments of conversation, body language.

There's no doubt now.

She just hopes she's not too late.

In the distance a door slams. A dull, muted thud.

Elin feels sick, her body flooded with adrenaline.

Time feels compressed, folded down to nothing. How long will it take? Three minutes? Four?

She breaks into a run.

87

The sliding doors slowly part, spitting her out into a mass of whirling snow.

Elin steps forward onto the decking, breathing heavily: she hasn't stopped running since leaving Lucas's office.

Steadying herself, she scans the area in front of her, squinting through the snow. The pool cover is retracted, the water lurid, obscenely bright above the underwater spotlights. Steam is snaking into the air, but as it ebbs and flows, she can make out a figure by the main pool.

Lucas. She was right. She knew if he wasn't by the indoor pool, he'd be here.

But he's not alone. Everything she's assumed — it's true.

She starts jogging toward him, kicking through the snow. Snowflakes are coming at her face, her eyes like tiny, feathered bullets. Adrenaline is spiking, making her clumsy, her feet giving way on the soft powder. She has to consciously shift her weight backward to prevent herself from slipping.

Finally, she reaches the main pool. Lucas is slumped across one of the loungers on the far right-hand side. He tries to turn his head toward her, but the movement is puppetlike, jerky. His eyes roll back in his skull, revealing slivers of reddish-white.

Am I too late?

Picking up the pace, she skirts the side of the pool until she reaches him.

"It's okay, he's coming around." Cecile is standing over him, bent at the waist, trying to prop him upright. There's something of the nurse in her demeanor, fussing, maternal, but Elin isn't fooled.

"You can stop the act, Cecile." Her voice is slow, calm, the simplicity of her words projecting a confidence she doesn't feel. "I know it's you. You were the one working with Margot. Not Lucas."

Cecile contemplates her, frown lines picking at her forehead.

She returns Elin's deliberate tones, but they're laced with condescension, as if she's talking to a child. "No. I found him here like this. I'm trying to help."

Elin knows instantly that Cecile's chosen the wrong reaction: faced with an accusation, she should be wild, incredulous. Defensive. Not this: this measured superiority.

It gives her away.

A noise comes from Lucas: a liquid, throaty sound.

She studies him. He's shifted position so she can see the left side of his face. Above his eyebrow, his forehead is sticky with blood, a clotted mass around his temple. His skin is pale, damp from either sweat or snow. Elin clears her throat. Her mouth feels dry, empty of saliva.

She needs to play for time.

"I know it's you. You gave it away. You were clever, until the last few moments."

Cecile's expression is inscrutable. "Gave it away?" she repeats.

"Yes. What you said back then, in Lucas's office. *'From now on, I'm going to do what I want. To hell with anyone who stands in my way.'* That expression . . . I realized I'd read it somewhere before. A blog, protesting about the hotel being built. Someone described Lucas using those very words. The same comment on Twitter too." Elin hesitates. "You were trolling your own brother, because this is what it's about, isn't it? Him."

The words roll across the space between them, but they don't seem to find Cecile: she seems buffered, unreachable.

"An expression?" Her face curls up: a mimic of disbelief. "You're accusing me because of a turn of phrase?"

"It's not only that." Elin straightens up to her full height. "I smelled chlorine on the mask in Lucas's study. I kept noticing it in places it shouldn't be . . . when I found Laure in the lift and when I was attacked in the stairwell leading from the penthouse, but it didn't register, not until today. You swim every day, don't you?"

Cecile looks at her, silent, the wind pulling her hair about her face. Still, no emotion.

"That's how I guessed you'd bring him here, to the pool. Either the indoor pool, or this one. It's your comfort zone, isn't it? The one place you feel at home."

"You don't know what you're talking about." Cecile's voice is empty. "What you're saying, it's supposition. Nothing more."

"It's not. This isn't just about the hotel, the sanatorium's past. It's personal, between you and Lucas. He's done something, something you can't forgive. Something that's made you seek revenge."

"No, I —"

Elin continues, sensing a weakness. "This, what's happened, everyone you've killed, you've been clever, making it about the sanatorium, as though it were all about the past, but it's not." She fixes her eyes on Lucas. "It's about him, isn't it? He started this."

Cecile takes a step back. It's now the façade slips: she falters, before recovering. "No, look, I —"

Moving forward, Elin's boots are buried deep in the snow. "What did he do, Cecile?

Tell me what he did."

Cecile's face crumples, her features collapsing as if someone had crushed them underfoot. A strange, bitter noise escapes from deep inside her throat.

"It's not about what he did. It's what he didn't do. None of this started with Lucas." Her face twitches. "It started with Daniel. Daniel Lemaitre. He raped me." She gestures to Lucas, hand jerking out erratically. "He knew, and did nothing about it."

88

There's a heavy silence. A silence Elin hasn't experienced since she's been here. She can feel the wind dropping, the snow, for the first time, falling straight to the ground.

"Nothing to say?" Cecile's gaze flickers to Lucas. Beside her, the water shimmers, steam coiling into the air.

He looks at her beneath heavy lids, unresponsive.

"Come on, you were there that night, Lucas, weren't you? After Daniel's birthday party, in Sion. His eighteenth. You drove us back, a group of us, to Daniel's place. We stayed over, everyone crashed in the living room."

Cecile's tone is still lacking in emotion, a void where feeling should be.

Elin knows that this type of emotion is always dangerous. Unlike a fiery, passionate rage, a cold, bitter anger like this can't burn itself out. It's gone past that point and hardened into something solid. Unbreakable.

"It wasn't one of those clichés," Cecile continues. "A stranger, dragging me off to some dark alley. He was my friend. Your best friend. Practically part of the family, and I was sixteen, Lucas. A kid."

"Cecile, don't —" Lucas's words are slurred.

"What is it, Lucas? You don't like hearing what you tried to ignore?" Her expression hardens. "Daniel and I were kissing, laughing about needing to be quiet, not waking anyone. Then he started pulling up my dress, nudged my legs apart. I tried to say no but he clamped his hand over my mouth, and then he raped me." She shakes her head, self-recriminatory. "I did nothing. Froze. The opposite of what I thought I'd do in a situation like that. Just let him do it."

Lucas watches her, tiny flakes of snow catching in his hair.

"When he finally climbed off me, I turned my head to you. You pretended to be asleep, but I'd seen your eyes open. I knew you were awake, had seen what he'd done."

He clears his throat. "That isn't right, Cecile, you know it isn't."

"It is, Lucas. It sounds unbelievable, doesn't it? That you wouldn't have done something? Tried to stop him? I thought so too. The next day, I kept running through it in my mind, wondering why you didn't pull him off, but I gave you the benefit of the doubt. Thought you weren't sure what you'd seen, or didn't want to embarrass me." She steps toward him.

Elin tenses. Despite the cold, she can feel sweat beading on her forehead.

"I never thought that would be it, Lucas. I kept waiting for you to say something, ask me what happened, if I was okay." Cecile hesitates, a new rhythm, curious, autonomic, to her words. "I had it all planned out: what would happen after we talked, how we'd go to our parents, tell the police."

Lucas, too, has sensed something awry in her robotic tone. He's rousing slightly, trying to change position, lift himself higher, but the sedative she's given him is making his movements slow, labored.

"But it didn't happen, did it, Lucas?"

"Cecile, I was a kid. We both were. I didn't know exactly what happened, how to handle it."

"No." Her eyes harden. "You weren't a kid. A kid might lie once, but not twice." She turns to Elin. "A few weeks later, I managed to tell our parents." Her words are crisp, precise. "They asked you, didn't they, Lucas? I know they did. They asked you and you lied. Pretended you hadn't seen anything."

Elin sees the first flicker of emotion, and with it a glimpse of something in Cecile's hand — a blade, overhead lights bouncing beads of reflection off the metal. She can feel her fingers juddering at the sight, has to clamp them into a fist to stop the movement.

"After everything I'd done for you . . . all those hours in the hospital, then at school, standing up for you against the bullies. This was the one thing I needed you to do for me, and you couldn't do it. Couldn't put your head above the parapet."

Lucas's expression changes, a jerky move from shock to guilt. His bloodshot eyes roam across Cecile's face before he hangs his head. "I'm sorry."

"No," Cecile says flatly, her grip on the knife tightening, knuckles turning white. "Sorry doesn't do it now, Lucas. Because you didn't stand up for me and tell the truth. Mama and Papa tried to cover the whole thing up. Thought there was an 'explanation.'" She rolls her eyes. "They knew I had a crush on him, so I never worked out if they simply didn't believe me or just took the easy way out. Chose not to rock the boat because they were friends with the family, and Daniel was Papa's golden boy. All they said was that it was over, that bad things happen sometimes and there was no point going over it, making myself upset." She gives an icy smile. "Even when I found out I was pregnant, they told me not to make a fuss. I had an abortion, and that was the end, in their eyes."

Lucas turns his head. Elin knows why he

can't look at Cecile: guilt. He's trying to literally block it out, block Cecile out.

"Things were never the same after that." Cecile takes a breath. "When I tried to swim, all I saw, with every stroke, was his face looming over me. Every pore, every freckle. His body pushing down on mine, proving it was stronger than me." She pauses. "It made me feel . . . tiny. That all the strength I had in the pool . . . it was imagined. Nothing compared to his strength, his power." Cecile steps forward again, twisting the handle of the knife between her fingers.

Lucas's eyes spring open, sensing the movement.

"That's how he made me feel, you know. Like nothing." Cecile holds up her hand, only a tiny gap remaining between finger and thumb. "That small. A fraud. Every time I got in the pool, I couldn't perform. The racing, my career . . . it was over."

"But you never spoke to me about it." Lucas's words are still slow, indistinct. "I didn't know how it had affected you."

"You didn't ask, Lucas. You didn't ask because it was easier to look the other way. Daniel was your friend and you chose your friend over me."

She falls silent. Elin watches her, sensing there's more to come.

"I suppressed it, tried to be normal. I gave up on swimming, went to hotel school in

Lausanne. I started to convince myself I could have a different future, that I wouldn't be defined by what Daniel had done." Cecile kicks at the snow on the decking with her feet. "That's when I met Michel. A year or so later, I tried to get pregnant. Nothing happened. We had tests, and the specialist said I couldn't get pregnant. I had an infection after the abortion. . . . It made me infertile."

Elin tenses. She doesn't like Cecile's tone. The unnatural coherence, the discipline of her words . . . it feels wrong.

"That's when our marriage started crumbling. Michel left eight months later. He said it was because I'd changed, but I knew it was because I was damaged. He wanted someone whole, someone who functioned properly."

"You should have told me," Lucas says. "You should have told me all this."

But it's as if Cecile can't hear him. She carries on, relentless. "That's when you called, told me about your plans for the sanatorium, asked me to be a part of it." She gives a grim nod. "I knew that was my chance to confront Daniel, make him acknowledge what he'd done."

"You spoke to him?" Lucas shifts position on the lounger. Blood is trickling down his face, running from his eyebrow to his cheek, but he doesn't reach up to wipe it away. His focus is on Cecile.

Cecile moves closer, right beside him. Her

posture would almost be casual, if it weren't for the knife in her hand. "Yes. A few weeks after I came back. I told him you'd asked me to work for you, wanted to know if he was okay with it."

"What did he say?"

"That he was fine with it. There was nothing. Not even a flicker." Cecile's eyes darken. "You know, I used to wonder whether he ever thought about it. If what he'd done had eaten him up over the years, that when he closed his eyes at night, he remembered me, but seeing him then, I knew he didn't. I knew he'd never be held accountable, not even by himself. He'd swept it aside, maybe even convinced himself that I'd wanted it, or maybe he didn't even remember." She hesitates. "Either way, he'd reduced me. Compartmentalized me. Just like the doctors did here. The doctors who were trusted to make people better."

Cecile turns to face Elin. "You see, that's where you're wrong, about this not being about the sanatorium, what happened here. This place, its secrets . . . they were the final straw." Her gaze flicks back to Lucas. "You tell her, Lucas. Tell her the truth about this place."

89

Lucas's voice is low, still slightly garbled. "Before the build started, Margot contacted us, asking questions about one of her relatives. Margot had found out from a clinic in Germany that she'd been transferred here, to the sanatorium. We searched, couldn't find anything in the official files. I said we'd look into it."

"Margot contacted you directly?" Elin clenches her hands together then releases. Her fingers are freezing now, numb at the tips.

"Yes. We looked as she'd asked, found something in a cupboard in one of the old wards. A box. You could tell it hadn't been opened for years. Inside, I found documents, photographs, patient files. Diaries. All women. I started reading, and I realized that these patients . . . they didn't have TB. That wasn't what they came to the sanatorium for."

Elin absorbs what he's said, feels a horrible

sense of inevitability about what's coming next.

"The patients were referred from the clinic in Germany. While they were here, they participated in trials. It started off as experimentation for new treatments, then it seemed to" — his voice falters — "escalate. The more we dug, the more we found. Photographs, records, but you could tell from the images, the notes, that they weren't experiments anymore. They'd become something else."

"It was abuse." Cecile's voice is barely audible. "The age-old abuse of power; it was an exploitation of vulnerable women." She meets Elin's gaze. "The women had nothing clinically wrong with them. They were sent to the clinic in Germany by their fathers, husbands, doctors, under the guise of a medical condition, but often it was simply because their behavior went against the status quo. Of what was acceptable for women at the time. They had too many ideas, were too outspoken. It wasn't uncommon." She turns her face to the floor, disgust marring her features. "Some of them, the unlucky few, were transferred here."

Nodding, Elin keeps her voice level. "So why didn't you bring the files to light right away?"

"Lucas said the negative press would affect the hotel. All he wanted was to carry on with the build." Cecile grimaces. "Daniel had the same reaction when we told him. 'It's in the past. Forget it.' "

"Cecile, that's not fair." Lucas tries to sit up. "If people knew what had happened, there would have been an investigation, it would have affected the plans for the hotel."

"Nothing was going to stop you, was it? The hotel, it was all that mattered." She glances at Elin. "Lucas and Daniel already knew about the grave in the photograph, that there were more. It got flagged during the survey of the site. Lucas chose to ignore it. Carry on. Another bribe. Another person choosing to look the other way."

Lucas winces as he shifts position. "I didn't see why something that happened so long ago should affect what this place had the potential to become."

"But that's it, Lucas. Can't you see? The point is, it's still happening. Every abuse of power, every rape, every harassment. It's still happening." Cecile crouches down next to him, her face close, only inches from his. "It's too easy, isn't it? To turn the other cheek. Ignore the consequences. Even worse, we're complicit in it. Not just men, it's women too."

"Women?" Elin moves forward a step, hoping Cecile doesn't notice.

"Yes. Adele. She was with Lucas's building manager when they found Daniel's body. His girlfriend. She was bought off, like he was. Lucas gave her a job here on a highly inflated

534

salary, good enough to keep her mouth shut."

That explains the link between the pair. The Instagram photo. "We found a photograph of Adele and Lucas together, here in the hotel. A party. It looked like an argument."

"Yes. She was asking for more money." Lucas's voice is muffled.

Elin turns back to Cecile. "But you killed Daniel, Cecile. Murdered him. Why would you have wanted Adele to talk?"

Cecile looks at her, her eyes bright, glittering. For the first time, Elin can see real emotion. "Because I never wanted to be anonymous. When I killed Daniel, I expected to get caught. I wanted my story to be told, those women's stories to be told. I wanted people to ask *why* I'd killed him like I had, but no. Everyone wanted to cover it up."

"But you could have gone to someone, the police, the press. Told your story that way."

Cecile looks at her in disbelief. "If I went to the press myself, I knew it would have been my word against his. No one believed me back then, so why would they this time? The only way to get justice was to do it myself. Make them pay."

Elin stares at her, everything pulling into sharp focus; a macabre, raw logic. Revenge in its most brutal form, tipping the power balance back the other way.

"So why the gap between killing Daniel and Adele?"

535

"I was waiting for the right time. When I found out Adele was asking Lucas for more money, something snapped. I knew she had to go."

"And by that time, you had Margot on board, too, didn't you? She was vulnerable, so you groomed her."

"I wouldn't call it grooming. She was simply open to suggestion. Her mother had recently died. She'd developed a fixation about her relative."

"A fixation?" Elin repeats. "She was ill, Cecile. She had a serious form of depression. Psychotic depression. I found printouts in Laure's desk. I assumed they were hers, but she was researching it because she was worried about Margot, wasn't she? Laure had depression herself, she knew the signs."

Cecile swipes her hand through the air impatiently, dismissing Elin's words. "It doesn't matter what you call it. The reason behind it is what's important."

"Cecile—"

"No. It's true. Before Margot's mother died, she asked her to find out what happened to Margot's great-grandmother. Her disappearance . . . it had scarred every generation of their family. Consumed her grandmother, now her mother too. All they wanted was answers. But when Margot found out what the truth really was, it didn't give her any peace. It unleashed something dark.

The envelope you found with the photographs inside . . . she carried it with her everywhere. She was obsessed by it."

"And you seized on that obsession, didn't you? Her vulnerability made her a willing puppet. You used her. She helped you, didn't she? With the murders?"

"That's how I knew," Lucas says quietly. "That's how I worked it out, in the tunnel. When I realized Margot was working with someone else, something clicked. I knew it had to be Cecile. Only she could know about the tunnel's existence, and only she knew the truth about what happened to Margot's great-grandmother. I knew she could have exploited that, got Margot to work with her."

"But why lock me in?" Elin says.

"I wanted to talk to her. Brother to sister. Give her a chance to explain. But I didn't get that chance. She was waiting for me. She didn't want to talk."

"So what did you ask Margot to do?"

"Restrain them. She didn't have the stomach for anything else." Cecile gives a slight smile. "Anyway, her involvement is Lucas's fault. All she wanted was recognition, an acknowledgment of what happened at the sanatorium, her great-grandmother's story to be told. Some kind of memorial, a mark in the sand, for those women's voices to be heard, but Lucas did nothing."

"I was planning the archive room . . ."

"But you never went through with it. You had no real intention of completing it. It was just to get Margot off your back. Even worse, you offered her a job to assuage your guilt. As if that would be enough." Cecile looks at him in disgust, her cheeks shining now, a mixture of tears and snow. "And you put those glass boxes around the hotel. Fetishizing the sanatorium's past, using it as entertainment for the guests. After everything you knew."

"So you decided to flip it on its head . . ."

"Yes. I put the victims on display, just like the doctors did with those women in the photographs."

"But what about Laure?" Elin's voice catches on her name. "Why kill her? She was Margot's friend, your colleague."

"She was the same as all the rest in the end. Cowardly." Cecile wipes a hand over her face. "It started with her fling with Lucas. He'd treated her badly. She was upset and bitter, started asking questions about the build, the bribery and corruption claims. She was planning to publish it on a blog to expose him, but never went through with it. When she got back with your brother, she decided to forget it all."

"So you got involved," Elin says, a flutter of trepidation in her throat as she watches Cecile's hand, holding the knife, move closer to Lucas's face.

A nod. "That's when I upped the stakes. A few months ago." Cecile jerks the knife upward to emphasize her point. "Got Margot to give her the memory stick with the redacted files. We thought she'd be intrigued, want to find out what was going on, but she balked. Said she didn't want to be involved. Even when Margot showed her the unredacted files, the full story, she wasn't interested."

"But that's a normal reaction. She was probably scared."

"No." Cecile's face twists, now a violent, angry red. "It wasn't. She wanted to look the other way. Like Lucas. Like Adele." Her eyes flash. "Even Margot in the end. Even she'd had enough, wanted to stop."

"But why *kill* Laure? She was no threat to you."

Elin tries to take a deep breath, but her chest is tight. Not from the cold, but from anger. Despite her fear of what Cecile's about to do next, she feels unmoved by her justifications — justifications for horrific acts that only make sense to her.

"It was necessary. When Lucas and I came back early from our trip, Laure knew I was planning something. She called me the night before she vanished. She wanted to stop me from doing anything. When I said no, she told me she had leverage."

"The memory stick."

"Yes. I'd had someone hack into the clinic's database to retrieve the electronic files, but I knew they were traceable back to me. That's why she disappeared. She hoped I'd assume she'd run, but I knew she was here. Watching, ready to expose me."

"So that's why Laure was keeping the encrypted memory stick on her, disguised." Elin works it through in her mind. "But you weren't going to give her the chance to use it, were you? That's why you abducted her."

"Yes. With Margot's help. Margot was the one who messaged you from Laure's phone to lure you up to the penthouse. And Laure had contacted Margot to try to convince her to stop me. Margot arranged to meet Laure to talk, early."

"Before I went to the penthouse . . ."

"That's right. It was a trap. Margot wasn't waiting for Laure. It was me."

"And you killed her."

"Yes. It was easy. Straightforward. She didn't know a thing about it. I thought I had everything in hand, but I made one mistake."

"Leaving the memory stick on her body."

Cecile nods. "I knew she had it on her, but I didn't realize that she'd transferred the files to another memory stick, disguised it as a lighter. It worked. I was looking for the old one, so I didn't find it on her."

"That was the delay in coming up to the penthouse."

"Yes. But it doesn't matter now. It worked out, like it's all working out here." Cecile straightens, hauls Lucas to standing. "Elin, please. I don't want to hurt you. We're alike, you and I. Loners. Fighters. Demanding answers, justice." Her hand is shaking around Lucas's waist. "Putting up with selfish brothers. Let me finish what I've started."

Her eyes have narrowed to slits, her fair hair now wet from the snow, plastered against her skull.

Lucas coughs, his legs buckling under him.

Elin doesn't move; she can see the fine point of the knife pressed against Lucas's neck. She inches forward. She has to do this carefully.

"I can't leave," Elin says steadily, still moving. "This is not the right way. You might think it is, but it's not."

"Leave." The voice is louder now. More insistent. Tears are spilling down her cheeks.

"Cecile, I can't. We can talk, get things straight before you decide what to do. I understand —"

"Understand?" Cecile shakes her head. Elin senses that something has shifted in her tone. *She's losing control.* "No one knows what I've been through. No one. How can you understand, Elin?"

"I know, but I can at least try to, can't I? If we talk it through again —"

"Talk? That won't do anything. I need action. *This*" — she presses the knife harder against Lucas's throat, making the skin around the edge of the blade whiten and pucker — "this is what I need to do. This. For me. For all those women."

"Cecile —"

"No. Don't even try to stop me . . ." Cecile's voice has tipped into a scream, her eyes locked on Lucas. "All everyone does is try to stop me. From telling the truth, getting payback . . ."

Lucas's face is paralyzed, a frozen mask of fear. Elin can tell the sedative's wearing off — he's finally able to understand what's happening, how much danger he's in.

It's now or never.

Elin makes her move, lunges toward Cecile, arms outstretched.

90

The movement is enough to set Cecile off-balance. Grimacing, she falls sideways, her left arm flailing as she tries to right herself.

Elin feels a flicker of hope: if she can isolate her, pin her down . . .

But it doesn't work — the angle is off.

It happens in slow motion — Cecile's torso twisting as she falls toward the pool, her grasp tight enough to pull Lucas with her. He crashes on top of her, briefly submerging her, water arcing into the air.

Cecile isn't under for long. Only seconds later, she surfaces, water streaming down her face.

Already, she's on top of Lucas, arms flailing violently above her head before her hands clamp tight around his neck.

Reality hits Elin: Cecile's a strong swimmer. Strong enough to take them both down. Panic flares in Lucas's eyes. In Elin's, too: this is the worst-case scenario.

I can't go in the water.

Her mind is blank with terror — knife sharp. Blinding.

The familiar fear consumes her. The scene in front of her tips, veers; that tunneling of her senses. Piece by piece, everything stripped away.

The surface of the pool dances with movement: thrashing water, Lucas's arms jerking, Cecile's hands scrabbling wildly, pushing his head backward into the water.

But still, Elin's body is hostile, it refuses to move. She feels snow on her face, and sweat, but she can't move, can't reach up, wipe it away.

Lucas finally reacts, as if the water has shocked him out of any remaining lethargy.

Rallying, he reaches up, forces Cecile backward, away. He starts to swim toward the side.

It doesn't work: barely drawing breath, Cecile swims beside him. She strikes out with her elbow, catches him in the throat, in his windpipe.

Once, twice — sharp, swift jabs.

Lucas cries out, his eyes flashing in fear before his head slips beneath the surface of the water.

The sight rips a memory free — an echo of that summer day. Of Sam. Of the case a year ago. A memory of her own inaction. Her fear, paralysis.

I can't let it happen again.

Elin reaches up to her neck, clasps her hands around her necklace.

Keeping her hand clamped around the hook, she yanks on it hard, feels the chain give and then break completely. One half falls, hitting the soft powder snow; the other remains in her hand.

Elin takes a deep breath, hand clenched tight around the necklace, and dives into the water. She breaks the surface cleanly, not letting herself think, forces herself up and around. She swims up behind Cecile.

Cecile doesn't even turn. All her focus is on destroying Lucas.

Elin is now facing Cecile. Still grasping the hook in her hand, she jerks it up, between her fingers, thrusts it toward Cecile's face.

Hand vibrating with tension, she moves it in a rapid, circular motion until she can feel resistance. Though blunted, she feels the hook gouge Cecile's cheek, finding purchase in the soft skin.

Elin retracts her hand, jerks it sharply back.

There's a cry of pain. It's enough: Cecile's grip on Lucas loosens.

The knife falls from her hand.

Elin puts her right arm around Lucas's chest, tries to pull him away, hoping he can at least catch his breath. She notices the knife slipping below the choppy surface of the water, a fragmented glimmer of metal.

Without hesitation, she lurches forward,

grabs at it with her left hand.

Cecile does the same, blood streaming from her cheek. Their fingers clash, but Elin gets there first. Tightly clasping the handle, she rotates it away from Cecile through the water.

A moment of distraction, but Cecile takes advantage of it: she goes for Lucas again. He's resisting, pulling away from them both, trying to hold on to the edge of the pool, haul himself out, but the effort is too much. His hands are wet, slipping off the snow-covered tiles.

Cecile's on him in seconds, pulling him from behind, wrestling him back into the water.

"Cecile. Stop. Let him go."

"No." Her voice is shrill. "He has to pay for his lies."

"He will. I know what you want, what you wanted all along. You wanted your story to be heard. Justice. Recognition." Elin takes a breath. "You've got that, Cecile. We now know what happened to you, to them. Those women's stories, they'll be told now. You've spoken their truth. And yours. Killing Lucas doesn't give you anything you won't have already."

"He turned his back on me." The words are shouted, but they've lost their strength, power. She's sobbing, the movement pulling up through her body so hard it makes her shudder.

546

"I know, but, Cecile, you've told him how you feel. He has to live with that. Not you. Not anymore."

Elin holds her breath, waiting. Watching.

Time seems to drag as Cecile moves backward through the water, releases her grip on Lucas.

Elin carefully wraps an arm around his chest, and pulls him toward the ladder at the side of the pool. Getting out first, she slowly helps him from the water. As the freezing air hits his skin, he immediately starts shivering with whole-body convulsions.

Elin stands up on the side, cold air biting into her flesh, and looks back at Cecile.

She's on her back in the middle of the pool.

Arms and legs outstretched, she's floating, her eyes tracing the snowflakes falling from the sky.

91

Five weeks later

"We're early." Will glances down at his watch. "There's a few minutes before the funicular goes."

Elin nods. Already her face is burning, the thought of leaving weighing heavy. Neither she nor Isaac are good at this: good-byes.

As she hovers on the curb, her eyes fix on Isaac's back. A tiny white feather has worked its way through the seam of his blue puffer jacket. It catches in the breeze, flickering from side to side before coming loose, flying away.

A bus trundles down the road in front of them, kicking up bits of salt, grit. The metal grille at the back is full, packed tight with skis and snowboards. Waiting for it to pass, she follows Isaac across the road to the station.

The concrete building isn't pretty. It's spare, functional, the blunted edges of the flat roof brutally splicing through the raw beauty of the snowcapped mountains behind.

Beyond, the sky is a brilliant blue. Not the pale blue of an English winter's day, but a deep, explosive color that makes the white of the mountains whiter, the streaky haze of cloud something definite and solid.

It's been like this for days, so long that it's hard to remember what the highs and lows of the storm were like, how it made her feel — the sharp, gripping waves of panic coming with each hour of wind and snow.

"It's busy," Isaac says as they walk into the station.

He's right. People are gathering in messy clusters: an elderly couple, teenage girls with rucksacks hanging low against their backs, a large group of schoolchildren.

A small kiosk on the left is selling coffee and pastries. The bitter, buttery scent makes her stomach growl.

"You wait here. I'll get the tickets." Will's already walking toward the counter, dragging their bags behind him. Though they need the tickets, Elin knows he's deliberately giving her and Isaac the time and space to say good-bye.

Isaac scuffs the toe of his shoe into the asphalt, his face pinched. "It's weird, saying good-bye like this. I've just gotten used to you being around." He stops, fingers tightening around the water bottle in his hand.

She can't look away from him: his eyes, his hair, the anxious expression on his face. It feels wrong, leaving him here alone.

"Then come with us," she says abruptly. "We'll book you a ticket. Just stay for a few weeks with me, see how you feel."

"Not yet. I want to try to get back to normal life. See how it goes." He presses his lips together, looks away. "I can't stop thinking, you know, about how I doubted her. Just before you told me she was dead, I was burning the photographs I had of her in my wallet. I thought she'd betrayed me, when the whole time she was there. I could have found her, instead of . . ." His voice splinters.

"Isaac, there's no point in beating yourself up. The situation was horrible. I doubted you, too, didn't I? When I found out about the accusations of intimidation, I jumped to conclusions when I should have just asked you about it." Even now, the thought of what she did — calling the university — makes her face burn.

"But you and I hadn't seen each other for years. Our relationship was strained. I can see why you might have doubts, but Laure and I were engaged. I shouldn't have questioned her. I should have known."

"How could you? Laure hid in the outbuilding deliberately. She knew it wasn't used, that she wouldn't be found. There were no cameras, no obvious way you could have found her."

"I know, but it's like a bug in my mind,

racing around and around. The fact that she was there, so close, all that time."

"That's why I think you should come back with us. Distract yourself." She smiles. "Mainly with my crap cooking. You can take over the kitchen if you like."

Elin takes a step toward him, reaches out a hand, then withdraws it, chiding herself.

I'm doing too much. Too full-on.

Several beats pass.

Isaac hoists his rucksack higher up on his shoulder. "I will come and visit," he says finally, his gaze finding hers. "It's not just words."

"I know."

"I mean it. It won't go back to what it was before. It's different now, isn't it? You and me. We're different."

"Okay." She'll take that. *Different.*

"I'll say good-bye to Will, then I'd better go." Isaac glances over to the kiosk.

"Will, mate, I'm going." Isaac raises his voice as Will starts walking toward him, tickets in hand. They do the half-hug thing, then fist-bump, before Isaac steps away.

He turns to Elin, pulls her close. She can feel tears hot at the back of her eyes. *Why does this feel so wrong? Leaving him?*

As they separate, she can hear the loud grinding of machinery — a clunking mechanical whirr. The funicular's nearly here.

"Before I go, there's something I wanted to

551

give you." Raising his voice above the sound, he reaches into his bag. "I had this copied for you. Will said you didn't have any photos of Sam, the three of us, in your apartment."

Elin almost can't look at it, but she makes herself.

It's a photo of the three of them on the beach, sand streaked up their legs. A lopsided sandcastle sits behind them, dotted with paper flags.

Her eyes lock on him. *Sam.* Her little brother.

Finally, a real picture. One to replace the flawed, messy flashbacks inside her head.

92

The funicular starts to move, and with it their surroundings — sky and snow give way to trees and snow-tipped chalets, 4×4s snaking up the narrow mountain roads.

Picture postcard.

Elin puts her fingers to the window. She can feel Will's eyes on her.

"Are you going to get the necklace fixed?" he says.

On autopilot, she reaches up, feels for it, but of course there's nothing there. She shrugs. "I don't know." She likes the empty swoop-hollow of her neck. It feels lighter, somehow. Free.

Will clears his throat. "Are you sure you're ready to leave Isaac?" He puts his hand in hers. His palm is warm.

She forces herself to meet his gaze. "I think he's going to be okay. Knowing that Cecile's been arrested . . . he said it helps."

"Do you know what's happened to Lucas?"

"Yes. Berndt told me this morning. He's

been arrested for his role in what happened; getting rid of Daniel's body and disposing of the evidence, covering up the truth about the sanatorium's past." She pauses. "He's admitted to knowing about the documentation, the graves, and bribing officials so none of it would be revealed."

A few beats of silence. "And what about you?" he prompts. "Are you okay with us going?"

"I think so." It feels strange, though; the thought of leaving, because she wasn't only leaving this place, she was leaving other things behind — Isaac, Laure, and a version of the truth she'd carried inside her for so long, it had defined her. *Become her.* Now she's got to live with something new.

"I'm more concerned about you. The walking wounded."

"On the mend." Will raises a hand to his stomach.

The gesture is so him, so low-key, so understated, she's seized by a sudden urge to hold him. Touch him. Open up in a way she's always resisted before.

She pulls him toward her, holds him in a clumsy rough embrace, breathing in the familiar scent of his skin. "I'm sorry for what happened." Her voice sounds strange. "I never meant for you to have to deal with any of this. You . . . you mean everything to me."

"I know," he whispers into her hair. "It's

over now. We can move on."

"Speaking of which." Breaking away, she unzips her bag, withdraws a magazine. The cover's folded, so she pushes it back with her fingers.

Will scans the cover. "*Living Etc?* Where did you get that?"

"At the supermarket in Crans. Cost me about twenty quid, but . . ." Elin flicks through the pages, finds the one she wants. "That one." She jabs at the page. "That sofa there. What do you think?"

"What for?"

"Our new place."

He's silent for a moment, then smiles. "I like it."

Elin's about to reply when she feels her phone buzzing in her pocket.

She pulls it out, and inspects the screen.

"What is it?" Will looks over her shoulder.

"Work." Her eyes trace the words on the screen. "They were fine with me taking a bit longer because of Isaac, but they need to know by next week."

Will nods, surveying the view through the window. Elin follows his gaze. They're nearly at the bottom of the valley. Chalets have given way to houses, snow-covered vineyards. Only some of the vines themselves are visible, thin dark smears rising through the snow.

He turns back to look at her. "So, have you made a decision?"

"I think so."

Next to them, a passenger reaches up, opens one of the windows. Tilting her head up, Elin can feel the cool breeze move over her face. It's early in the year still, not quite March, but she thinks she can sense it — the taste of spring in the air.

New life.

EPILOGUE

He's only one carriage back.

If they were to glance over, they might see him there. He's the one leaning against the window, the only one not taking in the view.

There's a small group in front of him — Middle Eastern. They're passing a bottle of water between them, speaking in rapid Arabic.

Every few minutes, they point at something through the smeared glass: a chalet, a church, the crumbled remains of a wooden outbuilding. They don't notice him. No one's even met his eye.

A Swiss family is behind him — mother, father, two girls no older than ten. The girls are dressed in brightly colored ski clothes — rainbow stripes that crinkle as they move. The younger girl, red-haired, freckled, is chewing on an overstuffed baguette, her cheek resting against her older sister's chest.

The mother takes a photograph of them and the father sighs, annoyed. He's laden with ski poles, a rucksack, a thick down coat slung over his arm.

Neither looks at him as he cranes his head over the group in front.

He glances back at Elin. She's smiling, gesticulating as she says something to her boyfriend. She's animated, something he hasn't seen in her for a long time.

It's clear she's oblivious to him, just like she was oblivious in the hotel, oblivious to what happened by the plunge pool, and exactly whose hand it was at the small of her back. *Pressing. Pushing.*

He doesn't mind: the anonymity suits him. There's no hurry, is there?

He's found it's best to wait until someone's relaxed, has let down their guard.

That's the sweet spot, isn't it?

That tiny space between happiness and fear.

- Human graves have been discovered by specialist Swiss police units at Le Sommet, a luxury Swiss hotel recently converted from a tuberculosis sanatorium.
- The graves were discovered by police during an investigation into three murders carried out in January at the hotel.
- Archived records show at least 32 women from Germany were sent to the Sanatorium du Plumachit, ostensibly to recover from tuberculosis.
- Other regions and European countries are now examining records amid fears that this could be the start of a flood of investigations.

Swiss police have found 32 human graves near the hotel Le Sommet in the Swiss resort of Crans-Montana, where it is alleged that women were illegally interned and both physically and mentally abused in the late 1920s and 1930s.

Anomalies consistent with potential graves were uncovered at the site, formerly known as the Sanatorium du Plumachit, where patients were housed for the treatment of tuberculosis.

The Valais Police Judiciaire made the discovery while investigating the sequence of recent murders at the hotel, reports *Le Matin.*

One of the suspects revealed that the motive for the murders lay in the hotel's past as a sanatorium, leading police to examine the site in more detail.

The gravesite is on the northeast side of the hotel, where it is believed the women were buried decades ago, before the sanatorium closed as antibiotics began to be used in the treatment of tuberculosis.

Forensic scientists from the Valais Police and the University of Lausanne have found 32 graves on the grounds using ground-penetrating radar and soil samples.

The sanatorium failed to record these burial locations, and forged documentation was found stating that the patients had been sent elsewhere to be buried. However, previously hidden documentation confirms that many women died under unknown circumstances, most likely from injuries sustained during abuse carried out under the guise of medical treatment.

All of the women are believed to have been transferred from the Gotterdorf Clinic in Germany. It is not yet known whether these patients had tuberculosis or if this diagnosis was invented in order to have the women admitted.

It wasn't uncommon at the time for women to be placed in medical care and admitted for treatment against their will and without medical justification. Many women were interned in clinics across Europe at the behest of a male guardian or family member, as a way of taking control — of an inheritance or of independent thought and ideas.

Prosecutor Hugo Tapparel of the Valais Police said, "We are studying the findings of the report. We'll be reaching out to the victims' families and discussing suitable next steps as work continues."

A relative of one of the women remarked, "We believe all of these women were under the care of Dr. Pierre Yerly, a prominent pulmonary surgeon who was known for his experimental treatments. Once the investigation has concluded we're planning to erect a memorial in remembrance of the victims."

ACKNOWLEDGMENTS

I would like to express my thanks to everyone who has helped bring this book to life and into print. I genuinely didn't know how many people are involved in helping a novel move through these stages and I feel hugely privileged to have benefited from their expertise and insight.

A massive thank-you to Jeramie Orton, my wonderful editor at Pamela Dorman Books, for her enthusiasm for Elin and her story. Her forensic attention to detail and hard work has helped the novel shine and become the absolute best it can be. I couldn't have wished for a more professional or intuitive editor to bring my book to readers in North America. A wider thank-you to everyone at Pamela Dorman Books and the Viking team, and a special mention to Jane Cavolina for her razor-sharp eye with the copyediting.

I also want to thank my brilliant editor Tash Barsby at Transworld in the UK and the team there. I can never thank you enough for wanting to bring this book to life and investing so much skill and time into developing and honing the story — you have changed my world in the best possible way.

Huge thanks to my amazing literary agent, Charlotte Seymour, who spotted something in my writing and has believed in this story from the very beginning (and took such a keen interest in my scrapbooks!). You have found me the perfect publishers. Your unwavering confidence in my work means the world to me.

Another thank-you is also extended to the wider team at Andrew Nurnberg Associates, especially the wonderful rights team and the co-agents who have sold my book in more countries than I could have imagined. A special thank-you to the tireless Halina Kościa, whose e-mails have brought such wonderful news. You have a habit of "making my week"! Thank you also to my foreign publishers for taking the story to their hearts.

A big thank-you to all of the people who kindly lent me their thoughts when I was researching the book, especially the Valais Police in Sion. Thank you for being so patient and generous with your time. The "what if" conversations we had unlocked so much of the novel, and even though Elin was left to her own devices, we ultimately accept your argument that the Swiss police can get anywhere and at any time. Any factual inaccuracies in Swiss police procedure are either my error or to fit the story.

I was also lucky to have support from several members of the British Association of Snowsport Instructors. In particular, Jaz Lamb of BASS Morzine, who answered many questions and also provided an introduction to the mountain rescue team in Portes du Soleil and one of their leaders, Jeremy Helvic — *merci*.

Within Crans-Montana, Stéphane Romang pointed us toward some great resources around the legacy of sanatoriums in the town. Many other mountain people helped inspire certain scenes. Kindred spirits.

On a more personal note, thank you to Axel Schmid and family for introducing us to the very special place that is Crans-Montana in the Swiss Alps — it is the unique atmosphere and dramatic landscape there that inspired me to write this novel, and I'm grateful for it every day as our family's "happy place." See you at Amadeus.

A massive, sparkly thank-you to my parents and sisters — where it all began. Thank you for fostering such a love of reading and for encouraging me to write. My childhood was all about words — endless bedtime stories, audiobooks, and the weekly trips to the library. You have listened and given so much time and love and inspiration (and food!). Without you, none of this would have been possible and I'm so happy I can share all of this with you. Thank you also to my wonderful friends both off- and online for their unwavering support for my writing and my book — your kindness and advice (and coffee supply) have been invaluable.

Thank you to my grandmother, who used to speed-read at least a book a day and lent me many of her favorite novels, and my grandfather, who, despite his macular degeneration, would read my short stories even if it took him an impossibly long time. You both would have loved following my journey and I hope, somewhere, you're following it from afar.

Finally, thank you to my daughters, Rosie and Molly, and my husband, James, for your enthusiasm and passion for the story from the very first step. Thank you for sharing a love of the mountains, for the six a.m. starts, and for helping with the tricky scenes and forcing me to go that little bit further. Having people cheering me on and believing in my writing through thick and thin is what keeps me sitting down and writing day after day. I'm so proud of you all and I honestly don't know what I would do without you . . . FTB.

ABOUT THE AUTHOR

Sarah Pearse grew up in Devon, UK, and studied English literature and creative writing at the University of Warwick before completing a postgraduate diploma in broadcast journalism. She lived in Switzerland for several years before returning to the UK. *The Sanatorium* is her first novel.